Quilting
On A
MIDSUMMER'S
NIGHT

A Quilters Club Mystery

ABSOLUTELY AMAZING eBOOKS

Habent Sua Fata Libelli

ABSOLUTELY AMAZING eBOOKS

Manhanset House
Shelter Island Hts., New York 11965-0342

bricktower@aol.com • tech@absolutelyamazingebooks.com
• absolutelyamazingebooks.com

The Absolutely Amazing eBooks colophon is a trademark of J. T. Colby & Company, Inc.

Library of Congress Cataloging-in-Publication Data
Rockwell, Marjory Sorrell.
Quilting On A Midsummer's Night, A Quilters Club Mystery #19.
p. cm.
1. FICTION / Mystery & Detective / Amateur Sleuth.
2. FICTION / Mystery & Detective / General.
3. CRAFTS & HOBBIES/ Quilts & Quilting.
Fiction, I. Title.
ISBN: 978-1-955036-55-9, Trade Paper

July 2023

Quilting
On A
MIDSUMMER'S
NIGHT

A Quilters Club Mystery

(Book 19)

Marjory Sorrell
Rockwell

Quilter Club Mysteries

Quilters Club Mysteries

By Marjory Sorrell Rockwell

Quilt Block (Book 13)
A Thimbleful of Murder (Book 14)
Sew Be It (Book 15)
Stab Stitching and Other Dangers (Book 16)
A Golden Needle and a Silver Bullet (Book 17)
A Backstitch Murder (Book 18)

Available from
AbsolutelyAmazingEbooks.com

William Shakespeare (1564-1616)
by John Taylor, 1610
The Chandos portrait
National Portrait Gallery, London.

"Lord, what fools these mortals be!"

-A Midsummer Night's Dream

Table of Contents

Chapter Seven
"All that lives must die ..."

.

Chapter Eight
"What's in a name?"

.

Chapter Nine
"Come and take choice of all my library ..."

.

Chapter Ten
"I must to the barber's, monsieur,
for methinks I am marvelous hairy about the face."

.

Chapter Eleven
"Foul whisp'rings are abroad ..."

.

Chapter Twelve
"When we are born, we cry that we are come
to this great stage of fools."

.

Chapter Thirteen
"My love is thine to teach."

.

Chapter Fourteen
"The nature of bad news infects the teller."

.

Chapter Twenty-Two
"Like a dull actor now,
I have forgot my part ..."

.

Chapter Twenty-Three
"Un-thread the rude eye of rebellion,
and welcome home again discarded faith."

.

Chapter Twenty-Four
"And cursed be he that moves my bones."

.

Chapter Twenty-Five
"Nothing can we call our own but death ..."

.

Chapter Twenty-Six
"... His foul and most unnatural murder."

.

Chapter Twenty-Seven
"Though she be but little, she is fierce."

.

Chapter Twenty-Eight
"The baby beats the nurse,
and quite athwart goes all decorum."

.

Chapter Twenty-Nine
"The direful spectacle of the wreck ..."

.

Chapter Thirty-Seven
"Full oft we see cold wisdom waiting on superfluous folly."

.

Chapter Thirty-Eight
"If you poison us, do we not die?"

.

Chapter Thirty-Nine
"Plead you to me, fair dame? I know you not ..."

.

Chapter Forty
"O gentle son, upon the heat and flame
of thy distemper,
sprinkle cool patience."

.

Chapter Forty-One
"Poison more deadly than a mad dog's tooth."

.

Chapter Forty-Two
"Like a barber's chair that fits all buttocks."

.

Chapter Forty-Three
"Life's but a walking shadow ..."

.

Chapter Forty-Four
"And when I am forgotten, as I shall be,
and asleep in dull cold marble, where no mention
of me must be heard of, say, I taught thee."

.

Chapter Fifty-Nine
"Good counsellors lack no clients:
though you change your place,
you need not change your trade."

.

Chapter Sixty
"Let's kill all the lawyers."

.

Chapter Sixty-One
"Sound trumpets! Let our bloody colours wave!
And either victory, or else a grave."

.

Chapter Sixty-Two
"A man can die but once."

.

Chapter Sixty-Three
"Why, I can smile and murder whiles I smile."

.

Chapter Sixty-Four
"Farewell, a long farewell to all my greatness!"

.

Chapter Sixty-Five
"The dove pursues the griffin; the mild hind
Makes speed to catch the tiger; bootless speed,
When cowardice pursues and valor flies."

.

11

Chapter Sixty-Six
"So we grew together,
like to a double cherry, seeming parted,
but yet an union in partition,
two lovely berries moulded on one stem."

.

Epilogue
"The evil that men do lives after them."

INTRODUCTION

"A murderer and a villain ..."
-Hamlet

As you might gather from the accompanying quotes, this Quilters Club mystery revolves around a troupe of Shakespearean actors who visit the little town of Caruthers Corners, Indiana. Maddy and the other members of her quilting bee get involved when a famous thespian drops dead in the middle of a Shakespeare-in-the-Park performance of *A Midsummer Night's Dream*.

I hope you will enjoy reading it.

This is my 19th book in the Quilters Club mystery series. You can find them all – either as ebooks or sturdy trade paperbacks – on Amazon as well as other online venues. I didn't intend to write this many books, but the characters kind of ran away with the story, reappearing time after time in my mind with new adventures.

These whodunits have covered such mysteries as those Lost Boys who disappeared into Never Ending Swamp, Commander McBragg's missing dinosaur bones, buried Viking treasures, nuclear threats, fake seances, and flying saucer sightings.

Readers tell me that Maddy and her friends Cookie, Bootsie, and Lizzie remind them of people they know ... or would like to know. And those same readers say they have fallen in love with Maddy's grandchildren: clever Aggie and brainiac N'yen, along with their sassy BFF Sissy.

They also like the quilting themes. That's important.

However, the books are really about the town of Caruthers Corners. Sure, I made it up, but based on some very real places in northeastern Indiana that I know so well. Thanks for letting me take you on a personal tour.

I'm glad you enjoy these stories. Without you, I would just be talking to myself.

-Marjory Sorrell Rockwell

Shakespeare in the Park quilt pattern by Judy Martin.

CHAPTER ONE

"This is very midsummer madness."
-Twelfth Night

Maddy Madison was enjoying the summer. Hotter than usual, thanks to insipient climate change. Icebergs and glaciers were melting, she'd read. But the nights in her small Indiana town of Caruthers Corners were reasonably comfortable, thanks to the nearby Wabash River. It seemed to bring a cooling breeze along with its lazy brown waters.

Maddy and her husband Beau were looking forward to an outing this Friday night, a special event sponsored by the Walters Foundation. This was a non-profit fund controlled by Maddy's twin sister Maisie Walters. Being that June 24 was Midsummer, a traveling theater troupe had been engaged to present Shakespeare's *A Midsummer Night's Dream* as an outdoor performance in the Town Square.

Summer solstice – when the earth's pole tilts closest to the sun –measures as the longest day of the year. That actually lands on June 20, but because the old Julian calendar marked it differently, the date for Midsummer generally remains as June 24.

Midsummer celebrations have taken place since the Stone Age. The early church created the Feast of St. John the Baptist to coincide with Midsummer. That's because, according to

The Gospel of Luke, John was born six months before his cousin Jesus, fixing the date as the 24th.

Midsummer's Night is said to be "a time when faerie folk pass into the human world at Twilight and offer blessings." People reflect on the coming harvest season and the beauty of Mother Earth. Traditions include singing and dancing, jumping over bonfires, and searching for the magic fern flower at midnight. Celebrations sometimes feature outdoor festivals and plays.

The Merry Times Players was a popular roadshow headed up by a highly respected Shakespearean actor named Adolphus Everly Anderson. Aficionados know that Addy Anderson was a two-time winner of The Burbage, a prestigious award for actors who have made their mark in productions of the Bard's works. Notable winners have included Sir Laurence Olivier, Sir Ian McKellen, John Philip Kemble, Edmund Kean, and Sir John Gielgud.

This award was named in honor of Richard Burbage, the great actor who worked directly with William Shakespeare from the beginning of both their careers. From 1594, Shakespeare and Burbage were among the leaders of Lord Chamberlain's Men, an acting company which later became known as the King's Men. They were part owners of the famous Globe Theater.

Adolphus Everly Anderson was renowned for his portrayal of Puck, the mischievous fairy in *A Midsummer Night's Dream,* the one who replaces Bottom's head with that of an ass. Puck is based on the *púca,* a prankish faerie creature of Celtic mythology. William Shakespeare was not shy about appropriating ideas from other cultures, myths, or even the Geneva Bible.

He commonly borrowed from other people's works, copying liberally from Latin and Greek literature as well as from writers like Geoffrey Chaucer, John Gower, Raphael

Holinshed, and Giovanni Boccaccio. *Hamlet* was taken from an old Scandinavian tale; *Romeo and Juliet* was inspired by someone else's poem; *The Tempest* was based on a true account of a shipwreck. Adapting the work of other writers was very common at the time.

A Midsummer Night's Dream is an exception, considered by many critics to be an original story. However, some see influences of Ovid's *Metamorphoses*. The recurring theme of *Metamorphoses*, as with nearly all of Ovid's work, is love. Here, Shakespeare examined the flip side – jealousy.

Written circa 1595, historians believe the play was created for (and performed at) an aristocratic wedding. The plot of this lighthearted fantasy revolves around the wedding of Duke Theseus of Athens and the Amazon Queen Hippolyta. Under the light of the moon, in a forest inhabited by faeries, Puck concocts a magical potion that makes people fall in love. Thus, four members of the wedding party find themselves bewitched in this sly mix-'em-match-'em examination of love, jealousy, and marriage.

This Merry Times performance was scheduled to take place in the Town Square, the 10-acre green that faces the Caruthers Corners Town Hall. Summer concerts were common at the gazebo. An open-air performance on a warm Midsummer Night was a perfect community event.

But the presentation of *A Midsummer Night's Dream* was never completed. Adolphus Everly Anderson died of a heart attack in Act 3 Scene 2.

Maddy Madison did not believe his death was from natural causes. She had good reason to suspect murder. But how to prove it?

Was this a job for the Quilters Club?

CHAPTER TWO

**"Once more unto the breach, dear friends,
once more."**

-Henry V

Those of you who have followed Maddy's adventures in previous books know that the Quilters Club is a small quilting bee comprised of four friends: Lizzie Ridenour, director of the Quilting Heritage Museum; Cookie Bentley, head of the local Historical Society; and Bootsie Purdue, founder of the Strays & Rescues Animal Shelter. Maddy Madison, wife of a former mayor and mother-in-law of the current mayor, was the group's de facto leader.

What you also may know is that this foursome has a well-earned reputation as amateur sleuths. To Bootsie's husband's chagrin – Jim Purdue was the town's police chief – they had solved many local mysteries without any help from law enforcement. From the Lost Boys who disappeared into Never Ending Swamp to the ghost that haunted Beasley Manor to patchwork quilts stuffed with rare 1890 "watermelon dollars." They even thwarted a madman from poisoning the town's water supply, uncovered secrets of the Potawatomi effigy mound, and solved the mystery of the legendary Madison Meteorite. You can look it up.

However, recently having accused the wrong person of a murder, the Quilters Club had abandoned its role as a quasi-detective agency. They had been certain that a state park ranger had killed a philandering college professor while inspecting bat populations in an Indiana cave. Turns out, the prof had accidentally bumped his head. No murder here at all. How could they have been soooo wrong?

No more detecting, no more snooping, they vowed.

Therefore, the idea of looking into the on-stage death of Adolphus Everly Anderson was not a popular subject for Maddy to broach at their next meeting. But Anderson's death bothered her.

The group met on Tuesday afternoons to work on quilts. Their current project was sewing baby quilts for an orphanage in nearby Burpyville. A bumper crop of unwed mothers had strained the sanctuary's resources. Baby quilts and crib quilts were in short supply.

The most popular sizes are 30" x 40" for newborn quilts, 30" x 30" for preemie quilts, and 36" x 56" for regular crib quilts. Patterns being used for the project included the Turnstile Block, the Dresden Burst, the Giant Star, the Sawtooth Star, and the Simple Triangle.

Maddy held up the morning's paper. **ACTOR DIES ON STAGE** blared the headline on front page of the *Burpyville Gazette*. "I think we should look into this," she said.

"What's to look into?" asked Cookie. "He had a heart attack."

"I'm not so sure about that."

"What makes you question that actor's death?" asked Bootsie. "Doc Medford ruled it a coronary thrombosis."

"I know the play pretty well," replied Maddy. "As you'll remember, I was in a college production of *A Midsummer Night's Dream*. So I noticed that Adolphus Everly Anderson changed the words to one of the lines just before collapsing."

"What did he say?" asked Cookie. She, like Maddy, had attended the performance. But the historian had been visiting the restroom when the actor collapsed mid-sentence. A weak bladder. Fortunately, a half-dozen Porta Potties had been placed in a semi-circle beyond the koi pond like a gypsy encampment. It was a bit of a hike.

"You know the part in Act 3 about *'ghosts, wandering here and there'*?"

Cookie nodded. "Of course, I do." Having an eidetic memory, she knew the exact words better than her friend. Probably better than the actors themselves.

She picked up the lines:

"My fairy lord, this must be done with haste,
"For night's swift dragons cut the clouds full fast,
"And yonder shines Aurora's harbinger,
"At whose approach ghosts, wandering here and there,
"Troop home to churchyards. Damnèd spirits all,
"That in crossways and floods have burial,
"Already to their wormy beds are gone,
"For fear lest day should look their shames upon.
"They willfully themselves exiled from light,
"And must for ayfe consort with black-browed night."

Maddy nodded. "Yes, that's the passage."

"So?"

"Well, instead of *'And must for ayfe consort with black-browed night,'* Puck actually said *'You must look to the murderer on my right.'* Then he toppled over. Dead by the time he hit the ground."

"A-are you saying he actually named his killer?" stammered Lizzie. Blowing a strand of henna-red hair out of her eyes with a puff of breath. She'd missed this week's appointment at Helen of Troy, the salon that did her usually immaculate coiffure. Fussy about her looks, she didn't feel properly dressed without her complete makeup and perfectly styled hair.

Maddy shrugged, a faint tilt of her shoulders. Her own silver hair riffling with the motion. "That was my thought."

"So who was standing on his right?" asked Bootsie, thinking like a policeman's wife. Looking to identify the guilty perp on the spot.

"That would be Hermia," said Cookie. Picturing the scene in her mind's eye. When she had excused herself to the restroom, the scene had locked itself into her brain like a photographic snapshot.

"Hermia? Is that an actor?" Lizzie had skipped the performance. She hated opera, Shakespeare, and poetry recitals. Instead, Lizzie had watched a TV movie with her husband Edgar. That Robert Redford epic about a mountain man called *Jeremiah Johnson* – her outdoorsy husband's pick. He loved rough-and-tumble survival movies.

"Hermia is a character in the play," explained Maddy. "The daughter of Egeus, an Athenian girl who is in love with Lysander – she was played by an actor named Carl Leicester."

"Carl? Don't you mean Carla?"

"No, Carl's a he."

"I thought you said Hermia was the *daughter* of Egeus."

"The character is a female. But here – like in Shakespeare's day – women's roles were played by men."

"Men?"

"That's right," confirmed Cookie. "Merry Times does 'classical performances.' In Shakespeare's day it was considered unseemly for women to appear on stage, so all characters were played by male actors."

"So you're saying this Carl Leicester is the murderer?" asked Bootsie, trying to follow the conversation. The plump pixie-haired brunette was easily confused.

Maddy smiled weakly. "Only if you believe Adolphus Anderson's last words."

"Also if you believe that he didn't die of a heart attack," Cookie pointed out. The blonde historian was always the logical one.

"Yes, that too," admitted Maddy.

"Why would you doubt Doc Medford?" asked Lizzie. The county's part-time coroner was also everyone's family doctor. Dr. Franklin Delano Medford's office was unfortunately (but conveniently for a coroner) located next door to Yost & Yost Funeral Home. He'd maintained a medical practice there for nearly 40 years.

"Because it didn't look like a heart attack to me," Maddy defended her opinion. "Instead of clutching his chest, he grabbed his belly before he fell over."

"That doesn't sound like a heart attack," agreed Bootsie. Years ago, she'd had training as a paramedic. "Most heart attacks involve discomfort in the center or left side of the chest that lasts for more than a few minutes. The discomfort can feel like uncomfortable pressure or pain."

Lizzie looked it up on her iPhone: "Says here that 'Many people think that a heart attack is sudden and intense, like the "Hollywood" heart attack depicted in the movies where a person clutches his or her chest and falls over,'" she quoted. "'The truth is that many heart attacks start as a mild discomfort in the center of the chest. Someone who feels such a "non-Hollywood" warning may not be sure what is wrong.'"

"Still sounds fishy to me," observed Bootsie. "Clutching his stomach. Saying the actor on his right has murdered him."

"But Doc Medford ruled it a heart attack," argued Lizzie.

"I love Doc. He's been my physician most of my life," said Maddy. "But you'll remember that he misdiagnosed Ethel Osbourn's pregnancy. Turned out to be a tumor."

"He's not an obstetrician."

"He's everything else," observed Maddy. "The sign next to his door proclaims that he's a general practitioner, oncologist, radiologist, podiatrist, and reflexologist, as well as the county coroner and a forensic pathologist."

"That's quite a mouthful."

"Even so," said Maddy, "he's not infallible."

"Okay, okay. Maybe it's possible it wasn't that actor's heart," Cookie gave in. "But then what was it?"

"Could be lots of things," said Maddy. "I'd guess poison. But it could have been anything from an electric shock to an artificially induced blood clot."

"Or a sonic beam that makes the brain explode or a blow dart dipped in curare or a deadly virus from Wuhan or even an eat-your-brain earwig, " added Lizzie. Being sarcastic. She had a sharp tongue at times.

Bootsie had other causes of death to suggest. "Or a drug overdose. Or acute respiratory arrest. Or an undiagnosed advanced terminal illness, such as cancer. Or postpartum hemorrhage."

"Are you daft," scoffed Lizzie. "Men don't get postpartum hemorrhage."

"Yes, some of that sounds highly unlikely," sighed Cookie. "But I get your point. That it could have been lots of things besides a heart attack"

"Still seems suspicious to me," said Bootsie. "People don't just drop dead in the middle of a play. Things like that just don't happen."

"So should we investigate?" Maddy called for a vote.

"Play detective? I thought we said we weren't going to do that anymore," Lizzie reminded them. "We made a big mistake with that park ranger. Practically ruined the man's life."

"But if we don't," responded Bootsie, "this Carl Leicester might get away with murder." A cop's wife, she believed in bad guys getting their due.

"How could he have killed anybody?" challenged Lizzie. "Nobody saw him do anything. He was simply standing next to this Aloysius Anderson."

"Adolphus Anderson," Maddy corrected.

"Lizzie's right," said Cookie. "Hermia was merely standing there beside Puck. She – or he – didn't lay a hand on him. There are nearly 300 witnesses to that fact."

"Poison, it had to be poison," said Maddy.

"How about we ask Doc Medford to show us the toxicology report?" suggested Bootsie.

"I'm still betting it was his ticker," murmured Cookie. "But checking the toxicology report is a good idea. That should settle whether he was poisoned or not."

"And we should look into Carl Leicester," suggested Maddy. "What motive might he have had? Was there any bad blood between him and Adolphus Everly Anderson? What's his history? Does he have any prior arrests? Stuff like that might be helpful to know."

Lizzie looked pained. "Are you sure about this? I wouldn't want to falsely accuse anybody else. Honestly, I will feel guilty about that park ranger till the day I die."

"Me too," admitted Cookie. She pushed her wire-frame glasses onto the bridge of her nose. She didn't really need prescription lenses after her recent cataract surgery, but wore them because she thought it made her look more serious, like a proper historian.

"Girlfriends, *we* aren't accusing Carl Leicester of anything," explained Maddy. "The victim did that. I distinctly heard him say '*You must look to the murderer on my right.*'"

"I've heard of deathbed confessions," grumbled Lizzie. "But I've never heard of a deathbed accusation. Have you?"

"This seems to be one," shrugged Maddy.

"Are you absolutely certain you heard him say that?" pressed Cookie. Obviously perturbed that she'd missed that part of the play. With her infallible memory there would have been no question about what was said.

"Yes. That's exactly what he said. Pinky swear." Maddy stuck out her hand, locking her small finger with Cookie's fifth digit.

"Oh, okay," sighed the blonde historian. "I'm in. I'll go along with my best friend."

"Count me in too," nodded Bootsie. "As long as you promise we'll be discrete. No pointing fingers publicly at this Carl Leicester until we have him nailed. Jim would lock us all up if we accused the wrong man again."

"Lizzie?"

"Oh, okay," the redhead gave in. "Just don't make me cite any Shakespeare sonnets. I failed English lit in college, as you'll remember. That left psychological scars. I never want to read *Romeo and Juliet* or *Macbeth* again!"

"I thought *Romeo + Juliet* was one of your favorite movies," said Maddy.

"It is. But that's because it starred Leonardo DiCaprio – not because it had anything to do with Shakespeare."

CHAPTER THREE

**"All the world's a stage,
and all the men and women merely players ..."**
- As You Like It

Cecilia LaToya Jackson aspired to be an actress. Sissy had received great reviews for her recent performance in the Caruthers High production of *West Side Story*. One of those modern "colorblind" presentations, she had starred as Maria.

"Is N'yen coming home this weekend?" Sissy casually asked over breakfast. N'yen's parents, Bill and Kathy, lived in Chicago, but Maddy's grandson considered Caruthers Corners his second home – or third home if you counted his dorm room at Northwestern. Even though he was only 16, the little brainiac was studying astrophysics under the university's Early Admission program.

"Yes. And you will be pleased to know he may be staying for awhile. His school is on summer break."

Sissy often had breakfast with the Madisons. She was practically a member of the family, being N'yen's official girlfriend. And her grandfather was Beau's old Army buddy. "Way cool," she murmured, helping herself to another piece of watermelon Danish.

Caruthers Corners was considered the watermelon capital of northeastern Indiana. Its annual Watermelon Days – a three-day festival – was a big tourist draw. At the recent event, Sissy took first place in the Junior Quilting Competition with a Rose of Sharon design. Lizzie Ridenour – predictably – took the top prize in the adult competition with an amazing Triple Double Diamond Star quilt of her own creation.

"Aggie's coming home too," said Maddy. Her granddaughter – Tilly's oldest – would be a sophomore at Yale when school reconvened for the Fall Semester.

"Dope."

"Beg pardon?"

"Excellent, I mean. Aggie is my best-est girlfriend."

Beauregard Madison shambled down the stairs and made his way into the kitchen, joining them at the breakfast counter. Now fully retired, Maddy's hubby had taken to sleeping later. It was nearly 9 o'clock. Caruthers Corners being plunk in the middle of farm country, most folks were early risers. "Coffee please," he greeted them with a lopsided grin. "I desperately need caffeine."

"Here you go, Pooh Bear," Maddy handed him a cup. That new Keurig made excellent coffee, a big improvement over her old electric percolator.

"Good to the last drop," he saluted them with his cup before taking a sip.

"This happens to be the Dunkin Donut brand," his wife pointed out. "If you want Maxwell House, you have to go over to Cozy Café." Maddy's twin sister owned the town's only diner, that aluminum-fronted eatery on South Main. Cozy Café was known for its "Never-Ending Cup of Coffee for Only 50¢."

"This'll do just fine," he grinned. "I'll get my Cozy Café fix at lunch." This was the day he met with Police Chief Jim Purdue, a holdover from when he'd been mayor. Jim had been his best bud since high school – "back in the Mesozoic Era," as they put it. Now in their mid-60s, they had been friends for a long time.

"Ask Jim if I can get a peek at the coroner's findings on the death of Adolphus Everly Anderson. I'm particularly interested to see a toxicology report."

"Who – that actor fellow?"

"Adolphus Everly Anderson was one of the most famous Shakespearean actors ever," opined Sissy. "Right up there with Patrick Stewart and Kenneth Branagh." She had been there the night Anderson died. The entire Drama Club was – a class assignment from Mrs. Grady, the club's sponsor.

"The Quilters Club is looking into his death," said Maddy.

"I thought you'd given up being a sexagenarian Nancy Drew," Beau winked at his wife, flirting.

"I prefer to think of myself as a *sexy* Nancy Drew," replied Maddy, serving him a plate of watermelon pancakes. One of his breakfast favorites. Particularly with a big slab of butter and plenty of syrup.

"You are that indeed, my dear," he said, slathering the pancakes with Aunt Jemimah (now rebranded as Pearl Milling Company). He liked the sweet wheatish flavor, no matter what they called it.

"Hey, no lovey-dovey talk in front of an innocent teenager," chided Sissy.

"When N'yen gets here this weekend, we'll see who's talking lovey-dovey stuff," laughed Maddy.

"Yeah, well –"

"Jim's not going to show you Doc Medford's reports," Beau got back to the subject at hand. "You know he's never approved of the Quilters Club butting into police business."

"He would if you asked. You used to be his boss."

"Mark Tidemore is mayor now," he named their son-in-law – Tilly's hubby. "Ask him to get Jim to give you that report, if you want to see it. I'm not going to meddle."

"Oh? You think *I'm* meddling?"

Beau laughed. "Dear, that's what the Quilters Club does when it isn't making quilts – meddle in murders and mysteries and things that should be left to the police."

"You know I think the world of Jim Purdue. But sometimes the police need a little extra help. That's where the Quilters Club comes in."

"Get serious. You gals have no official status. Jim would probably arrest the lot of you for 'interference in a police investigation' if his wife wasn't a member of your little gang of vigilantes."

"Vigilantes? We're simply doing our civic duty. You know, like a neighborhood watch."

"Well, watch me go out the door. I'm heading down to Slick Vic's for a haircut; then meeting Jim for lunch. But I'm not going to bring up that actor's death."

"Vic always trims your hair too short on the sides. Tell him to use the Number 8 clippers."

"Vic Davone doesn't take instructions from anyone. He's a tonsorial maestro."

"Vic is more of a follicle fascist– a haircut dictator."

"*Tsk, tsk*. You grownups should not be fighting in front of children," interjected Sissy. Her plate now empty.

Maddy laughed. "We're not fighting; we're bickering. And you're nearly 17, hardly a child."

"In that case, I'm going to have another watermelon Danish. An adult portion."

~ ~ ~

Bootsie Purdue was walking her dogs that morning. She had adopted six mutts from the Strays & Rescues shelter. Her husband had acquired a retired K-9 named Mörder through police channels. She was adept at jockeying six leases at the same time with all the skill of a Borax 20-mule team driver. The German Shepherd ran loose on his own, sniffing and marking his territory and happily wagging his tail.

"Hey there, Mrs. P," called Petie Hitzer, the next-door neighbor. A former police deputy, Petie and his wife Suzy Q managed Old MacDonald's Dairy. A small operation, the dairy farm had a contract to supply milk for Sealtest. It still delivered to a few local customers too, a holdover from when Petie's parents ran the farm.

"Hi Petie," she replied, pulling back on the leashes to slow down her rambunctious canines. She didn't bother trying to restrain Mörder. The K-9 only complied with commands in German, a language she didn't speak.

"Didja hear about that Merry Times acting troupe?" asked Petie. "Word is, the dead actor's brother is coming in to take over the traveling show, replace him as Puck in *A Midsummer Night's Dream*."

"They're still around?"

"I'm told they're holding up at Highliner Hotel over in Burpyville waiting for the brother. They plan a re-do of the show this coming Friday, even if it'll be a week past Midsummer night."

"A re-do?"

"Yeah, like they say, the show must go on."

"I suppose so."

"I'm thinking about taking Suzy to see the play. We skipped the earlier performance. But that guy dropping dead got our attention."

"I missed it 'cause I was out of town," said Bootsie. "Maybe I can talk Jim into taking me to this make-good performance. I'd like to see it."

"Let's just hope nobody drops dead this time around."

CHAPTER FOUR

"There is a history in all men's lives."
- Henry IV, Part 2

Founded in 1829 when a wagon train broke down on the banks of the Wabash River, Caruthers Corners is a town that values its heritage. The annual Founders Day celebrates those three hardy pioneers who led the wagon train – Jacob Caruthers, Ferdinand Jinks, and Col. Beauregard Madison. There's a statue of the three men on the far side of the koi pond in the Town Square.

Maddy's husband – Beauregard Hollinsworth Madison III – is a direct descent of one of that hapless trio, giving him a revered status among the town's elite. Beau is a tall, lanky man who reminds you of that farmer in those *Babe* pig movies. His term as mayor was uneventful, but well thought of.

If Maddy considered the women in the Quilters Club her closest friends, Beau would claim their husbands as his best buds. The four couples had been a tight-knit group since high school.

Edgar Ridenour (Lizzie's hubby) was a retired bank president. He and Beau were fishing pals, sharing ownership in a 20-foot Roughneck 2070 SC, a boat that could handle the uncertain depths of the Wabash. Beau's grandson N'yen often joined them in their pursuit of Ol' Calvin, a legendary catfish lurking near the Route 101 bridge. Chief Jim Purdue sometimes tagged along.

Ben Bentley (Cookie's second husband, Bob Brown having been killed in a tractor accident) was the county's largest landholder. He and Beau played poker with the guys at the Fire Department every week. Skilled at cards, Ben often took the pot. "The rich get richer," complained Beau's son Freddie, the town's Fire Chief, not always a good loser.

Jim Purdue (Bootsie's spouse) was, of course, Chief of Police. He and Beau kept a weekly lunch date. And the two families often vacationed together, enjoying trips to Disney World and other theme parks.

All four men served on the Caruthers Corners Town Council, technically the bosses of Mayor Mark Tidemore. Mark was married to Beau and Maddy's daughter Tilly. It was that kind of small town, not exactly a "bubba system," but one where everybody participated in civic affairs, everybody knew his or her neighbor. There was no political tribalism to contend with; Mark had run unopposed in the last mayoral election.

The only differing factions seemed to be among the descendants of the Town Founders. The Jinks relatives (mainly Johnsons and Crackletons) were bitter that their ancestor had been "all but written out of history." The Madisons felt Jason Caruthers had "stolen" the town's name. And those few Caruthers who were still around had a grandiloquent view of their place in the town's history.

That's why everybody was taken aback when Squeaky Beasley filed a legal petition to change the name of the town to Beasleyville.

~ ~ ~

Major Samuel Elmsford Beasley – known as "Old Sam" – was a passenger on that 1829 wagon train which led to the establishment of the town. A retired military man heading West with his family, he reportedly had a bellicose nature. History books identify Major Beasley as being the leader of that infamous massacre of Potawatomi in the Battle of Gruesome Gorge. As travelers to northeastern Indiana know, Gruesome Gorge is now the name of a canyonesque state park.

Several years back, the Quilters Club had exposed a fake quilt that was said to pictorially document that Ol' Sam had founded the town. A letter from a Beasley descendent claimed: "*Major Beasley helped found the town of Caruthers Corners. It was originally named Beasleyville, but in a political upset the name was changed by a vote of the early settlers led by Jacob Abernathy Caruthers.*"

However, experts disagreed. *The History of the Indian Territory, 1800 - 1900* by Nelson Lawrence Chadwick clearly stated that Major Samuel Beasley played "a minor role" in the founding of the town. And it was *never* known as Beasleyville.

As a professional historian, Cookie hated it when people tried to revise the past. She was familiar with the Winston Churchill quote that "History is written by victors." But there were no victors in the Beasley family. Ol' Sam had been exposed as a sadistic killer of peaceful Potawatomi. His descendants had nothing to brag about.

Seriously, who wanted to name their town after a mass murderer?

~ ~ ~

Sissy lived with her grandfather. Buck Jackson had been Beau's sergeant in Vietnam where they had fought gooks.

That's what they called Vietnamese back then. Nonetheless, he was pleased that Sissy was dating N'yen Madison. It was like the union of two kingdoms, the Jacksons and the Madisons. He liked that idea, kinda like fate stepping in to reaffirm their longtime relationship. Wars made for long-lasting friendships.

Sissy didn't give it a second thought. To her, N'yen was her soulmate. Having been raised in the South, she had a syrupy romantic viewpoint of Life. Love at first sight. Love is forever. Stuff like that.

N'yen was ethnically Vietnamese. But he'd never set foot in that faraway country. Having been born in Chicago, and adopted at an early age by a couple of purebred Midwesterners like Bill and Kathy Madison, he knew little of Asian culture, other than his taste for food like *phở* or *bún chả* or a fish dish called *Chả cá Lã Vọng*.

Sissy grew up with ham hocks and collard greens and black-eyed peas – although she preferred MacDonald's fare, particularly Big Macs ("two all-beef patties, special sauce, lettuce, cheese, pickles, onions on a sesame seed bun") and those delicious thin-cut French fries slathered with bloody-red ketchup. Yum.

In some ways they were an odd couple – she seeped in superstition and faith; him driven by science and logic. But somehow it worked. Balanced them off, you might say.

~ ~ ~

"Chief," said Det. Harry Teague, standing at the door of Jim Purdue's cramped office, "I've got a message here that might interest you." Harry was the Caruthers Corner's Police Department's lead detective – that is to say, its only detective.

"What's that?"

"You remember that park ranger who beat the rap on the murder of that college professor?"

"You mean the prof who bashed his head while looking for bats in that cave down south?"

"Yeah, Marengo Cave. Everybody thought that ranger – Hugo Marston – killed him, but that Vietnamese kid used your K9 dog to prove his innocence."

"Yeah, Mörder was trained to be a cadaver dog. Worked for the Chicago police before he got retired." Chief Purdue cocked his head. "What about Marston?"

Harry looked down at the paper in his hand. "According to this text from the North Dakota Bureau of Criminal Investigations, they've arrested Hugo Marston for homicide. Says he killed a man who made a pass at his wife."

"I'm not surprised," said the Police Chief. "That guy certainly had some anger management issues."

CHAPTER FIVE

"I pray thee, gentle mortal, sing again."
-A Midsummer Night's Dream

Razor's Edge is a two-chair barbershop that's located down the alley and under the backside of Kupnick's Pharmacy. Folks go there for a quick trim or styling.

Despite the two chairs, there's only one barber – Victor Davone. Been that way for 40 years. His only competition hereabouts is Gabe Hilty's Snippets Inc. The two men seem to have cornered the haircutting market, each having his own set of customers, as loyal as fraternal orders.

To his customers, Slick Vic Davone is known as "the singing barber." Instead of the chitchat and gossip found at Gabe's, Vic's clients get to sample of his crooning while he clips – a repertoire of old standards such as "Blue Moon," "Too Marvelous for Words," "Come Rain or Come Shine," and "They Can't Take That Away From Me."

Vic likes to compare himself to Perry Como, the pop singer who had been a barber before getting his big break with Freddie Corlone and His Orchestra back in 1933. That eventually led to an RCA recording contract and a series of popular television shows. Vic was still waiting for his big break, a fantasy that a talent scout would one day sit down in his chair and be swept away by his smooth rendition of "Smoke Gets In Your Eyes" or "Willow Weep for Me."

But that had never happened.

Nonetheless, Slick Vic continued to serenade his captive audiences. This morning, as Beauregard Hollingsworth Madison III got his hair trimmed, Vic was belting out an enthusiastic version of "Don't Let the Stars Get In Your Eyes." Mark Tidemore – Beau's son-in-law – was waiting his turn in one of the straight-back chairs that lined the far wall, his foot gently tapping to Vic's *a cappella* music.

"I hear those actors are going to reprise their Shakespeare-in-the-Park performance," said Beau when Slick Vic finished his song and began to shave his neck with a straight razor.

Mark nodded. "That guy dropping dead stopped the play. Rather than giving the town a refund, they opted to put on another performance. It's scheduled for next Friday in the Town Square. Their manager, a guy named Bartholomew, arranged it."

"Was Merry Times obligated to do that? I'd think the death of an actor would be considered an act of God. A legal out."

"Poor fellows, their contract didn't cover *force majeure*. And they didn't have any insurance. I gather money's been tight for them in recent years and they've been cutting corners."

"That's surprising," commented Beau. "Adolphus Everly Anderson is a fairly famous actor."

"True. That's why we asked Maisie's trust fund to hire them for this summer conclave. Thought it would add a touch of culture. As you know, the Watermelon Fest is our biggest annual event, but it's essentially an agricultural fair."

"Who's going to replace Adolphus Anderson?"

"Turns out, his brother is a famous Shakespearean actor, too. Agamemnon Anderson – you may have heard of him?"

"No, can't say I have."

"Well, he has inherited the Merry Times Players from his brother. And now he's on his way here to take over the reins."

"Interesting. You say this guy's a big-deal actor too?"

"Pretty famous in Shakespearean circles. He and Adolphus were very competitive. Sibling rivalry and all that. Had a big falling out after Adolphus beat him out for a Burbage Award. They hadn't spoken in years, I'm told."

"Yet, Anderson made his brother his heir?"

"Guess blood is thicker than bitterness."

"You know, Maddy and her Quilters Club cronies think there's something suspicious about that actor's death."

Mark Tidemore shook his head. "Doc Medford ruled it a heart attack. That's good enough for me."

"Maddy claims the man clutched his stomach instead of his chest. She suspects he was poisoned, wants to see a toxicology report."

"Don't think one was done."

"Too bad."

"You were at the play. Did you see him grab his stomach?"

"Not really. I'm hate to admit it, but I dozed off. Didn't see the big death scene."

"Well, I was sitting there in the front row," replied his son-in-law. "I don't remember him grabbing his stomach. But then I wasn't expecting him to keel over dead in the middle of a speech. That caught everyone by surprise. Do you think Maddy could be mistaken?"

"Dunno. But you know how she is when she gets a bee in her bonnet."

"Yes, she can be very single-minded. My daughter Agnes takes after her."

"Maddy says the guy not only grabbed his stomach, but that he also he changed the lines in the play."

"If that really happened, you'd think someone else would have noticed. There were close to three hundred people in that audience."

"True, but she's convinced herself."

"Doesn't matter – case closed. Who cares whether Adolphus Everly Anderson died of a heart attack or from eating a bad tuna sandwich?"

"Careful what you say there," chuckled Beau Madison. "I hear those actors had dinner at Cozy Café before the play. Maisie might not appreciate you suggesting that her food killed someone."

~ ~ ~

Maisie Walters was whipping up today's luncheon special, Watermelon Gazpacho. That was popular summer fare for Cozy Café customers – light and chilled and tasty. In the background, WZUR's mid-morning Easy Listening Hour was playing "Too Marvelous for Words," the version from Frank Sinatra's 1957 album, *Songs For Swingin' Lovers!* The words seemed to ooze out of the diner's Bose sound system. It reminded her of local barber Vic Davone; he had sung that very number at last month's Lion's Club talent show. Slick Vic had a pretty good voice for a guy without any music training.

Maisie preferred WZUR's programming – news and easy listening – over WABL's Howlin' Horace and his hard rock playlist. To her, Heavy Metal was a term for "metalloids with a high atomic density." That's what she'd been taught back in high school, long before the advent of highly amplified, harsh-sounding rock music.

10:00 to 12:00 – this was the lull between breakfast and lunch, a period that rarely saw customers. While Cozy Café employed a cook and waitresses, Maisie usually prepared the daily specials herself. Just because she was rich (that inheritance she and Maddy got from the Hoople Quadruplet Foundation had been like winning the lottery), she hadn't neglected management of the diner. Besides, she *liked* to cook.

That's why Maisie was surprised to see the revolving door admit a customer at precisely 11:30. It was Police Chief Jim Purdue, Bootsie's husband.

"Hi there, Jimbo. You already ate that dozen donuts you bought this morning?" she greeted him with her usual affability.

The Police Chief frowned. "Those donuts were for my deputies. I only had one. My wife has me on another stupid diet."

"Which one? Keto? Paleo? Calorie Counting?"

"The Deprivation Diet. Anything I want I can't have."

"Sounds tough."

"Tell me about it," he groused.

"What's up?" She was eager to get back to mixing her gazpacho. Lunch hour was looming.

"I dropped by to ask you to speak to your sister."

"Maddy?"

"Only one you got, far as I know." Maddy and Maisie were fraternal twins, the secret love children of Herbert Hoople – one of the famous quadruplets – accounting for their late-in-life acceptance into the Hoople family. And huge inheritances!

"What do you want me to tell her? That she has an overdue parking ticket?"

"It's a little more serious than that."

"Okay, shoot."

"That's not a thing you want to say to a man carrying a gun." He patted his sidearm, a Glock 17L.

"Good point. But back to Maddy?" Although the two women had grown up separately, unaware of their sisterhood, Maddy and Maisie had become quite close in recent years. They worked back-and-forth coordinating their philanthropic donations.

"Your sister has got it in her head that that actor's death was actually murder," sighed Jim Purdue. "She's got her Quilters Club cronies all stirred up. They want to reopen the case, despite Doc Medford's finding of death from natural causes.

"A heart attack, I heard."

"That's right. Nothing to investigate here. The coroner's report settled the matter – a myocardial infarction to be precise."

Maisie leaned her elbows on the counter. "You sure you just don't want your wife meddling in your business? I know that's got to put strain on your household."

"That's not the point. There's simply no evidence suggesting foul play."

"I haven't talked with Maddy in a couple of days. Likely she'll call this afternoon or tonight. If so, I'll ask her about her theory."

"Theory? It's pure imagination, I'm telling you!"

"Okay, whatever. I'll see what she has to say. Anything else?" She needed to get back to her gazpacho. It had to be chilled just right.

Jim Purdue glanced at his wristwatch – 11:45 on the dot. "I may as well take a table. I'm meeting Beau here for lunch in fifteen minutes. Maybe I could start with a cup of your Good-to-the-Last-Drop coffee?"

CHAPTER SIX

"Let's choose executors and talk of wills ..."
-*Richard II*

Agamemnon Anderson put down the telephone, a quizzical look crossing his angular face. A lawyer in Indiana had just informed him of his brother's death. No big deal that that jerk Adolphus was dead – a heart attack, they said. Not like the two of them had ever been close. But the big news was that, being Addy's only living relative, he'd inherited the Merry Times Players, his brother's theatrical touring business.

What luck! He was about to be booted from the repertoire cast of The Bard's Traveling Road Show. He'd been drunk during their performance of *As You Like It* in Phoenix. So what if he liked a nip now and then before a big show? There had been more than 3,000 people in the audience at the Phoenix Civic Auditorium. Not that he got stage fright – he'd been doing this for years – but a sip of Wild Turkey always took the edge off.

To heck with his boss and those two-bit actors he was forced to perform with. He would now be a direct competitor, owner of his own touring company. The lawyer told him that Merry Times was marginally profitable. Undoubtedly, he could turn the company around with his enormous acting talent and loyal fan following. He was a star in search of headlines!

Agamemnon was a tall man – 6-foot-2 in his leather boots, handsome by most standards. Looking more like Adolphus's twin than a younger sibling, he had the same aquiline nose and prominent cheeks and lightning-bolt blue eyes as his brother. He often wore a satin cape and a foppish wide-brimmed hat. All a part of his thespian persona.

He quickly got back on the phone and booked a flight to Burpyville Regional Airport for Monday. The Merry Times actors were holed up in a hotel there, awaiting him to come take over his new property. It would be an arduous flight – Phoenix to Dallas, Dallas to Indianapolis, Indianapolis to Burpyville. The first two legs were on wide-bodied jets, 747s. The last jag on a twin-prop commuter plane. He hated small planes.

The lawyer had told him that the Merry Times manager, a guy named Benjy Bartholomew, had re-booked the troupe to repeat *A Midsummer Night's Dream* next Friday. He was expected to step into the role of Puck. No problem there. He knew the part, could do it in his sleep. Thanks to Addy's untimely death, this performance could draw a lot of valuable publicity his way.

Next, he scribbled a note of resignation to The Bard's Traveling Road Show. He left it under the manager's hotel-room door, then pulled out his aging PC laptop and sent off an email firing his agent. No need to be paying an agent his usurious 10% when you'd be working for yourself in the future.

He had told the lawyer to have Adolphus cremated and send him the bill. He'd scatter the ashes at Stratford-upon-Avon come his next pilgrimage to William Shakespeare's birthplace. He tried to go every three or four years, a spiritual connection to the scribe who wrote the words he recited night after night. A pretty good living, thanks to "the greatest writer in the English language."

Some might say Milton or Dante were greater, but Agamemnon subscribed to the opinion of Marchette Chute, a critic known for her insightful biographies of Geoffrey Chaucer, Ben Johnson, and William Shakespeare. She summarized it like this:

"William Shakespeare was the most remarkable storyteller that the world has ever known. Homer told of adventure and men at war, Sophocles and Tolstoy told of tragedies and of people in trouble. Terence and Mark Twain told comedic stories, Dickens told melodramatic ones, Plutarch told histories and Hans Christian Andersen told fairy tales. But Shakespeare told every kind of story – comedy, tragedy, history, melodrama, adventure, love stories and fairy tales – and each of them so well that they have become immortal. In all the world of storytelling he has become the greatest name."

Shakespeare wrote plays of such magnificent beauty and universal ideas that they are still performed the world over in thousands of productions and a great variety of interpretations. By actors like Agamemnon Anderson.

And best news of all, with Adolphus gone, Aggy would be acknowledged at last as "America's Most Celebrated Shakespearean Actor" – even if it was by default. So much for that stupid lawsuit!

~ ~ ~

Benjamin Jerome Bartholomew had been manager of Merry Times Players for the past twelve years, since its very inception, serving as righthand man to Adolphus Everly Anderson. He'd helped Addy start the touring company, handled all the legal details, booked the town-to-town appearances, arranged for the travel and hotels, oversaw the finances and payroll, managed both the roadies and actors and stagehands.

It was a thankless job.

Adolphus Everly Anderson might have been a great actor, but he was also a loathsome and penurious owner. Fortunately, Benjy Bartholomew had possessed a knack for dealing with the Great Man: an obsequious nature that showered Adolphus with flattery, stroked his overinflated ego, pumped up his innate narcissism. Addy wallowed in it, unconcerned with day-to-day details, divorced from real life, eschewing responsibility, knowing that Benjy would take care of everything.

Truth be told, the job was demeaning and unpleasant, but Benjy loved it. A failed actor, he found managing an acting troupe quite satisfying. It allowed him to remain close to the stage and the performers that he worshipped. He loved the hustle-and-bustle of putting on a show, the brightness of the footlights, the applause of the audience – even if he only shared them second-hand from backstage.

Benjy Bartholomew would have done anything for the Merry Times Players. Now and then he went without pay, his sacrifice helping the company meet its payroll. But sometimes – with the uncertainty of theatrical bookings – the cast went wanting also. This unreliable cash flow was becoming more common these days. Bookings were falling off, as if culture and refinement were on the wane.

"We are becoming a nation of illiterate savages," Adolphus Anderson had complained loudly.

Benjy Bartholomew tended to agree.

Then came that fateful performance of *A Midsummer Night's Dream ....*

The death of his employer threw Benjy into a deep depression. What would become of Merry Times? What would be the fate of his beloved actors? They were like children to him, like kindergarten tots who spent their days playing in a literary sandbox.

Then, he heard from Addy's lawyer. According to a handwritten will found among his personal effects, Adolphus Everly Anderson had left everything to his brother. The conditions of the will required Agamemnon Anderson to keep the Merry Times Players intact, assume management control, continue its performances throughout the Midwest as usual.

This was indeed good news. Merry Times would carry on. The actors would enjoy continued employment. And – best of all – he got to continue with his only-one-degree-of-separation from the stage as day-to-day manager.

"'I can no other answer make, but thanks, and thanks.'" he said to no one in particular. Shakespeare had a saying appropriate for every situation, he reminded himself. He was happy with this surprising news from afar.

CHAPTER SEVEN

"All that lives must die …"
-Hamlet

Beau slid onto the stool next to Police Chief Jim Purdue. They often ate at the counter, a holdover from when they were teenage boys and Cozy Café was still called Morty's Delicious Diner.

Of course, Mortimer Longacre was long dead now, having sold the restaurant to Maisie Walters a few months before getting kicked in the head by a horse. Everybody agreed Maisie was a much better cook. And she knew how to treat her customers right, placing a cup of hot coffee on the counter in front of Beau Madison before he even ordered it.

"What's today's lunch special?" he asked. After all these years, neither he nor Jim bothered looking at a menu. They knew it by heart. Only the specials differed.

"Gazpacho."

"Hm, think I'll pass on that," he said. "I can never decide whether it's a soup or a liquid salad. What's Jim having?"

"Tenderloin," his friend interjected.

"Me too then," decided Beau.

"Coming right up." Maisie had already popped two breaded pork tenderloin cutlets into the deep fryer in anticipation of their orders.

One foodie website describes the pork tenderloin as "a classic Hoosier dish, with a thinly pounded, breaded, and deep-fried portion of meat hanging over the edges of a bun. At its best, the breading is crisp and crunchy, the meat juicy and well-seasoned, and the bun toasted enough to hold up to the grease, with a few condiments to top things off. Often comically oversized, the tenderloin edges might need to be nibbled at before going for a full bite, or sliced off and eaten with a knife and fork."

The pork tenderloin was invented in 1904 by Nicolas Freienstein, the son of German immigrants. The sandwich was a riff on wiener schnitzel. He'd been selling food off a pushcart on Courthouse Square in downtown Huntington, Indiana, but in 1908 opened Nick's Kitchen where he introduced the tenderloin sandwich as a regular part of his menu. Now it's considered the state's unofficial sandwich. Not surprising, considering that Indiana is fifth in the country for pork production.

"The pork tenderloin sandwich is central to the state's cultural identity," it has been suggested. "Some say it's exactly like the people in Indiana: simple, not too showy, sometimes a little too big for its britches." Well, that sounded about right.

~ ~ ~

Jim Purdue began nibbling at the overlapping edges of his tenderloin. "Beau, you've gotta get Maddy to calm down about that dead actor," he said. "She's got my wife all riled up, asking to see Doc Medford's official autopsy report."

The lanky man took a big bite off his sandwich. "Show the report to her," he replied. "If it says this Anderson fellow died of a heart attack, that oughta take the wind out of her sails."

"I suppose so. But the report's not very detailed. Doc was so convinced that a heart attack was the obvious conclusion, he just gave it a lick and a promise."

"Get him to amend the report," suggested Beau. "Add some more medical gobbledygook. Pad it a bit. Give 'em the medical definition of a heart attack, talk about how stress or whatever can bring one on. That oughta do it."

"Aw, you know how stubborn Doc can be. Almost like dealing with Maddy. They both can be mulish." He looked up, slightly embarrassed by his words. "You know what I mean," he apologized.

Beau waved his friend's concern away. "You don't have to tell me," he laughed. "I live with her. But I love her."

Bringing a Pyrex pot over, Maisie refilled their cups. Keeping true the diner's promise of the "endless cup of coffee." Having been listening, she said, "D'you boys really think you can keep my sister away from a murder? Good luck with that."

Jim ran his hand across his nearly bald head. "The Mayor wants me to keep a lid on this," he said warily. "As you know, the Town Council voted to bring in a big PR firm to help us promote tourism as a year-round thing, not just the once-a-year Watermelon Fest."

"We have Founders Day," said Maisie.

"Yeah, yeah, big deal. Nobody outside the town limits cares about that. " He looked up, embarrassed again. "Aw, you know what I mean, Beau. I know you're descended from a Founder. No offense intended."

"None taken."

The Police Chief was preaching to the choir. Both he and Beau Madison were on the Council and had been involved in the unanimous vote. Talks were underway with a public relations firm out of Indy called Gimble & Gimble. They were the ones who came up with the award-winning campaign for the Watermelon Growers Association – "Watermelons Put a Smile on Your Face" – those ads that show a little boy's face peeking from behind the smiling curve of a watermelon slice.

"Gimble & Gimble is costing an arm and a leg. They were the ones who suggested Merry Times as a way to beef up our summer fare."

"There is that," sighed Beau. "Does kinda put us between a rock and a hard place."

Jim looked up at Maisie, still standing there behind the counter, coffee pot in hand. "Did you go to that Shakespeare-in-the-Park outing?" he asked.

"No, I was never into that highbrow stuff. Did my duty by feeding them dinner before the show."

"Did they all have the same thing?"

"Yes, my Chicken Chasseur."

"One of my favorites," noted Jim.

Beau spoke up, "That's what the guy who died ate?"

"Hmph," snorted Maisie. "Are you suggesting maybe he died of indigestion?"

"Now, now," Jim calmed her. "Nobody's saying that."

Beau remembered his conversation that morning at the barbershop, with Mark the Shark practically accusing her of poisoning Adolphus Everly Anderson. What poisons were in fashion these days, he idly wondered as he finished off his sandwich and washed it down with cream-laden coffee. Back in Socrates' day, hemlock was *de rigueur*. In the 19th Century, arsenic was known as "the inheritor's powder," a hard-to-detect method of getting rid of a bad husband or a rich uncle. The Japanese seemed to choose ricin or tetrodotoxin. These days Russian spies seem to reply on radioactive compounds like polonium-210 or a Novichok nerve agent.

Of course, some people died from eating a bad oyster. President Zachery Taylor supposedly died of gastroenteritis caused by eating cherries. And King Henry I died from eating a "surfeit of lampreys." Sophocles died by choking on a grape seed. Mama Cass choked on a ham sandwich. Rocker Jimi Hendrix strangled on his own vomit. And Tennessee Williams was said to have choked on a bottle cap.

Odd that at this moment, Beau thought of a line from *Hamlet* he had memorized in high school: *"Thou know'st 'tis common; all that lives must die, passing through nature to eternity."*

Yep, it's just like they say: No one gets out of this life alive.

~ ~ ~

Turns out, Adolphus Everly Anderson had enjoyed a roast chicken with vegetables as his last meal. That's the same food singer John Legend likes to eat before a performance.

"I have a regimen," Legend once told an interviewer. "It's not for any real reason – I'm not superstitious. Once I kind of settled on what I liked before my show I just kept eating it every time. It's very simple. It makes me feel like, 'I'm ready to go sing now.'"

And after a show, Legend prefers to drink a simple cup of tea. Adolphus Anderson never got as far as the tea – or a Jack Daniels, as the case may be.

"Roast chicken doesn't sound dangerous," commented Jim Purdue when Maisie stepped away to wait on another customer – Phil Kupnick Jr., owner of Kupnick's Pharmacy. Being located just across the street, he ate lunch here every day without fail.

"Didn't Elizabeth Taylor almost choke on a chicken leg?" said Beau.

Jim took another bite of his sandwich. "But *she* didn't die ... and Addy Anderson didn't choke to death, according to Doc Medford."

"Hmm, good point."

"Roast chicken sounds pretty bland. Not a likely candidate for food poisoning. Besides, Maisie said she prepared the meal herself. Can't get safer than that."

"True," agreed Beau.

Phil Kupnick waved from his nearby table. "Beau, Jim – how you guys doing?"

"Just fine, Phil," answered Beau. "You?"

"All good. Tell Maddy her prescription's ready. She can pick it up at her convenience."

"Will do." His wife took Atorvastatin (20 MG daily) for her cholesterol. A precaution after that stroke a few years ago.

"Hi Phil," nodded the Police Chief. "You got any more of them watermelon-flavored Starbursts? I surely do love them little candies."

"Hard to keep 'em in stock. They go quick." Starburst was hands-down the most popular candy in Indiana. Manufactured by Wriggly, the chewy soft taffy comes in many fruit varieties – Tropical, Sour, FaveREDs, Summer Blast, etc. No surprise that watermelon was the bestselling flavor in Caruthers Corners.

"Can you hold a box back for me when you get in a new shipment?"

"Will do. I expect another delivery this week. But we've been experiencing some supply-chain problems due to the pandemic."

Caruthers Corners had avoided the worst of Covid thanks to the entire town getting vaccinated as a test group. Luckily, the formulation of the Mod-Tim vaccine they received also

had been resistant to many of the variants that followed –
from Omicron to Alpha (B.1.1.7) to Delta AY.4.2.

"What about this Monkeypox?" asked Beau. "Do we need
to worry about that?"

"Not likely. We don't have many monkeys around these
parts," joked the pharmacist.

Beau chuckled politely. "Good news is that Monkeypox is
not as contagious as the Covids," he added. He wasn't one to
kid around about serious matters.

"Too bad about that actor," said Phil, turning back to his
gazpacho. "He seemed like a nice guy."

"You met him?" Chief Purdue's radar went up.

"Just in passing. He came by the drug store before his
performance that day. Bought some Rolaids."

"Rolaids?"

"Yeah, said he had a stomach ache."

CHAPTER EIGHT

"What's in a name?"
-Romeo and Juliet

Mayor Mark Tidemore held a press conference that afternoon. Microphones had been set up on the steps of the Town Hall. He looked pretty dapper with his $1,800 Kincaid No. 3 suit and fresh haircut. About a dozen reporters had shown up for the event. A good turnout, in his estimation.

Mark cleared his throat and made eye contact with members of the Fourth Estate. "Thank you for coming," he began. "As you know, the town of Caruthers Corners has been petitioned by a lawsuit to change its name. However, the Town Council rejects that concept. Like it or not, the town has been known as Caruthers Corners for nearly 200 years. No need to change maps, signage, deeds and other documents just to satisfy the ego of a single individual with a grudge over his antecedent's anonymity. We will strongly oppose any attempts to rewrite history. We have filed an opposition."

Penny Heath, a reporter with the *Burpyville Gazette*, raised her hand. "Who was this Major Beasley mentioned in the lawsuit – the guy they want to name the town after?"

"I'll take that one," Cookie Bentley leaned into the microphone, her blonde hair shading her face. As county historian, she was sharing the podium with the mayor. "Major Samuel Elmsford Beasley was a member of the wagon train that brought the first settlers here. His wife was killed in an altercation with local Indians. In a vicious act of revenge, Major Beasley led a well-armed militia against a peaceful village of Potawatomi, murdering men, women, and children in what has become known as the Massacre of Gruesome Gorge. This infamous act of genocide is an unremovable stain on the town's history."

That brought a hush over the assembled reporters.

Not one to be deterred, Lucius Plancus with WZUR was up next. "Who is this John Beasley that filed the lawsuit?"

Mark adjusted the mic. "I've never met Mr. Beasley. But I'm told he's a great-great – I'm not sure how many greats – grandson of Major Samuel Beasley. He recently returned to town, after living many years in Massachusetts. His aunt runs the Beasley Heritage Museum in Hobson's Landing, Massachusetts. That's about all I know."

Cookie added: "The Historical Society had dealings a few years ago with the Beasley Heritage Museum. John Beasley's aunt – one Eunice Smith-Cardwell – owned a quilt that she claimed was proof of Ol' Sam's prominent role in founding this town. But the quilt turned out to be fake, a modern-day fabrication that she had sewn by hand herself. Nice needlework, I might add – but a total scam."

"So there's no basis to this claim?"

"None."

"Anyone else?" the Mayor surveyed the crowd.

Darlene Baxter had a question. She was normally the weather girl on Channel 4, but today was subbing for a sick colleague. "Will the question of renaming the town actually go to trial?"

"We don't think so," Mark flashed a winsome smile at the Barbie Doll blonde. "I expect Judge Cramer will quash the petition after he examines the facts."

Lucius Plancus raised his hand again. The big redhead was known to be tenacious. "What about the Jinks descendants? They have long opposed the name of Caruthers Corners. Do they have any involvement with this proposed change?"

"None at all."

"Do you expect them to make a new claim for *their* ancestor?"

"That ship has sailed," smiled the Mayor. "Time has settled any of their disputes as to the town's name."

"How does your father-in-law feel about this?" persisted the WZUR reporter. "Isn't he a descendant of Col. Beauregard Madison, one of the leaders of the wagon train?"

"Indeed he is, and proudly so," nodded Mark. "He's also a member of the Town Council. They took a vote last night affirming the town's desire to keep its name just as it is."

"And the Historical Society supports that position," reiterated Cookie Bentley.

"Any more questions?" asked Mark Tidemore.

Darlene Baxter called out, "I have one small request."

"Anything for the pretty lady in the front row."

"Could my camera crew get some footage of you across the street in front of the statue of the Town Founders?"

"No problem."

"And one more thing."

"Yes?"

"Could Channel 4 televise a debate between you and this John Beasley? We would give it a half-hour time slot following the *6 O'clock News*."

Mark the Shark held up his hands as if warding off her request. "Sorry, the only time Mr. Beasley and I will come face-to-face is in a courtroom. But, as I said, I doubt that will ever happen. He has no case."

"But –"

The Mayor took a deep breath, smiled as expected, and then declared, "That concludes our press conference. Thank you for coming."

~ ~ ~

Penny Heath caught up to the Mayor as he headed back to his office. "Excuse me, but I have another question," she called after him.

Mark Tidemore turned to examine her – a genuine Lois Lane type, a gonna-bust-this-town-wide-open reporter. He knew she was married to one of Jim Purdue's deputies, Det. Harry Teague, so he was inclined to be more generous than he might have been with other pushy journalists.

"Now what? Are you trying to sneak in a one-on-one interview?" he teased.

"No ... well, yes. But on a different topic. I wanted to ask about Adolphus Everly Anderson, that actor who died during your Shakespeare-in-the-Park event last Friday night."

Mark gave a faint tilt of his head. "Most unfortunate," he acknowledged. "And the play was going so well. I was sitting there in the front row. But by the time I got to him, he was gone. A heart attack, Doc Medford says."

"May I see a copy of the coroner's report? Public information and all that."

"Don't see why not. Pretty dull reading I'm afraid."

"Thanks."

"I'm curious. You've already covered the man's death. A front-page story. Why the ongoing interest?"

"Well, it's not every day that a world-famous Shakespearean drops dead in the middle of a performance."

She paused, then added, "And I hear the Quilters Club thinks he might've been poisoned."

That stopped Mark Tidemore in his tracks. His mother-in-law was meddling again. That wouldn't do. He'd have to put his foot down. "Where did you hear that?" he wanted to know.

"Oh, I have my sources."

He wondered if Chief Purdue had let something slip to his deputy, who had tipped his wife to the Quilters Club's theory. "Doc Medford says a myocardial infarction. That's good enough for me. Like I said, you can look at the coroner's report."

"Does Chief Purdue have any suspects?"

"Suspects for what? As I just said, this was ruled a natural death."

"Word is, the Quilters Club is claiming Adolphus Anderson made a 'deathbed accusation,' saying one of his fellow actors murdered him. Is that true?"

"Of course, not. Anderson died on stage in front of three hundred witnesses. No one heard him utter any dying words."

"Not dying words – more like a clue in delivering his lines."

"Who have you been talking with – Maddy? Bootsie? Cookie? That blabbermouth Lizzie?"

"You know I can't reveal my sources."

"Fine then. Play it that way if you want. You want to see that coroner's report, file a Freedom of Information Act request."

~ ~ ~

Beauregard Madison stuck his head inside the door of Kupnick's Pharmacy and called, "Hey Phil."

Phil Kupnick Jr. was behind the soda counter, making a milkshake for Donny Kinsinger. Chocolate, it looked like. He waved and replied, "Hi Beau. Nice seeing you at lunch. Maisie's gazpacho sure hit the spot, perfect for a hot day like this."

"I'll have to try it sometime," Beau allowed. But he was just being polite.

Kupnick added whipped cream to the top of the chocolate milkshake, placed a cherry on top, and slid it across the counter to Donny. "There you go," he said. "That'll be four bucks."

The boy counted out the change, then took a sip of the brown liquid. "*Mmm,*" he smiled happily. "Goooood."

"Glad you like it, Donny."

Then Phil Kupnick looked up at his visitor. "Anything I can get you, Beau. A milkshake? Wait, I know. You came by for Maddy's cholesterol pills."

"That's it," nodded Beau, stepping into the drug store and looking around the shelves as if considering buying a candy bar or a pack of gum. An old-fashioned drug store, Kupnick's offered everything from corn plasters to comic books, vitamins to vaporizers. A marble lunch counter running down the side; a pharmacist's counter across the back.

"Gimme just a minute." Phil Kupnick raced back to the pharmacy section and picked a white paper bag from an alphabetical lineup. He checked the name, then hurried back to the front. "Here you are."

"Got a question," Beau said matter-of-factly.

"Yes?"

"You say that actor came in to get some Rolaids?"

"That's right. Said his stomach was upset."

"What time was this?"

"A little after dinner. I stayed open late that night to pick up the Shakespeare-in-the-Park trade. Business was pretty brisk."

"Would that have been a symptom of an oncoming heart attack."

Phil Kupnick leaned forward, elbows on the marble counter. "I'm not a doctor, Beau. Just a humble pill-pusher. But I doubt it. He said it was indigestion."

~ ~ ~

Maddy pulled out her Playbill, the one that had been handed out to attendees of the Shakespeare-in-the-Park performance. There on the cover, it announced:

Merry Times Players present William Shakespeare's A Midsummer Night's Dream, a Comedy in 5 Acts.

She flipped through the pages until she came to one titled **WHO'S WHO IN THE CAST**. There, the fifth listing, last on the page, was the one she was looking for.

CARL LEICESTER (*Hermia*). Merry Times Players work includes: Antipholus in *The Comedy of Errors*. Mistress Quickly in *The Merry Wives of Windsor*. Iris in *The Tempest*. Celia in *As You Like It*. Cressida in *Troilus and Cressida*. Duke of Somerset in *Henry VI Part 1, Henry VI Part 2, Henry VI Part 3*. Flavius in *Julius Caesar*. Ophelia in *Hamlet*. Lady Macduff in *Macbeth*. Goneril in *King Lear*. Sextus Pompey in *Antony and Cleopatra*. Portia in *The Merchant of Venice*. Rosaline in *Romeo and Juliet*.

Interesting, thought Maddy. But this doesn't tell us much about the guy, just that he's a second-string actor who gets the minor parts. Mostly playing females.

Odd perhaps. But nothing here that makes him look like a killer.

She didn't bother turning the page.

~ ~ ~

Bootsie was trying to wheedle her husband into getting Doc Medford to reconsider his verdict. Surely, the old curmudgeon (Doc, not her hubby) could come up with a dozen possible causes for Adolphus Anderson's death.

There was a phenomena known as Sudden Unexpected Death, or SUD for short. She had looked it up on Google.

A sudden death is any kind of death that happens unexpectedly. These include:
- suicide.
- road crash or other transport disaster.
- drowning, falling, fire or other tragedy.
- undiagnosed advanced terminal illness, such as advanced cancer.
- sudden natural causes, such as heart attack, brain hemorrhage, or cot death.
- sudden death from a communicable disease such as COVID-19.
- sudden death from a serious illness that was known about, but where death wasn't expected, for example epilepsy.
- murder.
- war or terrorism.

It was obvious that Sudden Unexpected Deaths have many different causes.

Among natural causes are fatal arrhythmias, acute myocardial infarction, intracranial hemorrhage/massive stroke (cerebrovascular accident), massive pulmonary embolism, and acute aortic catastrophe. With so many potential causes of SUD, wasn't it reckless to pick a heart attack out of a hat as the answer.

And if a heart attack might be uncertain, then what about an unnatural cause ... like murder?

Even so, Chief Jim Purdue was having none of it. "Ain't my call," he tried to convince his bumptious wife. "If Doc ruled it murder, I would investigate. As long as he sticks with heart attack, there's nothing for me to investigate. End of story."

"But can't you ask him to take a second look?"

"Not my job. Let it go, Little Bear."

"But, Big Bear –"

"Enough or I will be forced to arrest you for interfering with a police investigation."

"You can't do that."

"Why not?"

"Because you said Adolphus Anderson died from natural causes so there's no investigation to interfere with."

"Oh yeah, want me to get out my handcuffs?"

"Promise?" she giggled.

CHAPTER NINE

"Come and take choice of all my library ..."
- *Titus Andronicus*

ookie Bentley could kick herself for going to the potty during Scene 3 Act 2 of *A Midsummer Night's Dream*. She'd missed the death of the actor playing Puck. Not that she was being ghoulish. Just that she could have confirmed Maddy's observations, what with her trick memory. Maybe picked up some other clues. Highly Superior Autobiographical Memory (HSAM) is a condition that has been identified in fewer than 100 people worldwide.

Cookie recalled a squib that had appeared on gossipmonger Matt Drudge's Internet blog, a report about a falling out between Adolphus Anderson and his actor brother Agamemnon over The Burbage Award. Adolphus's younger sibling felt he'd been cheated out of it by some backstage hanky-panky with the judging committee. No evidence of misconduct ever surfaced. But, according to Drudge, the two brothers never spoke again.

Another interesting report – actually just a one-liner – in *Financial Times* suggested there had been a lawsuit between the Andersons over the use of the tagline "America's Most Celebrated Shakespearean Actor." Apparently, based on his two Burbages, Adolphus handily won the case.

~ ~ ~

Cookie decided to do more research. After all, her memory was only as good as what she had previously seen or read. She couldn't recall a fact that she'd never been exposed to before.

She took the morning off and drove over to the Burpyville Public Library. Being Director of the Historical Society, she had the flexibility of making her own hours.

You might ask why she chose the Burpyville Public Library? After all, the Caruthers Corners Library was located in the Perricock Science & History Museum – the same building as the Historical Society. In fact, only a few steps away from her office. But unfortunately its chief librarian, Dorothy Stargazer, was still rebuilding the book collection after the devastating 2018 Northeastern Indiana Tornado had blown away the old library building with all its contents. Burpyville had a much larger reference section, some 30,000 volumes in all – intact.

The Burpyville Public Library was a massive stone building, constructed in 1927 by Andrew Carnegie's Library Endowment Fund. In all, Carnegie had donated some $40 million to build 1,670 public library buildings across the United States.

Taking a table in the Reference Room, Cookie started by skimming books about William Shakespeare. Much of it, she already knew.

Born in April 1564 in Stratford-upon-Avon, a small market town in the West Midlands of England, he was the third of eight children. Known as the Bard of Avon, he wrote 39 plays, 154 sonnets, three narrative poems, and various verses.

Sources from William Shakespeare's lifetime spelled his last name in more than 80 different ways, ranging from "Shappere" to "Shaxberd." In the handful of signatures that have survived, the Bard never spelled his own name "William Shakespeare," using variations or abbreviations such as "Willm Shakp," "Willm Shakspere" and "William Shakspeare."

Shakespeare attended Stratford's local grammar school, where he mastered reading, writing, and Latin. Shakespeare's parents were probably illiterate. His father signed his name with a mark. His wife and children almost certainly were, though his daughter Susanna could scrawl her name.

In November 1582, 18-year-old William wed Anne Hathaway, a farmer's daughter eight years older than himself. She was three months pregnant at the time. Daughter Susanna was followed by twins Hamnet and Judith in 1585. His son died in childhood, but probably contributed his name to the play *Hamlet*. The spellings were interchangeable in Shakespeare's day.

Nobody knows what William Shakespeare did between 1585 and 1592. Some have speculated that he worked as a schoolteacher or joined an acting troupe. But by the end of these "lost" years, he had established himself as a successful playwright. A competitor, Robert Greene jealously denounced him in a pamphlet as an "upstart crow." Ben Jonson called him the "Swan of Avon" in a poem.

The Globe, an open-roof public theater, was built in 1599 by Shakespeare's acting troupe, The Chamberlin's Men. Shakespeare and the other actors owned shares in the theater. About 20 actors, half of them owners. It burned down in 1613, but was rebuilt the following year.

Shakespeare often performed in his own plays. *The First Folio of 1623*, a posthumous collection of "Mr. William

Shakespeare's Comedies, Histories, & Tragedies" lists him as one of "the Principal Actors in all these Plays." It has been recorded that he preferred to play "kingly roles" as well as the Ghost of Hamlet's father.

Fellow actors among The Chamberlain's Men included Richard Burbage and his older brother Cuthbert, John Heminges, Henry Condell, Augustine Phillips, Richard Cowley, William Kempe, and Thomas Pope. Richard Burbage played the leading role in the first performances of many of William Shakespeare's plays, including *Richard III*, *Hamlet*, *Othello*, and *King Lear*.

~ ~ ~

Turning to books about famous Shakespearean actors, Cookie noted that many talented performers had carried on the torch. By the time of the Restoration, William Charles Macready was drawing applause as the lead in an adaptation of *King Lear*. During the 1740s, Charles Macklin was achieving acclaim as Shylock in *The Merchant of Venice*, and David Garrick was winning fame as the lead in *Richard III*. By the 19th Century, John Philip Kemble and Henry Irving were playing Hamlet, while Sarah Siddons and Ellen Terry were doing Lady Macbeth.

In 1936, Orson Welles produced *Macbeth* with an all-black cast (a production that came to be known as *Voodoo Macbeth*). In 1937, he produced *Julius Caesar*, costuming actors in Nazi uniforms. For *Othello*, he filmed it in a Turkish Bath. Welles acted in theatrical versions of *Julius Caesar*, *Romeo and Juliet*, *Macbeth*, *Twelfth Night*, and *Hamlet*, among others. And he brought several adaptations to the screen also.

Many consider Sir Laurence Olivier the best Shakespearean actor ever. Others who followed in his footsteps include Sir Ian McKellen, Sir Kenneth Branagh, Sir Ian Holm, Sir Patrick Stewart, and Sir Mark Rylance. Notable females include Dame Judi Dench, Dame Maggie Smith, Dame Diana Rigg, and Dame Vanessa Redgrave.

Richard Burton (in pre-Elizabeth Taylor days) established himself as a formidable Shakespearean actor with a memorable performance of *Hamlet*. He was called "the natural successor to Olivier," but (in Cookie's opinion) squandered his talent on the movies, booze, turbulent romances, and tabloid covers.

~ ~ ~

Next, Cookie's research turned to various touring companies.

Since 1982, Shakespeare & Company has been sending tours of The Bard's plays into middle and high schools, colleges, and other venues all over the Northeast. These performances reach more than 20,000 students, teachers, and audience members each year.

Another interesting troupe came from the American Shakespeare Center. Founded in 1988 as the Shenandoah Shakespeare Express, the ASC National Tour is a traveling company that uses Shakespeare's staging conditions to perform his plays – "on a bare stage, surrounded by audience, under universal lighting, with a company of actors playing multiple roles." ASC has performed in 48 states, one US territory, and six foreign countries, establishing itself as one of America's most respected touring theatre companies.

The list of touring groups was long, ranging from The Acting Company to Aquila Theater, National Players to RSC in America (an offshoot of Royal Shakespeare Company).

Then Cookie came to the two she'd been looking for – Merry Times Players, headed by Adolphus Every Anderson, and The Bard's Traveling Road Show, featuring Agamemnon Anderson. Although both were national touring companies, Merry Times seemed to spend much of its season performing in the Midwest, while The Bard's seemed to concentrate its bookings in the Southwest.

She ran her finger down the page. Each listing enumerated all the actors in the troupe. Adolphus was at the top of the column for Merry Times. Agamemnon was number three on The Bard's entry in the directory.

"Looks like Adolphus was winning the brotherly competition for Top Thespian," she murmured to herself. "Addy owned his own company; Aggy was only one step above being a spear carrier."

The librarian at the front desk whispered, "*Shhhh*. Quiet please."

CHAPTER TEN

"I must to the barber's, monsieur,
for methinks I am marvelous hairy about the face."
-A Midsummer Night's Dream

Slick Vic was sweeping up for the day. Enough hair lay on the floor to create a Sasquatch. He was humming "That Old Black Magic" as he swept. He preferred the Sinatra version over the Johnny Mathis recording or the Margaret Whiting album. He considered himself a purist.

He began to sing:

"That old black magic has me in its spell
That old black magic that you weave so well
Those icy fingers up and down my spine
The same old witchcraft when your eyes meet mine ..."

He did a little dance step as he swept.

Looking down, something caught his eye, a glittery object among the pile of follicles. What was that?

Bending over, he picked up a gold cufflink. Now that was strange, he thought. Most of his customers were working-class stiffs who had never owned a shirt with French cuff sleeves. About the only time around here anyone wore cufflinks was for a school prom. Those white puffy shirts that you rented with a tux usually included a set of cufflinks and studs that served as buttons.

But this cufflink was much too fancy for a prom. If he wasn't mistaken, those were diamonds inset in the square gold surface. That must have cost someone a pretty penny.

He turned the link in his fingers, inspecting it in the afternoon sunlight streaming through the barbershop's large plate-glass window. What was that? he asked himself as he noted a tiny catch. Flipping the surface upward with his thumb, he discovered a small compartment inside the link. Now that was odd. He'd never seen a cufflink with a hidden compartment before.

He tried to count the glittery specks of diamonds on the face of the cufflink. Must have been close to 50. And the backside of the link was stamped 18k in minute letters. This had to be very valuable.

Who could have dropped it?

How could he find the owner? Run a notice in the Lost and Found classified ads in the *Burpyville Gazette*? No, that wouldn't work. Not everybody read the paper anymore, it circulation dwindling.

Didn't WZUR carry a Swap Shop program on Saturday mornings? Yes, but its audience was mostly housewives looking to buy Bradford Exchange commemorative plates and other collectibles. Or working guys hoping to find a used chainsaw or a spare tire or a bowling ball.

Maybe one of his customers would come looking for it. That was the best bet. If nobody claimed it in a reasonable amount of time, finders keepers. Maybe he could sell it at Joe's Pawnshop down in Pitsville. Joe Prizvak bought gold and silver.

Shrugging, he tossed the link in a drawer filled with combs and clippers. May as well wait and see if anyone came round to claim it.

CHAPTER ELEVEN

"Foul whisp'rings are abroad ..."
-Macbeth

Lizzie Ridenour loved juicy gossip. The redhead always got an earful when she had her hair done at the Helen of Troy Spa & Beauty Salon. Margie Yost was like a taxi dispatcher, tracking the comings and goings of everyone within a two-county radius. She talked non-stop, telling all while coiffing Lizzie's hair. That's why Elizabeth Kay Ridenour maintained a weekly appointment at Margie's salon.

Today was no different. The topic being the death of that famous actor. You'd think she was talking about the fiery car-crash of James Dean or Elvis falling off his toilet from an overdose.

Margie was quick to admit she'd never seen a performance of any of Shakespeare's plays. She was more into soap operas. *Days of Our Lives* was her favorite. She recorded it on her DVR. The show had been on the air since 1965, long before Margie was born. Yet she followed the tumultuous lives of the Horton family, residents of a fictional Midwestern town, as if they were her next-door neighbors.

No surprise that Margie had not been at the Shakespeare-in-the-Park performance of *A Midsummer Night's Dream*, but she'd talked with dozens of customers who had. She had all the dirt, like a street sweeper at the end of the daily rounds.

A sampling:

—Doris Swartzendruber didn't remember Adolphus Everly Anderson clutching his belly. "But then I didn't have a good seat. I was behind Wanda Schaeffer, Fat Karl's wife. She really needs to go on a diet."

—Rita Rutaberger had an unobstructed view in the front row due to her wheelchair. Her health had been on the decline recently. She swore she heard the actor give a death rattle after hitting the ground. "Sort of an *Agggggh*. I don't remember what he said before that."

—Molly Dougan (née Heidecker) didn't know anything about that Oberon character changing his lines. "I was having trouble understanding what they were saying in the first place. That Elizabethan English is hard to follow. All those *anon*s and *perchance*s are confusing. Who speaks like that?"

—Missy Yager, owner of the Clothes Horse Boutique, was making out with her new boyfriend at the time, and didn't see anything.

—Doris Swartzendruber had dropped her husband Roger's hot dog while trying to put mustard on it and was down on her hands and knees searching for it in the grass, causing her to miss the entire death scene. She was very disappointed at failing to witness this "historic moment."

—Marnie Zarn, a teacher's helper at Daisy Mouse Kindergarten, thought the actor had tripped. She didn't notice anything unusual other than that. "I'm not sure why they stopped the play," she said. "Did he hurt himself?"

—Birdie Longstreet had a different view. She recalled that a hunchback troll jumped out of the bushes and "stabbed the actor with a long silver dagger." But Birdie was known to have a wild imagination, always seeing green-skinned space aliens and Elvis and Bigfoot in her backyard. No one else in the audience saw a "hunchback troll" or a "silver dagger."

—Michael Allen Palley was the best witness she'd spoken with so far. An accountant by profession, he had a no-nonsense, organized mind. "Yes, the man put his hand to his stomach, but I don't remember the lines he said before falling. I thought he might've been having been a stroke."

Lizzie took all this in as Margie fussed with her hair, combing at the springy red curls and clipping here and there with long thin scissors. "So there's nobody to back up Maddy's story?"

"Nobody I've talked with. But keep in mind there were 300 or so people there. I've only covered 30 or 40 so far."

"I'll check in next week. I think I'm due for a dye job."

~ ~ ~

Margie Yost may have preferred *Days of Our Lives* to Shakespeare's plays, but when you examined the two storylines, *Days of Our Lives* vs. *A Midsummer Night's Dream*, there were interesting parallels. Both dealt with love, family, marriage, death, and sex.

Compare them:

The plot of A Midsummer Night's Dream *revolves around the marriage of Theseus and Hippolyta. One of its subplots involves a conflict among four lovers. Another follows a group of six amateur actors rehearsing the play which they are to perform before the wedding. Puck the fairy makes both boys fall in love with the same girl. The four run through the forest pursuing each other while Puck helps his master play a trick on the fairy queen.*

Then check out *Days of Our Lives*. Soap.com gives a summary of a recent episode. Rather than fairies and enchantments during a wedding, you have omens and marriage proposals.

Disaster Strikes After Ava Ignores a Bad Omen and Accepts Jake's Proposal

Today on Days of Our Lives, *Ava throws caution to the wind, Jake protects his lady, Sarah pulls a knife on Gwen, Kristen takes her war with Chloe to HR, and Sonny gets a surprise.*

That's kind of Shakespearean, right?

As the BBC puts it, "Like today's soap operas, Shakespeare's plays featured characters and language that were, in their time, every day, relatable and topical. He poked fun at figures of the establishment, referenced current affairs, and used the latest words and slang of the day."

So, were William Shakespeare's plays merely the soap operas of their time?

CHAPTER TWELVE

**"When we are born, we cry that we are come
to this great stage of fools."**
-King Lear

The Historical Society maintained genealogy charts for most of the families in Caruthers Corners. With her weird memory, Cookie Bentley could recite many of them on demand, like the Bible's Book of Genesis with all its "begats." Cookie could not recall a Squeaky Beasley – and she had an infallible memory. But a little research at Ancestors.com turned him up with no great effort.

But she'd learned nothing particularly new: Just as she'd been told, John "Squeaky" Beasley was the nephew of Eunice Smith-Cardwell, the woman who ran the Beasley Heritage Museum in Massachusetts. Smith-Cardwell was the old fraud who had promoted Major Samuel Beasley's role in founding the town, based on a pictorial quilt displayed in her small museum.

Problem with that theory, Ol' Sam's wife – the woman who had supposedly sewed the quilt – had died during an Indian attack *before* the town's founding. When the Quilters Club pointed out this discrepancy, Eunice Smith-Cardwell confessed to the fraud, how she had created a phony quilt in an attempt to enhance her ancestor's historical standing.

Now her nephew was trying to do the same thing – without benefit of a quilt to back him up – merely an unsubstantiated lawsuit. The man was a scoundrel, in Cookie's opinion.

~ ~ ~

Chief Jim Purdue dropped by Razor's Edge for a quick trim. He didn't have enough hair for much of a cut, his male pattern baldness having left him with a shiny dome. The narrow circle of hair ringing the back of his head didn't require much care.

"The usual," he said to Slick Vic as he slid into the padded barber's chair.

"Sure thing, Jim," replied Vic Davone as he jacked the chair another notch higher. Now pushing 80, he had been cutting Jim Purdue's hair since he was a boy with bushy locks. From those unruly curls to a butch cut to that youthful mullet to a combover to the few sprigs that were left – Vic had been there for the entire capillaceous history of Jimmy's hairline.

The Police Chief settled back in the comfortable chair. He often fell asleep in the middle of Slick Vic's rendition of "You'll Never Know" or "It's Only Make Believe." More of a catnap, because his haircuts never took very long.

Vic rummaged in a drawer for a Number 2 guard for his clippers. That size was perfect for cutting hair short but with minimal scalp exposure. Jim liked what hair he had left to look shorter but fuller. Something comfortable but official.

As Slick Vic pawed through the combs and attachments, a little gold object caught his eye. It was that damned cufflink he'd found. He'd almost forgotten about it.

"Jim, take a look at this," he held it out for the police chief to inspect. "Found it on the floor yesterday. Some customer must've dropped it. Looks like it could be valuable. Says its 18 carat gold on the back side. And those shiny flecks look like real diamonds to me."

"What is it – a tie stud?"

"No, a cufflink. And look at this – it has a little compartment. What would you put in there?"

"A pinch of snuff?" shrugged Jim Purdue.

"Maybe."

"Don't know anyone round here who would wear such a fancy thing. Have you had any new customers lately?"

"No, same old, same old."

"Nobody just passing through?"

"Come to think of it, I did one of those actor fellows. Y'know, one of those thespians putting on that Shakespeare play."

"Thespians?"

"That's a fancy name for actors. Learned that from my Reader's Digest Word-A-Day calendar," Vic said proudly. "Comes from Thespis, the Greek who's credited with being the first actor."

"My wife has one of them calendars too," nodded Jim Purdue. "She's always trying out new words on me. Last week it was 'Pandiculation.' The other day it was 'Gubbins.'"

"'Pandiculation,' I remember that one. But what's 'Gubbins'?"

"An object that has little or no value."

"Don't guess you could say that about this cufflink. I'm betting it's worth a bundle. It's made of gold."

"Have you tried to research it?"

"No, how would I do that?"

"On the Internet, I'd say. Local jewelers –" meaning shops in nearby Burpyville "– wouldn't have a clue about something like this. I'd call it an oddity."

Slick Vic looked pained, as if suffering from a toothache. "I wouldn't know how to go about searching the Internet. Don't even own a computer."

"I could have Tommy do it. My deputy's a whiz. Ain't nobody smarter with a computer, unless it's N'yen Madison."

"That little Chinese kid?"

"Vietnamese. But born here in the United States."

"Yeah, I hear he's real smart."

"Already in college at sixteen."

"Okay, here you go," the barber handed Jim the cufflink. "You take custody of it. Have one of them boys check out what it's worth. But, remember, if nobody claims it, it's mine. Finders keepers."

"No problem. But sounds like it could belong to that actor. People like that wear fancy things. Puffy shirts and all that. Do you remember which one it was who came in?

"'Fraid not. You know I'm not one to make small talk. Just do my singing routine while I clip."

"Yeah, everybody gets a kick outta that."

"What I can tell you is that fellow liked my rendition of 'I Am the Very Model of a Modern Major-General.' Even joined in on the chorus."

"What's that song from?"

"*The Pirates of Penzance*, of course. He said he'd done the road show version a few years back. He had a very good voice."

"Wonder if it was the actor that dropped dead."

"No, not him. They ran a picture of that guy – Adoofus Anderson – in the paper. My customer was a different fellow. Much younger, I'd say. And gay as a goose."

CHAPTER THIRTEEN

"My love is thine to teach."
-Much Ado About Nothing

"**H**i, everybody, this is my drama teacher," Sissy introduced Estelle Grady, a reed-thin lady with unplucked eyebrows and mousy-brown hair. Her plain-Jane appearance was belied by a broad smile and a twinkle like an electric spark in her hazel eyes.

Maddy and the Quilters Club looked up from their work on baby quilts for that orphanage over in Burpyville. "Oh, happy to meet you," responded Maddy. "Sissy has such great thing to say about you. Yours is her favorite class."

"Thank you," the woman said. "And Cecilia is one of my favorite students."

"I brought Mrs. Grady over to meet you because she has something important to tell you. She heard Puck change his lines, too."

"Really?"

"Yes," nodded Estelle Grady. "I noticed the changes in Puck's scripted lines the moment he spoke them. As you can imagine, as a drama teacher I'm quite familiar with William Shakespeare's plays. I know many passages from the Bard's tragedies and comedies by heart."

"What did you hear him say?" Maddy asked timorously.

"The end of that passage that goes, '*And must for ayfe consort with black-browed night...*'"

"Right."

"Well, I heard him say, '*You must look to the murderer on my right.*' I thought that was a strange thing for him to say, don't you?"

"Exactly," said Maddy. "We think he was identifying his killer."

"His killer?"

"Yes," said Bootsie. "We think he was murdered."

"By whom?"

"Carl Leicester. He was standing on Puck's right."

"No," Estelle Grady shook her head. "Hermia was on Puck's left. Oberon was at stage right."

"Stage right – why didn't I see that," gasped Cookie. "In English-speaking cultures, 'stage left' and 'stage right' refer to the *actors'* left and right when facing the audience."

"Sometimes the terms 'prompt' and 'bastard/opposite prompt' are used as synonyms," added the drama teacher. "I would think Adolphus was talking traditional stage blocking."

"Let me make sure I understand this," said Lizzie. "You're saying the actor on Adolphus Everly Anderson's left was actually on his right?"

"Kind of."

Cookie nodded. "The person on *his* right would be facing the audience, making him on *our* left."

"So who was on Puck's right right?"

"The character on Puck's right was Oberon."

"Who's this Oberon?" asked Bootsie.

Mrs. Grady had the answer. "In *A Midsummer Night's Dream*, Oberon is King of the Fairies."

Bootsie frowned. "That's not what I was asking. I want to know who's the actor playing Oberon. We now know that *he* is the murderer!"

"Oh," Mrs. Grady said. "That would be Harvey Wallace Wallberg."

Bootsie said, "We need to take a closer look at this Wallberg guy. We've been wasting our time with Carl Leicester."

Everyone seemed to agree.

"I'm glad that's all straightened out," said Estelle Grady. "You can forget about Carl Leicester and his brother Bob."

"Bob?"

"Oh, I thought you knew. There are two brothers – twins – in the cast, Carl and Bob. But never mind them, now that you've figured out who Addy Anderson was talking about."

"Thank you for all your help," said Cookie. Frustrated that she hadn't picked up on two actors with the same last name. She hadn't bothered to read the credits in the Playbill.

"Yes, thanks for your help," sighed Lizzie. "We wouldn't want to accuse the wrong man – again."

Sissy said, "I know you all believed that Maddy heard what she said she heard. But I thought you'd want to know Mrs. Grady confirms it."

"Yes, but the big thing is she cleared up this business about stage right and stage left," said Cookie. "Showed us that we were looking in the wrong direction."

~ ~ ~

Cookie had once read a book titled *Who's Who on the Shakespearean Stage*, a lengthy tome written by a former *New York Times* theater critic. With her freak memory, she was able to call up the pages as if thumbing through a physical book. This guide to modern-day thespians had listed Harvey Wallace Wallberg as "a talented interpreter of such characters as Mark Antony (*Julius Caesar*), King Duncan (*Macbeth*), Oberon (*A Midsummer Night's Dream*), Duke Frederick (*As You Like It*), Proteus (*Two Gentlemen of Verona*), Lucius (*Titus Andronicus*), and King Edward (*The Raigne of King Edward the Third*)." Wallberg's reviews were generally good. He had accumulated several awards, but never The Burbage. *Stagecraft* Magazine had once described him as "promising."

But there was nothing here that would point to him as a murderer.

Problem was, most folks in the audience didn't know the lines of *A Midsummer Night's Dream*, so a few changed words wouldn't stand out to them. No wonder so few people noticed.

~ ~ ~

Lizzie heard back from Margie Yost. The proprietor of Helen of Troy Spa & Beauty Salon had been surveying more customers about what they saw at the abbreviated performance of *A Midsummer Night's Dream*. And as *gossipmeister supreme*, she had been making dozens of phone calls. Margie had the inquisitiveness of an investigative reporter; the well-tuned ear of a pollster; the relentlessness of a telemarketer.

"I didn't want to wait till your appointment next week," declared Margie. "Thought it best to give you a call and report on what I've heard so far."

"Thanks, you're the best."

"Yes, I am, aren't I? But, to the point: The *Burpyville Gazette* estimated there were close to 300 people attending that Shakespeare-in-the-Park performance. I've spoken to nearly 100 of them. I've found 67 people who recall Adolphus Anderson clutching his stomach before collapsing. And 38 who thought he mangled his lines before dropping dead. Most chalked it off to the confusion of a dying man. And 96 of them said they would go see a re-do of the performance. Also, I picked up four new customers from my calls."

"Well done," said Lizzie. Already fidgeting to share this info with the Quilters Club. This proved Maddy was right, sorta. Oberon had changed his lines and clutched his stomach. But did that mean he was poisoned? Not necessarily.

Nonetheless, they were getting closer to the truth. She could feel it in her hair follicles. Yes, very close.

"Shall I schedule a double appointment for you next week – give you the works?"

"Of course," said Lizzie. Feeling obliged.

~ ~ ~

Bootsie was frustrated over the fact that they now knew who was responsible for Adolphus Everly Anderson's death, but were powerless to do anything about it. The victim himself had pointed to Harvey Wallace Wallberg as his killer. Case closed, right?

Not really. Doc Medford was sticking with his findings, and as long as he did, her husband wasn't going to listen to the Quilters Club. Nobody would. It irked her that the menfolk dismissed them as a bunch of busybodies without any brains. Or at least that's the way it sometimes felt.

If she could only think of a way to get the facts out in the open. Telling her husband wouldn't accomplish anything; it would be like water off a duck's back. And putting out the rumor through Margie Yost would amount to nothing; hadn't Lizzie already gone down that road? Beau didn't want to hear about it; the Town Counsel had its own agenda. And you couldn't just buy a billboard outside of town that announced THE MURDERER IS … That would get you sued for defamation.

Maybe Maddy would have an idea how to stir the pot. She was clever about things like that. Yes, she would have to discuss this conundrum with her friend Maddy.

~ ~ ~

"Hi Penny, your husband gave me your number," said Maddy, speaking a tad loudly as people sometimes do on the phone. "I hope you don't mind me calling this late."

"No, not at all, Mrs. Madison. What can I do for you?" She knew Maddy Madison was a big deal in little Caruthers Corners, her husband being descended from one of the town's Founding Fathers. But more than that, the woman belonged to the Quilters Club, those amateur detectives posing as a quilting bee.

"I have a tip, but can you promise not to reveal your source? My friends might think I'm jumping the gun by telling you this."

"I once spent a night in jail on a Contempt of Court charge for refusing to reveal a source."

"And your husband married you despite your criminal record?" Maddy joked.

"He's trying to rehabilitate me," came the dry reply.

"Okay, here's the scoop. The Quilters Club has reason to believe an actor named Harvey Wallace Wallberg murdered Adolphus Everly Anderson. Probably used poison."

"And how do you know this?"

"Because of where he was standing."

CHAPTER FOURTEEN

"The nature of bad news infects the teller."
-Antony and Cleopatra

Burpyville *Gazette* crime reporter Penny Heath found Harvey Wallberg in Room 304 of the Highliner Hotel. A once-elegant turn-of-the-century brick structure, the Highliner had, as they say, seen better days. However, the impoverished acting troupe could not afford to stay in four-star establishments.

"Greetings, fair lady," Wallberg bowed to his visitor. She was a pretty blonde with a trim figure wrapped in a two-piece business suit. Just his type. His mother had been a sales executive with Amway. His former wife had been a loan officer for a large Cincinnati bank. He liked women who had a professional air about them. But then again, he liked young boys too. He was flexible in his sexual preferences.

"Are you Harvey Wallbanger?" Penny inquired. Confusing his name with the mixed cocktail.

"Wallberg," he corrected with a tinge of irritation. "Harvey Wallace Wallberg, the celebrated thespian who won a Tony for his rendition of Mark Antony's speech in the 1999 revival of Shakespeare's *Julius Caesar*. That's who I am."

"My apologies, can't read my own handwriting," she smiled, holding up her stenographic notepad as if displaying Exhibit A. The page was covered with chicken scratches – a mixture of Gregg shorthand and tiny cursive scribblings. "You were one of the stars of that Shakespeare-in-the-Park presentation over in Caruthers Corners – right?"

"Indeed I was. I play Oberon, King of the Fairies."

"Were you on stage when your colleague died?"

"Yes, I was standing precisely next to Addy when he collapsed. A heart attack, they tell me."

"I hear you will be reprising the performance on Friday."

"That's true, my dear lady. As soon as Addy's replacement gets here. He's flying in from Arizona."

"His replacement?"

"His brother – Agamemnon Anderson. He will be taking over management of the Merry Times Players. So I dare say my employment remains secure."

"Addy – that's Adolphus Everly Anderson?"

"Yes, indeed. A two-time winner of The Burbage, he was acclaimed for his stage interpretation of Puck. He will be sorely missed on the American theater circuit."

"Did you know him well?"

"I would say so. I have been with Merry Times for four seasons now. And also I appeared with him in a summer stock production of *As You Like It* a dozen or so years ago, before he founded this touring group."

"Did he have heart problems?"

"Not that I know of."

"Was he under any undue stress?"

"Just paying the bills. It was nip and tuck sometimes. America does not appreciate classical theater like it once did. Audiences are smaller. Fees are penurious. This is not a profession to get rich in, unless one can cross over to motion pictures like Kenneth Branagh or Laurence Olivier did."

"Do you –?"

"Excuse me, but exactly who are you?"

"Penny Heath with the *Gazette*. I thought I told you."

"Do you do theater reviews?"

"No, but –"

"Then I have nothing more to say," he sniffed. "Excuse me, but I must take my afternoon nap. That's the key to a good performance. Clears the mind, relaxes the body. Good day to you, my fair damsel. May angels sing thee to thy car."

"But –"

"So long, farewell, auf wiedersehen, adieu. In short, beat it."

Not much of a story here, Penny told herself as the door closed in her face. Those Quilters Clubbers must be off on the wrong foot again, like when they falsely accused that park ranger earlier in the year.

Those batty old gals must be losing their touch.

A shame. She liked them a lot. But another misstep would ruin their credibility as crime fighters. It would be like that 1997 *Thunderbolt* comic book, where you discover the superheroes were really supervillains. False accusations weren't something to take lightly.

Nonetheless, she would file a story about the theater troupe getting a new owner – a straightforward changing-of-the-guard announcement. The fact that the previous owner had died during a local performance provided enough human interest to get the piece a few column inches. And maybe she could play it up as exclusive. That never hurt.

Then she could get back to working on a bigger story, a series of burglaries down near Amish Acres, just off 73. The Managing Editor's mother had been one of the victims. You could bet he would give that story plenty of play.

CHAPTER FIFTEEN

" 'Tis best to weigh the enemy more mighty than he seems."
-Henry V

Lizzie Ridenour was very wealthy. She owned the controlling shares in the Caruthers Corners Savings & Loan, the bank that her grandfather had founded. Her husband Edgar had been its president until his retirement a few years ago. But even so, Lizzie's net worth didn't compare to the enormous riches that had made up the totality of the Hoople Quadruplets Trust Fund.

Those famous quads had toured the world, getting paid for public appearances, product endorsements, merchandising, licensing, motion picture rights, even several clothing lines. However, all that easy revenue had evaporated when it became known that the Hooples were not true quadruplets, not even biological brother and sisters, but instead a phony scam perpetrated by those unscrupulous tricksters, Henry and Henrietta Hoople. Fortunately for their heirs, Henry and Henrietta had put the money away in a Trust Fund and hired a former Mob lawyer to administer it in ways to keep the IRS and other creditors at bay. Barnabas Soltairé was very good at his job.

That massive wealth had been divvied up on the death of the remaining two "quadruples" (as they liked to be called), so Maddy's share was greatly diminished. But even so, it still dwarfed Lizzie's holdings. And you can rest assured that it takes a lot of money to make Lizzie's net worth seem small.

Nicolas Bergamachi, Lizzie's Italian-born grandfather, had started up the bank back in the mid-1800s. He was a bit of a robber baron, amassing a huge fortune by giving out high-interest loans to watermelon farmers and small business owners. It added up to a tidy sum.

As the bank's largest shareholder, Lizzie Ridenour had plenty of moolah to play with. So she hired a private detective to sniff out who might want to see Adolphus Everly Anderson dead.

~ ~ ~

Odell Lumley was a licensed private investigator out of Indianapolis. Not the two-fisted Phillip Marlow or Mike Hammer type, he did most of his work on a computer, searching records and databases and sometimes even the Dark Web.

Didn't take him long – a few hours actually – to come back with a preliminary report:

CASE # 17A-304
SUBJECT: Adolphus Everly Anderson
PROFESSION: Actor, Theater Manager
CURRENT STATUS: Deceased, Suspected Homicide

PEOPLE WITH POSSIBLE MOTIVES:
• Agamemnon Sophocles Anderson, the subject's estranged brother. They once engaged in a lawsuit over stage billing. No love lost here. The only heir.

• Harvey Wallace Wallberg, actor in Merry Times Players. Second lead. Past conflicts over billing, pay, roles. Bad blood here.

• Carl and Bob Leicester, twin actors in Merry Times Players. Homosexuals, they often play female roles. Physical altercation with subject over workplace harassment. Made verbal threats in front of witnesses.

• Herbert Golding, actor in Merry Times Players. Plays multiple roles. Was caught on video attempting to steal box-office proceeds. Adolphus Anderson blackmailed Golding, using a threat of turning the video tape over to police to keep him working at slave wages. (Note: This information came from another member of the acting troupe, Tom Turlington.)

• Tom Turlington, actor in Merry Times Players. Plays both male and female roles. Celebrated for his performance as Lady Macbeth. Straight, but has complained of sexual harassment from Adolphus Anderson. Big mouth, untrustworthy. "Not a guy who has your back," according to one coworker.

• Mildred Ann Fleming, a former girlfriend of Adolphus Anderson. Works as a hostess at a Ruby Tuesday in Chicago. A single mother, she was impregnated by Subject. He had to take out a restraining order when she began to show up at his performances and cause a scene.

• Ryan Hicks, a former business manager. Unsuccessfully sued Adolphus Anderson when the actor broke a management contract. Arrested for stalking Subject with a loaded handgun in his possession. Considered dangerous.

Any one of the above named people has motivation to do Subject harm. To narrow the list down will require another week's extension of my services. Let me know if you'd like for me to continue.

Sincerely,
Odell Lumley
Private Investigations R Us
Indianapolis, Indiana

Hmm, thought Lizzie, pleased with the report. This seemed like a good list to start working with. The Quilters Club was obviously on the right track, having already identified Harvey Wallace Wallberg and the Leicester twins as likely suspects.

CHAPTER SIXTEEN

"I like this place and could willingly waste my time in it ..."
-As You Like It

Agamemnon Anderson took a taxi directly from the Burpyville Regional Airport to the Highliner Hotel. He frowned as he pulled up in front of the faded brick building. Things must be going poorly for Merry Times if they were reduced to staying at a rundown fleabag like this. His inheritance seemed to be shrinking before his very eyes. Drat and double drat!

Nonetheless, Aggy had to admit he liked the weather here. Pleasant for a summer's day. He'd had enough of that blast furnace called Arizona. He took a deep breath as he walked up the steps, thinking: I will make the best of this. My brother's death is a windfall. This will be a new beginning for me! Onward and upward! To the heights.

At the front desk, he asked the clerk to call Benjamin Bartholomew's room. As the Merry Times' manager, Benjy was his brother's second-in-command. "Have everyone meet in the dining room at 3 p.m.," he announced his arrival.

Everyone was prompt, crowding into the small dining room with its stained yellow wallpaper and cut-glass chandelier. It wasn't clear whether this promptness was to impress their new boss or curiosity over their own fates.

Harvey Wallace Wallberg was first in the room, looking as regal as a king of fairies might be. He was followed by Martin Hubble, who played his queen. Next came Herbert Golding, one of the leads as the Duke of Athens. Beside him was Tom Turlington, who portrayed the Queen of the Amazons. Shuffling in after them were the Leicester twins, Carl and Bob, along with Henry Trout and Stuart Henley – the play's four bewitched lovers. Others – spear carriers and stagehands and roadies –crowded behind them in the doorway.

"Ah, you're all here," bellowed Agamemnon in his best stage voice. "Looks like I'm your new overseer. Is everyone willing to carry on at Merry Times with me at the helm?

There was a universal agreement, no dissenters. No one dared.

"Very good. I understand we have a performance this week – a make-good, as it were. I assume no rehearsal is necessary. *A Midsummer Night's Dream* is your forté. You've performed it hundreds of time – from Maine to Missouri. I will be stepping into my brother's role as Robin 'Puck' Goodfellow, a part I've played many times with other touring companies. If you have any questions, speak up."

"So it will be business as usual, no changes?" asked Benjy Bartholomew. Always concerned with job security for the troupe. His ducklings, as it were.

"Exactly," barked Agamemnon. "Other than I expect to do a much better job of directing this outfit than my stupid brother ever did."

"You and your brother didn't get along," Herbert Golding stated. "We all know that. But we don't want to get caught up in the middle of a family feud."

"Nothing to get caught up in. Addy's dead, so there's no feud."

"Yes, but –"

"That's enough on that topic. Anything else?" He surveyed the room. No hands were raised, no one speaking. "Guess not," he concluded with a wicked smile. "So shall we get on with it?"

Under his breath, Herbert Golding muttered, "Family feud? Looks like you won!" But no one heard him say this *sotto voce* as he left the room.

~ ~ ~

Five minutes later, Agamemnon fired Benjamin Bartholomew, the company's longtime manager. "Thanks for all you have done, my friend. I can take it from here," he said. "Give me a forwarding address and I will mail you any outstanding salary that might be due."

"But –"

"'*Fairies and gods prosper it with thee! Go thou further off; Bid me farewell, and let me hear thee going.*'"

"But, Mr. Anderson –"

"*Adieu, adieu.* Begone with you!

So much for "no changes."

CHAPTER SEVENTEEN

**"A hundred thousand welcomes: I could weep,
and I could laugh; I am light and heavy: Welcome."**
-Coriolanus

"**H**ail, fair sir, I bid thee a hundred thousand welcomes," Harvey Wallace Wallberg proclaimed grandly. He sat facing Agamemnon Anderson at a table in the hotel dining room. The new owner of Merry Times had appropriated the space to meet one-on-one with each of his actors and stagehands. These meetings had all the trappings of a tribunal, a court where fates were being decided, careers either affirmed or snuffed out like a candle.

Agamemnon Anderson looked dyspeptic, his eyes sallow, a snarling frown on his lips. He'd just got off the phone with some reporter from the local paper, confirming that he now headed up the Merry Times Players. He hated theater critics, but run-of-the-mill reporters could be a source of valuable publicity, more likely to value his pretty words than cast aspersions on a particular performance. Yet interviews were unnerving, often leaving him ill-temper and exasperated. Forget that admonition in *Henry VI Part II* of "*Let's kill all the lawyers.*" He'd much rather go after those blasted newspaper reporters.

"You are now the captain of our ship," Wallberg continued blithely.

"Hmph, I feel I've just been made captain of the *Sea Venture*." Anderson named the ship whose wreck off Bermuda had inspired Shakespeare's *The Tempest*.

"I am sure you will right the vessel, good sir," answered Wallberg, at his obsequious best. He had his own plans for this revival of the Merry Times Players, with him as puppet-master pulling all the strings. He just needed to assert himself with this new owner. This might well be his big moment, a turning point in his theatrical career.

"There is much to fix," murmured Aggy Anderson.

"Fix?"

"Have you not seen? Reviews of your recent performances have been sour. I dare say the company's stagecraft has not been up to par. The ship is scraping bottom."

"I quite agree. I tried to tell that to Adolphus, but he turned his ear away. I have many good ideas; I am sure you will like them upon hearing."

"Yes, yes, we must have a chat some day soon. In the meanwhile I have much to do."

"I sometimes felt that Addy stood in the way of my success. He would seldom give me roles of any stature. It was most debilitating, I assure you."

"I take it that you did not enjoy working for Adolphus?"

Harvey Wallberg tried to be diplomatic. "I must confess your brother was not the best employer I have ever had. His attitudes were very restrictive to my career. However, I'm confident you will better appreciate my talent. I'd like to take on the role of Macbeth in a future production. I have a wholly new interpretation in mind. I'm sure you will be most impressed."

Agamemnon Anderson snorted. "Don't be daft. Macbeth is one of my parts. I'm the lead actor in this troupe."

"But –"

"Now, now. Don't overvalue your worth. Your roles are only to make my performance look good, nothing more."

"How insulting!"

"My eye for talent is unerring. Anyone will tell you so."

"But what about my place in this company?"

"You are fortunate to be keeping your job. Your thespian skills are lacking. You would be little more than a spear carrier in a better company."

"T-that's not fair –" Harvey Wallberg sputtered.

"Enough sniveling. You are lucky I don't fire you. Is that stated clearly enough?"

"But –"

"Begone with you, you bacon-fed knave. I have important work to do. Heading up a theater company requires a lot of sweat and fever. But mark my word, I'm going to whip Merry Times into a world-class troupe of Shakespearean performers, far from the ragtag group of jesters that it is today."

"Marry trap with you, sir! You're just as big a blackguard as your brother Addy."

"What say you?"

"Never mind my stingless words. I'm going to my room. Good day, foul sir!"

"Practice your lines, you lizard-tongued idiot. This make-good performance in Caruthers Corners will be a proper chance to show our mettle. There will be lots of press coverage. Reporters are coming from all over to see how we bounce back from that unfortunate death mid-performance last week. And to see *me* offer my own interpretation of Puck."

"What a lack-brained blowhard. He'll get his comeuppance," Harvey Wallberg muttered under his breath as he slammed the door behind him.

Agamemnon looked up at the sound of the door banging closed. "Wonder what got into him," he said to himself. "His skin is thin as parchment."

~ ~ ~

Next up was Tom Turlington. That went quickly. "Turly, old sod, you're not delivering as Queen of the Amazons. Fact is, you're not tall enough to carry it off as a mighty Amazon warrior queen. You're only 5-foot-2, for Hermes sakes. I am switching you with Martin Hubble. He's not very good, but he's big, over 6 feet, the proper height for an Amazon. From now on you are Queen of the Fairies. Do you know the part?"

"It is not much of a part."

"Take it or leave it. Lots of hungry actors out there."

"I will take it."

"Excellent. Now get thee from my sight, thou loathsome and venomous toad. I have others to see."

~ ~ ~

"I enjoyed your video," Agamemnon Anderson grinned maliciously. He could have been mistaken for a Zoroastrian demon. Evil seemed to bubble from his very skin.

"What video?" replied Herbert Golding. His voice betraying a nervous tremor.

"Don't be sly. You know the video of which I speak. That surveillance tape of you with your hand in the till."

"Where did you get that?"

"One of your colleague was holding it for my brother. Adolphus was afraid you might kill him to get it back, so he asked someone to safekeep it."

"Turlington, it had to be that rat Turlington."

"Turly has the makings of a long-term member of this little repertoire company. You, however, do not."

"Wait, I can explain —"

"Too late for that, I'm afraid."

"Fie! I paid all the money back. It was like a short-term loan. Your brother was all right with it, especially when I added a generous interest payment. Everything was settled between us. The slate was wiped clean. He told me so."

"Yet he held onto the tape."

"He was using it as leverage, a threat. I was kicking back half my salary. I can keep doing that."

"Did you kill my brother? Not that I mind. I'm just curious."

"He died of a heart attack."

"Not according to a rumor I heard. There are some old biddies over in Caruthers Corners who think he was poisoned."

"Poisoned? Ridiculous!"

"Don't worry. We'll never know for sure. I had ol' Addy cremated. Always told him I'd see him in Hell. Well, at least I gave him a fiery send off in that direction."

"Don't kick me out of Merry Times. You need me for the upcoming reprisal of *Midsummer Night's*."

"Nay, not so. I've hired Laurence Linklater from The Bard's Traveling Road Show. He will be here in two days. Larry could do your role in his sleep. He's one of the few from the Bard's repertoire company that I could stomach. And he doesn't steal from his betters."

"Are you sure you want to do this? It might be risky for you."

"Oh, is that a threat?"

"If you think I killed your brother, what makes you think you're safe?"

"Ha! I fear you not, you horse pizzle."

"Perhaps you should."

"Begone with you, knave. *'Good night, good night! Parting is such sweet sorrow, that I shall say good night till it be morrow.'* "

~ ~ ~

Who was next on the list?

Carl and Bob Leicester came shuffling in, laughing and giggling and ribbing each other like a pair of schoolyard children.

"Quit that," Carl sniggered.

"No, you quit."

"Boys, sit down," ordered Agamemnon. He indicated the ladderback chairs opposite his side of the table. He had a malevolent smile on his face, blue eyes gleaming in the incandescent light. One would have easily cast him as Mephistopheles in a production of Christopher Marlowe's *The Tragic History of the Life and Death of Dr. Faustus.* "I have serious business to discuss. You must pay attention."

"Yeah, sure."

"Okay."

Their new boss seemed to be energized, as if feeding off the previous firings and demotions. "I hear very positive things about you two," he nodded. "You do good females. And the twins in *The Comedy of Errors* could've been written just for you."

"Does that mean you are going to give us a raise? We are still getting minimum."

"Verily, we could use a raise. Even a pittance would be appreciated."

"Sorry, boys. That is not going to happen. Money is tight as a pauper's purse. My brother was not only a poor actor, he was also a poor businessman. You are lucky to have a job. This touring company is on the ropes. I'm afraid you will have to go hungry for a spate longer."

"Mother mercy –"

"Aw, pish."

Agamemnon gave them a fearsome smile, Satanic in its intensity. "Buck up, lads. Take it without complaint. You're on the good side of my ledger. Let's keep it that way. Now off with you. And send in the next half-wit."

CHAPTER EIGHTEEN

"We must not make a scarecrow of the law ..."
-Measure for Measure

The piece was buried on the second page of the *Gazette*, under a story about an upcoming car show:

ACTOR'S BROTHER
TAKES OVER PLAYERS

Exclusive to the Gazette
By Penny Heath

Renown Shakespearean actor Agamemnon Sophocles Anderson will be taking the reins of Merry Times Players from his recently deceased brother, Adolphus Every Anderson. Readers will recall that Adolphus Anderson died last Friday during his performance as Puck in a production of William Shakespeare's "A Midsummer Night's Dream," a free concert that was taking place in Caruthers Corners' Town Square.

Agamemnon Anderson confirmed that the play will be reprised this Friday night in the same locale, a do-over for those patrons who didn't get to enjoy the full performance due to Adolphus Anderson's untimely death.

"The show must go on," said the troupe's new owner. "My brother would have wanted it that way."

"We are excited to be continuing the tradition of our esteemed founder, Adolphus Every Anderson," commented Harvey Wallace Wallbanger in an exclusive one-on-one interview with this reporter. Mr. Wallbanger plays Oberon in the production.

Dr. Franklin D. Medford confirmed that the actor had suffered a coronary during the play's performance in Caruthers Corners. "A tragedy," he called it. Ironically, "A Midsummer Night's Dream" is one of Shakespeare's 17 comedies.

Yada, yada, yada ....

Penny was disappointed that her story had not made the front page. Even below the fold would have been okay. But it certainly deserved more than Page 2 at the bottom. It was a scoop ... sort of.

~ ~ ~

Harvey Wallace Wallberg wrote to the *Gazette*, complaining that his name had been misspelled. The paper did not print a correction.

~ ~ ~

Squeaky Beasley, it turned out, lived in the new Hoople Senior Living Center. That was the castle-like mansion atop one of the two hillocks overlooking the town of Caruthers Corners. Once it had been the former home of the world-famous Hoople Quadruplets, and more recently the abode for Maddy Madison and her extended family. Upon the death of her remaining "aunts," Maddy had signed the big stone monolith over to the town to become a low-cost retirement home – one wing for the needy, the second wing for the infirm, and the third devoted to memory care.

John "Squeaky" Beasley qualified as infirm, being confined to a wheelchair due to severe rheumatoid arthritis, a condition that twisted his body into a pretzel. At 83, he had returned to his hometown with little to do but cause problems with frivolous lawsuits. He'd retained J. Harold Wentworth, Esq., a shady lawyer from Burpyville. Wentworth had been on the verge of getting disbarred a few years back, but had escaped this fate thanks to some papers getting misfiled. Wentworth "knew the right people."

About two months ago, Squeaky Beasley sued Tom's Taxis for not having proper equipment to carry the wheelchairs of handicapped passengers. Judge Horace Cramer dismissed the case, observing that a folded wheelchair would fit neatly into a taxi's trunk.

Last month Squeaky had sued Wabash Acres for not renting him a house. After all, it was a retirement village and he was retired. But the case was thrown out of court when Wabash Acres produced records showing that its inventory was fully rented and no houses had been available. There were three houses up for sale, but Squeaky was not in the buying mode.

This month he was suing the town of Caruthers Corners, demanding that it change the name to Beasleyville.

The lawsuit stated in part:

"WHEREAS the hamlet currently known as Caruthers Corners was originally named Beasleyville in honor of its true founder, one Major Samuel Elmsford Beasley, and the name was illegally changed in 1833 without benefit of proper vote, we hereby petition that your honor revert the town's name to its legitimate form of Beasleyville."

Nobody expected the lawsuit to go forward. Katherine Ann "Cookie" Bentley, director of the Caruthers Corners Historical Society, filed an *amicus curiae* brief in which she affirmed that the name Caruthers Corners came into common use in 1829, and has remained unchanged from the town's incorporation until today. The name Beasleyville was never adopted and no records exist using that name.

Town clerk Tom Dancy filed a declaration attesting that there were no town records under the name of Beasleyville. He could find nothing in the town's archives to back up the lawsuit's allegation.

Historian Nelson Lawrence Chadwick (author of *The History of the Indian Territory, 1800 – 1900*) submitted his expert testimony that there was no basis for the claim that Caruthers Corners had ever been known as Beasleyville. "My extensive research shows this to be a myth started within the past twenty years – likely by members of the Beasley family," he wrote in his deposition. "No historical documents support this fatuous assertion."

Squeaky was not happy.

Having been turned down at Wabash Acres, he had managed to secure a room at the Hoople Senior Living Center. Wheelchair bound, he'd been assigned a room on the ground floor. Proper ramps had been installed. Egress and ingress was convenient. Only a year ago, this room had served as Beau Madison's painting studio. Refurbishment had added a bath, pocket kitchen, and sleeping alcove. He found it quite comfy.

No one was sure where John "Squeaky" Beasley was getting the money to fund his frivolous lawsuits. Financial need was a criteria for housing at the Senior Living Center. A portion of the rent was covered by the generosity of the Madison Foundation.

Speculation was that Squeaky was acting as a frontman for his aunt, Eunice Smith-Cardwell, the woman who ran the Beasley Heritage Museum back in Massachusetts. It was likely that family money was being funneled into his foolhardy quests. The ultimate goal being the renaming of the town.

Squeaky was a mean-spirited and bellicose man, not the kind of relative anyone wanted to share Thanksgiving dinner with. Someone said he received a generous monthly stipend ... to stay away from Massachusetts.

~ ~ ~

Mayor Mark Tidemore settled down in a plush leather chair facing the oversized oak desk in Judge Horace Cramer's chambers. Judge Cramer was a wizen man with a shock of white hair topping an angular face. His robe was hanging on a coat rack near the door. This was his lunch hour, so he was eating a tuna salad on white at his desk. He liked Mark, so he'd had his bailiff pick up an extra one for him too. The coffee came from an urn in the corner of the room; it tasted like mud.

"So, Mark, what's on your mind?" Judge Cramer inquired as he took a big bite from his sandwich. The call had been somewhat impromptu, the mayor asking for a private audience. So Cramer had fitted him in between hearings.

"It's that jerk John Beasley –"

"Squeaky? Yes, I'm familiar with his little crusades. He and that shyster lawyer – don't repeat me on that! – have appeared before me on several time-wasters in recent months. One or two more frivolous lawsuits and I'm going to have him bound over for psychological evaluation."

"The man's a nutcase, that's for certain. I hate to be spending city money on this crazy claim that the town should be named after his long-dead ancestor. Who wants to name their town after a psychotic mass murderer?"

"I see your point. But what can I do for you? I can't exert undue influence on a case in my courtroom."

"Just wanted some friendly advice. Is there any way to settle this matter without dragging it through the courts?"

"You'd know all the legal options, Mark. You used to be a lawyer, and a pretty good one in my opinion. As I recall, they used to call you Mark the Shark."

"I'm feeling pretty toothless at the moment."

Judge Cramer lowered his voice. "Here's my advice, but I will deny we ever had this conversation. Squeaky likes being back in Caruthers Corners. And he's very comfortable in that subsidized apartment at the Hoople Senior Living Center. I'd think a clever fellow like you could pull some strings to get him thrown out, if he doesn't agree to drop this stupid lawsuit."

"Evict him?"

"Just find a reason to threaten him with eviction. I predict he'll fold like a rickety lawn chair on a hot summer day."

CHAPTER NINETEEN

"Ay, is it not a language I speak?"
-All's Well That Ends Well

Mrs. Jefferson Grady – Estelle, that is – had enjoyed meeting Sissy's Quilters Club friends. She and her husband were fairly new to town, but she'd heard stories about them, four clever women who solved crimes when not sewing patchwork quilts. "A quartet of aging Agatha Christies," someone had called them.

This was Estelle's first year at Caruthers High, where she taught theater and acted as school sponsor for the drama club. She liked working with youngsters. And she enjoyed imparting her skills and knowledge in the theater arts.

Before marrying Jeff Grady, she had been a professional actress with several Broadway credits under the stage name of Cecilia Connors. Maybe sharing a first name with Sissy was what attracted her to the girl. That and Sissy's obvious talent.

Among Cecelia Connors' career highlights were the lead in *My Boy George*, a musical which ran three years on Broadway; second lead in *Death of a Darling*; and a supporting role in *Clementine Kicks Up Her Heels*, which got great reviews. Also, she starred opposite Ian McKellen in a Broadway revival of *Macbeth*. Without a doubt that was the pinnacle of her career, winning her a Tony for Best

Performance by a Featured Actress in a Play for her nuanced interpretation of Lady Macbeth.

That Tony – plus a Master's Degree in Theater – made her a shoo-in for the teaching job at Caruthers High. She'd moved here with her husband when he took a position as CEO of ZapData.

Located within the barbed-wire confines of the Caruthers Corners Industrial Park, ZD (as locals call it) is a fast-growing data processing company. Jefferson Archer Grady had an advanced degree in Computer Science from Stanford. Previously, he'd been a division manager for Google. And he was a two-time winner of the Oncom Icon Award. Hiring him had been a "no brainer" for ZapData owner Haim Goldberg.

~ ~ ~

"Why is Shakespeare worth studying?" asked Sissy Jackson. She preferred musical theater. All those talky Shakespeare plays were hard to understand with that funny-sounding Elizabethan English.

Mrs. Grady liked these kinds of questions. "Shakespeare wrote about timeless themes – life and death, youth versus age, love and hate, fate and free will – topics just as relevant today as they were back then," she explained.

"Maybe so, but his plays are like opening a dusty old history book. You know, stories about *Julius Caesar*, *King John*, or *Antony and Cleopatra*."

Mrs. Grady couldn't help but smile. "He wrote comedies too. *The Merry Wives of Windsor*, *Much Ado About Nothing*, *The Taming of the Shrew*."

"I like *Kiss Me Kate*. That's a fun Cole Porter musical with a modern-day storyline. An updating of Shakespeare for modern times."

"True, but the original also is worthy of your attention. *The Taming of the Shrew* offers a brilliant commentary on the War Between the Sexes."

"But all the character dress in old fashion costumes and speak funny."

"That's the beauty of it. Shakespeare's characters have an emotional reality that transcends time. His plays depict familiar experiences – family squabbles, falling in love, betrayal, greed, ambition. His characters teach us about ourselves."

"So do modern playwrights. I love plays by Rogers and Hart, Stephen Sondheim, Neil Simon, and Lin-Manuel Miranda."

"Don't forget about Harold Pinter, Tennessee Williams, Edward Albee, Eugène Ionesco, and Arthur Miller."

"Arthur Miller, wasn't he married to that movie star?"

"Yes, Marilyn Monroe – the sex symbol."

"I liked her in the movies *Bus Stop* and *The Misfits*. And she was funny in *Some Like It Hot*."

"Marilyn Monroe had underutilized talent," the drama teacher allowed. "But back to William Shakespeare. He is considered the greatest writer in the history of the English language."

"English language? I can hardly understand anything he says. All those funny words and strange sentences."

Mrs. Grady chuckled. "I suppose it can be a challenge when you take Elizabethan English, toss in some archaic words, set it to iambic pentameter, then speak it with a British accent."

"My point exactly," agreed Sissy.

CHAPTER TWENTY

"My words fly up,
my thoughts remain below ..."
-Hamlet

N'yen arrived that same afternoon. He was driving his 2003 VW Beetle, a gift from his grandparents after finally getting his driver's license. He pulled up in the driveway of Beau and Maddy's new house on Mellon Pickers Row, a somewhat larger replica of their Victorian home that had been destroyed by the 2018 tornado. This new structure had extra bedrooms, including a large suite for N'yen when he visited.

Vietnamese by birth, Nguyễn Văn N'yen had been adopted by Bill and Kathy Madison following the death of his real parents in a car accident. He assimilated into the family quite quickly, particularly with Bill's parents. He called Beau and Maddy "Grampy" and "Grammy."

Now, the boy had another tie to Caruthers Corners – his girlfriend Sissy Jackson. They were going steady. Pretty serious for a pair of 16-year-olds. But N'yen considered himself mature. Hadn't he been admitted to college at 16? Wasn't that the same age as Romeo?

"Where is everybody?" he called out as he burst through the front door. He had little luggage, everything he needed waiting for him in his suite. "Is Sissy here?"

"Come on back. I'm in the kitchen," came Maddy's voice. "I'm baking a watermelon upside down cake."

"Yummy," he answered. That was one of his favorites.

Seemed like watermelon was an ingredient in most everything people in this part of Indiana ate. The town owned the large watermelon cooperative that had once been Aitken Produce. It claimed 42% of all watermelons grown in the state.

"Sissy said she'd join us for dinner," his grandmother continued. "We're having rack of lamb with watermelon glaze, forbidden rice, and grilled asparagus. You know how your Grampy likes his rack of lamb."

"Me too." The boy idolized Beau Madison. And the feeling was mutual, Beau having overcome the fact that he'd fought against relatives of N'yen in Vietnam. You had to look forward, not backward.

"My, look how you've grown," said his grandmother. "You must be an inch taller."

"Half inch."

"Have you heard about Aggie?" His cousin Agnes was the daughter of Mark and Tilly Tidemore. And Matilda "Tilly" Madison Tidemore was N'yen's dad's younger sister. Beau and Maddy had three children – Bill, Tilly, and Freddie. But you practically needed a program to follow this twisted family tree.

"What about that pushy, headstrong cousin of mine?" N'yen asked. Despite their constant quibbling, he and Aggie were actually quite close. Being junior members of the Quilters Club, they considered themselves aspiring detectives. A part of an inner circle.

Even so, N'yen was making a name as a young astrophysicist at Northwestern. He'd even had a quasar named after him. Aggie was a pre-law student at Yale, following in her father's footsteps. Before becoming the town's mayor, he'd been a lawyer whose well-earned nickname was Mark the Shark.

"Aggie just completed her summer term. She made the Dean's List."

"Whoop-de-doo, so did I."

"Now, now. Be gracious. I'm proud of you both."

"Thanks, Grammy."

"Sissy has news too. She was just picked as the lead in Caruthers High's upcoming production of *Romeo and Juliet*."

With a swipe of his finger, N'yen stole some cake batter from the ceramic mixing bowl. His pink tongue licked it away like a lizard catching a bug. "Wow! Everybody seems to be getting into William Shakespeare. You just had a roadshow production of *A Midsummer Night's Dream*. Now, a school production of that play about star-crossed lovers."

"You heard about that actor dropping dead during the performance of *A Midsummer Night's Dream*?" his grandmother said, moving the bowl out of his reach.

"Yep. Who hasn't? It was all over the news. Guess he was pretty famous in classical acting circles."

"That's what I'm told," she replied, carefully pouring the cake batter into a mold. "They're going to put on the play again this coming Friday. The first one got disrupted by Adolphus Everly Anderson's dropping dead in Act 3, so they're going to try again."

"Maybe I'll take Sissy to see it. Get her in a Stratford-on-Avon mood for her *Romeo and Juliet* role."

"She'd probably like that." Maddy paused. "You know, I don't think that actor's death was a heart attack like they're saying," she added.

"Oh? Murder most foul, you think? Is this a job for the Quilters Club?"

"You might say we're informally looking into it." She pushed the cake pan into the heated oven and closed the door with a firm *klang*.

"Count me and Sissy in. I've missed investigating crime. Been so busy with my studies. I'm tracing an electromagnetic variance I've discovered in the Gamma Quadrant of the Milky Way. Neat stuff, if I do say so myself!"

"Aggie's on her way home, too. She'll be getting in tomorrow afternoon."

"Great, we junior members of the Quilters Club stand ready to help solve this murder."

"Suspected murder, I should say."

"Okay, suspected. But what makes you *suspect* this Anderson guy didn't die of a heart attack?"

"He clutched his stomach before collapsing. Wouldn't a heart attack cause him to go for his chest?"

"In the movies, heart attack victims often grab their chest and grimace in pain. But that's not very accurate. It's unusual for a heart attack to produce intense pain. More commonly, a heart attack is described as a sensation of intense pressure, like an elephant sitting on your chest."

"Yes, but if you had an elephant on your chest, you wouldn't grab your tummy."

"I suppose that's true." He opened a watermelon-shaped jar to snag a cookie. He knew his Grammy kept it filled. "Did you see him go for his belly?"

"I did. So did the entire audience, not that anyone has brought it up. Also there was something else."

"What?" He munched down on the chocolate watermelon macaroon.

"He changed the lines he was supposed to say. Most people wouldn't have noticed, but I know the play pretty well. I played Hermia in a college production of *A Midsummer Night's Dream*, so I knew the lines by heart."

"You're saying he changed the lines right before he collapsed?"

"Yes. He said, '*You must look to the murderer on my right.*' That's not in the script."

"Was he saying the murderer was the person standing next to him?"

"That's the way I took it."

"Who was standing on his right?"

"The actor playing Oberon – a fellow named Harvey Wallace Wallberg, according to the program."

"So how did he kill this Anderson guy?"

"The only thing I could come up with is poison."

"That should be simple to determine. A toxicology report should tell all."

"Unfortunately, Doc Medford didn't do one. He's convinced it was the ol' ticker."

"So bring in an outside forensic pathologist. That should take care of that."

"Aren't they expensive?"

"Grammy, you're rich. You can afford it."

"Oh yes, I forgot. I'm not used to having so much money."

"You and Aunt Maisie got the biggest slices of the Hoople Quadruplets Trust Fund pie. You two could be diving into piles of money like Scrooge McDuck."

"What do you know about Scrooge McDuck? I thought you were into Marvel superheroes – Spider-Man and Iron Man and The Incredible Hulk."

"I am, but that doesn't mean I don't know other comic book characters. After all, I read."

"Well then, what have you read about the death of Adolphus Everly Anderson?"

"The best coverage has been by Penny Heath, the crime reporter with *Burpyville Gazette*. She's written an article every day. You remember her from the business with that park ranger down at Marengo Cave? She reports that the

Mayor's Office refuses to release Doc Medford's autopsy. She says the *Gazette* is filing a Freedom of Information request to see it."

"Can the *Gazette* do that?"

"I've been reading up on that. The Access to Public Records Act (APRA), Indiana Code 5-14-3, provides that a person has the right to access information regarding the government and the official acts of public officials and employees. The statute also states that government officials have a responsibility to provide that information upon request. So I expect she'll get it."

"That will be interesting."

"Not so much, if a tox screen wasn't done."

"Oh."

"What about that forensic pathologist?"

"Where would we find one?"

"Dunno. But I know a professor at Northwestern I can ask. He would know."

"Call him now.

"The Mayor's Office may oppose that too."

"The mayor is Aggie's dad. We'll see about that."

~ ~ ~

"Pooh Bear," Maddy greeted her husband when he came home from fishing, "N'yen got in."

"Yeah, I see his little yellow bug in the driveway. Where is that rascal."

"Off meeting Sissy, where would you think?"

"Young love."

"Yes, I can remember that," she smiled.

"We were only a few years older than those two kids. But young people grow up so fast these days. I blame it on the Internet."

"Probably," she agreed. Her husband blamed most things on the Internet. Before that, it was television.

Beau rambled on. "Wish N'yen had gotten in early enough to go fishing with us. Boy's got a knack for it."

"He was running late. Traffic was heavy, he said."

"Oh well. Guess I better get out of these dirty clothes. It was pretty muddy out there today."

"Did you hear any news from Jim on that dead actor?" Her hubby and Edgar Ridenour had been out for their weekly sortie on the Wabash. They fished mostly for catfish and bass. Today, the Police Chief had taken off the afternoon to join them. He often did.

"Jim says there's nothing to report. Death by natural cause doesn't fall under police jurisdiction."

"He's just being stubborn. Or lazy."

"Hon, that's one of our best friends you're talking about."

She made a face to show her frustration. "I know, I know. But something's not right here. And Jim and Mark and you and the entire Town Council seem to be turning a blind eye."

"The Town Council is just trying to avoid any bad publicity ... especially when there's no proof of anything untoward."

"Politics, that's what it is."

"Do I need remind you the mayor is your son-in-law – and I'm president of the Town Council?"

"Everybody is just trying not to scare the tourists. But Watermelon Days has come and gone. Visitors will be pretty scarce till next year."

"Mark is trying to change that. Have more public events to attract people to visit our little town –"

"Like the Shakespeare-in-the-Park performance," she scoffed. "How's that working out?"

"C'mon, we've hired Gimble & Gimble to help us develop our tourism. They're a pretty fancy public relations outfit – and expensive. Don't want to waste all that money chasing phantoms or seeing murders where none exist."

"Beau, I'm sure Adolphus Anderson was murdered."

"Doc Medford disagrees with you. And he has a medical license."

"We just need to find more clues," she insisted.

"Forgot to tell you, Phil Kupnick sold a pack of Rolaids to that actor before the performance. Said the man had indigestion."

"See!" she got excited. "That's proves he had a stomach problem. He'd ingested poison."

"Not necessarily," replied her husband. "I looked it up. About 1 out of every 3 people who have heart attacks do not feel any chest pain. Sometime the pain is felt in the stomach area, where it may be taken for indigestion."

"Appendicitis can be mistaken for indigestion too. But that doesn't mean it wasn't poison."

"Or that it was."

"We'll find out for sure. N'yen got me the name of a forensic pathologist who can conduct an outside analysis. A Chicago company called Midwestern Pathology Institute. I wrote to them, asking if they could help us with Adolphus Anderson's death."

"It's a good bet they will. Sounds like this Pathological Institute's one of them experts-for-hire companies. You pay the price; they deliver the testimonial."

"What's wrong with that? The more experts the better, right?"

"If you say so, dear," sighed Beau Madison.

"By the way, how was fishing today?"

"Nothing biting. Except mosquitos."

CHAPTER TWENTY-ONE

"Too much to know is to know
naught but fame."
- Love's Labour's Lost

Harvey Wallace Wallberg liked to quote a passage from his favorite book, a memoir titled *The Actor Uncovered* by Michael Howard. He always intoned the words in his deep baritone voice as if making a speech:

> "Olivier searches – as all good actors do – for transformation. From Richard III to Shylock to Archie Rice in *The Entertainer*, he wants the experience of revealing hidden elements that exist in himself and in the great villains and heroes of the world. And, of course, as a star he was given the opportunity to accomplish total transformations. Genius and non-genius actors alike make the same demands of themselves. They are concerned with transformation, not with celebrity."

It is clear that in reciting this passage, Wallberg identified himself as a "genius actor" like Sir Laurence Olivier. And that his lack of any greater success than being part of a traveling repertory company like Merry Times – i.e., that is, his failure to achieve "celebrity" – was of little concern to him. His art, that of creating a transformation that affects an audience, was all that had any true importance to him.

He was an *artiste*!

The lie to his words was found in the fact that as of late he had been applying for teaching positions in the theatrical departments of community colleges throughout the Midwest. A steady paycheck and a less mobile lifestyle trumping his high-minded pursuit of art.

At heart, Harvey Wallberg was an unhappy man, disappointed by his lack of recognition in the acting field, bitter at his failure to win leading roles on Broadway, angry over the lack of recognition he received when walking down a city street, despondent with the dead-end direction of his acting career.

Truth is, he didn't long for a transitory thing like "celebrity." He aspired to a much higher goal – that of "fame."

~ ~ ~

Odell Lumley filed his second report. The Indy private eye emailed it to Lizzie along with his latest invoice.

It read:

CASE # 17A-304-B
SUBJECT: Adolphus Everly Anderson
PROFESSION: Actor, Theater Manager
CURRENT STATUS: Deceased, Suspected Homicide
Here is the status of each of the individuals identified in my previous report as having a motive to kill Adolphus Everly Anderson.
• Agamemnon Sophocles Anderson, the subject's estranged brother. Best motive, in that he inherited his brothers theater company. Also they were bitter rivals. However, he was in

Phoenix, Arizona, at the time of Adolphus Anderson's death. No accomplice identified, no known relationship with any members of Merry Times. Unlikely that he murdered his brother despite the cui bono element. Analytic ranking: 30%

• Harvey Wallace Wallberg, actor in Merry Times Players. Anger Management issues. Psychological profile indicates it more likely he would commit murder by physical means – knife or gun – rather the careful planning required with poisoning. Was known to have had disagreements with Subject over casting choices. Made threats. Analytic ranking: 70%

• Carl and Bob Leicester, twin actors in Merry Times Players. Both are practicing homosexuals who gender identify as female. Poison is a murder weapon favored by women. Being twins, they are close and might act as co-conspirators. Carl seems to be the more dominate of the two. Analytic ranking: 50% and 40%

• Herbert Golding, actor in Merry Times Players. Unlikely, for fear of previous crime being exposed. Subject had left a copy of video with Tom Turlington along with instructions to turn it over to police if anything happened to him. Known to be unassertive. Analytic ranking: 20%

• Tom Turlington, actor in Merry Times Players. Unlikely, in that his diary reveals unrealized homoerotic feelings for Subject. Turned Golding video over to police as instructed. No motive. Analytic ranking: 20%

• Mildred Fleming, a former girlfriend of Adolphus Anderson. She was on her job at Ruby Tuesday in Chicago at the time of Subject's death. Numerous witnesses. Not a viable candidate. Analytic ranking: 5%

• Ryan Hicks, a former business manager. Died in a 20-car pile-up on US 80 two month's before Subject's death. Analytic ranking: 0%

Based on these rankings, focus should be placed on Harvey Wallace Wallberg. This concludes my research. Please let me know if you require further efforts from my firm.

Sincerely,

Odell Lumley

Private Investigations R Us

Indianapolis, Indiana

~ ~ ~

"I've been meaning to tell you girls about this." Lizzie produced her private detective's report at their next meeting. "I hired an investigator out of Indy. He did an analysis, but didn't come up with much. See here –" she pointed at the paper "– he suggested we focus on Harvey Wallbanger –"

"Harvey Wallberg," Cookie corrected.

"– and maybe those twins. As you can see, he eliminated a lot of suspects."

"Persons of Interest," Bootsie corrected.

"Many of them are people we haven't even heard of, like an old girlfriend and a former business manager. This investigator – Odell Lumley is his name – felt strongly that either this Wallbanger guy or those evil twins were the guilty parties."

"Odell Lumley, I remember him from an old case," noted Cookie.

"Of course, you do," teased Maddy. "You're like an elephant who never forgets."

"Hey, my little knack comes in handy sometimes."

"That's true," agreed Bootsie. "It's like having our own Encyclopedia Brown."

Lizzie interrupted this love fest. "Odell Lumley has a good reputation. His conclusions might save us some time. We should concentrate on his main, uh, Persons of Interest."

"That would be Wallberg," said Maddy.

"I thought we were already doing that," grumbled Bootsie.

"Right you are," said Cookie. "As we learned from Estelle Grady, he was standing stage right of the victim. So he's the main focus of our investigation."

"So we're all in agreement," nodded Maddy. "Wallberg is our man."

"My money's on him," agreed Lizzie. "Literally. I paid that private eye lots of money for this report."

Bootsie nodded. "We agree that everything points to this Harvey Wallace Wallberg."

"What's the next step then" asked Lizzie.

"I say we should brace him," said Maddy.

Bootsie was eager to do just that. "Yes, let's see what he has to say when we confront him face-to-face."

"Okay, It's a plan. Let's go interview this Harvey Wallberg," proposed Cookie. "I'll drive."

"Where to?" asked Lizzie.

"Petie Hitzer said the actors were staying sat the Highliner in Burpyville," said Bootsie.

"They could be anywhere by now," said Cookie."

"Don't worry," Bootsie reassured them. "I'll call my husband. The police department will know where to find him."

"Why would Jim help us?" asked Maddy. "You know he disapproves of our investigations."

Bootsie laughed. "Do you remember that Greek play *Lysistrata*? We studied it in college – World Lit 101."

"Yes."

"Need I say more?"

CHAPTER TWENTY-TWO

"Like a dull actor now,
I have forgot my part ..."
- Coriolanus

Everybody piled into Cookie's new Range Rover Sport L461 – it was the mid-size crossover 4x4 hybrid model – roomy, deluxe, and expensive at $115.625, but the Bentleys could well afford it – and drove over to Burpyville together.

The Highliner Hotel was easy to find on Anthony Wayne Avenue, just off the intersection with Highway 21. The brick façade was chipped and dirty, looming over them like a rotten tooth. The faded green awning over the entrance was tattered. Cigarette butts littered the sidewalk, indicating the spot where guests loitered outside to smoke. The boxwood plants on each side of the glass doorway were brown from lack of watering. There was no valet service, but luckily they found a parking space out front.

"This is where they're staying?" Maddy asked, her nose slightly wrinkled.

"That's what Harry Teague's wife said," replied Bootsie. "According to her, we'll find Wallberg up there in Room 304."

"Penny Heath should know. She interviewed him for the *Gazette*." Maddy didn't think it necessary to mention that she was the one who had sicced Penny Heath onto Wallberg in the first place.

Bootsie was happy to take credit for coming up with the address. Cookie was saying, "I can't believe your husband asked his deputy do that for us."

"*Lysistrata,*" Bootsie repeated. As if that explained all.

"I don't remember that play," said Lizzie. "I failed World Lit 101."

Cookie patted her hand. "It's that Greek play by Aristophanes. The one where Lysistrata persuades the women of the warring cities to withhold sex from their husbands and lovers as a means of forcing the men to negotiate peace."

"Oh, that one. A Battle Between the Sexes theme, right?"

"Right," said Bootsie. "Let's just say, I won the battle."

Lizzie studied the hotel's depressing façade. "What a dump," she said, echoing that famous Bette Davis line.

"C'mon, let's go in," urged Cookie, pocketing her car keys. She hoped her Range Rover would be safe parked at the curb on this forlorn side street. Anthony Wayne *Avenue* indeed! The narrow side street barely accommodated parking spaces *and* a thoroughfare!

The foursome cautiously entered the lobby, a cavernous room with slow-moving ceiling fans and drooping potted ferns. Threadbare couches were scattered about the room. The carpet had holes in it. The desk clerk looked to be about twelve years old. "May I help you?" he greeted them, adjusting his bowtie nervously. "We have a group rate."

"Oh no, we're not staying," responded Maddy. Perhaps a little too adamantly. "We'd like to see one of your guests, a Mr. Harvey Wallace Wallberg."

The desk clerk – MANAGER, his nametag said – cleared his throat. "I'm most sorry, ladies. Mr. Wallberg is out. I believe he said he was going on picnic."

"A picnic?"

"Well, out in the countryside. To that swamp north of Caruthers Corners. Strange, he didn't have a picnic basket. Just an empty pail."

"Never Ending Swamp?" said Cookie. "We just came from Caruthers Corners. I can't believe we drove all way down here for nothing."

"Shall I take a message for Mr. Wallberg."

"No thanks, we'll come back."

"Would you like to see Agamemnon Anderson. He's the gentleman in charge of those ... actors. He's up in his room. I'll be happy to ring him, if you like."

"No thank you," said Cookie politely. "No need to bother the boss. At least not yet." Agamemnon Anderson had been on the job for only a day or so. He would have no insights to share.

As they turned to go, Maddy paused with a Columbo-like after-thought. "How about Mr. Carl Leicester?" she suggested. "Is he here?"

Lizzie was taken aback. "Why do we want to see him?"

"May as well get a close-up look as long as we're here. He was number two on your investigator's list."

"Hmm, good idea," said Bootsie. "I've been curious about him. After all, he was standing on the other side of Adolphus when he dropped dead."

So Cookie turned to the manager and asked curtly, "Well, what say you, young man? Is Carl Leicester here – or is he on a picnic too?"

The manager swallowed, then nodded his head toward an archway. "I'm not sure which one he is, but most of those actors are in the dining room."

"You have a dining room?" blurted Lizzie, as if she were here from the Health Department.

"We o-only serve breakfast and s-sandwiches," he stuttered. "The actors like to gather in there in the afternoons. They call it Tea Time, but they only drink coffee and eat sugar cream pie."

"Do tell," said Bootsie. She owed her rounded figure to extra helpings of sugar cream pie. Made with butter, cream, and sugar (with a light dusting of nutmeg), this thick custard concoction is considered the unofficial state pie of Indiana.

"Not now," Cookie wagged a finger at her friend. "We're here to meet people, not have a snack."

"Couldn't we join them for Tea Time?"

"Bootsie," chastised Lizzie. "Remember your diet."

"Jim isn't sticking to his. I should get some latitude too." She'd gone off her Atkins routine recently and was looking like an over-inflated love doll. Fortunately, Jim Purdue liked Ruebenesque women.

"Barbara Jo Purdue, listen to yourself. Is there any food you don't like?"

"Broccoli," she said. "I don't care for broccoli."

"What about Chicken and Broccoli?" Lizzie piped up. "You're always ordering that dish when we go to the Golden Dragon down in Pitsville."

"That's Chinese food. It doesn't count."

Maddy gave a Heaven-Help-Me roll of her eyes. "Come along, girls," she shooed them through the archway. "We're on a mission, remember?"

"Oh, okay."

The so-called dining room was a collection of mismatched tables and chairs, most of them occupied by well-groomed men sipping coffee from ceramic mugs. The mood in the room was glum. Everyone sat around with a hangdog look on his face. You'd think they were attending a wake.

Herbert Golding sat by himself, muttering under his breath, not a happy man. Henry Trout was stuffing his face with sugar cream pie, looking like a well-fed chipmunk. Other members of the troupe lingered at nearby tables, drinking their coffee, looking stoic.

"What have we here, pray tell?" Tom Turlington stood up to greet the newcomers. "More hotel guests?"

"I'm afraid not," Maddy said with a pleasant smile. "We're looking for one of your colleagues, a Mr. Carl Leicester. He plays Hermia in *A Midsummer Night's Dream*."

"Sometimes he does. Are you ladies fans?"

"Yes, that's it," Lizzie spoke up. "We admire his work."

"That's right," said Bootsie. "Is he here? I'd love to get an autograph."

Turlington shrugged. "You will find him over there at the corner table with his brother." Obviously losing interest in the women the moment they showed attentiveness to any actor other than himself. Narcissism was rampant among thespians. Merry Times had an excess of such out-of-control egos.

The four visitors turned toward the corner Turlington had indicated. "Oh my," said Maddy as she stared at the table's occupants, two young men who looked exactly alike – mirror images. Being a twin herself, the subject fascinated Maddy. But separated at birth, she had grown up unaware of her twosomeness. And she and her sister Maisie looked nothing alike, being fraternal twins. However, these two guys were drop-dead doppelgängers – it was like seeing double.

"You're identical twins," she blurted.

"Yes ma'am," smiled one of the young men. "That we are – Carl and Bob Leicester."

"Which is which?"

"Doesn't matter. We're interchangeable."

"The program listed Carl Leicester as Hermia in last week's play."

"That's right," said the young man, "but it could've been either of us. We swap off parts. You know, mix it up for variety. It gets stale portraying the same character week after week."

"But which one was it last week?" asked Bootsie. Getting a little irritated by this verbal runaround.

"Don't remember," grinned the actor.

"That doesn't make sense," said Cookie. "You would remember if you were standing on stage next to Adolphus Everly Anderson when he died. That's like people remembering exactly where they were when they heard Kennedy was shot."

"JFK was long before my time," said the actor.

Having a super memory, Cookie had trouble with the idea of someone forgetting. "Seriously, which one of you was it?"

"Why are you asking?" the other twin spoke up. "What does it matter which one of us was standing there when Addy departed this mortal coil?"

"That's right," nodded the first man. "'*Death, a necessary end, will come when it will come.*'"

Maddy pressed on. "We have a few questions for the brother who was on stage with Adolphus Everly Anderson."

"By what authority?" smirked one of the twins.

"My husband is Chief of Police in Caruthers Corners," bluffed Bootsie.

"Does that make you a deputy?" laughed the young man. Unimpressed.

"You're Carl," said Cookie, eying the twin who was speaking. "At least, you're the one who was on stage at the time of Adolphus Everly Anderson's death. No doubt about that."

The man turned his pale eyes on the blonde historian. "What makes you so sure of that?"

"You and your brother may be identical twins, but there is one minute difference. You have a freckle near your left ear. I see that your brother doesn't. I remember the freckle. It was you on stage as Hermia last week. I assume your brother was playing the other role, Helena. You were both fairly well disguised under your make up. But your makeup didn't extend up to your ear."

"Okay, so I'm Carl. But enough of these games. *'More of your conversation would infect my brain.'* "

"An easy one. *Coriolanus*, Act 2, Scene 1," Cookie identified the quote. That eidetic memory at work.

"Hm, you certainly do know your Shakespeare."

"Why are you afraid to answer our questions? *'Go, prick thy face, and over-red thy fear, thou lily-liver'd boy.'* "

"*Macbeth*, Act 5, Scene 3," he matched her.

Cookie smiled pleasantly at Carl Leicester. "If I can stump you with a quote, will you agree to speak with us? If you get it right, we will leave."

"*'I scorn you, scurvy companion,'*" he sneered. "Yes, I accept your challenge."

"That was *Henry IV Part II*, Act 2, Scene 4," she replied. "Now are you ready for my quiz?"

"Indeed. *'Lead on Macduff.'* "

She didn't bother identifying his phrase from *Macbeth*. Instead she recited:

> "*Good friend for Jesus sake forbear,*
> "*To dig the dust enclosed here.*
> "*Blessed be the man that spares these stones,*
> "*And cursed be he that moves my bones.*"

"Aha! That's not Shakespeare," retorted Carl Leister. "I know all the plays, all the sonnets, all the narratives."

"Wrong," Cookie said. "That's from his epitaph. You will find it inscribed on his tombstone!"

Carl Leicester scowled. "But he didn't write that."

"Some people say he did, just as others say he didn't write the plays."

"No fair. But I'll give you credit for cleverness. What do you want to ask me?"

"Do you know who killed Adolphus Anderson?"

Both Carl and his brother Bob looked shocked, the same expression of dismay appearing on the two faces simultaneously. "No, of course not," exclaimed Carl, the one with the freckle ... or maybe it was a birthmark.

Were they being sincere? Or were they – as one might expect – good actors?

Cookie tilted her head, ruffling her blonde hair. "Adolphus said you did."

"What? Did he appear to you like Banquo's ghost and impart that accusation?" he replied sarcastically.

"No," said Maddy. "He changed the lines in his speech just before he dropped dead beside you. He said, '*You must look to the murderer on my right.*' And you were standing to his right."

"No, I was at stage left."

"Who can be sure what he meant," said Maddy. "But he changed the line. That means he was referring to either Hermia or Oberon."

"Oh that," Carl's brother Bob laughed. "I heard him say that. He was always throwing in stuff like that, changing lines. He was very mischievous."

"That's right," nodded Carl. "Doing the same lines over and over, night after night, is very boring, so he would threw in lines like that for his own amusement. Nobody in the audience ever complained. Most of them don't know the actual words anyway. They just come to see the plays because they think watching Shakespeare makes them an intellectual. The pretentious rubes."

"Hey, I'm one of those rubes," said Maddy. "You should have more respect for your audiences."

"We give them a good performance," shrugged Carl. "They get their money's worth, I dare say."

"Deliberately mangling his lines?" said Lizzie. "That doesn't sound like giving audiences their money's worth."

"Addy Anderson owned Merry Times. He could do anything he liked. Let's be honest – he was a megalomaniacal jerk. He had no respect for Shakespeare! And no respect for his fellow actors. Much less the audience. What's more, he was a cheap bastard, refusing to pay us fair and honest wages!"

"Doesn't sound like you're a big fan of your former boss."

"'*Nothing in his life became him like leaving it,*'" snorted Carl.

"And that goes for his stingy brother too," added Bob. "He deserves his own fate, I dare say."

CHAPTER TWENTY-THREE

**"Un-thread the rude eye of rebellion,
and welcome home again discarded faith."**
-King John

Agnes Tidemore arrived home early Tuesday afternoon. Her father and mother had driven down to pick her up at Indianapolis International Airport. The flight from Tweed-New Haven Regional Airport (HVN) to Indy (IND) was uneventful, despite its two stops. On the last leg of the trip she'd enjoyed a comfortable aisle seat.

Aggie was delighted to see her parents. She hadn't been back to Caruthers Corners since the funeral of Aunt Hilda and Aunt Helga. Her mother's mental health had been improving; she no longer saw fairies and unicorns. Her father reported that the town was running smoothly, the only hiccup being last week's death of an actor during a Shakespeare-in-the-Park performance. That had made the front page of the *Burpyville Gazette*, though thankfully it had faded quickly to the interior pages. Good press was essential to keep tourists attending the annual Watermelon Fest, he emphasized. The Town Council had hired a PR firm. He was thinking of initiating an ad campaign. "Catch Up With Your Friends in Caruthers Corners" was a theme under consideration.

They played catch-up all way home, Aggie talking about her grades, her favorite professors, classmates. She liked college.

Aggie was eager to see her dog Tige. He was a long-haired dachshund mix, a cute little scamp that she and her Grammy had found as a giveaway puppy on the side of the road near Wabash Acres some ten years ago. She had really missed Tige during her time away at college. Yale was too far away for weekend visits.

Almost as much as she'd missed her dog, she had missed her cousin N'yen. True, he'd been away at college too – that little genius was in an Early Admission program at Northwestern – but the two had grown up together, junior members of the Quilters Club, helping their "aunties" solve whodunits ranging from lost Viking treasures to mob hits to legendary werewolves. They made a good team.

Now they were off on separate career paths, N'yen studying to be an astrophysicist, Aggie planning to become a lawyer like her dad. The glue that held them together these days was Cecilia LaToya Jackson, still her best friend and N'yen's steady girlfriend.

Aggie knew N'yen was already home … well, at his suite in Grammy and Grampy's new house on Melon Pickers Row. She was sure he and Sissy were waiting for her to meet them there.

"Dad, can you drive faster?"

Mark Tidemore chuckled. "Wouldn't do for a local mayor to get pulled over for speeding," he told her. "Besides, not having your law degree yet, you couldn't defend me."

"Dad, you're still a member in good standing with the Indiana bar. You could defend yourself."

"You know what Abraham Lincoln said about that – '*He who represents himself has a fool for a client.*' "

Aggie leaned forward from the backseat so her father could hear her. "Actually Lincoln didn't say that. The old adage first appeared in a 1682 book, *Humane Prudence, or,*

The Art by which a Man May Raise Himself and Fortune to Grandeur by William De Britaine."

"That's quite a mouthful. Have you read it?"

"No, never. I just now looked it up on my iPhone." She held up the device for her father to see in the rearview mirror."

"Well, you can't argue with the Internet," laughed Mark Tidemore.

"One thing, dear," her mother spoke up. "Don't get involved in my mother's latest shenanigans – her idea that that actor was murdered."

"Tell me more about it."

"Forget it, Aggie," her father chimed in. "Doc Medford ruled the death a myocardial infarction – a heart attack. Nothing untoward here."

Tilly continued, "Your grandmother has this silly idea he was poisoned, just because he grabbed his stomach instead of his chest."

"Are you sure he did that, Mom?"

"Of course, dear. I was sitting there in the front row with your father. I saw it myself."

"Does Grammy know you saw that too?"

"I asked your mom not to tell her. It would just fuel her nutty conspiracy theories."

"Grammy's conspiracy theories aren't nutty. She's been right more often than wrong," huffed Aggie.

Mark the Shark sighed. "We all love your Grammy. But you've got to admit she missed the mark last time around, falsely accusing that park ranger of murdering that bat expert in Marengo Cave. Practically ruined the guy's life."

"I know, I know. But he certainly looked guilty."

"If your Uncle Jim's K9 dog hadn't sniffed that blood on that limestone ledge..."

"Yes, I know," she repeated. "N'yen helped with that, proving him innocent."

"Are you talking about that man I thought was a Morlock?" murmured her Mom.

"That's the one," nodded Aggie.

"How silly of me. What was I thinking? I used to have so many crazy ideas."

"All is good now," Mark Tidemore patted his wife's hand.

"Yes, dear. But I am certain I saw that actor clutch his stomach."

CHAPTER TWENTY-FOUR

"And cursed be he that moves my bones."
-Shakespeare's Epitaph

Aggie met up with her cousin N'yen and friend Sissy at the Dairy Queen. The soft-serve ice cream stand had been rebuilt after the 2018 Northeastern Indiana Tornado devastated a third of the town, the DQ included. But somehow it didn't seem the same. Maybe she was just getting older and childhood memories were starting to fade? Things seemed smaller somehow ....

N'yen and Sissy had already ordered double-scoop cones, his symbolically chocolate, hers orange, and had licked them down to the rim of the wafer cones. "Grab some custard and join us," N'yen called to her.

"Custard?" frowned Sissy. Being from the South, she didn't know this local parlance for soft ice cream. To her, custard was a sweet sauce made with milk, eggs, and sugar.

"Frozen custard is a cold dessert similar to ice cream, but unlike ice cream it's made with eggs in addition to cream and sugar," Aggie explained.

N'yen chimed in with a brief history: "Frozen custard was first commercialized on Coney Island, but was more widely introduced to the public at the 1933 World's Fair in Chicago. Since then, the dessert's popularity had spread throughout the Midwest. Per capita, Milwaukee has the highest concentration of frozen custard shops in the world. Caruthers Corners only has the DQ."

He was such a know-it-all.

After dutifully listening to her cousin's lecture, Aggie stepped to the window and ordered a cup of pistachio. Her blond hair, now cut in a bob, glistened in the late afternoon sunlight. She looked properly grown up, trim and neat and curvy. After all, she had just turned 19.

Joining N'yen and Sissy at the round cement table, she commented, "You're eating a cone. I thought you preferred parfaits."

N'yen shrugged. "That was back when I was a kid."

"You're still a kid to me," she retorted.

"Hey, you're only two years older than me."

"Nearly three years."

"Would you two enjoy your ice cream and quit fussin' and fightin'?" said Sissy, taking a big lick at her cone with a wide pink tongue. "I like this stuff. What did you call it – frozen custard?"

"Uh-huh. Right up there with sugar cream pies as a true midwestern dessert."

Aggie gave her cousin the stink eye, but dipped her plastic spoon into the lump of pistachio ice cream. Or custard, depending on your nomenclature. "Okay, on another subject," she said, "we need to help Grammy look into the death of Adolphus Everly Anderson."

"Junior members of the Quilters Club, unite!" declared her cousin. Sort of like shouting, "Avengers assemble!" He was a big comic book fan, a Marvel Maniac.

Aggie continued unabated. "We need to determine whether that actor died of a heart attack ... or was poisoned."

"How do we do that?" asked Sissy.

"We need a toxicology report. Tests that determine whether he has any signs of poison in his body."

"But your Grammy said Doc Medford didn't do one," Sissy countered. "So how do we get a test. They've already planted that dead man at Pleasant Glades, I heard."

"Exhume the body," stated N'yen. As casually as if suggesting they have another cone of ice cream. "Grammy's gonna hire an outside forensic expert to do the examination. Already sent off the letter to one in Chicago."

"Exhume the body," Aggie repeated the words, trying on the idea for size. "Can we do that?"

"I'm not suggesting *we* dig him up," said N'yen. "We're not grave robbers, for goodness sakes."

"Good to hear that," replied Sissy. "'Cause I'm not going into that spooky old cemetery at midnight with shovels."

"Question is, who has the authority to order an exhumation?" mused the boy.

"My daddy," said Aggie. "He's the mayor."

CHAPTER TWENTY-FIVE

"Nothing can we call our own but death ..."
-Richard II

Robert Bob Roberts Jr. had been manager of the Highliner Hotel for four years now – his first job out of high school. Being manager also meant acting as desk clerk, concierge, maître d', and building custodian. His mother provided maid services, cleaning the rooms after each visitor, what few guests there were. She also got paid as a part-time cook. Everybody agreed that Amelia McNeill Roberts made an excellent sugar cream pie.

This past week had been a windfall for the Highliner, what with the Merry Times theater group taking all the available rooms while waiting to give their make-good performance over in Caruthers Corners. Robby Junior had been forced to give up his own room and move in with his mother when the new owner of Merry Times showed up. Robby planned to pocket that room fee himself, not putting the extra occupancy on the ledger.

The hotel was owned by a blind trust that was holding it for the land value. Rumor had it that the Burpyville City Council planned to buy the building by eminent domain as a teardown. That blind trust – a construction company, some said – planned to build a civic auditorium on the site. A questionable insider deal. That's why he didn't feel guilty about nicking the unofficial room rental.

Part of his management deal included two rooms being set aside, one for him, another for the maid. After his dad died in a bizarre taffy-pulling accident, he'd hired his widowed mother. With the free rooms, they had been able to sell their family home for a pretty penny and invest the money in Blue Chip stocks. If the market held up, they would be able to cash out soon, quit these miserable jobs, and move to Costa Rica. He'd heard you could live cheap-but-good in that lush Central American country. Robby Junior spent his spare time studying Spanish.

His reverie was interrupted when he heard the bell on the front desk ring. Having a full house kept him hopping. Probably someone wanting more towels or complaining about the lack of hot water. The plumbing system was on the fritz this week. Matter of fact, it was unreliable most of the time. The hotel needed a new water heater, but the blind trust that owned the place wasn't very responsive about repairs.

"Yesss?" said Robby Junior, plastering a phony smile on his face as he popped out of the tiny office behind the counter. At 22, he was a gangly guy with slicked-back blond hair and jug-handle ears. His starched white shirt was topped with a bright-red bowtie. He wore a plastic nametag that identified him as **MANAGER**.

Standing on the other side of the wooden counter was that new owner of the acting troupe – *Agamemnon Sophocles Anderson, Th.D.*, he'd signed the ledger when he checked in. A tall, imposing man with a beaked nose and startling blue eyes, this Anderson guy carried himself with the regal posture of a King Richard II or Henry V. Roles he sometimes played. However, this morning he looked a bit green around the gills, his face pale as a wraith, eyes slitted, a grimace on his thin-lipped mouth. Jet lag was Robby Junior's first guess.

"*Agggggh,*" gasped Agamemnon Anderson, then collapsed to the floor.

Robby Junior rushed around the counter to inspect the fallen guest. Staring down at the man on the threadbare carpet, he wasn't sure what to do. He didn't know how to apply CPR or render some kind of First Aid. "Ma!" he shouted. "Call 9-1-1."

His mother shuffled out of the backroom office, took one look, and began dialing. "We need an ambulance!" she screeched into the telephone. "And hurry!"

Robby Junior bent over the prone figure and shook his shoulder, as if trying to rouse him. "Dr. Anderson, Dr. Anderson," he called urgently.

Agamemnon Anderson opened his eyes and stared up at the hotel manager. His lips barely moving, he whispered, " *'Truth will come to sight; murder cannot be hid long.'* I've been kilt by a poisoner's potion. They can cancel Friday's performance!"

Then he died.

~ ~ ~

Burpyville Police Chief Frank Crenshaw looked down at the body. "Well, that's two," he said.

"Two what?" replied his deputy.

"The second actor to die within a week."

"D'you think they're related?"

"Don't you?" said the Police Chief. "I don't believe in coincidences."

His deputy – a Barney Fife type named Homer Woodall – raised his eyebrows. "You saying we got us a serial killer who's going after actors?"

"Well, they're both dead. And two brothers dying from heart attacks in the same week seems to stretch credulity, wouldn't you say? I better call Jim Purdue over in Caruthers Corners and let him know we may be sharing a case."

CHAPTER TWENTY-SIX

"... His foul and most unnatural murder."
-Hamlet

"I think mine's a murder," said Chief Frank Crenshaw. He was a handsome man, with a square chin and flinty eyes. He held his iPhone 13 Pro Max flat in the palm of his hand, speaker on, talking into the slit on the bottom edge. Sometimes it made him feel like Dick Tracy with a two-way wrist radio.

"What makes you say that?" came Jim Purdue's hoarse voice. The two Top Cops knew each other well, running PDs in adjacent towns. And Crenshaw had once dated Jim's Bootsie when they were in high school together.

"Cause he said so before he died."

"Was your vic shot? Stabbed?"

"Poisoned, I'd guess."

"That's what Beau Madison's wife keeps saying about mine. But I don't have a lick of evidence."

"Did you do a tox workup?"

"Doc Medford didn't think one was necessary."

"Dig the guy up."

"Too late," sighed Chief Purdue. "His brother had him cremated."

"And now his brother's dead."

"At least you have time to run toxicology on him before he gets cremated."

"Don't know if he's getting the ashes-to-ashes treatment or not. We can't find any living relatives. Nobody knows if there's a will or any instructions. The body hasn't been officially claimed. Not much to go on."

"Does anyone in that acting company know his last wishes,"

"'Fraid not. They only met him this week for the first time."

"With him dead, who's in charge?"

"That's not entirely clear. Agamemnon Anderson fired the manager t'other day. Fellow named Benjy Bartholomew. Packed his bags and left town the same day he got the pink slip."

"Is this Bartholomew a Person of Interest?"

"Naw, he's been in a Chicago hospital last few days. Seems a Greyhound ran over his foot as he getting off at the 95th/Dan Ryan Station."

"Ouch. Guess that leaves him out.

"Ever since Bartholomew left, that actor Harvey Wallace Wallberg's been behaving like he's in charge. Says they plan to put on the performance tomorrow night without this dead guy. Bringing in another actor from outta town, Wallberg says."

"That a fact?"

"Just repeating what this Wallberg guy said. I've got him and some other actors undergoing routine interviews. Just took a break to give you a call."

"I appreciate that, Frank.

"Let me get back to quizzing these oddballs. I'll let you know what the tox screen comes up with. I got Herman Vox on it. If my guy died of a particular poison, chances are your guy died from the same thing."

~ ~ ~

The interviews plodded along. Chief Crenshaw found himself getting bored. Nothing helpful here. He could barely stay awake.

"Did you hear what I said?" Harvey Wallberg raised his voice. Jostling the police chief out of his somnolence.

"Uh, yes, of course."

"I'm telling you Aggy Anderson brought it on himself," repeated the actor. He was sitting across from the police chief belly-up to a dull metal table in the Interrogation Room of the Burpyville Police Department. It looked just like the ones you see in movies, a bare concrete chamber with a picture-window-size one-way mirror along the far wall.

"Brought what on himself?" asked Frank Crenshaw, trying to pick up the thread of conversation.

"Bad luck."

"How'd he do that?"

"The Curse of the Scottish Play."

Chief Crenshaw screwed up his face with puzzlement. "A curse?"

"Yes," he said. "– *Macbeth*."

"I don't follow you," frowned the policeman.

Harvey Wallberg quickly explained: "Goes back to King James VI of Scotland. He had this obsession with demons and witchcraft. So in 1603 when he was crowned King James I of England, his new subjects – particularly suck-up authors – were eager to please him. Christopher Marlow wrote *Dr. Faustus* in 1604. Willie Shakespeare wrote *Macbeth* in 1606."

"So what?" Chief Crenshaw found all this nonsensical.

"*Macbeth* was cursed from the beginning. A coven of witches objected to Shakespeare using real incantations in his dialogue – '*eye of newt*,' all of that – so they put a curse on the play. At least, that's the legend that persists to this very day."

"D'you believe that stuff?"

"Absolutely. History records that the play's first performance was filled with disasters. The actor playing Lady Macbeth died suddenly, so Shakespeare himself had to take over the part. And real daggers were mistakenly used instead of stage props for the murder of King Duncan, which resulted in that actor's actual death. Lot of unfortunate mishaps like that."

"What's this got to do with Agamemnon Anderson's death?"

"Like I told you, he said '*Macbeth*.' Everybody knows that uttering the play's name aloud in a theatre causes bad luck."

"Yeah," said Chief Crenshaw, "I guess dying would be considered bad luck."

~ ~ ~

Tommy Turlington wasn't much of a suspect in Chief Crenshaw's opinion. But he was methodically interviewing all the actors one-by-one. A hunch told him Agamemnon Anderson's murderer would be found among the troupe of actors. Anderson was their new boss, an intrusive interloper who had not made himself popular with his new colleagues.

"Who among you disliked this Agamemnon fellow enough to kill him?"

"No one, I'm sure."

Crenshaw leaned back in his chair and tented his fingers. "Well, somebody slipped him a mickey. Poisoned him. Was it you?"

"Lord, no. I didn't know him well enough to hate him. I was happy to be keeping my job. Actors don't get a lot of steady work."

~ ~ ~

"He fired you. That's a motive for murder," said Chief Crenshaw.

"I was ready to move on," grumbled Herbert Golding. "He did me a favor."

"So why are you still here in Burpyville?"

Golding shrugged. "Room was paid for through the week. Might as well take advantage of it while I formulate my plans."

"And what are those plans?"

"To move on."

~ ~ ~

Carl and Bob Leicester were interviewed together. They did everything together. Identical twins, Carl was three minutes older than his brother. Therefore, he generally took the lead.

"The Macbeth Curse?" laughed Carl. "Pish! That's a silly superstition."

"True," nodded Bob. "Like stepping on a crack will break your mother's back."

"That was Harvey Wallberg's theory," said Chief Crenshaw, an attempt to goad them.

Carl all but giggled. "Harvey is an old fool. His ambition is great, but his talent is small as his —"

"We tolerate his antiquated ideas for the sake of his companionship," interjected Bob. "There are few opportunities for friendship when your life is on the road, performing in one strange outpost after another."

"So you count Harvey Wallbanger –"

"– Wallberg," Bob corrected.

"– as a friend?"

Carl quoted, " *'Most friendship is faining, most loving mere folly ...'*"

Bob added, "*'Then, heigh-ho, the holly. This life is most jolly.'*"

Frank Crenshaw shook his head wearily. These actors sure talked funny.

~ ~ ~

The women felt vindicated when Chief Purdue and Chief Crenshaw concluded that they were dealing with two homicides. But the question remained: Whodunnit?

"Jim and Frank finally agree with us that someone murdered those two actors," said Maddy. "That's progress."

"Yes," said Bootsie. "Problem is, they have no solid leads."

"Logic says the most likely suspects are those actors in the Merry Times troupe," opined N'yen.

"But what's the motive?" asked Cookie.

"Ambition. Jealousy. Money. Professional differences," Aggie ticked off the list on her fingers like a counting game. "Any one of the Seven Deadly Sins."

"Maybe we're dealing with a psycho serial killer – you know like Hannibal Lecter in *The Silence of the Lambs*," suggested Lizzie. She tended to get a little phantasmagorical in her thinking.

Bootsie huffed, "Nobody's eating these actors with flava beans."

"There has to be something we're missing," said Maddy. "Something we've overlooked. Nobody commits a murder without leaving clues."

"What could we have overlooked?" exclaimed Lizzie, throwing her hands into the air. "We've been over this at least a hundred times!"

"That's the $64,000 question," replied Sissy, although at 16 she was much too young to have ever seen the TV quiz show that gave rise to that phrase.

CHAPTER TWENTY-SEVEN

"Though she be but little, she is fierce."
-A Midsummer Night's Dream

"**N**o," said Aggie's father. "Nobody is digging up that actor."

"But the body needs to be exhumed," insisted the girl. "Dr. Medford should have done a toxicology screening. He needs to correct that error."

"No," repeated her father.

"But, Daddy, it's for the public good. People are saying Adolphus Everly Anderson was poisoned. That question should be answered."

"No, that's not possible."

"Of course, it is. You're the mayor. All you have to do is –"

He cut her off. "I mean, it's not possible to dig him up because he was cremated."

"Cremated? You mean ashes in an urn?"

"That's likely where you will find them. An urn was buried in Pleasant Glade on Sunday. A quiet affair, there was no ceremony. On instruction of the brother."

"What brother?"

"A guy named Agamemnon Anderson. He's an actor too. As the sole heir, he'll be assuming control of his brother's business. Arrived on Monday, according to what I've been told."

"Do you think he poisoned his own brother to take over Merry Times?"

"Doesn't seem likely. He was in Arizona at the time of Adolphus Anderson's death."

"Maybe he hired someone. Or had a minion infiltrate Merry Times. Has Uncle Jim checked out all those actors?"

"What's to check out? There's no crime here. Just a man dying of a heart attack at an inconvenient time."

"But Grammy says –"

"Yes, yes, I know – poison. But there's no evidence of that."

"That's why we needed a toxicology report."

"A little late for that now."

"But Daddy –!"

"Sweetie, go hang out with your friends Sissy and N'yen. Have a watermelon milkshake at Cozy Café. Put it on my tab. Save your Quilters Club's detecting for a real crime, okay?"

CHAPTER TWENTY-EIGHT

**"The baby beats the nurse,
and quite athwart goes all decorum."**
-Measure for Measure

The Quilters Club were needle-and-thimble sewers. They eschewed machine stitching, so each handmade quilt took them a little longer. The time it takes to make a quilt depends on the size, the complexity of the blocks, and the quilting itself. Full-sized patchwork quilts can take anywhere from days to years. A typical baby quilt could take up to 3 days, but a skilled quilter like Lizzie could do one in a day or less.

As one online blog put it: "Making a baby quilt can take a mere 12 hours depending on your level of expertise and quilting method. If you're machine quilting and highly experienced, you can put together a baby quilt in a couple of hours. On the other hand, if you're a newbie or are quilting by hand, it may take you a while."

Bootsie usually took two days to sew a 24" x 36" baby quilt; Maddy, and Cookie could do a baby quilt with a simple pattern in one day. Lizzie could knock out one in an afternoon. Of course, we're talking plain blocks, flange binding, and straightforward diamond quilting across the squares.

When it comes to fabrics for baby quilts, cotton is always a good choice. In fact, it's one of the most popular options, a material that's been used for generations. The primary reason is that cotton is soft and highly absorbent, gentle against a baby's skin. Organic cotton fabric is always preferable, as it is grown without the use of chemicals and fertilizers.

Charm Packs are an easy way to make a simple baby quilt with a large variety of different but coordinated fabrics. To make a 42" x 42" charm pack baby quilt you will need 64 five-inch squares – usually two Charm Packs.

Charm Packs are bundles of quilt fabric cut into specific sizes. Pre-cut bundles have been a longtime favorite with quilters because they shorten your cutting time and give you "an affordable way to purchase an entire collection of fabric without breaking the bank."

Duvets, quilts, and pillows are not recommended for babies under a year old. Not only might they make a baby too hot, they also pose a risk of suffocation (SIDS). Once your baby is over a year old, it's considered okay to use a duvet.

~ ~ ~

Being faster at sewing than the others, Lizzie Ridenour had completed her quota of baby quilts for the Our Lady of Mercy Children's Home. With all the hubbub about *A Midsummer Night's Dream*, she now decided to try a quilt pattern known as Shakespeare in the Park.

Designed by famed quiltmaker Judy Martin, Shakespeare in the Park is a relatively simple pattern made entirely of squares and triangles. Adaptable to any style and color scheme, Martin describes it as her most popular pattern.

The Shakespeare in the Park quilt captures the magic of spending an evening under the stars, the complex mix of stars and swirls mimicking the kinetic action found in Shakespeare's plays. Lizzie liked making "scrappy quilts" – that is, leftover bits from other projects, anything from old garments to unused pieces of fabric. She saw this as a chance to get creative in piecing together colors and textures.

But she knew the Shakespeare in the Park wasn't for everyone. As one quilter blogged:

> What have I gotten myself into?
>
> It has about a million pieces to it. Started cutting them out yesterday.
>
> I thought no biggie - all rotary cut - wrong!
>
> There are 2 triangles that have to be cut a certain way and my brain cannot figure it out so I used templates. I need a total of 90 of these two.
>
> By evening my neck was sore and my brain was fuzzy. I hope I haven't bitten off more than I can chew.
>
> It looks like it will go together well though.
>
> Anyone else make this one? I know I saw one on the board. It's a really pretty pattern.

Another quilter who tried a Shakespeare in the Park design posted:

> My niece is getting married in August, and this is her wedding quilt. It's mostly batiks (who knows how many different fabrics / solid purple batik backing), wool batting, and machine quilted with nylon on top and Bottom Line in the bobbin. The rebel in me decided to do concentric circles a half-inch apart, rather than continuous line spirals, or something like that. (What the blankety-blank-blank was I thinking! I'll be snipping threads from circle-jumping for weeks, because I got lazy and didn't do it as I went along.) I started it in July '09, finished the top in Jan '10, and just finished the quilting this week (about an hour before my guild meeting ... just in time to bring it for show and tell). I still have to block it and put the

binding and label on, but I thrilled I'm going to have it finished on time!!! Since the pic was taken, I've soaked it in ice water to remove the water-soluble blue and white markers (the cold water in AZ is NOT cold enough to do the job), washed it in hot water with Synthropal with two dye catcher sheets (I think I prewashed the backing, but nothing else, plus added 4 tons of starch along the way.), and dried it in a hot dryer. No need to call the quilt police. I got the effect I was going for, lots of puckery goodness and texture that hides my still-developing-confident-beginner-free-motion-quilting skills (long winded way of saying my circles aren't the smoothest). No, there isn't bleeding of the dark onto the light, and if there is, I can't find it. I slept under it last night, just to see if it works, and it does ... ha ha! I'll wash it again, after the binding, as my cat insists on sitting on my lap, when I hand-stitch the back, and the fabrics could be a bit softer. My theory is enjoy the quilt and use it until it's nothing but shreds! If my niece puts it up in a closet, I'd be crushed!

~ ~ ~

Cookie also took a brief break from making baby quilts, turning her attention to a Romeo and Juliet pattern, a design that looked like a field of multicolored flowers. Measuring 47" x 48", this beautiful hand-stitched hexagon quilt was, in Cookie's view, just as romantic as it sounded. With a cotton quilt top and a velvet backing, it indeed provided a dazzling design.

And it was a lot more fun than making a plain, practical crib quilt.

~ ~ ~

Watching Cookie's progress, Bootsie vowed to try a Romeo and Juliet quilt of her own; that is, when she finished with her baby quilt allotment. The slowest member of the Quilters Club, she was always running behind in her production of the little quilts.

However, Bootsie wasn't interested in the flowery design that was being tackled by her friend Cookie. Instead, she would be going for a pictorial quilt that featured actual scenes from the 1968 *Romeo and Juliet* movie starring Leonard Whiting and Olivia Hussey. In her opinion, that Franco Zeffirelli version was the most romantic of any film based on a William Shakespeare play. This quilt would remind her of that movie.

Tacky maybe, but she liked those kind of designs. She was fond of kitschy Keane paintings of big-eyed children and Thomas Kincaid oils depicting idyllic cottages in the forest. She even had a black velvet painting of Elvis in her kitchen.

Bootsie's taste was simple. But it fit her uncomplicated personality.

~ ~ ~

Sissy Jackson had been sewing baby quilts, too – but given her class load and play rehearsals, her quota was much smaller. Even so, she was running well ahead of Aunt Bootsie in her quilt production.

The teenager had stuck with a basic Log Cabin pattern, the most popular of any quilt design. And one of the easiest. That's because she was going for quantity, doing her share for those little unclaimed children at the orphanage.

Sissy could identify with them. She'd never known her absentee father, and her druggie mother was constantly in rehab. That's why she'd come here to Caruthers Corners to live with her grandfather. Buck Jackson was her official guardian. And the Quilters Club had become her extended family.

Under Aunt Lizzie's tutelage, Sissy was showing great promise as a quilter. She had started racking up prizes in Junior Competitions. But in another year she would move up to the adult category at Watermelon Days. That would put her up against pros like Aunt Lizzie and Abigail Wagler and former state champion Holly Eberhart.

Yes, she would have to up her game! But she was looking forward to it.

~ ~ ~

As for Maddy, she always seemed to be working on several quilts at the same time, bouncing from one to another several times a day. Even so, it always felt good to finish a quilt. Near the end of her baby quilt quota, she decided to start working on a 60" x 60" quilt called A Midsummer Night's Dream. Designed by quiltmaker Alison Thompson, its description read:

> An homage to William Shakespeare. The wreaths are on a garden wall covered in ivy. Each wreath has a quote from Midsummer Night's Dream and fruit or berries or flowers appropriate for the quote. All drawn by me from nature, hand applique and hand quilted. Took 3 years to complete.

Three years, my foot, thought Maddy. I can do this one in less than three weeks.

You can find the A Midsummer Night's Dream pattern on The Quilt Show website, where members are allowed to upload images of their latest projects. An accompanying photograph shows nine circular wreaths beneath hanging ivy, all on a light tan quilt front. Quite elegant!

The site features several other Shakespeare-inspired designs, including a King Lear pattern and new variations on the Shakespeare in the Park design.

~ ~ ~

Having worked on this orphanage project for several months now, the baby quilts, lap quilts, and crib quilts were starting to pile up. Pretty soon the gals would begin delivering them to Our Lady of Mercy Children's Home in Burpyville.

Quilting was lots of fun, Maddy told herself. But even more enjoyable when your quilts were serving a worthwhile purpose. Like these.

CHAPTER TWENTY-NINE

"The direful spectacle of the wreck ..."
-The Tempest

By noon on Wednesday, Maddy had finished her batch of crib quilts and bundled them up with a sturdy cotton twine for delivery to the orphanage. She carted the half-dozen bundles out to her new Audi S7 and loaded them into the well of the hatchback. The quilts spilt over into the backseat and rear floorboard.

Keeping under the 55 MPH speed limit, she headed down 21 (the Burpyville Highway) to make the delivery. She was driving alone, since no one had been available to accompany her. Lizzie had her weekly hair appointment. Cookie was busy giving a deposition to lawyers in the Squeaky Beasley lawsuit. And Bootsie had nobody to spell her at the animal shelter, both volunteers being out with a summer cold. Who knew where N'yen and Sissy were off to. Aggie had gone over to the Town Hall to see her dad.

She thought about asking her daughter Tilly to ride along, but this wasn't Mrs. Gottman's day to watch the "Terrible Trio," as Aggie called her younger sisters. So much for that. Maddy loved her grandchildren, but she wasn't prepared to drive to Burpyville and back with those wiggling, squealing brats jumping up and down in in the back seat. Besides, the car was filled with bundles of quilts.

Turning on the radio to keep herself company, Maddy tuned to WZUR. It was Easy Listening Hour, hosted by Snooky Smith. "Moon River" – the Andy Williams version – was playing. When Snooky wasn't performing with his band, he subbed as a DJ. Everybody had to make a living.

She could barely see out of the rearview mirror due to the bundles piled in the back. Those small quilts had been quite a challenge, due to the quantity needed in a short span of time.

Crib quilts are a relatively new phenomena. Around 1750, cribs, rocking cradles, and small beds began to be listed in the inventories of libraries and museums. "It is supposed that the making of small quilts goes with the making of small beds," postulates *Les Nouvelles du Patchwork.*

Until the middle of the 19th Century, it was customary for children to sleep in bed with their parents, or in a servant/caretaker's bed. By 1841, *The American Woman's Home* was suggesting, "The baby shall not sleep in his mother's arms at night except when the weather is very cold. A crib near his mother ... and a light cover are the best conditions for a good sleep."

Wrapping up babies to protect them from the cold was the purpose of the small quilts. But they displayed the same creative designs as full-sized patchwork quilts. Lizzie was the most talented quilter among them, but Maddy could certainly hold her own. Each of the crib quilts in her bundles were miniature works of art.

Listening to Snooky Smith spin his Golden Oldies, she wasn't paying attention to her rearview mirror and didn't see the panel truck coming up fast behind her. It wasn't until the truck's front bumper collided with the rear of her Audi did she know it was there.

Ka-chunk!

Maddy felt the car lurch forward like an F-14 jet being catapulted off an aircraft carrier. She struggled to maintain control of the wheel. Even so, she felt her SUV jackknife, wheels leaving the asphalt, sending her into a bumpy field of soybeans.

Fortunately, Indiana is mostly flatlands, with no cliffs or sharp inclines along most country roads. So the Audi didn't flip, although the plowed rows were like driving over a washboard. She came to a stop next to a scarecrow, though she wasn't sure what this straw man was doing in the middle of a soybean field. Crows weren't particularly fond of soybeans, were they?

The airbags deployed upon the car's journey across the bumpy field, punching Maddy in the chest hard enough to create a painful bruise. The Audi S7 comes with frontal, side-impact, front-knee, and rollover airbags as standard, a total count of 10 in all. To a passenger, it was like being hit by an angry mob from all sides at once.

Airbags contain sodium azide and sodium hydroxide, which create high temperature thermal gases that inflate the bag. These substances can cause a thermal or alkali burn when an airbag goes off. Maddy suffered a serious burn on her left arm.

Ow-eee!

Through a crack between the puffy bags she could see the panel truck speeding away, its mission accomplished. Was this intended as a threat of some kind? If so, why? Or was someone trying to do her serious harm? She fished out her iPhone and dialed 9-1-1. She knew the call would go straight to the Caruthers Corners Police Department.

"What's the nature of your emergency?" asked the dispatcher.

"Is this Myrtle or Elvina?"

"Myrtle."

"Myrtle, this is Maddy Madison. A truck just ran me off the road on the Burpyville Highway. Think I may have broken an axle. The airbags, they –"

"You say you broke your arm?"

"No, I burnt my arm. My car's axle may be broken."

"Is your car on fire?"

"No, no. Just disabled. I'm fine, more or less. Jim may want to call Chief Crenshaw over in Burpyville and have him try to head off that truck. It was a blue panel truck, a Chevy I think. I didn't get a look at the driver."

"On it. Calling the Chief. Notifying Burpyville. Summoning an ambulance. Dispatching an officer to the scene – Tommy Truehart most likely. He's not far away."

"Forget the ambulance, I'm okay."

"Standard procedure. Just sit tight."

"But –"

"Stay on the line till Tommy gets there. He's en route."

"But –" she repeated.

"Remain calm. You may be in shock."

"No, I –" But Maddy didn't bother finishing the sentence. She could hear a siren wailing in the distance.

CHAPTER THIRTY

**"Yet does this accident and flood of fortune
so far exceed all ..."**
-Twelfth Night

Beau got word about his wife's automobile accident from Chief Jim Purdue. "She's okay," his friend was quick to assure him. "But your car may need a few repairs. I had Flynn's Texaco tow it in."

"Where is she?"

"Home. Tommy Truehart dropped her off. She refused to go to the hospital."

"But she's all right, you say?"

"Just a few bruises, a slight burn on her arm from when the airbags deployed. Otherwise fit as a fiddle."

"What happened?"

"A panel truck ran her off the road. You know how people drive on Burpyville Highway."

"What did the driver have to say?"

"He kept going. Hit and run. Myrtle alerted the Burpyville PD to set up a roadblock. But they didn't catch him. Disappeared like a phantom."

~ ~ ~

"Well, hello there, Miss Agnes Millicent Tidemore," Doc Medford greeted her. His glasses were perched low on his nose, a sign that he'd been going through the stack of papers that cluttered his desk. Medicare invoices and patients records. "What brings you to our little town? I thought you were off wowing them at Yale."

"Summer break."

"How are you doing in your studies. Pre-law, as I recall."

"Made the Dean's List last semester."

"Way to go, young lady." He paused to adjust his glasses. "What brings you to the office? It's not time for your annual checkup. No female problems, I hope."

She smiled, a perfect row of teeth. "I'm fine. Just wanted to ask you about that actor who died."

"You too? Your grandmother has been causing quite a foofaraw. Little too late to prove it one way or another, I'm afraid."

"So my Daddy told me. I hear his brother had him turned into a crispy critter."

"Cremated, yes."

"What makes you so sure it was a heart attack?"

Dr. Franklin Delano Medford removed his glasses to polish them. "I've seen a billion coronary thrombosis cases. This one fit the bill. Man was fine, then dropped dead. Most obvious explanation."

"How would a poison have been different?"

He cleared his throat, as if preparing to give a lecture. "Depends on the poison. Lots of items fall under that definition. Poisoning symptoms can mimic other conditions, such as seizure, alcohol intoxication, stroke, insulin reaction – even a heart attack. I'll give you that. But with some poisons you get dizziness, restlessness, perspiration, nausea, diarrhea, vomiting, difficulty breathing, soreness in joints, skin irritation, even burns. Depends on whether it's a poisoning

169

from agricultural or industrial chemicals, drugs, biological poisons, or radiation."

"That's quite a range."

"Exactly. But I'll take Occam's Razor."

"The principle that the simplest explanation is likely the correct one?"

"There you have it."

Just then, the phone on his desk rang. At least Aggie thought it was on his desk. He had to plow through the pile of papers to find it.

"Yes?" he answered. "Yes," he repeated shifting his gaze to Aggie. "Thank you. We'll both be over right away."

"What was that?" Aggie asked nervously, somehow aware that it involved her.

"Your grandmother," Doc Medford said. "She's been in a car accident."

CHAPTER THIRTY-ONE

**"To mourn a mischief that is past and gone
is the next way to draw new mischief on."**
-Othello

Maddy's youngest son Freddie was the Caruthers Corners Fire Chief. Since the paramedic team reported to him, it didn't take long for him to get word of his mother's automotive mishap. Within minutes of Maddy arriving home, his red vehicle pulled into the Madison driveway on Melon Pickers Row, lights flashing.

"Mom," he shouted as he ran into the house, "are you all right?"

"Of course, dear," came her reply. She was reclining on the big white couch in the living room, her feet elevated by a plump pillow. A steaming cup of watermelon tea sat on the end table within easy reach. She relied on watermelon tea as a panacea for most ills – from bad colds to tummy aches. The tea was her special blend. The concoction may have had a touch of Johnnie Walker in it.

"You should've let my boys take you over to Burpyville Memorial. Something may be broken. At your age, bones are brittle."

"*Tsk, tsk,*" she said. "Your father and I are not the old fossils you think we are. Doc Medford gave me a clean bill of health at my annual checkup just a few weeks ago. No osteoporosis. I'm solid as a rock."

"But —"

"Don't you worry, Freddie. I'm fine. Just a little sore. The airbag hit me in the chest like a prizefighter's punch."

"My point exactly. You had a stroke only a few years ago."

"That had more to do with a blood clot to the brain than a thump on the chest. Just relax, dear."

At that precise moment Beau Madison rushed into the house, not even bothering to close the front door behind him. "Maddy, sweetheart, are you all right?" he called frantically.

Maddy remained calm, comfortably reposed on the big Haitian cotton couch. "As I was telling Freddie, I'm perfectly fine. Just a little shaken up. The driver of that panel truck hit my Audi from behind, then kept on going. You would've thought he could have stopped to make sure I wasn't injured. My car wound up in the middle of Burt Lazenski's soybean field."

Freddie took his fire chief's cap off to brush his hair back. His face was horribly scarred from a long-ago fire when he worked in Atlanta. "That driver oughta be arrested. Reckless driving. Leaving the scene of an accident."

"He got clean away," Beau repeated what the police chief had told him. "The Burpyville cops were waiting for him, but he never showed up on that end. No sign of a blue panel truck."

"I think it was a Chevrolet cargo van. Hard to say what year."

"The Chevrolet Express haven't changed styles in years. It's maintained the same basic style for 27 years," noted Freddie. He was something of a car buff. "Those vans are like time capsules from the 1990s, the epitome of the If-It-Ain't-Broke-Don't-Fix-It school of design. With a 4.3 liter V6 engine and rear-wheel drive, it gets the job done."

"Well, it certainly did a job on my Audi. Banged it up pretty good. I think the axel may be broken. At least, that's what Buddy Flynn said."

"Buddy knows his way around a car," said Freddie. "If he said it's broken, it's broken."

"Forget the danged car," grumbled Beau. "What I can't understand is why that driver didn't bother stopping to see if you needed help."

"Probably panicked," shrugged their son.

"I dunno about that," mused Maddy. "I'm pretty sure that bump was deliberate."

~ ~ ~

Within the next hour, all the members of the Quilters Club – Maddy's BFFs –were gathered around her bed. "Holding court," as Beau described it.

He and Freddie had insisted she get some bed rest. Nonetheless, the big Victorian house was abuzz with activity. Daughter Tilly had rushed over to help, although it was unclear what help was needed. Aggie and N'yen and Sissy were there too. Oldest son Bill and his wife Kathy (N'yen's dad and mom) were said to be driving down from Chicago. Maddy's fraternal twin sister Maisie had delivered bowls and bowls of delicious food.

It was almost like a wake, Maddy thought.

She pronounced all this hubbub as "Much Ado About Nothing" (to steal the phrase from Shakespeare.) The Bard was a topic of much discussion for the Quilters Clubbers – now that there were *two* murders of Merry Times actors to consider.

~ ~ ~

Penny Heath heard about Maddy's automobile accident from her husband. Although the couple professed to maintain a "firewall" between their respective jobs, a certain amount of pillow talk took place. Harry Teague had phoned his wife at the *Gazette* to give her the scoop. She posted the story for tomorrow's addition, then set out for Caruthers Corners in her late-model Volkswagen Passant to get a follow-up interview with Maddy Madison. She could practically smell a big story here.

Penny parked haphazardly in the Madisons' driveway, grabbed her palm-sized voice recorder, and headed toward the front door of the massive Victorian-style house. Just as she was about to knock, a voice called out, "Hold on, I'm right behind you."

She looked around to see a small black girl with frizzy brown hair and bright green eyes. Her dress was dizzying with its measles-red polka-dots. It was that Vietnam kid's girlfriend, if she wasn't mistaken. What was her name – Cecily? No, Cecilia. Sissy, they called her.

"My hands are full," said Sissy. "Can you get the door?" The girl's arms were loaded with folded crib quilts. Her contribution to the Our Lady of Mercy Children's Home project. Since she didn't drive, one of the senior members of the Quilters Club would help with the delivery. She was dropping them off at Maddy Madison's house.

"Here you go," Penny held the door wide.

"Thanks." Sissy could barely balance the tall stack.

"Uh, I was hoping to interview Mrs. Madison."

"C'mon in. I'm sure she won't mind. She reads your articles all the time."

"Oh – she does?"

"Yep. Says she admires your spunk."

174

"Spunk?"

"Yeah, you got spunk, she says. Ever'body likes spunk."

Sissy stacked her crib quilts on the kitchen island and ushered Penny Heath upstairs to Maddy's bedroom. She'd moved up there after everybody left to let her get some rest.

"You got yourself another visitor," announced the girl.

Maddy looked up from a book she was reading. *Shakespeare for Beginners* (Book 3) was its title. *Understanding A Midsummer Night's Dream* was the subtitle. "Oh, Penny," she said. "Do come in. I'm so glad you're here."

"Thank you for seeing me," replied the reporter, unobtrusively switching on her recorder. She looked very official, wearing her green two-piece pantsuit and black horn-rimmed glasses.

"I'm so pleased you dropped by," said Maddy. "I'm hoping I can convince you to do a short piece about my 'accident.' I want to get a message out there."

"A message?"

"That's right. Somebody deliberately ran me off the road. I'm not sure whether he was trying to kill me or scare me. But he rammed me hard from behind, sent me off into Burt Lazenski's soybean field. I got a bit bruised up, but as you can see I'm okay. No whiplash, no concussions, no broken bones."

"This was deliberate, you say?"

"Absolutely."

"And what's the message."

"The vehicle that rammed me was a blue Chevrolet Express cargo van. It hit my Audi hard, so there's undoubtedly some serious damage to its front end. If you can get that description out there, someone will surely turn it in. Then we will know whose behind Adolphus Everly Anderson's murder."

"You still think that actor was murdered?"

"Yes, poisoned."

"And you think your wreck is connected to the murder?"

"What do you think?"

Penny paused for a moment, then said, "Quite possibly."

"Will you help me?"

"Give me a minute. I need to phone in a few additions to the story I filed before the morning edition's deadline."

CHAPTER THIRTY-TWO

*"When sorrows come, they come not single spies,
but in battalions."*
-Hamlet

Everybody showed up again at the Madison household on Melon Pickers Row by 9 a.m., scurrying about the kitchen, carrying platters of eggs and oatmeal and pancakes up to Maddy's bedroom, turning the big sunny room into the site of a festive indoor picnic.

Maddy was sitting up in bed, feeling much better after a good night's sleep. She had fared better than her Audi S7. Other than a white bandage on her arm (the burn), there were no other signs of injury or impairment. The Audi had been totaled.

In addition to her Quilters Club pals and the "kids," the picnickers included daughter Tilly, Marybelle Olsen, Freddie's wife Amanda, Mary Alice Hegler, Florence Kilroy (the minister's wife), Myrtle Dobbler (her sister Elvina was on duty at the PD), and such assorted neighbors as Dizzy Duncan, Elaine Bjorn, Margaret Swartzendruber, and Janey Baumgartner.

Assessing the situation, Beau quietly slipped out the garage door and made his way to Cozy Café where he shared coffee and donuts with Jim Purdue. Mark Tidemore joined them. Maddy's sister Maisie was holding down the fort, refilling their cups with that "endless" coffee.

Jim passed around his copy of the *Burpyville Gazette*. The morning edition carried Penny Heath's report of Maddy's so-called accident. The headline blared:

Local Dignitary Targeted In Murder Attempt

Exclusive by Penny Heath

Madelyn "Maddy" Madison, mother-in-law of Caruthers Corners mayor Mark Tidemore, reportedly was the intended victim of a hit-and-run driver yesterday morning. Mrs. Madison's Audi S7 was struck from behind by a blue Chevrolet Express panel truck on Highway 21 while traveling east toward Burpyville. The driver sped away without stopping. Mrs. Madison's vehicle veered off the road, coming to rest in an adjacent field. Although bruised, she was not seriously injured thanks to the deployment of the Audi's airbags.

"I am sure it was deliberate," said Maddy Madison in an exclusive interview with the *Gazette*. "Someone tried to kill me."

Mrs. Madison's Audi S7 was declared a total loss. The front axle was broken and the rear bumper was severely damaged. The engine was cracked, according to Ronald "Buddy" Flynn, owner of Flynn's Texaco.

According to the police report, it is thought that the van incurred significant front-end damage from the collision.

Readers are alerted to be on the lookout for a light blue Chevrolet Express cargo van, a boxy panel truck like those used for delivery or light hauling. A reward of $2,000 is being offered by the *Gazette* for any information leading to the arrest of the van's driver.

"Harry Teague's wife might be a big help," commented Chief Purdue. "We should be getting sightings on that blue panel truck with a bashed-in front pretty quick. Unless the driver's been able to hide it somewhere. But it can't be far away. My boys and the Burpyville Police cut off both ends of Highway 21. That blue truck's gotta be somewhere between the two towns."

~ ~ ~

Penny Heath sat at her desk in the newsroom, checking her story in the morning paper. Good placement, page one below the fold. Not headline news, but pretty close. Her Managing Editor was pleased that she'd scored a first-person interview with the victim. She would be able to play this out with several follow ups. Yes, she was a good crime reporter. And being married to a cop didn't hurt either.

The story was pretty accurate, Penny thought. Except for that offer of a reward. Her publisher would kill her when he read about the $2,000.

~ ~ ~

By noon, the Maddy's visitors had faded away, leaving time for a quick nap.

The Quilters Club – minus their leader – repaired to the downstairs family room where they worked on their crib quilt quota. Lizzie and Maddy had finished theirs. Cookie and Sissy weren't far behind. Bootsie still had a way to go, so Lizzie was pitching in to help her.

Cookie's husband Ben had sent some farmhands over to Buddy's Texaco station to retrieve Maddy's quilts from the wrecked vehicle. The bundles were piled along one wall of the family room, like bales of cotton waiting for a steamboat. Aggie joined her friend Sissy in working on a baby-sized quilt; N'yen began tallying the number of finished quilts in the room. Our Lady of Mercy Children's Home was certainly going to receive a windfall.

"Jim has got Tommy Truehart running matches on blue Chevy Express vans against local zip codes," said Bootsie. "Nothing showing up yet."

"Maybe we should hire Lizzie's private eye to follow some of those actors, see if someone slips up, gives us a clue," suggested Cookie, looking up from her sewing. "One of them has to be connected to a blue panel truck."

"Odell doesn't do that kind of detective work," Lizzie shook her head, ruffling the red hair. "Most of his sleuthing he does at a computer."

"A computer?" said Bootsie. "That's what Tommy is doing."

"Odell can search the Dark Web, that place on the Internet where bad guys hang out."

N'yen spoke up: "I can do that. But I doubt these are the kind of bad guys you'd find on the Dark Web."

"Internet searches can only take you so far," said Cookie. "We need some eyes-on."

"Right," nodded Aggie. "Sometimes it takes some old-fashioned legwork.

Sissy made a face. "What kinda gumshoe is this guy anyway?"

"He's not a gumshoe, dear," corrected Lizzie. "He's a professional private investigator."

"Somebody needs to keep an eye on our main suspects," said Aggie.

"Why don't we do it ourselves?" proposed N'yen. "We could divide into teams. Keep an eye on the top Persons of Interest listed in that private eye's report – Wallberg and the twins."

"Now that's a good idea," said Bootsie. Smiling like Poppie Fresh, the puffy wife of the Pillsbury Doughboy.

"You mean follow them?" asked Lizzie.

"Why not?"

"Yeah, why not?" echoed N'yen.

"Because Grammy is still bedridden," Aggie pointed out.

"Fiddlesticks," said Maddy, shuffling into the room, wrapped like a mummy in a diaphanous lilac bathrobe. "Doc merely said for me to get some rest. And now I'm rested."

Lizzie raised her perfectly plucked eyebrows. "So we're going to spy on them?"

"Surveille them," Bootsie amended.

"I like the idea," nodded Cookie.

"Let's do it then," said Maddy.

"Well, okay," Lizzie acquiesced.

"Oh boy," said N'yen.

"Yeah," said Sissy.

"Forsooth and anon," said Aggie. But she was just being a smart aleck.

CHAPTER THIRTY-THREE

**"Speak the speech, I pray you, as I pronounc'd it
to you, tripping on the tongue ..."**
-Hamlet

William Shakespeare wrote in Elizabethan English. This linguistic period fell somewhere between Geoffrey Chaucer and the Modern English we speak and write today. The language was less than 100 years old at the time. There were no dictionaries. And most documents were still written in Latin.

Shakespeare was something of a philological pioneer. He introduced over 1,700 original words to the English language as well as using existing words in new, inventive ways. It's truly amazing that one person could have such an influence on a language.

We owe him a lot. "It's Greek to me" (*Julius Caesar*), "elbow room" (*King John*), "heart of gold" (*Henry V*), "dead as a doornail" (*Henry VI, Part II),* "wild-goose chase" (*Romeo and Juliet*), "in my heart of hearts" (*Hamlet*), 'neither here nor there" (*Othello*), and "such stuff as dreams are made on" (*The Tempest)* are just a handful of the many well-known phrases that Shakespeare invented.

Among his plays, *Love's Labour Lost* is best known for its clever wordplay and puns. Most people think *The Comedy of Errors* is the funniest play. Others say *Twelfth Night,* describing it as "the kind of play that can seem as fresh the twelfth time you see it as the first."

~ ~ ~

N'yen had a Shakespeare joke:

> "Why did Puck cross the road?
> He saw someone he knew Oberon the other side."

"That's funny," clapped Sissy. A fan of her boyfriend's silly wordplay.

"Oh yeah, how about this?" Aggie matched him:

> "Did you hear about the chicken who walked out of a production of *Hamlet*?
> He heard somebody threaten to murder most fowl."

Sissy thought about it a moment, then came up with:

> "Those are so bad, thou hast been Bard from making any more Shakespeare puns."

"Groan," giggled Aggie.

"Hey, I thought that was pretty good," said N'yen. But Aggie knew he was just sticking up for his girlfriend. That was okay with her. She expected that.

They were waiting there outside the Highliner Hotel in Burpyville. The little VW was as crowded as a sardine can. The summer heat hovered in the high 80s. Air conditioning in a Beetle is iffy at best. The threesome had been assigned to trail Harvey Wallace Wallberg, report on where he went, make note of any suspicious movements.

Maddy ("Out of my deathbed," she joked) and Bootie were assigned to follow one of the Leicester twins; Cookie and Lizzie were to follow the other. Which was which didn't matter, the twins as interchangeable as bookends.

The three surveillance teams were in place, Quilters Club on the job.

~ ~ ~

Harvey Wallberg came out first and flagged a passing taxi. Burpyville had many more cruising cabs than Caruthers Corners, which relied on Tom's Taxis, a single-cab service.

N'yen followed behind the taxi in his sputtering Volkswagen bug, with Sissy wedged into the front seat beside him, Aggie crammed into what passed as a backseat. Aggie was nervous with her cousin behind the wheel, but he had finally passed the test for his driver's license. The boy might be a certified genius, but the mechanics of driving a car seemed to elude him. (No Asian stereotype intended ... he was just an inexperienced driver.)

The taxi headed west along Highway 21, racing toward Caruthers Corners. N'yen held back several car lengths to avoid Wallberg spotting them. The road was fairly straight, so the boy's driving was not as scary as Aggie expected. She had offered to drive – her skill was as flawless as a female Tony Stewart – but he refused to let anyone else behind the wheel of his first car.

As they cruised past the fields of soybeans and corn and watermelon, Aggie ruminated about Anthony Wayne Stewart, one of her idols. Nicknamed "Smoke," Tony Stewart was a NASCAR Hall of Fame stock car driver. He had won 13 driving championships, the only driver in history to win a championship in both IndyCar and NASCAR classes.

She thought about taking a course in fast driving. There were nearly a dozen race car tracks near New Haven, but the one that appealed to her was Lime Rock, a classic 1.53 mile, 7-turn course founded by Skip Barber in 1975. The school had turned out such drivers as A.J. Allmendinger, Andy Lally, Juan Pablo Montoya, and Marco Andretti. Even celebs like Paul Newman, Patrick Dempsey, and Tom Cruise had trained there.

With her trust fund, she could afford to buy a Ferrari 333 SP. Her dad would bust a gasket. But she thought racing might be the thrill of a lifetime, putting pedal to the metal, winding through the hilly terrain of the Berkshire Mountains at 120 MPH.

Her reverie was broken as the taxi they were following slowed down. What was going on?

At that curve where Highway 21 circles the town, N'yen was surprised when the cab continued straight, leading them onto South Main Street. He proceeded carefully, cruising along the narrow thoroughfare past the Dollar General Store, past the Dairy Queen, past the silver-fronted Cozy Café, past the squat concrete bunker of the Police Department, past the redbrick building of Kupnick's Pharmacy.

"WTF," said Sissy. "He's stopping at the Town Hall."

Aggie frowned. "That's where my Daddy works."

CHAPTER THIRTY-FOUR

"Hide not thy poison ..."
-Henry VI

As Chief Purdue would later describe it, Tommy Truehart "struck pay dirt." The deputy's computer search turned up a match for the cufflink that Slick Vic found on his barbershop floor while sweeping up.

"Here you go, Chief," said Tommy as he slapped a two-inch-thick printout onto Jim Purdue's desk. "Found 'em – the very cufflinks in question."

The Police Chief stared down at the slab of paper. "Can't you just give me the Cliff's Notes version?" he implored. Sometimes his deputy's zealous enthusiasm turned into overkill. Ask him for a sentence and he'd give you *War and Peace*.

"Well, sure. First off, this cufflink is rare. It was designed by an artist named Wynona Burns. She's a pretty big deal in the jewelry world. Only two sets were ever made, so it shouldn't be hard to figure out who this link belongs to."

"You don't say?"

"I found the cufflinks listed on the website of a fancy New York jewelry store called Preston Peterson & Sons. Here's what it says about them." He pointed to the top sheet, a printout of the webpage itself.

"These cufflinks were inspired by the 16ᵗʰ-century noblewoman and queen consort Catherine de Medici. History tells us she was a notorious poisoner and kept her murderous potions inside a locket-style ring. Wynona recommends that you keep something less dangerous than arsenic or nightshade inside the hidden compartment inside each link. Nose candy, anyone?"

"D'you think she was suggesting people use these cufflinks to carry sniffs of cocaine or crystal meth?" frowned Tommy.

"Maybe, but somebody could just as easily use it in the Catherine de Medici manner – for hiding poison."

"Does that mean the actor whose hair Vic cut was the one who poisoned them Anderson brothers?"

Chief Purdue chewed on his lip before answering. "Don't rightly know. But I think we should get Vic Davone to look over a photo lineup of those Merry Times actors. See whose hair he cut."

"Where'm I gonna get their pictures?" Tommy asked. For a technically smart guy, he could be dense sometimes.

"Same place you got this," he indicated the printout. "Don't you keep telling me you can find *any*thing on the Internet?"

"You got it, Chief."

"One more thing, Tommy. Bag that cufflink carefully and send it over to Burpyville PD. Ask 'em to analyze it for any residue they might find inside that secret compartment. Looking for poison. Herman Vox, the crime scene tech over there, can work miracles."

"Yessir."

"Guess you better hand deliver it. Not only is it an important piece of evidence, it looks expensive."

"You got that right, Chief. That website listed them links at $5,000 a pair. Said they was made of –" he glanced down at the printout to get it correct "– 18k yellow gold, satin finish, approximately 50 points of F/G Vs 1/2 diamonds."

Chief Purdue bent to examine the squarish cufflink more closely. "Diamonds, you say? Better not lose it. I'd have to take it out of your paycheck."

CHAPTER THIRTY-FIVE

"We came into the world like brother and brother,
and now let's go hand in hand,
not one before another ..."
-The Comedy of Errors

The Quilters Club had been waiting for better than an hour when the Leicester twins came out of hotel together, holding hands, more like girlfriends than siblings. They were giggling and whispering and nudging each other as the strolled down the sidewalk.

Apparently they had a rental car, a silver Toyota Corolla parked down the street. The Highliner had no parking garage or adjacent lot. Guests, the few it had, were forced to park along Anthony Wayne Avenue.

When the two actors got into the same car, Maddy's idea of two teams following each of them was scrapped. She and Bootsie abandoned their Buick and scurried down the street to climb into the backseat of Cookie's Jeep Grand Cherokee. Better to have one surveillance vehicle than a procession conspicuously following that rental car.

Cookie already had the engine running and pulled away from the curb the second she heard the car's rear door slam with her two friends inside. The silver Toyota was only a block or so ahead of them by the time the Cherokee got rolling.

"Stay a little way back so they won't spot us," instructed Bootsie. Being a police chief's wife, the plump woman with the pixie 'do considered herself an expert in investigative techniques.

"Barbara Jo Purdue, I've seen enough television cop shows to know how to tail another car," said Cookie, eyes glued on the vehicle driven by the twins.

"Hey, just trying to help."

"Ladies, pay attention," Maddy urged. "They seem to be heading toward Highway 21."

"Bet they're going to Caruthers Corners," declared Lizzie. An easy assumption since that's where 21 went. There were no other options, the Burpyville Highway a straight shot between the two towns. Other than Wabash Acres or the old Star-Lite Drive-In, there were few sideroads and only a scattering of farmhouses before hitting the town limits.

"If the killer is one of those twins, which one do you think it is?" Cookie made idle conversation as she drove, her speed matching the car in front.

"I'd pick Carl," answered Maddy. "The program listed him as playing Hermia. so it would've been him standing to Puck's right."

"Bob," guessed Bootsie. "Those are tricky boys. And they refused to confirm which was which. I'd bet they traded parts that night."

"My thinking is that Carl and Bob Leicester could be in this together," said Lizzie. "They seem very close. And like that old saying goes, 'Those who play together, slay together.'"

"What old saying's that?" frowned Maddy.

"Some old saying – whatever."

"Maybe Lizzie should have her private investigator cross-check his list to see who had a motive to kill *both* Addy Anderson and his brother," suggested Cookie, smoothly changing the subject.

"*Humph*, I think it's cheating for Lizzie to use a detective," complained Bootsie. "I thought the Quilters Club was supposed to solve crimes on its own."

"This isn't a game," snapped Lizzie. "We're trying to catch a double murderer. Any way we can do that should be considered fair play."

"Everybody calm down," said Maddy. "Being wrong about that park ranger has made us lose our confidence. We need to get our edge back if we want to solve these horrible crimes."

"Maddy's right," sniffled Lizzie. "I can't bear the thought that we almost sent an innocent man to jail."

"Not so innocent now. Remember, Jim just told me the guy murdered a man in North Dakota." Bootsie felt that this vindicated their lapse in judgment. A crook was a crook was a crook, as her husband often said.

~ ~ ~

Up ahead, the silvery Toyota made a sudden right turn.

"Whoa," said Cookie, hitting the brakes.

"What's going on?" Lizzie blurted as Cookie made the sharp turn.

"Rosencrantz and Guildenstern just veered into Wabash Acres. Where they go, we go."

Originally conceived as a retirement village, financial straits had broadened Wabash Acres' inhabitants to include couples looking for starter homes and working stiffs in need of affordable housing. The construction quality was questionable, built to barely outlast its original elderly homeowners. Even so, it had once been considered a ritzy part of town before the 2018 tornado had wrecked the town's economy along with a third of its buildings.

"Why there?"

"Maybe they spotted us and are trying to make a run for it," speculated Lizzie. The banker's wife had a turn for the dramatic. She saw them as a latter-day Bonnie and Clyde – or Bonnie and Bonnie. Or Bonnie and Bonnie and Bonnie and Bonnie.

"I doubt that. This is the only road into the Wabash Acres. There's no other exit," said Cookie. She was picturing the map of the housing development in her mind's eye.

"Maybe they're trying to lose us in this labyrinth of streets," speculated Bootsie.

"The streets aren't that complicated," said Cookie. "They're laid out in a simple grid. I'd guess they're going to visit somebody."

"Who could it be?" wondered Bootsie, eyes focused on the silver Toyota moving along two blocks ahead of them. "Do we know anybody who lives here?"

"Lots of people," replied Maddy. "My real-life aunt, for instance."

"Who?"

"Emily Polk, my biological mother's sister. Poor old lady has Alzheimer's now. My Foundation pays for her caretaker."

"Oh, I'd forgotten."

"Doesn't your twin sister Maisie own Wabash Acres?" asked Cookie. Already knowing the answer.

"Yes, that was part of her Hoople inheritance. People who live here say she's a good landlord. I think she helps subsidize some of the rents and mortgage rates."

"That's nice of her," commented Bootsie. She wished somebody would help subsidize *her* mortgage payment. Money was tight, living on a policeman's salary.

"My bank holds most of the mortgages in Wabash Acres. I doubt it subsidizes much. Edward Durkin, the manager, is pretty tightfisted, I regret to tell you."

Everybody in town knew Durkin. The local answer to the Grinch, he never put money in the collection plate at Pleasant Glade. Rev. Kilroy prayed for his immortal soul, as if that would loosen his purse strings. His wife always bought her clothes off the sale rack at the Clothes Horse Boutique. He bought his suits at Barney's Discounts. People called him "Tightwad Teddy" behind his back.

Suddenly, Cookie hit the brakes, nearly throwing Maddy and Bootsie into the front seat. Lizzie almost smacked against the windshield, only saved by the tight seatbelt.

"What the heck?" screamed Lizzie. Realizing how close she came to a concussion. If her lips had been puckered, she could have kissed the windshield.

"Sorry," Cookie apologized. "The Toyota stopped in front of that house halfway down the block."

"Who lives there?" Lizzie stared into the distance at the bungalow, studying it for a moment. It was a one-story brick-fronted prefab. Probably two bedrooms and 1 ½ baths. There was an attached garage, but the door was closed. The lawn was neatly manicured. Sprinklers spewed a rainbow of water onto the grass as the nozzles clicked in a semi-circle.

"Dunno," Maddy said. Many of the houses in Wabash Acres looked alike, there only being five styles used in the construction. She wasn't as familiar with this corner of the development as with the block where her aunt lived.

"Can you make out the house number?" asked Cookie, peering over her glasses. "I could identify who lives there by that. My memory thing."

"Not from here," said Bootsie. "My eyes aren't what they used to be."

"I'm afraid to pull up any closer."

"Guess we'll just have to wait to find out," Maddy told them.

CHAPTER THIRTY-SIX

"O, how full of briers is this working day."
-As You Like It

"**L**ook at that," said Aggie, leaning forward to stare out the VW's windshield. "The taxi stopped in front of the Town Hall."

"Why would Harvey Wallace Wallberg be going there?" mused N'yen.

"To pay a parking ticket?" guessed Sissy.

"Doubt that. He's not driving a car. He took a taxi all way from Burpyville. That's got to be a big tab if he's paying by the meter."

Aggie considered the situation for a moment, before speaking. "Maybe he's going to see my Daddy," she said.

~ ~ ~

"Thank you for meeting with me on such short notice, Mayor Tidemore," said Harvey Wallace Wallberg, accepting a chair in front of the large mahogany desk. A wide toothy smile was plastered on his squarish face.

"What can I do for you, Mr. Wallberg?"

"I'm sure you heard about our little acting troupe losing another member – first Adolphus, now Agamemnon."

It was a rhetorical question, but Mark Tidemore murmured his condolences nonetheless. "Yes, sorry for your loss."

"I'm taking over temporary control of the company," he continued as if not hearing the mayor's response. "And I'm here to confirm our performance of *A Midsummer Night's Dream*."

"Confirm –?"

"Alas, yes. For Friday night. We are like a phoenix rising from the ashes. Acting is not just our livelihood, it is indeed our very life. We'd still like to put on the play."

Mark gave a thoughtful frown. "I'm not sure that's a good idea, Mr. Wallberg. It might be better if we simply let the community get over this calamity. No need to drag it out."

"As the Bard said, '*Perseverance, dear my lord, keeps honor bright.*' I must insist that we be allowed to honor our contract."

"No need to do that. I'm sure that under the circumstance, the town can forgive any contractual obligations. No payments need be returned. "

"Yes, but –"

At that moment the office door flew open and Aggie Tidemore entered the room with the momentum of a whirling dervish. "Dad, got a moment?"

"Aggie, I'm in a meeting."

"Oh, sorry. But I've got a quick ..." She paused midsentence, as if just noticing her father's visitor for the first time. "Say, aren't you that famous actor, Harvey Wallace Wallberg?"

The flattery snared his attention. "Why yes, I am. Maybe not quite so famous as you suggest, but I've been receiving good notices on our tour." A lie, but what would this kid know?

"Everybody says you're one of the best Oberons ever."

"Do they now? It is indeed one of my better roles. But wait till you see my Puck when we give our next performance in your Town Square."

"You're going to do another performance?"

"Verily, that is what I am here to discuss with your father."

"Cool."

"Aggie," Mark Tidemore caught her attention. "That decision hasn't been made yet. Why don't your run along and let me and Mr. Wallberg discuss that possibility."

She turned to the actor. "Before I go, could I get your autograph?"

"I'd be delighted."

"Aggie!" repeated her father.

"Maybe next time," she said to Harvey Wallberg before leaving the room with a fluttery toodle-oo wave in his direction.

~ ~ ~

"He was there to book another performance," Aggie explained to N'yen and Sissy.

"I can't believe you just walked in there and confronted him," said Sissy with awe. As if she were addressing Joan of Arc or Rosa Parks.

"It was my Daddy's office. Nothing unusual about me popping in."

"You don't think he got suspicious, do you?" worried N'yen. His head was buried against the stirring wheel. He could be such a Nervous Nellie.

"No way. I blew some smoke at him about being a famous actor and he ate it up. Wanted to give me his autograph."

"Like you're collecting autographs of famous murderers," N'yen chided.

"I could start."

"Don't get ahead of yourself," cautioned Sissy. "We don't know for sure that Harvey Wallbanger is the guilty party."

"True, but he has a very strong motive. After getting the two Anderson brothers out of the way, he's trying to take over the Merry Times Players. He was in there with my Dad claiming to be the troupe's new manager."

"That's one way to succeed," observed N'yen. "Murder your way to the top."

CHAPTER THIRTY-SEVEN

**"Full oft we see cold wisdom waiting
on superfluous folly."**
-All's Well That Ends Well

The two actors had disappeared into the boxy Wabash Acres bungalow about fifteen minutes ago. The four women sitting inside the Grand Cherokee were starting to get impatient.

"What are they doing in there?" whined Lizzie. "Why are they taking so long? We can't wait out here forever. I gotta pee."

"There's a rec center about two blocks over that way," Maddy pointed. "It has a restroom. If they come out before you get back, we'll follow them but circle back later to pick you up."

"No, don't leave me here in Old People's Town," pleaded Lizzie. "I might get arrested as a trespasser."

"No need to worry," teased Maddy. "I'm sure you can pass as a senior citizen."

"That's not funny."

"Technically we all qualify as senior citizens," Cookie said. "Anyone who has reached 50 is eligible to become a member of AARP. Senior discounts are available from many retailers and restaurants for folks 55 or older. Social Security benefits can begin at age 62. And being 65, we qualify for Medicare."

"Thanks for that enlightening information, Miss Know-It-All," huffed Lizzie. The slender redhead spent a lot of time at Helen of Troy Spa & Beauty Salon, refusing to accept the ravages of time.

"Relax, Elizabeth Kay Ridenour. Jim and his deputies know you. Nobody's going to arrest you for trespassing," Bootsie assured her friend.

"Okay, okay. But promise you won't go off and leave me," replied Lizzie.

"I promise we won't leave you," sighed Cookie.

"Pinky swear?"

"Pinky swear." The two women locked digits and repeated the childish chant:

> "Pinky, pinky,
> "Whoever tells a lie
> "Will sink down to the bad place
> "And never rise up again."

"Hurry it up," Maddy interrupted them. "Lizzie, you go pee. Cookie, you and Bootsie stay here with the car, ready to pick us up. Me, I'm going to take a stroll down the street and get the house number. And maybe I can see something through that big picture window in front."

Climbing out of the Cherokee, Lizzie headed in one direction, Maddy in the other. Cookie and Bootsie remained in the waiting car.

"We look pretty suspicious, parked here," griped Bootsie. "Right out in the open."

"There's no other place to park. If we pulled into someone's driveway, the homeowner might call the police."

"Forget the police. Wabash Acres has a strong Neighborhood Watch," Bootsie muttered nervously. "We're gonna get caught. I just know it."

"Relax, Barbara Jo Purdue," Cookie mimicked her friend's earlier comment. "You know the police chief."

~ ~ ~

Tommy Truehart was on his way to Burpyville with the cufflink. The deputy drove just under the speed limit, trying to be a good role model for other motorists. He was singing a Bruce Springsteen anthem – "Born in the USA" – at the top of his lungs.

Bruce Frederick Joseph Springsteen A/K/A "The Boss" was his favorite singer. Some of Tommy's friends preferred Heavy Metal and Techno Rock, but he was an old fashioned kind of guy. Socially inept, most of his buds were online gamers, nerds scattered around the globe. Even his local friends he saw more often online than in person. He hung with such misfits as Pinky Bjork and Gary the Gollum. He played Tower Defense using an avatar known as "Beelzebub666." His biggest competitor was N'yen Madison, that Asian kid from Chicago. The boy was really, really good, but he hadn't been playing as much now that he was in college. You had to be some kind of genius to get admitted to Northwestern at 16.

Tommy's family was poor, so college had been out of the question. Mostly he lived with his aunt. His job as a police deputy was a good career path for a guy like him. Chief Purdue was a pretty good boss, demanding but fair. The Chief valued his computer expertise. The word 'hacker' was never used.

As Tommy's cruiser passed the entrance to Wabash Acres, he saw a familiar car disappearing into the rabbit warren of the development. That Jeep Grand Cherokee belonged to Ben Bentley's wife, the lady who ran the Historical Society. Its color stood out, the only Hydro Blue

Grand Cherokee in town. Wonder what she was doing out here in the boondocks?

His glance had noted other people in the Cherokee, likely Mrs. Bentley's cronies, those Quilters Clubbers. He knew Chief Purdue's wife was one of them. Mrs. Madison too. Those busybodies liked to play detective, a hobby that drove his boss cross-eyed crazy. But it was hard to complain about these activities when one of the so-called offenders was your own spouse.

Tommy had the impulse to turn into Wabash Acres and see what they were up to, but he was on an important mission. Crime scene tech Herman Vox was waiting for that cufflink.

More important than that, the deputy was waiting to get that list from Preston Peterson & Sons of the buyers of these limited-edition links. He'd contacted the jewelry store before leaving for Burpyville. The store manager was checking with a lawyer to determine whether he should insist on a subpoena before turning over the names. But the guy said he didn't anticipate a problem.

If Vox found any trace of poison in the cufflink's secret compartment, and they could trace its ownership back to one of those actors, *ergo* (as those Greeks like to say) he'd have the killer. And solving a double homicide ought to be enough to get him a raise. Maybe even a promotion to sergeant.

His mother would be so proud of him. Maybe she'd quit complaining that he was just "a worthless lump of sod" who spent all his spare time sitting in front of a computer playing "stupid games."

His computer skills were proving to be valuable. Beelzebub666 ruled!

He smiled to himself as he drove past Wabash Acres, his cruiser pointed straight toward Burpyville. "Carry on, Quilters Club, he said to himself as he passed by.

CHAPTER THIRTY-EIGHT

"If you poison us, do we not die?"
-The Merchant of Venice

Harvey Wallberg had kept the taxi waiting outside the Town Hall. A scowl on his face, he climbed into it and slammed the door behind him. Obviously, the meeting with the mayor hadn't gone well. The yellow vehicle lurched away from the curb, made a U-turn in the middle of Main Street, and drove down the block.

The three youngsters ducked down as the cab passed the parked Beetle. Peeking up a moment later, they watched as the cab pulled into a slot in front of the Caruthers Corners Police Department.

"What's he want there?" whispered N'yen.

"Maybe he's going in the cop shop to give himself up and confess to the murders," posited Sissy.

"Fat chance of that," said Aggie. "He's too arrogant to give himself up. You should've seen him up there in Daddy's office, posturing and posing, acting like he was a visiting potentate."

They watched the actor stride into squat concrete building like Henry V confronting the Battle of Agincourt. Head held high, chin thrust forward, his momentum like a military charge.

"I'd sure like to be a fly on the wall in that police station," mused Sissy, staring at the wide glass door as it closed behind the visitor.

"Hey, that's a good idea," said N'yen. "Just call me Jeff Goldblum – The Fly!" With a wide smile, the boy stepped out of the domed-shaped Beetle and raced down the sidewalk toward the Police Station, his feet making *smak! smak! smak!* sounds against the hot concrete.

"What the heck?" said Sissy as she watched him push open the wide glass door and disappear into the fortified building.

"Your boyfriend is crazy," concluded Aggie.

"You don't have to tell me," she replied.

They might as well have been watching Daniel as he walked into the lion's den.

~ ~ ~

Det. Harry Teague was the only cop in the station, unless you counted Elvina Dobbler, the daytime dispatcher. Chief Purdue was across the street at Kupnick's Pharmacy getting briefed on various types of poisons. Tommy Truehart was making a run to Burpyville to deliver that cufflink to Herman Vox. And the other deputies were all out on patrol. Harry Wallberg looked around as if trying to decide whether he was in the right place or not.

"*Tut!* I demand to speak with the High Sheriff," he announced loudly.

Harry was taken aback at the man's appearance: wide floppy hat with a purple plume sticking from the band, a gray waistcoat over a frilly pink shirt, tight pants, boots up to his knees. He looked like a cartoon character, Bugs Bunny doing

Shakespeare. "This is the police department. There's no sheriff here."

"Then your police chief will do."

"He's out. You may have to make do with me. I'm the department's lead investigator."

"Then you will do perfectly. I am here to learn what progress you're making with the investigation of the deaths of my colleagues, Adolphus Everly Anderson and Agamemnon Anderson."

Harry leaned his elbows on the counter and cleared his throat. "As far as the Adolphus Anderson case, we're following up on some promising leads. You'll have to ask the Burpyville PD about Agamemnon Anderson; that's their case."

"Promising?"

"That's right, but I can't go into details. It's an active investigation, you know."

"I see, I see."

"Pardon me, but what's your name? I assume you're one of those Merry Times actors."

"'Tis true. I am Harvey Wallace Wallberg, the troupe's lead performer, as well as current manager of the group."

"Ah yes, Mr. Wallberg. I've heard of you."

"Of course, you have. As the Bard said, '*Some are born great, some achieve greatness, and some have greatness thrust upon them.*' I easily qualify for two of those three."

"Thank you for coming in, sir. We'll be in touch if we learn anything new."

Just them N'yen Madison pushed through the door. "Hey there, Harry Teague. Is Uncle Jim in?"

"Here's the Junior G-Man," he greeted the boy. They had both been involved in solving that suspected murder down at Marengo Cave. N'yen had helped prove that the death was accidental. "I'm afraid the Chief is doing some field research. Checking on common poisons."

"Poisons?" gasped Harvey Wallberg. "Why would he be doing that?"

"Just eliminating various possibilities."

"But there's no proof of poison, is there?"

"Not sure yet. Adolphus's body was cremated without being tested. We're still waiting for the toxicology report to come back on his brother."

"Romeo died of ingesting deadly nightshade," stated the actor grandiosely. "Juliet was likely paralyzed by tetrodotoxin from the pufferfish. Hebenon was used to do in Hamlet's father. Hemlock is mention by Macbeth's friend Banquo."

"You certainly know your poisons," said Harry Teague.

"Knowledge is a part of the craft. Poisons play a key role in many of Shakespeare's works."

The Asian boy broke in. "If you were gonna poison Adolphus and Agamemnon, what would you use?"

"*Moi*? I am but a humble actor, not a murderer. '*There is no sure foundation set on blood, No certain life achieved by others' death.*' "

"C'mon, I bet you've got a favorite poison," pressed N'yen.

"I could speak only theoretically ..."

"Go ahead. You sound like you've given it some thought."

"Well, a wee bit," he admitted.

"So what's a foolproof way to do it?"

Harvey Wallberg's ego got the best of him, drawing him into the speculation. "If it t'were mine to choose, I would pick something common but untraceable as to its source. Say, *Amanita bisporigera* – a fungi sometimes known as the Destroying Angel. This innocent white cap is considered the most toxic mushroom in North America."

"*Hmm,*" said N'yen. "A very good choice indeed. You can pick them yourself. Mix them in food. Symptoms take 5 to 24 hours to appear – delirium, convulsions, liver and kidney failure. And it leads to death."

Harry Teague looked impressed. "You know your poisons too," he whistled. "How did you learn so much about deadly mushrooms?"

"I read," the boy said.

CHAPTER THIRTY-NINE

"Plead you to me, fair dame? I know you not ..."
-The Comedy of Errors

N'yen made it back to the VW Beetle a few minutes after Harvey Wallace Wallberg climbed into the yellow cab. He and his friends watched as the taxi headed back toward Highway 21. Probably returning to his hotel.

Cranking the 2.0L air-cooled engine to life, N'yen jackknifed his little VW around, barely missing the curb, and set off in a cautious pursuit. Hanging back. No need to get spotted at this point. Wallberg would easily recognize both him and Aggie from their previous encounters.

"So what have we learned?" Sissy posed the question.

"That Harvey Wallberg is trying to take over the Merry Times Players," offered Aggie.

"And that he sure knows his poisons," added her cousin.

"I'll bet he's pretty pissed right now, having killed two people to get ahead – and your daddy turned him down for a performance that would allow him to play Puck, one of the lead roles in *A Midsummer Night's Dream*," Sissy summed it up. "Question is, what's he gonna do next?"

"Maybe he'll try to kill Aggie's dad, hoping the next person in line will approve the Shakespeare-in-the-Park performance," speculated N'yen. "That seems to be his *modus operandi*."

"His M.O," said Sissy. I've heard that term on TV. *Law and Order*'s one of my favorite programs."

"Hey –!" Aggie protested. "He better not try to poison my Daddy."

"You can't trust murderers," stated her cousin. Sounding like a warning.

"If Harvey Wallbanger murdered the mayor, who would be next in command?" asked Sissy. Her face squinched like a prune as she tried to work out this puzzle.

"Guess that would be Grampy," replied N'yen. "He's President of the Town Council."

Aggie looked horrified. "Are you suggesting that if Harvey Wallberg doesn't get his way he might try to kill Grampy too?"

"Who knows what a crazy man will do," said Sissy. As casually as if discussing which club a golfer might choose for his next shot. "I think this Harvey Wallbanger has been driven stark raving mad by his ambitions. Like Dr. Evil in them *Austin Powers* movies."

"To be technically correct, we still don't know for sure whether Harvey Wallberg is the killer or not," Aggie pointed out. Taking the other side of the argument.

"He has the best motive," argued N'yen, eyes glued to the road. The cab was a yellow dot in the distance.

"My money's on Harvey Wallbanger." huffed Sissy. "That man is guilty about *some*thing, He acts too suspicious to be totally innocent."

"I'll give you that," said Aggie. "We have to make sure he doesn't try to harm my Daddy or Grampy."

~ ~ ~

The taxi dropped Harvey Wallberg off in front of the Highliner. N'yen pulled his Volkswagen over to the curb at the far end of the block, afraid they would be spotted if he followed the taxi down the street. His caution was futile. As Wallberg walked up the steps to the hotel entrance, he paused, turned and stared fixedly at the little yellow VW. Making it clear he knew they'd been following him.

"Uh-oh," said Aggie. "I think we've been made."

"We'd better get outta here," gulped N'yen, putting the car into reverse and backing around the corner in a lurching start-and-stop manner. Turning around in the middle of the street, he drove away in the opposite direction, merging back onto Highway 21, speeding up as if being chased by the Hounds of Hell.

"I-is he following us?" sputtered Sissy, trying to look out the VW's small rear window.

"No, silly," said Aggie. "We're in a car. He was on foot when we got out of there."

"I'm pushing 60," responded N'yen. "He'll never catch us, even if he jumped back in that taxi and tried to follow."

"Slow down or you'll get a ticket," Sissy warned. "Speed limit's 55."

"Tommy Truehart patrols the Burpyville Highway," added Aggie. "He's pretty strict with speeding tickets, I hear."

"Beelzebub666? He's my bud. We play online games together. He'd give me a pass if it came down to it. He owes me a lot of gaming points. We could trade off some – tit for tat."

"Wouldn't that be bribing a policeman?" said Sissy. Concerned about this plan.

"Don't count on Tommy's goodwill," warned Aggie. "He's a cop first; gamer second."

"So you say."

"Slow down, Neesie," said his girlfriend. "You lose your license, you can't take me parking."

"Oh, that's a good point," said the boy, easing his foot off the pedal, dropping the speed down to 50. "Parking is the best part of owning a car."

"TMI," sighed Aggie, rolling her eyes.

~ ~ ~

At that same moment, Maddy was strolling along the sidewalk with the innocence of a senior citizen out for an afternoon constitutional. She wished she'd brought Aggie's dog Tige. That little mutt had been living with her and Beau while their granddaughter was off at college. A woman walking a dog would have dispelled any suspicions by curious onlookers.

The silver Toyota Corolla was parked haphazardly in the driveway. A number next to the door identified the house as 327. She would have to check the sign at the end of the block to figure out which street this was on. For some unknown reason, many of the byways in Wabash Acres were named after birds – Woodpecker Way, Oriole Avenue, Robin Road, Starling Street, cutesy names like that.

As she passed 327 slowly, head held high, as if enjoying the warm summer sun, out of the corner of her eye she was trying to get a glimpse into the house through the picture window. Unfortunately, the afternoon sunlight was reflecting off the plate glass, turning the surface into a large shiny mirror. Nothing to be seen other than her own image looking back at herself as she passed.

The garage door was closed. That was too bad. If she could have seen a license tag on a parked car, Bootsie could have talked one of the police dispatchers into running the plate. Who would the Leicester twins be visiting in Wabash

Acres? The actors were out-of-towners, not likely to know many local people.

The houses on both sides of the narrow street were brick-fronted pre-fabs, modest in appearance. In the yard of the house directly across from 327 was a big red **FOR SALE** sign. Next door Amazon deliveries were stacked of the step. Another house had a tricycle in the driveway. And another had a blue plastic wading pool in the yard. But there were no people to be sighted on this street in the heat of the afternoon.

Other than Maddy.

At the end of the block, she looked up at the green sign that topped a 7-foot-tall metal post. **Bluebird Lane**, it read. Hmm, who did she know on this street? Nobody came to mind. Her aunt lived on the other side of the development, on Pelican Place. She'd always thought that was a funny name for a street in the middle of Indiana, a location nearly 700 miles from the nearest ocean.

Now she had a decision to make – continue around the block, or turn and walk back past 327 Bluebird Lane to reach Cookie's Grand Cherokee. She could see it parked next to the curb at the far end of the block. Best she could tell, Lizzie hadn't returned from her pee break.

Flipping a mental coin, Maddy decided to head back the way she'd come. Maybe she could spot a name on the mailbox. *Step*, *step*, *step*. She was still sore from those stupid airbags.

As she passed the house, she squinted toward the square black box affixed to the wall beside the front door. Wabash Acres didn't allow mailboxes at the edge of the street anymore. Too many juvenile delinquents liked to drive by, knocking boxes off their posts with a baseball bat. The HOA had tried to remedy that by requiring boxes at the door. Fritz Berber, the mailman, wasn't happy with that decision, one that required him to walk from house-to-house rather than comfortably ease by in his right-hand-drive electric USPS mail truck.

Maddy could see a name on the box, but try as she might she couldn't quite make out the fancy lettering. Best she could tell, it spelled out G-R-A-C-E – Grace.

Did she know any people hereabouts named Grace? Not that she could think of. When she got back to the Grand Cherokee, she would ask Cookie. With her friend's mental gymnastics, she would be able to recite the entire genealogy chart for the Grace family.

No point checking out the car in the driveway. The Toyota Corolla was obvious a rental car, You could tell by the little barcode sticker on the side window. The barcodes are placed in the windows so a rental company can scan the car when it goes in and out of the lot, in order to keep track of it. There would be nothing to learn by checking the glove compartment for personal items or the dashboard for the odometer reading.

Keep walking, she told herself.

"Hey you," came a voice from the house. Somebody had stepped out the door – one of the twins.

Maddy froze.

Had she been recognized? Likely so. After all, the Quilters Club had interviewed them only yesterday in the Highliner's dining room. What excuse could she come up with for her presence here? That she lived down the street? No, the homeowner they were visiting would know better. That her sister owned Wabash Acre and she was running an errand for her? Nobody would believe that. Should she come clean, admit that the Quilters Club had been following them because they suspected them of murdering Adolphus Anderson and his brother? No, not a good idea to admit that to possible killers.

Holding her breath, she slowly turned to face the caller. "Y-yes?" she replied. Noncommittally.

"Do you live around here? I'm trying to find a place called Razor's Edge, a barbershop. Got my hair cut there the other day, but I don't remember how to get there. I asked my aunt, but she's not good with directions."

Maddy Madison found her breath returning. The twin hadn't recognized her. "Y-yes, it's behind Kupnick's Pharmacy on South Main Street. Just take a right onto the highway as you leave this housing development and keep going straight."

"Thanks, ma'am."

"You're welcome," she croaked hoarsely.

"Say, you look familiar. Do I know you?"

She smiled weakly. "Not likely, I don't get out much. I take care of my invalid husband. He has Parkinson's."

"Sorry to hear that."

"That new levodopa medication they have him on is helping with his tremors."

"Yes —well, you have a nice day." Nobody wanted to hear a recital of some stranger's health conditions. He stepped back into the house and quickly shut the door.

Maddy kept walking, picking up her pace as she neared the Grand Cherokee. Then she actually ran the rest of the way.

"What was that all about?" asked Bootsie as her friend slid into the backseat.

Maddy's eyes were as glassy as a Cat's Eye marble. "One of the Leicester twins. He asked directions to Vic Davone's barbershop. I can't believe he didn't recognize me!"

Lizzie turned in the front seat. "What would he want with Slick Vic?"

"Maybe he's looking for that cufflink Vic found," suggested Bootsie. Her hubby had told her about the

Catherine di Medici cufflink with the hidden poison compartment. Another clue pointing to the murderer.

"That's right," nodded Cookie. "Vic said he thought it might have been one of those actors. Either Carl or Bob Leicester would fit the bill."

Bootsie said, "Jim's going to have one of his deputies show Vic a photo lineup of all the actors. He should be able pick out his drop-in customer."

"Look, here comes Lizzie. I figured she'd get lost," said Cookie.

"Let's get out of here," urged Maddy as her friend climbed into the car. "I don't want to wait around for that twin to remember where he has seen me before."

CHAPTER FORTY

*"O gentle son, upon the heat and flame of thy distemper,
sprinkle cool patience."*

-Hamlet

Maddy's oldest son Bill and his wife Kathy had driven down from Chicago, but left in a huff when they discovered his mother was already out of bed and off playing detective. Bill vaguely frowned on his mom's extralegal activity. He was a straight-laced type who didn't approve of rule-breaking. He had been an Eagle Scout, a teacher's assistant in high school, and a dorm monitor in college. He had never had a parking ticket or a citation for speeding.

To assuage his feelings, Bill's siblings – Freddie and Tilly – took him to lunch at Cozy Café before he and Kathy headed back north.

"You'd think she would grow up," grumbled Bill as he worked his teeth around the edge of a pork tenderloin sandwich. Kathy was having the soup (tomato bisque today).

"Mom's always been like this," shrugged Freddie. His scars seemed etched onto his face. He was doing a tenderloin, too. It was one of Cozy Café's most popular items. That, and the watermelon burger.

"She's like a magical warrior," said Tilly, hinting that she still had one foot in a never-never land of dragons and unicorns. Also having the soup, she sipped at it daintily as if attending a Wonderland tea party..

"I can't believe we drove all way down here and Mom's not even around to greet us."

"A big clue came up in a case they're working on."

"We were worried about her."

"Don't worry about our Mom," said Tilly. "She's invincible."

"I don't know about that," laughed Freddie, picking up his fireman's helmet to head back to work. They had caught him coming back from a brush fire at Baumgartner's farm and he was both sooty and smelling of smoke. But that was a common demeanor for Maddy's youngest son.

"We have to get back to Chicago," declared Bill grumpily. "We have children to take care of. Our NGO keeps us running day and night."

"Yep, I understand. Duty calls." What Freddie didn't point out was that their mother had done more to raise N'yen than his adoptive parents had. Bill and Kathy were do-gooders with blinders on, cobblers whose own children had no shoes.

"Travel safely," Tilly said to her older brother. "We'll let you know when Mom catches that murderer. The Quilters Club is closing in on him ... or her!"

"Or them," added Freddie.

~ ~ ~

Chief Purdue returned to his office after spending a fruitless session with Phil Kupnick. Poisons were a confusing subject to say the least. "Harry, got time for a little errand?" he called to his chief investigator.

Harry Teague looked up from his paperwork. "What you need, Jim?"

"I got Tommy running over to Burpyville to see that crime tech, Herman Vox..."

"Yeah, I know Hermie. We're old buddies from my days at Burpyville PD."

"Probably should've sent you, but Tommy volunteered. Anyway, since he's gonna be tied up, can I get you to go over to Razor's Edge and show these pix to Slick Vic? See if he recognizes any of these jaspers as a walk-in customer he had the other day. That's the person who likely dropped that cufflink he found." He tossed a stack of photos – computer printouts actually – onto the cluttered desk. Tommy had found them on a Merry Times Players website.

"You got it." The detective ran his hand through his unruly shuck of hair, a brown mop that covered his head like a beaver pelt. "Need to get a haircut myself."

"If you do, get Vic to sing 'Sunny Side of the Street.' He does a great version of that. Makes me feel like dancing."

"Not me," said Harry Teague. "I got two left feet."

CHAPTER FORTY-ONE

"Poison more deadly than a mad dog's tooth."
-The Comedy of Errors

N'yen kept thinking about his conversation with that actor when they were at the Caruthers Corners Police Department. Harvey Wallberg had described his idea of a perfect crime, poisoning by toxic mushrooms. Maybe there was something to what he'd said.

After all, wasn't it the Quilters Club's theory that Adolphus Anderson had been poisoned? He'd died right there on stage in front of 300 witnesses. There were no bullet holes or stab wounds. Nobody had bashed him on the head or strangled him. He had simply dropped dead.

Doc Medford pronounced it a heart attack. But if it wasn't, what else *could* be the cause of death.

Poison, his Grammy had speculated.

But what kind?

N'yen was an avid reader. So he read up on the subject:

• Rat poisoning is a form of strychnine. It causes a paralysis that kills via respiratory failure. Ingestion can lead to internal bleeding, organ failure, coma, and death. There's no antidote for the poison.
• D-Con is another pesticide. With Warfarin as the active ingredient. it works by affecting blood clotting

to an extreme degree. Symptoms include nosebleeds, bloody diarrhea, extreme fatigue, and shortness of breath. In the end, you die.

• Arsenic is a metalloid element that kills by inhibiting enzyme production. This was a popular poison in the Middle Ages because it was easy to obtain and the symptoms (diarrhea, confusion, vomiting) resembled those of cholera. The bitter almond odor made it easy to suspect, yet difficult to prove.

• Cyanide is a toxic salt or ester of hydrocyanic acid. Prussic acid is a form of hydrogen cyanide used in polymers and pharmaceuticals. Hydrogen cyanide gas is used in spray pesticides and for executions in some prison gas chambers. Potassium cyanide is used in gold mining and plastics. These cyanide compounds inhibit essential aerobic metabolisms, causing death.

• Hemlock (*Conium maculatum*) was a highly poisonous biennial herbaceous flowering plant in the carrot family. A short time after ingestion, the alkaloids produce potentially fatal neuromuscular dysfunction due to failure of the respiratory muscles. Ingestion of about six to eight fresh leaves (or a smaller dose of the seeds or root) can be fatal.

• Polonium is a highly radioactive chemical element. If inhaled or ingested, it can kill in extremely low doses. However, the poison doesn't do its work immediately. And it's extremely difficult to come by. He remembered reading that the Russians used polonium-210 to murder spy Alexander Litvinenko a few years ago.

• Belladonna (*Atropa belladona*) – sometimes called Deadly Nightshade – is a plant high in the toxic chemicals solanine, hyoscine (scopolamine), and atropine. Eating a single leaf or eating 10 of the berries can be kill you.

N'yen checked off the list:

Strychnine was out because Adolphus had exhibited no shortness of breath. He had continued enunciating his lines up to the minute he dropped dead, even naming his killer as a fellow actor.

Warfarin was unlikely, because there had been no sign of bleeding. No nosebleeds, no ichorous symptom that would have alerted Doc Medford.

Could be arsenic, but no one reported the telltale odor of bitter almonds.

Symptoms of Cyanide poisoning include headaches, dizziness, confusion, fast heart rate, shortness of breath, and vomiting. Adolphus did not seem to experience anything like this.

Hemlock was famous as the poison that killed Greek philosopher Socrates. However, it was highly unlikely in this case, being native only to Europe and North Africa.

Polonium was out. This radioactive poison was nearly impossible to come by, only manufactured at a remote facility in Russia.

As for Belladonna, it grew wild, there for the picking. But one would have to know something about horticulture to identify this obscure plant. Likely you could find it in a place like Never Ending Swamp if you knew what to look for. This had been N'yen's pick as the mostly likely poison – largely because of its Shakespearean connection. Legend has it that Macbeth used wine made from Deadly Nightshade to poison Danes invading Scotland in 1040.

However, Harvey Wallberg had cited as his poison of choice as the Destroying Angel (*Amanita bisporigera*), a toxic mushroom. Perhaps it deserved a closer look.

N'yen clicked a few keys of his computer and read the following:

> The Destroying Angel (*Amanita bisporigera*) and the Death Cap (*Amanita phalloides*) account for the overwhelming majority of deaths due to mushroom poisoning. The toxin responsible for this is amatox, which inhibits RNA polymerase II and III. The damage (destruction of liver and kidney tissues) is irreversible. As little as half a mushroom cap can be fatal if the victim is not treated quickly enough. The symptoms include vomiting, cramps, delirium, and convulsions.

Yep, someone having eaten a Destroying Angel would certainly be clutching his stomach rather than his chest.

~ ~ ~

Deputy Tommy Truehart struck out on the poison angle. Herman Vox couldn't find any traces of a toxic substance – for that matter *any* substance – on the interior of the cufflink's secret "poison compartment."

"Clean as a whistle," Vox had said after careful examination under an electron microscope. His police lab was well equipped. "Doubt it was ever used to hold anything. Seems to be more of a decorative element than a utilitarian feature."

Bummer.

However, Tommy had more success with Preston Peterson & Sons, that fancy New York jewelry store. The manager got back to him with the news that the company's lawyer okayed revealing the names of buyers of the Wynona Burns cufflinks. It was a short list.

"We advertised that only two sets were made," said a guy who identified himself as Jamie Peterson. The owner's son. "But that's not entirely true. Wynona actually made four sets – two to sell, two for herself."

"So there was four in all?"

"Right. Four sets, eight cufflinks in all."

"And you sold two sets?"

"Yes, we sold them to a Melissa Alice Caldwell and a Frazier Allen Melrose, both regular customers of our salon. We know them quite well. Very substantial individuals. I can't see them being involved in a police investigation."

"Them names don't ring a bell. What about the other two?"

"Wynona kept them for her own personal use. Our arrangement specified she couldn't sell them."

"A dead end," sighed the deputy. "Thanks for your trouble."

~ ~ ~

Herbert Golding refused to give up his room, so when Laurence Linklater arrived early from Phoenix, he had no place to stay.

"I was assured I would have first-class accommodations," Linklater pounded his fist angrily on the counter. He was a burly guy and quite intimidating. Known for portraying characters like Falstaff and Titus Andronicus, his aggressive nature could be quite intimidating.

Robert Bob Roberts Jr., the manager-cum-bellboy, stepped back from the front desk, as if facing a madman.

"Excuse me, sir, but we have no vacant rooms. I would be more than happy to accommodate you if I could. However, the acting company has taken up every room we have."

"I demand to speak with Agamemnon Anderson. He assured me everything was arranged. Where is that cream-faced loon?"

"I regret to tell you, Mr. Anderson is deceased."

"I know Adolphus Anderson is dead. I'm talking about his brother Agamemnon."

"I'm afraid he is deceased too."

"Both dead, you say?"

"Yes, sir. Both of them."

"How can that be?"

"I'm sure I don't know, sir. In fact, I told the police exactly that."

"But Aggy hired me to join his acting troupe. What am I supposed to do?"

"I have no idea, sir."

"Who's left in charge of Merry Times?"

"I believe that would be Mr. Wallberg. He tells me he's the Acting Manager. I think he's in his room – Number 214, if you want to go up."

"Wallberg? Do you mean that stuttering idiot Harvey Wallace Wallberg?"

"Yes. Perhaps he will let you stay with him. 214 has two queen-sized beds. Normally, we would charge extra for room-sharing, but under the circumstance I will turn a blind eye."

"Stay with that old fop? I'd rather sleep on the front steps."

"I imagine the Hotel Association would frown on that."

"Then give me a room! Didn't the two deaths create vacancies?"

"Yes, sir. They both had occupied the same room. Now the police has designated that as a crime scene – although point of fact, Adolphus Anderson died on stage and Agamemnon Anderson died here in the lobby on the very spot you're standing."

"Ye gads!" He took a step backwards. "Is there nothing else?"

"Maybe we could put up a cot in the cloakroom ...?"

"Not for me. Move one of the lesser actors in there and give me that room."

"I'm afraid that sort of decision would be up to Mr. Wallberg. You should speak with him."

"That villainous blackguard. Harvey Wallberg is an infinite and endless liar, an hourly promise breaker. To blazes with him!"

"Whatever you say, sir."

CHAPTER FORTY-TWO

"Like a barber's chair that fits all buttocks."
-All's Well That Ends Well

Det. Harry Teague dropped by Razor's Edge that afternoon, a manila folder tucked under his arm. "Hi, Vic," he greeted the barber.

"A quick trim?" asked Vic Davone, eyeing the policeman's shaggy locks.

"I know I need one. Right now, I need you to look at some pictures, see if you recognize anyone."

"Oh, you're looking for that actor who dropped the cufflink. Jim said he might want me to look at – what did he call it? – a photo lineup."

"That's why I'm here. Can we use this table?"

"Sure thing. Mind if I sing while I look? Helps me concentrate."

"Help yourself," shrugged Harry as he spread the pictures across the table's glass-top surface. About twenty in all, a collection of 14 actors and assorted stagehands and roadies.

Slick Vic gave forth a melodic version of "A Pretty Girl Is Like a Melody" as he leaned forward to inspect the images one-by-one, his nose practically brushing the surface of each photo. His eyesight was notoriously weak.

Harry sat back in one of the two padded barber's chairs, enjoying the impromptu musical performance. He shut his eyes while Vic examined the photographs, nearly falling asleep while being serenaded with the Old Standard. He knew Irving Berlin wrote the song in 1919 as the theme for The Ziegfeld Follies. Fred Astaire danced to it in the 1946 movie *Blue Skies*. Woody Allen recorded a clarinet version with the Preservation Hall Jazz Band. Lots of singers have put out their own renditions, but he liked the Pat Boone version best.

Vic's singing abruptly stopped.

Harry's eyes immediately popped open. "Find anything?" he asked, sitting up in the chair. He could see that the barber was holding up two pictures, one in each hand.

"This is not a trick is it?" said Vic, giving the cop a sideways look.

"What d'you mean, a trick?" Harry Teague was confused."

"You know, a test. Trying to trip me up."

"How so?"

"No way I can pick out the right guy when you put duplicate photos in the pile."

"Duplicates?"

"Sure," nodded the barber, holding out the photographs in each hand. Exact images of the same actor. "There are two pictures of this guy. Why is that?"

Harry laughed. "Oh, one of those photos is Carl Leicester. The other is his brother Bob Leicester. They're twins."

"Well, I can't pick between them. But I'm sure it was one or t'other."

Det. Harry Teague was caught off guard. His money had been on that pompous fellow, Harvey Wallace Wallberg. He wasn't expecting Vic to pick the twins.

"I'm saying I can't tell from these pictures which one was my customer t'other day. But if you bring them both in here, I can tell you. I'm always able to recognize one of my haircuts."

Harry sat back in the chair. "I'll see if I can round them up. Meantime, as long as I'm here, you may as well trim my hair."

CHAPTER FORTY-THREE

"Life's but a walking shadow ..."
-Macbeth

At the end of the day, The Quilters Club – both the original gals and the junior members – met up to share their collective findings. Everybody crowded around the big island in Maddy's cheery kitchen. When she and Beau rebuilt their Victorian on Melon Pickers Row, it was much like their old home that had been destroyed by the 2018 tornado – only bigger.

As it turned out, Beau was at home. And Jim Purdue just happened to drop by "for a cup of coffee" (having received a heads-up from Beau). They were intent on keeping track of their wayward wives.

"It's been quite an afternoon," Maddy reported, going over their adventures with the Leicester twins, and relating the kids' observations about trailing Harvey Wallberg.

"Let me get this straight," said Beau. "You gals followed those twins? And the kids followed that fancy-pants actor Harvey Wallbanger?"

"Wallberg," corrected Aggie.

"Whatever," rejoined her grandfather. "That sounds dangerous. One of them is probably a killer."

"We were careful," said N'yen.

Beau scowled. "Careful? Aggie followed Wallbanger into her Dad's office. You braced him face-to-face at the Police Department."

"But, dear —" began Maddy.

"And you," said her husband, "prancing la-de-dah down the sidewalk in front of a couple of guys you think might be murders, are you crazy?"

Jim Purdue put his hands over his ears like one of those see-no-evil hear-no-evil speak-no-evil monkeys. "I'm going to pretend I didn't hear any of this," groaned the police chief. "I can't condone what amounts to stalking. There are laws against that, I might remind you looneys."

"Looneys?" chuckled his wife. "Think of us as a helpful Neighborhood Watch."

"But those weren't your neighborhoods," Beau carefully pointed out.

"Never mind," said Lizzie. "All Jim has to do is deputize us, then we'd be as legal as the mayor's parking spot in front of Town Hall."

"I can't go 'round handing out tin badges to every wannabe Sherlock Holmes in the county," grumbled Chief Purdue.

"Dear, we're not just any ol' wannabes," said his wife. "We're the Quilters Club. You know us all, like the back of your hand."

"Aw, Bootsie —"

Maddy got back to the topic at hand. "At any rate, we turned up some interesting dirt. That Wallberg guy is trying to take control of the Merry Times Players. That's plenty of motive for murder."

"That's right," nodded Aggie. "I heard him tell my Daddy that he was now running the show."

"I've already heard that," allowed the police chief.

"And those twins are up to something nefarious," interjected Bootsie. "We followed them to a house in Wabash Acres. Like Maddy said, one of them almost caught her snooping around."

"What were they doing there?" asked Beau, his curiosity piqued.

Maddy shrugged. "The twin I spoke with implied that it was his aunt's house."

Cookie looked puzzled. "I don't know of any Leicesters in Caruthers Corners. To have a different last name, she would have to be an aunt on their mother's side."

"Or be a married aunt on their father's side," amended Lizzie. Pleased to find a flaw in Cookie's usually perfect logic.

As a cop, Jim Purdue couldn't help being inquisitive. "Did you get the address? I can have Tommy check on who lives there."

"Yes, 327 Bluebird Lane," said Maddy.

Lizzie shook her head, making the red hair shimmer like tinsel. "That's a new one on me. But then, I don't know a lot of people in Wabash Acres." She and Edgar lived over on River Road, on the far side of town.

"I know a lot of people in Wabash Acres," said Bootsie. Her house backed up to the development. "But unfortunately I've never met anyone on Bluebird Lane."

"Me neither," Cookie admitted. Calling on her super memory. "Last time I looked over a street directory – about a year ago – that house was listed as unoccupied."

"327 Bluebird Lane?" said Sissy. "I know that address."

CHAPTER FORTY-FOUR

"And when I am forgotten, as I shall be,
and asleep in dull cold marble, where no mention
of me must be heard of, say, I taught thee."
-Henry VIII

"You know that address?" said Maddy, caught off guard by the girl's unexpected declaration. Everybody in the room was astounded.

"Yessum," nodded Sissy Jackson. "That's where my drama teacher lives. She's had the class over for a read-through of the new play we're prepping. A modern-dress version of *Oedipus Rex*. You know, that Greek play by Sophocles, the one about some guy marrying his mother. Weird stuff. I'm surprised the school's letting us put it on."

"Your drama teacher?" said Bootsie. "You mean that nice Mrs. Grady?"

Sissy nodded.

"That explains the name on the mailbox," Maddy blurted. "From a distance I read it as GRACE, but it was really GRADY. I got the last two letters wrong!"

"Hon, you may need glasses," said Beau. "You haven't been to the eye doctor in ages."

"True," Maddy admitted. "I hate getting my eyes dilated."

"Hmm," said Cookie. "The Gradys only moved to town about a year ago. That's why they weren't on the last city directory I saw."

"But why would those twins go to Estelle Grady's house?" wondered Lizzie. "How would they know her?"

Cookie snapped her fingers. "Simple. They're actors. She's an acting teacher. I'd bet they are her former students."

"That guy said something about an aunt," Maddy reminded them.

"Probably a term of endearment," said Bootsie. "Like Aggie and N'yen calling me Aunt Bootsie."

"Maybe, but it still shows a relationship," said Maddy, passing around more watermelon sugar cookies to go with their coffee. The kids eagerly helped themselves to the sweet confections. "The twins were at the Grady house as big as life."

"So what if the twins know somebody in town? Said Aggie. "That doesn't change the likelihood that one – or both –of them are cold-blooded murderers?"

"I'm sure Mrs. Grady wouldn't be hanging around with murderers," said Sissy.

"Yeah, my money is on that Wallberg guy," N'yen supported his girlfriend's viewpoint.

"Your money?" laughed Aggie. "You don't have any money. I had to pay for those frozen custards we had the other day at the DQ."

"Do too," argued her cousin. "I have a trust fund, just like you do."

"That's why I'm his girlfriend," joked Sissy. "I'm after his fortune."

"Children, behave," shushed their grandmother.

"Hey," said Aggie. "I'm not a child. I recently turned 19. Almost as old as you were when you married Grampy."

Lizzie smiled. "Oh, so you're about to get married?"

"Don't be silly, Aunt Lizzie. I don't even have a boyfriend."

"It's easy to see why," her cousin muttered under his breath.

"I heard that," she gave him the stink eye.

"What happened to that nice Bobby Elwood?" asked Bootsie. "I liked him. He was very polite."

"We took a break – about two years ago. I heard he's dating Joanie McPhee."

"Didn't she used to be your best friend?" asked Cookie, the one with the sticky memory.

"That was mostly in grammar school. We shared everything. Now, I guess we share Bobby."

"I'll let you gals sort out Aggie's love live," sighed Jim Purdue. "I've gotta get back to work. I still have a murder to solve."

"Dear, wasn't all our detecting at least a little bit helpful."

"Hm, let me see if I've got it straight. Those twins are innocent. That flamboyant new manager of Merry Times is innocent. Mrs. Grady is innocent. You're innocent. I'm innocent. If we only had a suspect!"

"What makes you think that Wallberg guy is innocent?" frowned N'yen.

"He may be a tad ambitious, but that doesn't prove he's guilty," said the police chief. "I need hard evidence before I can go around accusing a man of murder. We don't want to go through that again!"

N'yen had no more to say. He took the police chief's comment as a rebuke over the Quilters Club having falsely accused that park ranger of murder a while back. Wasn't fair, N'yen told himself. He was the one who had proven the guy's innocence with that blood splatter evidence. And Uncle Jim's own K-9 dog had been the one to sniff it out.

Maddy came to her grandson's rescue. "Think of this way, Jim. Every person we eliminate narrows down the list of possible killers."

"What list?" he threw up his hands.

"Calm down, dear," said his wife. "We're only trying to help."

"Help like this, I don't need. These murders are going to be solved with good old-fashioned police work. Herman Vox identifying the poison. Slick Vic Davone identifying the customer who dropped that cufflink. Tommy finding out from the jewelers who bought the links."

"But –"

"Gotta go. My deputies should be back at the station by now. Tommy with Burpyville's toxicology report. Harry with the results of his photo lineup. I expect to crack the case tonight – without the Quilters Club's help!"

"Good luck with that," snorted his wife.

Jim Purdue stood up abruptly, his face as red as a bad sunburn. "See you later, Beau."

His old friend saluted him with a coffee mug. "Bye, Jim. Let me know when you identify the killer. Town Council would like to get this murderer off the streets."

"And avoid any more bad publicity," Maddy muttered under her breath.

Her husband heard the remark. "Public safety is job number one," he said. "Isn't that right, Jim?"

"You bet," the Police Chief replied, slapping his cap on his slick head as he headed for the door. Not looking back. "So long. I got some work to do."

As the door closed, Bootsie sighed. "Poor Jim. He's more likely to find Bigfoot than solve this murder."

~ ~ ~

Deputy Tommy Truehart was settled behind the desk that he shared with Harry Teague. They sat facing each other when both were in the station at the same time. Today was one of those times, with Harry kicking back in his swivel chair, cowboy boots planted on the desk; Tommy hunched over his computer, his nose close to the screen.

Harry was waiting to get the Chief's go-ahead to bring those Leicester twins over for a face-to-face ID by Slick Vic Davone. If that didn't work, he would roust the boys to see which one of them could produce only one cufflink.

Tommy had just returned from Burpyville, anxious to give his report to his boss – no toxic substances found in the cufflink's poison compartment, no identification of the cufflink's owner. He wanted to get the meeting over with, take his lumps and move on to his next assignment. This was one of those instances of "Which do you want to hear first, the bad news or the bad news?"

Harry seemed half-asleep, waiting patiently for the Chief's return. Tommy was a different story. You would have thought he was about to pee in his pants. Both good cops, but personalities as different as night and day.

"Hi Chief," Tommy called when Jim Purdue came through the front door. Trying to catch him before Harry.

"Leave me alone," came the gnarly response.

"Uh-oh," whispered Elvina Dobbler. "Watch yourself, Beelzebub." She had a knack for sensing when the police chief was in a bad mood. This grumpiness often followed an encounter with the Quilters Club. You would have thought they were a dread business competitor, the way he carried on, huffing and puffing, scowling, throwing things around his office, slamming down the phone, acting like a man who had stepped on a bee.

"Just got back from Burpyville," Tommy continued, unabated.

"Turn up anything?" asked Chief Purdue. But you could tell his hopes were not high. He was clearly in a funk.

"Nary thing," the deputy admitted. "Herman Vox went over that cufflink with –" he almost said *a fine tooth comb* "– extra care, but didn't turn up a whiff of any kind of poison."

"So those actors weren't poisoned?"

"Didn't say that. Vox finished up the toxicology report while I was there. Showed that Agamemnon Anderson was poisoned with some kinda deadly fungus. Mushrooms, he said."

"Holy smokes," exclaimed Harry Teague. Feet coming off the desk. "Did you say mushrooms?"

"Yeah, I wrote the name down in my notebook." Tommy flipped open a steno pad. "Here it is, *Amanita bisporigera*. It's sometimes called a –"

"—Destroying Angel," Harry completed the sentence.

"How'd you know that?"

"Got it from that flibbertigibbet actor, Harvey Wallberg. He dropped by the station earlier today."

That stopped Jim Purdue in his tracks, hand paused on the doorknob to his office. He was the only one who had a private office, although it was hardly bigger than a walk-in closet. "What did you just say? That Harvey Wallberg knew what kind of poison killed Agamemnon Anderson?"

"That's what he told me," confirmed Harry.

"And that's the poison Herman Vox named," added Tommy.

"Congratulation, boys. We may just have our man," smiled Chief Purdue. Suddenly cheerful. "I told those Quilters Clubbers we'd solve these murders without their help. And we may have just done that!"

"Hold up, boss man. You may need a little more corroborating evidence than that to make your case," opined Elvina Dobbler. Studying online at Phoenix University to get a law degree, Elvina and her sister Myrtle knew more about legal matters than any of the cops in the building.

"Good point," the Chief noted. Reining in his excitement. "Tommy, did you hear back from that jewelry store? Might help if we can tie that cufflink back to Wallberg. Fungus might not leave traces on the surface of a tiny gold box."

"That's the other bad news," remembered the deputy. "The guy at Preston Peterson & Sons – he was one of the sons – gave me the names of the people who bought the two sets of those Catherine Di Medici cufflinks." He thumbed through his steno pad again. "Here it is, Melissa Alice Caldwell and Frazier Allen Melrose. Nobody we've ever heard of."

"Did you run 'em through NCIC?"

"Yes sir. Not hits. Squeaky clean."

Chief Purdue removed his cap to rub his slick head, a nervous habit. "Hard to believe that designer only made two sets," he muttered.

"Rarity," said Harry. "Makes 'em more collectible. Worth more money."

"Guess I can see that."

Tommy spoke up. "She actually made four sets, but only two to sell. Kept the other sets for her own use."

"Four sets?" shouted Jim Purdue. "Get that jewelry store guy back on the phone and find out if she still has those extra sets."

"But she wasn't supposed to sell them."

"Maybe she gave them as birthday presents to friends. Or raffled them off for charity. Or they were stolen by a burglar. Let's find out exactly where those links are."

"I'm on it, Chief."

CHAPTER FORTY-FIVE

"What is the city but the people?"
-Coriolanus

This was also the week that Mark the Shark saved Caruthers Corners – well, its name that is.

Having had enough of John "Squeaky" Beasley's frivolous lawsuit, Mayor Mark Tidemore decided it was time to play hardball. Acting in behalf of the town, he had deposed Beasley for the litigation the little twerp had instigated. Judge Cramer allowed it as part of the fact-finding between the parties.

Mark queried Squeaky about his lawyer and the legal fees he was amassing. The man in the wheelchair was loquacious, willing to talk freely about his quest to reestablish his family's name. Money was no object, he avowed.

That was exactly what the Mayor wanted, a sworn deposition about the vast sums Squeaky Beasley was spending with his lawyer, an ambulance chaser named J. Harold Wentworth. As an attorney himself, he knew these kind of lawsuits were not cheap.

Then, Mark took the transcript over to Marybelle Olsen, director of the Hoople Senior Living Center, where Squeaky currently made his home. Financial need was a major criterium for residency in the Senior Center. The calculation of a rental fee was based on a person's monthly income. Anyone who could afford big legal bills just might not qualify.

Mark had the foresight to bring along Michael Allen Palley, the accountant for the Senior Center. After a few hours with an adding machine, they had their answer. Ol' Squeaky was in trouble.

That very afternoon, Mrs. Olsen presented John "Squeaky" Beasley with an eviction notice, pointing out that his application contained false income statements. His initial response was to threaten suing the facility. But in the end he negotiated a settlement: firing his lawyer, dropping the lawsuit against the town, and keeping his room – with the understanding that his finances would no longer be questioned.

Squeaky was a practical man. A comfortable room at a reasonable rate trumped his aunt's vendetta against a town's name. She could go fly a kite. All that extra money had been going to pay the lawyer, not him. Besides, Ol' Sam Beasley was an infamous murderer of indigenous Americans. Who cared if a town was named after him or not? Certainly not Squeaky.

~ ~ ~

What's in a name? the Bard asked.

That depends.

Caruthers Corners was named after a Town Founder. Nearby Burpyville was named after a seed company. Pitsville got its name from the rock quarries that dot its landscape.

The Bottomless Sinkhole (a local karst formation) is not bottomless – you can see the chimney of a house that sank when the land collapsed. The Never Ending Swamp has been surveyed as 400 acres ("more or less"). Gruesome Gorge State Park is actually a pleasant place, despite its macabre history.

Maddy Madison's birth name was Taylor, but her genetic father turned out to be a Hoople (one of the famous quadruplets), who was actually a Crackleton (not a true quad at all). A very confusing family tree.

CHAPTER FORTY-SIX

**"You whose pastime is to make
midnight mushrooms ..."**
-The Tempest

Estelle Grady took pleasure in her weekly excursions to Never Ending Swamp. She never went far into the morass of tangled vines and tree roots and quicksand. She was into foraging, whether it was finding edible greens such as chickweed, dandelion, clover, chicory, cattail, and wild mustard ... or picking berries ... or collecting barks like pines, slippery elm, black birch, and yellow birch.

As Masterclass.com explains, "Foraging is the process of searching for and obtaining food sources or medicinal plants in the wilderness ... Some common food sources you can forage for are cattails, acorns and stinging nettles (if boiled), tubers, rosehips, weeds, yarrow, and plantain. Before you forage, you want to make sure that you know how to properly do so, because eating the wrong kinds of plants can be toxic."

Estelle Grady all but worshipped the late Euell Gibbons. Back in the '60s, he was a noted outdoorsman and health food advocate. Many considered him the "patron saint" of foraging. You older readers will remember him as the pitchman for Post Grape-Nuts ("They remind me of wild hickory nuts," he'd famously said). His book *Stalking the Wild Asparagus* had been a huge success at the time.

Mrs. Grady particularly loved wild mushrooms. There was one section of the swamp that yielded excellent specimens of oyster mushrooms, morels, and chanterelles.

Mushroom hunters in Indiana are rewarded with a wide variety of edible fungi. She was also very fond of Meadow Mushrooms (*Agaricus campestris*), a wild cousin of the domestic mushroom often sold under names like white button, crimini, or portobello. However, being ghostly white, they are sometimes confused with Destroying Angels, a potentially deadly variety.

She often served her husband a delicious chicken and mushroom dish with lemons and fresh parsley sauce. It only took minutes to make.

~ ~ ~

Deputy Tommy Truehart wasted no time getting back in touch with Jaimie Peterson, manager of Preston Peterson & Sons. Jamie said he was more than happy to contact designer Wynona Burns to ask about the two sets of Catherine Di Medici cufflinks she had reserved for her own personal use.

"She gave them as gifts," Jamie Peterson reported back. "I've got the name of the recipient if you want it."

Tommy did.

"Wynona is an amateur actress, appears in lots of Little Theater productions. She gave both sets of cufflinks as a thank-you to her former drama professor, a woman named Ceci Bennington."

~ ~ ~

"Well, that's a dead end," pronounced Chief Purdue. "No connection with our case, other than the woman was an acting teacher."

"Like Mrs. Grady?" said Maddy. That night she and Beau were having dinner with Jim and Bootsie at Cozy Café. Her sister Maisie had reserved the big corner booth for them. A special accommodation.

"Yeah, I suppose so," he said as he shoveled another bite of Maisie's famous Chicken Chasseur into his mouth. It was one of his favorite dishes.

"This chicken is delicious," Bootsie agreed. "You'll have to give me your recipe sometime," she said to Maisie.

The café owner made a face. "That's like asking Col. Saunders to reveal his 11 secret herbs and spices," she taunted.

"Oh, c'mon," Bootsie pleaded. "I promise not to tell another living soul. Well, other than Maddy here."

"It's a classic French chicken recipe. What's sometimes called Hunter's Chicken. Back in the day, hunters would bring home game meat, along with any mushrooms that they'd found on the way, and they'd cook this amazing dish with the ingredients they'd collected. This is a variation of that. Very simply an oven-roasted chicken with mushrooms and wine sauce. It's very popular with my dinner customers."

Maddy took up for her sister. "Keep your recipe a secret. If you give it to Bootsie, she'll start cooking it at home and Jim won't have to come here to get your Chicken Chasseur."

"Oh you," Bootsie Purdue waved away her friend's words. "I'd never do that. You know I hate cooking."

"That's why I treat Cozy Café like a spare kitchen," laughed her husband, taking another bite from his plate. "Always something good to eat here. At home it's catch as catch can."

"This sure is great chicken," Beau added his compliment. "Tender, tasty, just perfect."

"The trick is fresh ingredients," Maisie shared her technique. "The chicken comes from Adam Wagler's farm. The mushrooms I buy locally. The tomatoes and shallots are straight from Errol Baumgartner's garden. The herbs (tarragon and parsley) I grow myself."

"And the wine?" asked Jim.

"From Abner Newfield's vineyard down in Pitsville."

"His wines won an award last year," Beau noted. "I bought a couple of bottles of his Sauvignon blanc just last week. Got a good price. He was having a two-for-one sale."

"Fresh ingredients – then what?" Bootsie was still trying to get at the recipe.

"The rest is simple," relented Maisie. "I sear the chicken on both sides, move it to a sheet pan and finish roasting in the oven. This guarantees a crispy skin. While the chicken is roasting you then prepare the hunter's sauce."

"It's certainly delicious," agreed Maddy, taking another bite to savior the tomatoey wine sauce. She could taste the delicate touch of tarragon with its anise flavor.

"I always serve it with rice and a green salad. That was the menu for those Merry Times actors the night of their performance. That Adolphus Anderson had two helpings."

That got Maddy's attention. "All of them had the same dish?"

"Yes, they called ahead and made a reservation, selected the entrée in advance."

"But you don't normally take reservations," said Bootsie,

"I do for big parties. There were 20 people in that group. I had to bring in an extra cook."

"I thought you said you prepared Adolphus Anderson's meal yourself," Jim reminded her.

"I did, mostly. I oversee the cooks, do the main work. They help with the prep, the presentation, sometimes the serving."

"You said you brought in help?" Maddy pursued this new line of thinking. "Who did you get?"

"I usually call Lindsey Binkworthy and Carol Clarkson. Their day job, they work in the High School cafeteria. But Carol had the screaming meemies that night – she suffers PTSD from her stint in Desert Storm – so I called the woman who supplies my mushrooms. She's quite a good cook."

"Who's that?"

"Estelle Grady. She teaches drama over at the high school, but sure knows her way around a kitchen."

CHAPTER FORTY-SEVEN

"Presume not that I am the thing I was."
-Henry IV

"**T**hank you for making time to see me," Cookie Bentley smiled at the gray-haired lady in the pink pinafore. The historian had just been seated in the spartan living room at 327 Bluebird Lane. Estelle Grady was pouring steaming elderberry tea into dainty china cups, a welcome break in her midmorning routine.

"I'm happy to help," replied Mrs. Grady as she sipped at the hot liquid. "Enjoy your elderberry tea. I picked and dried the berries myself."

"Are you sure this is safe to drink?" asked Cookie, staring cautiously into the cup. "I've read that the seeds of *Sambucus callicarpa* are poisonous."

"An Old Wife's Tale," Mrs. Grady brushed away Cookie's concern. "Elderberry tea is rich in nutrients, can boost a healthy immune system, and contains no caffeine. Its anthocyanins help reduce cardiovascular risks, control obesity, fight diabetes, and cure a cold. I'm quite adept at foraging. Know the good plants from the bad ones."

"Hm, it has an interesting taste," noted Cookie, taking a sip.

"Elderberries tend to be sweet and tart. I add a pinch of cinnamon to enhance the flavor."

"Hm, I like it."

"Elderberries make a fine wine too."

"Oh really?"

"Yes indeed. I make that too. Matter of fact, I have a jug in the fridge, if you'd like to try it."

"Perhaps I'd better stick with the tea."

"As you like. I suppose it is a little early in the day to break out the wine.'""

"Now about my visit —"

"Genealogy, you said?"

"Yes, that's right. A survey. You see, the Caruthers Corners Historical Society maintains genealogy records of local families. Part of our Family Tree Records Initiative. We receive a state grant for this program. And now that you and your husband are a part of the community, we'd like to add you to our archives."

"I'm flattered. How do we go about this?"

"Two simple steps. First, fill out this Family Tree form at your leisure and return it to the Historical Society. Second, there's an informal interview."

"Okay."

Cookie produced a clipboard and mechanical pencil. "Your husband's full name?"

"Jefferson Archer Grady. Of the Great Lakes Gradys."

"And yours?"

My married name is Estelle Fiona Grady, but I was born a Bennington."

"Would you spell that for me?"

She did. Then said, "Uh, perhaps I should mention that I used to be an actress. My stage name was Cecelia Connors. Many of my friends still call me Ceci."

"I think I've heard of you. A stage actress, right? You won a Tony for Best Actress in that Broadway revival of *Macbeth*." Her eidetic memory was kicking in.

"Oh my, it's amazing that you remember. So few people do."

Cookie was quickly connecting the dots, her brain cells firing like pistons in a turbocharged 526" Big Blocked engine. No doubt Estelle Grady was the same Ceci Bennington who received the Catherine Di Medici cufflinks as a gift from the designer. And the same woman who sold mushrooms to Cozy Café. And the same cook who helped Maisie prepare that last meal for Adolphus Anderson.

It was all coming together.

"Are you all right?" asked Estelle Grady.

"Uh, yes, sorry. I was just savoring the elderberry tea."

"I thought you might like it."

"Yes, it's quite tasty." Cookie took another sip.

"Next question?"

"Let me see, yes, here we are. Do you have any siblings?" she continued, pencil poised.

"Just one sister. But she died in a car accident. Judith was her name."

"Do you have any children?"

"Alas, no. But I raised Judith's sons as my own."

"Sons?"

"Twins as it happens. Quite a handful."

Bingo! The Leicester twins. She was their aunt.

"Next. The year of your birth was ...?"

The questions droned on. But Cookie Bentley's mind was racing. She could hardly wait to get out of there and carry her discovery back to the Quilters Club.

~ ~ ~

Harvey Wallace Wallberg was getting a little long in the tooth, as they say. Too old to ever play Romeo. After all, in

Shakespeare's original story, Romeo was given the age of 16; Juliet only 13. And here he was, facing 63 (that is, if he kept up the lie about his birthyear).

Macbeth was a role better suited to his age. A mature king. A meaty part for an experienced actor. With nearly half a century on the boards, Wallberg considered himself seasoned.

Now that Adolphus and Agamemnon were out of the way, and Benjy Bartholomew fired, there was no one to block his dramatic goals. With him assuming control of the Merry Times Players (who was to stop him from doing that?) he could cast himself in any role he chose.

First, he needed to get that stupid mayor to let him proceed with a new performance of *A Midsummer Night's Dream*. That would establish his credentials as an impresario … and show his acting chops in the popular role of Puck. Not to mention generate some needed funds. Merry Times was all but broke.

Second, he would announce a tour with him starring in *Macbeth*. That would make his reputation as a lead. Next thing you know, they would be awarding him a Burbage!

"*'Give me my robe, put on my crown; I have immortal longings in me,'*" he quoted aloud from the Bard's *Antony and Cleopatra*.

Ambition burned hotly inside his chest. Or maybe it was just agita.

~ ~ ~

Mayor Mark Tidemore was glad to have that stupid lawsuit behind him. Beasleyville indeed!

Also, he was happy to have those Shakespearean actors out of his hair. Those deaths were something the town needed to put behind it. Forget reprising that play. It seemed to be as accursed as *Macbeth*.

Besides, he had other worries to deal with. If Caruthers Corners were going to develop another summer event in addition to the Watermelon Fest, he'd better come up with something fast. July 4th was nearly upon them, with its parade down Main Street and fireworks in the Town Square. But there was a long stretch between the 4th and Labor Day. An event was need to fill that gap.

The good news was that Maisie Walters was still willing to put up the money for a big to-do, part of her Foundation's philanthropic mission. And she had an idea: The Caruthers Corners Summertime Song Fest. Or maybe they would name it in honor of Herb Shriner, the Hoosier humorist and harmonica player. Or maybe after Maisie.

The idea was a night of music, a concert featuring local entertainers. Musical treats like Snooky Smith and His Smooth Cruisers, Hoagie Henderson & His Hoosier All-Stars, Little Mitzi McQueeney, Paul Whittaker and His Hoosier Hotshots, The Tommy Tucker Trio, Hinkie Dinkie Dixon, The Straw Hatters, even Slick Vic Davone. That would be quite a lineup. Every last one of them would be eager to participate. Gigs were hard to come by these days.

But first things first: 4th of July was upon them.

Nevertheless. Mark made a call to Police Chief Purdue. He intended to put a little pressure on Jim to clean up these so-called Shakespeare Murders sooner rather than later. If the police had to accept a little help from his mother-in-law and her Quilters Club cronies, so be it.

The town didn't need any unsavory situations that might scare tourists away!

CHAPTER FORTY-EIGHT

**"Let every eye negotiate for itself
and trust no agent."**
-Much Ado About Nothing

eau brought in the afternoon mail. Fritz Berber had been running late today. He placed the stack of letters on the tray along with Maddy's afternoon tea. She was in bed – resting.

Still sore, she could barely move. Maybe she hadn't fully recovered from the car crash after all. Those airbags packed quite a punch.

Sitting up to drink her tea, she took a quick look at the mail. Shuffling through the letters and flyers didn't reveal much of interest. A brochure from Food Lion listing this week's sale items. An electric bill. An offer for another credit card. A notice for an upcoming ½-price sale at the Clothes Horse Boutique.

One letter stopped her. The return address stated: MIDWESTERN PATHOLOGY INSTITUTE. Wasn't that the company N'yen had found for her? It specialized in expert witnesses, toxicology, serology, genetic testing, tissue procurement, wound ballistics, private autopsies, and such.

She quickly slit the envelope open with her fingernail. It read:

Dear Mrs. Madilyn Madison:

Thank you for your recent inquiry about our services. Unfortunately, we are unable to help you. A brief record check shows that the body in question, Mr. Adolphus Everly Anderson, was cremated per the request of his nearest relative. Therefore there are no remains to examine.

While we specialize in the examination of persons who die suddenly, unexpectedly or violently, the lack of a corpse precludes our ability to conduct an autopsy, toxicology testing, or other procedures necessary for proper forensic analysis.

We wish we could be more helpful. Please feel free to contact us if we might assist you at any time in the future.

Sincerely,
Dr. Cyril R. Pearson, MD
Executive Director, Midwestern Pathology Institute

Well, that was that.

~ ~ ~

N'yen was bummed that hiring a forensic pathologist was out. Aggie's father had confirmed that the actor had been cremated. There was no way to determine cause of death – and Doc Medford was sticking to his heart attack finding.

Another dead end.

Aggie had an idea. "What if Adolphus Anderson was an organ donor? There might be tissue samples to examine."

"How would we find that out?" said Sissy.

N'yen smiled. "It would be listed on his driver's license. Hold on, let me break into the Bureau of Motor database."

"You can do that?"

"Just watch me."

While her cousin bent over his computer, Aggie clicked on her iPhone. "Says here there are there are currently more than 3.5 million registered organ and tissue donors in Indiana."

"That's about one out of every two people," N'yen observed. "Still a long shot, but worth checking."

"Why would somebody give away their body parts?" asked Sissy. "You might need them on the Other Side."

"Spirits don't have organs and tissue," teased Aggie. She found the girl's Southern superstitions funny.

"Hmm, I never thought of it that way. If you can see through a ghost, it must not have any guts and stuff inside."

"That's one way to look at it," laughed N'yen, bent over his computer, fingers dancing on the keyboard.

"My preacher back home says a person's soul won't rest in peace if the body is not intact at the time of dying."

"That actor had all his parts at the time of death," Aggie assured her. "We're just checking to see if he gave them away afterwards. People do that to help living people who need a new heart or kidney or eye."

"Hey, here we are," shouted N'yen. "One white male named Adolphus Everly Anderson, aged 62, has a driver's license issue that was issued in Evansville, Indiana."

"And –?"

The boy gave a heavy sigh of disappointment. "We struck out. The organ donor box is not checked."

~ ~ ~

"No luck," Maddy reported to her friends. "That Midwestern Pathology Institute couldn't help us. They need body tissue and ol' Adolphus was cremated. Can't do much with just ashes, they say."

Lizzie had an interesting thought. "Maybe Doc Medford kept some tissue samples. Pathologists do that sometimes."

"But there was no autopsy," Bootsie reminded them.

"I don't understand why not," argued Lizzie. "Aren't they legally bound to do one in the case of a mysterious death?"

"But this death wasn't mysterious," Maddy reminded her. "According to Doc it was natural causes – a heart attack."

Cookie cranked up her eidetic memory. "The state's website says: 'Autopsies are performed mainly to determine the medical cause of death and to gather evidence for court. The coroner typically will not perform an autopsy if the manner of death is natural and the cause of death can be determined by past medical history or an external exam.'"

"So if he didn't do an autopsy, he didn't take any tissue samples?"

"Not likely," said Cookie.

"Back to Square One," sighed Maddy.

~ ~ ~

N'yen was scrolling on his Dell Precision 7730. Poking about. Trying to come up with another line of investigation.

Aggie and Sissy were playing Go Fish. The card game uses a 54-card standard deck (52 plus a pair of Jokers). Each player receives 7 cards. One player asks the other player for a card of a particular face value. If the player has that card, he hands it over. If not, he tells his opponent to "Go Fish," requiring him to draw from the Pool. Four cards of one face value forms a Book. When the cards are exhausted, the player with the most Books wins.

N'yen refused to play Go Fish, calling it a sissy's game. He would have preferred 3-dimensional chess. Or a more complicated game like *Magic: The Gathering.*

"Hey, take a look at this," said N'yen, nodding toward his computer screen. "I just pulled up a news release about that park ranger –Hugo Marston."

"Lemme see," said Sissy, scooting onto the gaming chair beside him. A tight fit, hip to hip.

"Me too," said Aggie, planting her bottom on the chair's padded arm. "I was dead-sure he had murdered that Northwestern professor."

"Neesie took a class under that professor," Sissy reminded them.

"Six degrees of separation," the Asian boy joked.

"Yes, you're a regular Kevin Bacon," said Aggie, rolling her eyes.

"Never mind that," he sniffed. "I picked this up from the website of the *Bismarck Ledger.*"

BISMARCK, NORTH DAKOTA – State Police confirmed the arrest of a former park ranger in connection with the death of a local rancher. Hugo Merriweather Marston, 44, allegedly bludgeoned Rick Edwin Burke, age unknown, in a dispute over Marston's wife. The altercation took place in a bar frequented by both men.

Hugo Marston gave a statement to the arresting officers. "Yeah, I killed him and I would do it again.

Ain't the first man I've knocked off for messing 'round with my wife."

When contacted by the Ledger, Trudy Marston said, "My husband is a very jealous man. I was not romantically involved with Rickie Burke. We were just good friends. Ask anybody. Wasn't no need to kill him."

Until recently, Marston worked as a ranger assigned to Fort Abraham Lincoln State Park. He was terminated in late May for "brawling," according to the ND Parks and Recreation Department's personnel records.

A fellow park ranger who spoke under the promise of anonymity said, "Hugo had a hair-trigger temper. You look at him cross-eyed he was ready to fight you. He broke one of my teeth. I don't know what set him off."

Another unnamed ranger described Marston as "a bad fit. He only lasted a few months."

A third co-worker called him "A wild card. Nobody you could depend on."

Police officials confirmed that Marston will be arraigned tomorrow. He is expected to plead guilty. Under North Dakota law, murder is differentiated from the other types of homicide by criminal intent. It is also the only homicide offense that can receive a life imprisonment sentence.

After reading the news release, Aggie turned to her two friends. "What's he mean, this isn't the first man he's knocked off?"

"He's just bragging. We proved he didn't kill that professor, Dr. Jonathan Livingston Segal."

"Did we?"

CHAPTER FORTY-NINE

"My dancing soul doth celebrate"

-Richard II

The 4th of July began with the big parade at 2 p.m. It was a hodgepodge of marching bands, beauty queens, and the Sons of Anthony Wayne scout troop. A flame-red firetruck led the parade, with Fire Chief Freddie Madison sitting atop the big engine waving at the crowd. Movie star Missy Montana was this year's Grand Marshal, riding in a red convertible behind the firetruck. Swami Bombay (né Juan Martinez) led Happy the Elephant. Other circus animals from Haney Bros. Petting Zoo and Exotic Animals Refuge followed – Sneezy the Baboon, Bashful the Tiger, Grumpy the Lion, Sleepy the Bear, plus Doc and Dopey the Horses. Along came 7-foot Tall Paul Johnson (a former sideshow giant) and his wife Martha Ray (a tattooed lady), smiling and waving. Andrew Linderman and his 9 children led Janus, their two-head calf. And that popular barbershop quartet known as the Straw Hatters brought up the end, singing a rendition of "Yankee Doodle Dandy."

The parade was followed by a potluck picnic on the Town Square.

Maddy had contributed 20 of her famous Upside down Watermelon Cakes. Cookie – true to her name – had baked several trays of macaroons and chocolate chips and snickerdoodles. Bootsie made a washtub-sized green salad. And Lizzie paid for a truckload of root beer to be delivered.

Cozy Café (Maisie, that is) delivered 400 pounds of her watermelon-fried chicken. Marybelle Olsen, Molly Dougan, Alice Schroeder, Francis Morgan, Lindsey Binkworthy, and Carol Clarkson helped with the serving.

Amish farmer Abram Wagler provided enough deviled eggs to feed everybody in town twice over. Old MacDonald's Dairy made up trays of sugar cream pies. The town's cooperative (formerly Aitkens Produce) supplied free watermelons. The Dollar General donated paper plates and plastic utensils.

And more: The DQ contributed free ice cream sundaes. N.L. Purdue paid for 800 pepperoni pizzas from the Papa John's in Burpyville. His younger brother Bobby Ray outdid him by buying 1,000 submarine sandwiches from Hoagie's Hoagies down in Pitsville. But Missy Montana (actually Louise Carol König, a local-girl-who-made-good) topped that by hiring a caterer out of Indianapolis to set up a temporary cook tent to turn out 2,000 grilled hot dogs. Food Lion provided a condiment table with ketchup, mustard, and relish – along with squeeze bottles of Kraft Cheez Whiz. Everybody agreed, it was quite a spread.

The 4th of July was a very festive day. Just after sunset Charlie Scherzinger and several of his ruffian pals set off 3,000-pounds of fireworks – rockets, roman candles, fountains, multi-shot cakes, spinners and Catherine wheels. The 20-minutes display cost the town about $10,000, but everybody agreed it was money well spent.

Beau leaned close to Maddy's ear. "You ready to call it a day?" The Tommy Tucker Band was beginning to play its selection of Golden Oldies. Couples were drifting over to the gazebo to dance. Kids were playing tag in the dark.

"I am a little tired."

"Doc Medford said you needed plenty of rest after that automotive mishap."

"I guess I have been pushing it a bit," she admitted. "But I honestly think the airbags did more damage than the wreck itself."

"Maybe. But the wreck might have done more damage without 'em."

"Good point."

Aggie appeared beside them, a young man on her arm. None other than Bobby Elwood, her onetime boyfriend. Was the "break" over, Maddy wondered. "Hey, are you guys leaving?" her granddaughter inquired.

"We were thinking of it," Maddy admitted. "Don't want to overextend myself."

"Yes, you'd best get some rest," Aggie encouraged. "Tomorrow we're back on the case."

"The case –?" said Bobby Elwood.

"The Quilters Club is looking into those actors' death," she said matter-of-factly.

"Do you have any suspects?"

"One or two," she dismissed his questions with a wave of her hand. The lovesick teenager who used to fawn at Bobby's every word had certainly grown up. She was now the one in charge. Female empowerment in the flesh.

"We're ducking out early."

"Party poopers," teased their granddaughter.

Maddy couldn't help noticing how Aggie had matured. Taller now, she was going to be a willowy beauty like her mother. In her sleeveless sundress, she looked like she had just stepped out of a magazine ad. Her blonde hair billowed about her angelic face like halo.

"If you youngsters stick around, a rock band is set to follow The Tommy Tucker Trio, some group called the Serial Killers.

"Oh, they're chill," said Bobby. "I heard them at a club in Muncie." He was going to Ball State. Somebody said he was majoring in Communications. "They sound like Foo Fighters meet Arctic Monkeys. You'll like them."

"Great, we'll stay and dance."

"Enjoy," said Maddy, wrapping her hand around Beau's arm. Ready to go.

"I'll pass the word that you flaked out if I see Aunt Cookie or any of the others," said Aggie, as she waved goodbye and pulled Bobby into the swirling crowd.

~ ~ ~

When Maddy and Beau got home, the street lights were casting an artificial moonlight along Melon Pickers Row, bathing their Victorian home in a pale blue glow, a scene so peaceful, they almost didn't notice the envelop on their doorstep. If it wasn't for the dagger that pinned it to the stoop they might have stepped over it without looking down.

"Is that a knife?" she pointed. Her words reminded her of the words of Lady Macbeth: *Is this a dagger which I see before me, the handle toward my hand? Come, let me clutch thee. I have thee not, and yet I see thee still.*"

"Little early for Halloween pranks," said her husband, bending over to pluck it from the wood. The dagger came up, the envelope still impaled on the pointy blade. "What's this?" he said, plucking off the paper and inspecting it carefully.

"Let's look at it inside," urged Maddy. "I don't like standing out here in the open."

Beau fumbled with his keys, unlocked the front door, and ushered his wife inside. He flipped on an overhead light, and used his penknife to carefully slip open the envelope and shake out the note inside. He laid it onto the coffee table and bent over to read the words printed on the ivory-colored paper.

WOE, DESTRUCTION, RUIN, AND DECAY;
THE WORST IS DEATH,
AND DEATH WILL HAVE HIS DAY.

"What's that?" said Beau.

"I'd bet it's a quote from Shakespeare."

"What's it mean?"

"I'm not sure, but I think it's intended as a death threat."

CHAPTER FIFTY

**"Sweet are the uses of adversity which,
like the toad, ugly and venomous,
wears yet a precious jewel in his head."**
-As You Like It

Police Chief Jim Purdue said, "Don't feel special, Maddy. We got one too. So did Cookie and Ben. I haven't heard from Lizzie and Edgar yet."

"Who would be sending death threats?"

"Some sicko," Jim answered. His view of psychology was pretty simple – nut cases and not-quite nut cases.

"Let's think through this," said Maddy. "What do we all have in common?"

"That's easy. The wives all belong to the Quilters Club," said Jim.

"And what are we doing right now that might irritate someone?"

"You're investigating the murder of those two actors."

Maddy nodded. "So it would appear that the person who left these threats is also the person who committed those two murders."

"That means if we can figure out who left these notes, we've got our murderer," said Aggie. "*Quod erat demonstrandum.*" She had dropped by after breakfast to check on her grandmother. She'd been concerned about her leaving the 4th of July celebrations right after the fireworks.

"Judging by the contents of those notes – verses from William Shakespeare – it has to be one of those actors," Maddy theorized.

"Makes sense," Beau nodded.

N'yen had come downstairs to meet Sissy for breakfast. "Did anybody get a glimpse of the sneak who left the notes?" he asked, pulling up a stool at the island.

"Not that we know of," the police chief admitted. "I've got a couple of men interviewing neighbors, asking if they noticed any strange cars on the street, checking if any of the neighbors have surveillance cameras or Ring doorbells."

"What did the other notes say?" asked Maddy. "Same as mine or something different?"

"Different. Ours said '*Thou know'st 'tis common; all that lives must die, passing through nature to eternity.*' And Cookie and Ben's note said –" he consulted a notebook "– Here we go, '*Death, a necessary end, will come when it will come.*' "

"I'm pretty sure those are all quotes from Shakespeare," observed Maddy, "although I'd be hard put to identify the plays they came from.

"I won't be surprised if Lizzie and Edgar got something along the same lines," commented Beau.

Sissy said, "Is it too late for breakfast? I'm hungry."

"Hold on, dear," responded Maddy. "I will whip up some watermelon pancakes. How does that sound?"

"Yummy. You'd think I'd be full, much as I ate at the 4th of July picnic yesterday."

"I'll say," exclaimed N'yen. "You had at least four hot dogs and two Philly cheese steaks. Not to mention those ice cream sundaes."

"Frozen custards," she corrected. "That's what you told me they were."

"Right. But you still ate enough to give a polar bear a stomach ache."

"Pancakes still sound good," she ignored him.

"Me too, if you don't mind," said Aggie. She'd danced into the wee hours of the night with Bobby Elwood, working up a new appetite. Eat your heart out, Joanie McPhee, she told herself.

"Jim, how about you – pancakes while I'm making them?"

"Why not?" he agreed. "No rules against eating pancakes on duty."

"I'll take some too," volunteered N'yen. "Long as everybody else is."

"None for me," demurred Beauregard Madison. "I had some earlier. At the breakfast your grandmother served at 9 o'clock."

"Sissy and I were up late," the boy offered an excuse for sleeping late.

"Back to those notes," said Maddy as she prepared a bowl of batter. "I take them to be warnings, trying to make us back off. Same thing with my car being run off the road. That means we're hitting a nerve."

"And what nerve is that?" asked Jim Purdue, trying not to sound too dubious while waiting to get his helping of pancakes.

"We've been poking around Harvey Wallace Wallberg ... and those Leicester twins."

"And my drama teacher," Sissy added.

"Eeny meeny miny moe," said Jim Purdue.

~ ~ ~

"It was a threat?" Lizzie had turned up at Maddy's house with her note. Edgar had found it this morning when he went outside to get the milk. Old MacDonald's Dairy still delivered to some local customers.

"What did it say again?" asked the police chief.

Lizzie held it at arm's length to read. She wasn't wearing her glasses, a vanity thing. "Let's see here. It says, '*He that dies pays all debts.*' I thought it was referring to one of the bank's mortgage holders passing away or something like that."

"What did Edgar think?" Beau wanted to know.

"He didn't say. Just gave me the note as he went out the door. He's off fishing again.'

"He didn't invite me." Beau sounded sulky about it.

"Me either," pouted N'yen.

"Don't feel rejected. I think that was just his excuse to get out of the house. Allow him to ignore this note. You know how he doesn't like to get involved in Quilters Club business."

Chief Jim Purdue looked up accusingly. "This isn't Quilters Club business," he warned. "This is official police business."

"Right, right, whatever you say," Maddy waved his words away as she prepared another batch of watermelon pancakes. Turned out Lizzie Ridenour hadn't had breakfast either.

~ ~ ~

Deputy Tommy Truehart found a video cam at neighbor's house – Mrs. Eunice Dancy, the elderly lady who owned the stately Queen Anne on the corner of Melon Pickers Row and North Main She was the mother of Tom Dancy, the longtime Town Clerk. Her surveillance camera had been blown off-kilter by that big windstorm last month. Old Tom wasn't very timely in helping his mom with home repairs. Its new angle picked up more of the street than intended.

Doing a quick playback, Tommy spotted a light-colored Toyota Corolla turn down the street at precisely 8:34 p.m. – slightly after dusk – when the fireworks display was going full force. Everybody's eyes would be on the nighttime sky, not on a quiet downtown street.

"Who do we know drives a Corolla?" asked Chief Purdue, thinking out loud. He did that a lot.

"Those Leicester brothers," said Bootsie. By now, she and Cookie had joined Lizzie at the Madison house. More pancakes were sizzling on the griddle.

"The twins?"

"Yes, we followed that silver Toyota – it's a rental car – all way from Burpyville to Estelle Grady's little bungalow in Wabash Acres," said Cookie Bentley. "I remember it had an Enterprise sticker on the back bumper."

"The car in the video has a sticker of some kind," confirmed Tommy Truehart, "but it's too grainy to read."

Everyone was gathered around N'yen's computer. He'd brought it down from his room in order to replay Mrs. Dancy's surveillance tape. She had turned it over to Tommy Truehart in return for him fixing the angle of her ADT video cam.

"Are you going to arrest them?" asked Aggie.

Chief Purdue looked unhappy. "Not enough evidence."

"Why not?" said Sissy. "We've got them here on tape."

"You can't see the drivers. And you can't read the license plate."

"But who else do we know that drives a Toyota Corolla rental car?" protested Aggie.

"There are 1.8 million rental cars in America," said Cookie, pulling the statistic out of her memory banks. "And

Enterprise has 1.1 million of those cars. A lot of them are Toyotas."

"Makes sense," said Beau. "The Toyota Corolla is the No. 1 bestselling car in the world." He'd learned that fact from his youngest son. Freddie was a car enthusiast, a big fan of Japanese cars – even though the Corolla was manufactured in Blue Springs, Mississippi.

"Why are Toyotas so popular?" asked Lizzie. She drove a Mercedes-Benz GCL.

"The Corolla is one of the most popular rental car models out there," Cookie quoted from memory. "It has good fuel economy, making it a great budget road trip option. It can fit 4 passengers comfortably and has good legroom for the people in the back seat. Its size also makes it an excellent choice for driving in cities and tight parking spaces."

Maddy voiced what they were all thinking. "We know Carl and Bob Leicester are driving a Toyota Corolla rental car. Trick is, how do we place them in that car in the video?"

CHAPTER FIFTY-ONE

"The course of true love
never did run smooth."
-A Midsummer Night's Dream

With the Leister twins moving to the top of their suspects list, attention shifted to the Grady family.

Cookie had returned to the Burpyville Library. Bootsie was working (behind her husband's back) with Myrtle and Elvina Dobbler to search the various law enforcement databases – NCIC, ProQuest Criminal Justice, SocINDEX, Nexis Uni, and the multidisciplinary Web of Science. Lizzie had asked her private detective to take a closer look at the twins.

With N'yen's help, Maddy was focusing on The Vault, the FBI's new FOIA Library, a public resource containing 6,700 documents and other media that have been scanned from paper into digital copies. It was interesting reading. She had to be careful not to get sidetracked by files on Al Capone or Marilyn Monroe or Martin Luther King, Jr. Even The Monkees.

Chief Jim Purdue met with Chief Crenshaw to coordinate their investigations. Crenshaw's staff had been checking out statewide registrations of blue Chevy panel trucks. Now they would also start checking out local rentals of Toyota Corollas. And Herbert Vox would process the four threatening notes for fingerprints.

Deputy Tommy Truehart hacked into the FBI's NICS and CODIS databases. Det. Harry Teague slogged on, setting up a look-see meet between Vic Davone and the Leicester twins at the jail.

Aggie and Sissy took to their computers.

Everybody was fully engaged in the investigation. There was no longer any grumbling about the Quilters Club butting in. You didn't threaten Jim Purdue's friends with impunity.

~ ~ ~

The Burpyville PD had the first hit. A crosscheck of blue Chevrolet Express cargo vans registered in the state turned up one belonging to Merry Times Players LLC of Evansville, Indiana. When questioned, the actors acknowledged that their company owned one, a 2014 Chevrolet Express 3500 with AWD and GM's 5.3L V8. The panel truck was used to transport props and lighting equipment from performance to performance.

Likely this was the blue truck that ran Maddy off the road. However, no one seemed to know where it was at the moment. "Maybe Benjy Bartholomew left it in a nearby parking garage," Tom Turlington surmised. "He left so abruptly after he got fired, nobody had a chance to ask him about it. Or about anything else."

~ ~ ~

CASE # 17A-304-B
SUBJECT: Adolphus Everly Anderson
PROFESSION: Actor, Theater Manager
CURRENT STATUS: Deceased, Suspected Homicide

Here is a closer examination of the individuals identified as Persons of Interest in the death of Adolphus Everly Anderson.

• Harvey Wallace Wallberg. Actor. Ambitious. Owes $32,312 in overdue credit card bills. One arrest for sexual solicitation of underaged male (case dismissed). Belongs to AA. Suspected relationship with Carl and Bob Leicester. Nothing to indicate a knowledge of mushrooms other than remarks to Det. Harry Teague and connection to Carl and Bob Leicester, whose aunt provides foraged mushrooms to local diner.

• Carl Castor Leicester. Actor. Few assets, $332 in credit card debt. Suspected relationship of convenience with Wallberg. Highly immature. Nephew of Estelle Grady (see below). Aunt provides foraged mushrooms to local diner.

• Bob Pollux Leicester. Actor. Few assets, $212 in credit card debt. Suspected relationship of convenience with Wallberg. Highly immature. Nephew of Estelle Grady (see below). Aunt provides foraged mushrooms to local diner.

• Estelle Bennington Grady. A/K/A Cecelia Connors. Drama teacher, former actress. Gave up stage career under mysterious circumstances. Raised sister's twin sons (Carl and Bob Leicester). Students love her. Provides foraged mushrooms to local diner. Considered a good cook.

• Jefferson Archer Grady. Professional in Technology Industry. Squeaky clean. Government Top Secret clearance while working at Google.

Common thread of foraged mushrooms links above Persons of Interest, but no conclusive evidence of anyone using them for murder of Subject and his brother.
Sincerely,
Odell Lumley
Private Investigations R Us
Indianapolis, Indiana

Lizzie's detective had more or less struck out.

~ ~ ~

Bootsie and the Dobbler sisters had slightly better success. They turned up the fact that both Carl and Bob Leicester had juvie records.

- Three charges of shoplifting for Carl; one for Bob.
- Both boys had received a suspended sentence for setting a high school classmate's hair on fire. The victim suffered second degree burns on his scalp. The dispute had been over an insulting comment made in a YMCA locker room.
- During their first year at Julliard, there were accusations of sexual solicitation ("Two for the price of one," an alleged john had quoted the offer), but the vice squad couldn't make the charges stick. The school delicately turned a blind eye.
- As an adult, two years ago, Carl had been arrested for grand theft auto – a 2013 Lamborghini Aventador that he'd tried to resell – a felony that usually comes with a fine of $10,000 and up to 30 months in prison. Somehow, the sentence had been suspended. How he escaped punishment was not

clear. It was thought Jefferson Grady pulled some strings. A Google exec at that time, Grady obviously had friends in high places.

Records showed that Carl Leicester was no Sunday School boy. Nor was his brother. But, as Bootsie admitted, there was not enough here to brand either of them a killer. Or to clear them from the Quilters Club's list of suspects.

~ ~ ~

"Got it!" shouted N'yen Madison that afternoon. He pumped his arm in the air like a gamer who had just made a big score. He was sitting in front of his Dell Precision 7730 with its Intel Core Xeon E-2186M 6-Core CPU, having completed his search.

"Yes?" said his cousin, her blonde hair shimmering in the ambient light of the computer screen. You could see the sprinkling of freckles on her nose.

"I just completed a crosscheck of Cecelia Connors – Aunt Cookie says that was Mrs. Grady's stage name in her younger days – with each one of the actors in the Merry Times Players. And I got a hit."

"I still can't believe my drama teacher is connected to those murders."

"Believe it, Cuddle Bug." N'yen's voice sounded confident.

Cuddle bug? Aggie rolled her eyes. "You found a connection between Estelle Grady and one of those actors?" she tried to re-focus the conversation.

"Yeah. I could have done it much easier if I'd had time to write an algorithm. As it was, I had to go back and forth between individual listings on IBDB."

"What's IBDB?" inquired his girlfriend.

"The Internet Broadway Database, the official archive for Broadway theater information. Kinda like the IMDb."

"The Internet Movie Database," Aggie Tidemore identified the second acronym for Sissy's benefit. Aggie had taken several film courses in high school. And she belonged to an informal film society at Yale. She was a movie buff.

"That's right," nodded N'yen. "IMDb is ultimately owned by Amazon; IBDB is backed by Playbill."

"So what did you find out?" insisted Cuddle Bug, tugging at his sleeve.

"Cecelia Connors appeared in a Broadway revival of *Macbeth* with Adolphus Everly Anderson in 1988."

"So Mrs. Grady knew one of our victims," said Aggie. "That doesn't prove anything."

"Nessie has a nose for clues," responded Sissy. "I'll bet there'll be more connections if we dig deeper."

"Get out your spade," said Aggie.

~ ~ ~

Det. Harry Teague phoned the Highliner Hotel and asked to speak with either Carl or Bob Leicester. Harry's wife had assured him the Merry Times Players were still at the hotel, despite the death of their new owner.

After a few minutes, Carl came on the line. "Pray tell, what does a noble policeman want with me and my brother? We have done naught to cause alarm."

"Just a minor matter in our investigation of Mr. Anderson's death."

"Heigh! Which Mr. Anderson – Addy or Aggy? Both are dead. As the immortal Bard said, '*The heavens themselves blaze forth the death of princes.*'"

Harry didn't think the man sounded very sincerely. But he continued politely, "Sir, would you and your brother be willing to come to Caruthers Corners for a brief interview? We'd be happy to send a car for you. It would be most helpful in our investigation."

"Fi to you. We will not come unless you legally compel us to do so. There is nothing in our civic duty that requires such inconvenience."

"But, sir —"

"Nay, we will not come. Good morrow to you, officer." And Carl Leicester hung up with no further ado.

Klunk!

Harry Teague sat there at his desk steaming. What to do? Wasn't likely that Judge Cramer would issue a subpoena for what was essentially a fishing trip. No way Harry could compel them to submit to an informal lineup.

Check and mate.

Or was it?

CHAPTER FIFTY-TWO

"For murder, though it have no tongue,
will speak."

-Hamlet

As the saying goes, "If the mountain won't come to Mohammed, then Mohammed must go to the Mountain." Det. Harry Teague couldn't convince Carl and Bob Leicester to come to Vic Davone, so he decided to bring Slick Vic to them. If that didn't work, he'd ask Judge Cramer for a subpoena requiring them to produce their cufflinks. See if one was missing.

"Fortunately, this is the afternoon I close the shop each week," Vic rambled on as Harry Teague drove him to Burpyville in the police cruiser. "Otherwise, it would be costly for me to do this. I have steady customers who depend on me."

"Uh-huh."

"Snippets Inc. only uses clippers. Razor's Edge does a smooth razor cut. There's a big difference. That's why I get so many customers – that and my singing."

"Uh-huh."

"How do you like the haircut I gave you the other day? Better than those cuts you were getting over in Burpyville, I'd bet."

"Downtown Barbershop was convenient. Just down the street from the Burpyville Police Department when I worked there. I got used to Gino Giacometti cutting my hair. He was good."

"Well, now that you're on the Caruthers Corners force, you oughta patronize local businesses. Forget Gino. You start coming to me regular and I'll take care of you."

"Yeah, sure."

"Am I going to be looking at a police lineup? Y'know, with a one-way mirror and the suspects lined up in front of me like in *Usual Suspects* – that's one of my favorite movies."

"No, nothing like that. This will be an ambush meeting. We're going to the hotel where they're staying and knock on their door. You take a quick look, identify the guy whose hair you cut, and we walk away. Wham-bam thank you, ma'am."

"Gotcha. I can do that."

What Harry didn't mention was he'd likely arrest the man Vic identified, else it would be impossible to tell one twin from the other. Suspicion of murder ought to satisfy Judge Cramer.

The rest of the ride into Burpyville, Slick Vic treated Harry to a mellow rendition of "Strangers In the Night" – Frank Sinatra's "dooby dooby doo" phrasing.

~ ~ ~

Carl and Bob Leicester had no inkling that Det. Harry Teague was headed their way. Creatures of habit, they went about their day in the usual way, settling at their regular table in the corner of the dining room and sipping the hotel's thick black coffee as they played backgammon. Carl was the better player, but more careless. His brother usually won. They played for money – Monopoly money – and Bob was several hundred thousand dollars ahead. Any time Carl fell short of these fake funds, he simply bought another Monopoly set and threw away the board. Each Monopoly game comes packaged with $20,580 in assorted bills.

Today, Carl was playing with IOUs. He planned to find a nearby Toys R Us later in the day to replenish his treasury.

Bob kept his ersatz winnings in a cigar box. Sometimes, Carl stole money from his brother's colorful Don Diablo Premiums box. Bob knew it, but pretended he didn't. In truth, everything they owned was community property – interchangeable between the twins whether it be clothing, shoes, used chewing gum, or Monopoly money. Often, on the road, they swapped off roles from night to night in various plays.

However, there was a certain division of labor between them. In school, Carl stole the test answers; Bob took the tests for both of them.

Thanks to their Aunt Ceci, they'd had the best education – boarding schools, private academies, Juilliard. Uncle Jeff had shelled out for tuition and other fees like a human ATM, thanks to their Aunt's relentless pressure on him. Nothing but the best for "her boys."

They had grown up with no sense of responsibility. Acting was all they knew. Now in their 30s, they were insipient sociopaths with no sense of right and wrong.

So what if some small-town cop wanted to interview them? To them, life was but a game of Catch Me If You Can.

~ ~ ~

Herbert Phillip Godfrey Golding was no fool. He'd been giving some thought to the death of Adolphus Anderson – and to that of his brother Agamemnon, too. He was not sadden by either's demise. They were horrible men who deserved nothing less. But he was not buying into that heart attack theory. Two brothers dying from a myocardial infarction within a week of each other was well beyond reasonable coincidence. Something fishy was going on here.

He knew this would not fare well for him. Having been fired by Agamemnon Anderson a day before his death would put Herbie on the list of people with a possible motive. No way was he going to let some hick cops pin the man's ill-timed demise on him.

What's more, a rudimentary investigation would likely turn up the surveillance tape that captured him with his hand in the cookie jar. If they didn't get him for murder, they would surely nail him for Grand Larceny. In Indiana, any amount of stolen money over $750 constitutes a Level 6 felony. That draws a fine up to $10,000 and imprisonment up to 2½ years.

Even worse, a homicide conviction could pull a life sentence – or the death penalty!

No way was he going to do jail time. Or hang.

Quickly packing his bags, he left by the hotel's back stairway, walked the three blocks to the Burpyville Municipal Bus Terminal, and bought a ticket to Cleveland. He'd picked the destination out of thin air.

That jerk Larry Linklater could have his room for all he cared.

~ ~ ~

Laurence Octavius Linklater was upset. He'd had enough of the Merry Times Players. Agamemnon Anderson had hired him under false pretenses. No fancy room had been waiting for him. The promised advance never materialized, just some lame excuse about money being tied up in a local bank.

Now Agamemnon was dead! And the Friday night performance of *A Midsummer Night's Dream* had been canceled. There was no guarantee of his future employment.

Larry wasn't a man to wait around for things to sort themselves out. He'd immediately phoned the manager of The Bard's Traveling Road Show and begged for his old job back. Then he packed his bags and vacated the cloakroom where he had been forced to bunk down in leu of an available room.

He hoofed it over to the bus terminal to book a ticket back to Phoenix. Low on cash, he couldn't afford to fly.

And whom should he bump into at the ticket counter? – that talentless hack, Herbert Golding.

"Hail, Larry, old friend, what are you doing here," Golding greeted him.

Sitting down his bags, Laurence Linklater wiped his brow and said, "Going back to the Road Show. I've had enough of this circus. And you?"

"I've got an offer from a dinner theater in Cleveland," he lied. "That's why I resigned."

"Yes, of course. I cannot blame you for abandoning this sinking ship."

"Opportunity awaits," Golding added awkwardly. It was obvious that Linklater didn't believe him, but who cared what this pompous twerp thought.

"Too bad Agamemnon died on us."

Golding nodded his agreement. "Yes, it was bad timing. You arrived much too late, and I am leaving far too soon."

"Fate plays what games it will," sighed Linklater. "I'm sure Cleveland holds a good future for you."

"Indeed, I look forward to it," he stuck with the lie.

As they sat there on the hard waiting room benches, Herbie Golding began to formulate a plan: What if he waited till the bus was ready to leave, then locked Larry Linklater in the men's room and stole his ticket to Phoenix? When he got there, he could tell the Traveling Road Show's manager that Larry wasn't coming, that he'd sent him in his stead. The Bard's Traveling Road Show was a decent Shakespearean troupe, it would make a good home for him. Bumping into Larry had been a stroke of luck.

"*'Fortune brings in some boats that are not steered,'*" Herbert Golding later muttered to himself as he climbed onto the bus. He was sure that he would like Phoenix.

~ ~ ~

Harvey Wallberg was moping in his room. He was finding that managing a traveling roadshow had its downsides. It had looked so easy when Addy Anderson did it. Wallberg had confiscated the Merry Times booking list, those venues that were part of the company's regular cross-country tour. But one-after-one he was getting postponements and cancellations, the result of bad publicity from having had two lead actors die within a week of each other. People were calling it "some kind of Macbeth curse."

Thing was, Harvey believed that was true – sort of. Everybody in the theater knew about the curse. He had even explained it to Police Chief Crenshaw. Did it matter who had helped it come to pass? Were we all not tools of fate?

He slammed down the phone in frustration. Kansas City had just given him a "no." So had Wichita and St. Lewis. His head was pounding. His throat was dry. Maybe he was coming down with something – the flu, maybe. Or perhaps it was just stress. He'd had no idea that managing this ragtag band of thespians would be so challenging. Perhaps his ambition had gotten the better of him.

Buttoning his waistcoat, he headed down the stairs to get a cup of coffee. The dining room had a help-yourself urn of coffee for hotel guests. A little caffeine would do wonders, he told himself. Settle his nerves.

As he passed the front desk, the manager called his name. "Mr. Wallberg, a moment please."

Harvey Wallberg whirled on the pipsqueak, taking in his Ichabod Crane physique and oversized ears. The red bowtie looked like something you'd find on a ventriloquist's dummy. "What now?" he snapped. "Can you not see I'm on a mission to wet my whistle. Too bad this donkey's stable does not have a true bar. An alcoholic libation is called for, dare I say?"

Robert Bob Roberts Jr. spoke firmly. "Mr. Wallberg, about the Merry Times bill—"

"What bill?"

"Your payment for the hotel rooms, it's due."

Wallberg took a step backward, as if confronted by a viper. "Blessed fig's end! Are you not running a tab?"

"I can't do that. The Merry Times credit card was blocked upon Mr. Adolphus Anderson's death. And the credit card produced by Mr. Agamemnon Anderson was declined. I'm afraid we will have to proceed on a cash-only basis."

"What say you?"

"If you want to keep your rooms, it will be pay-as-you-go."

"But, my good man, do you not realize the company's bank account has not been turned over to me yet? I have a meeting at the First Third National Bank at 10 a.m. tomorrow morning. I assure you sufficient funds are in place."

"I'm sorry, Mr. Wallberg, but I have no choice but to demand payment. My orders come directly from the hotel's owner – the Burpyville Civic Development Corporation.

Merry Times is occupying 20 rooms, the Highliner's entire inventory."

"Peace, fool, I am not the responsible party. Merry Times is not mine to claim. Seek your payment from each occupant. Tell me how much I personally owe and I will deposit that sum upon your desk. How now, is that not a satisfactory solution?"

"Well, I guess so." Robert Bob cursed this turn of events. Rather than dealing with one responsible party, he would now be relegated to chasing down a score of flaky actors, some of whom would pay him with crumbled dollars and pocketsful of loose change, others camping homeless in the lobby or crashing in their colleague's rooms.

Chaos awaited!

CHAPTER FIFTY-THREE

"Cry havoc and let slip the dogs of war."
-Julius Caesar

Harry Teague and his witness arrived at the Highliner Hotel in the middle of this madness. Actors and stagehands crowded the lobby, yelling, screaming, and pounding on the front desk. The manager looked like a frightened bird, a whooping crane with molting feathers. His red bowtie was askew.

"What's going on here?" Harry asked a man that he recognized as Tom Turlington, the actor who had played the Queen of the Amazons. His face had been in the photo lineup he'd showed Vic.

"Bastard's trying to kick us out. Didn't give us any warning. Just demanded payment out of the blue. I was told our rooms had been paid for in advance."

"Sorry to hear that, but I'm looking for the Leicester twins. I don't see them in this unhinged pandemonium."

"Saw them in the dining room earlier. I think they were planning to abandon this sinking ship and go stay someplace else. They have a relative who lives somewhere around here. She offered to put them up, they said."

Harry turned to Slick Vic. "You stay right here. Don't move an inch. I'm going to check the dining room."

"But –"

"Do as I say," the policeman ordered.

Harry Teague disappeared through an arched doorway.

"Wait," Vic feebly called after him. He didn't like being left in this madhouse, people yelling and shoving and acting crazy. But Harry was gone.

~ ~ ~

Estelle Grady was rising on the Quilters Club's list of suspects. Or Persons or Interest, as Bootsie called them.

Who would have thought? She'd seemed like such a nice lady, Sissy's favorite teacher.

Lizzie was upset that Mrs. Grady had not even appeared on the original report prepared by her private investigator. She was debating whether or not to refuse to pay him for shoddy work. Odell Lumley had not been cheap at $400 an hour. She expected more for her money. How could Lumley have missed the woman. She had been in a play with the victim. Could she have been a former girlfriend? Was there bad blood between the two? Could she have put poison in his Chicken Chasseur?

It would seem so.

Nonetheless, Lizzie advocated caution. She didn't want to repeat their *faux pas* with that park ranger.

Bootsie thought there was enough "circumstantial evidence" to charge Estelle Grady with a crime. She wanted to take the case to her husband, have Jim haul the woman in. *Lock her up!* as the chant goes.

Cookie wasn't so sure. She proposed more research. Checking out Mrs. Grady's curriculum vitae, talking to her references (surely she had to submit some to get hired at the High School), speaking to her neighbors in Wabash Acres.

Digging for more clues. Taking no chances of making a false accusation.

At this point, Maddy wanted hard evidence. So she suggested they stake the woman out, see what Mrs. Grady was up to, where she went, whom she met, what she did. If she had poisoned those two actors, might there not be a third person on her hit list? Were the Leicester twins in jeopardy? Was their visit to her house a case of the spider luring flies into its web? And what about Harvey Wallace Wallberg or Tom Turlington – were they in any danger?

"That a good idea," said Bootsie. "We do need eyes on. No telling whom that woman might poison next."

"Your husband warned us not to stalk people," Cookie reminded her friend.

"Staking someone out is not stalking," argued Bootsie. There being a distinction in her thinking.

"Good luck convincing Jim Purdue of that," scoffed Lizzie.

"We don't need my husband's permission," replied the pudgy brunette.

"Okay, okay," conceded Cookie. "How do we go about it?"

"Staking her out's gonna be tricky," advised Bootsie. "There's not much hiding space there on Bluebird Lane."

"True," agreed Cookie. "She would certainly spot us if we hung around too long. We'd be pretty visible parked at the curb up the street from her house."

"There's got to be a way," insisted Maddy.

"Hm, I have an idea," said Lizzie. "Let me make a phone call."

CHAPTER FIFTY-FOUR

"By her he had two children at one birth."
-Henry VI

Harry found the dining room empty except for a plump gray-haired woman wiping a table with a rag. "I'm looking for the twins," he said to her, flashing his police ID.

"You just missed 'em," she replied, inspecting the silver badge nervously.

"Where did they go?"

"Dunno. Said something about visiting their aunt."

He looked around the room. "Where is everybody?"

"Out front rioting. Didn't you see 'em? They gone berserk. Somebody's gonna get hurt. My son has called the police."

"Your son?"

"Robby Junior – he's the manager. Them crazy actors don't want to pay him for their rooms. To heck with them, I say. Let 'em spend the night in jail if they want a place to stay."

Just then Slick Vic stumbled into the dining room, breathing heavily, eyes wild. "There you are," he shouted at Harry. "I thought you'd abandoned me. Those people out there have gone freaking insane. They're trashing the lobby, breaking chairs, overturning furniture. I think they're going to lynch that desk clerk."

"The police are on the way. Let's get out of here."

"But you're the police."

"This is not my beat. Let the Burpyville cops do their job."

The plump woman spoke up. "What about my son? Are they gonna hurt him."

"I expect so. But I doubt they'll actually lynch him. They're just angry about being kicked out of their rooms. The police will sort it out."

"W-where are we going?" gibbered Vic Davone.

"To find the twins."

~ ~ ~

William Shakespeare was father to twins, Hamnet and Judith. So it's not surprising that twins should appear as themes in two of his more popular plays.

In *The Comedy of Errors* and *Twelfth Night*, the plots revolve around identical sets of twins.

As a summary puts it:

Set in the Greek city of Ephesus, *The Comedy of Errors* tells the story of two sets of identical twins who were accidentally separated at birth. Antipholus of Syracuse and his servant, Dromio of Syracuse, arrive in Ephesus, which turns out to be the home of their twin brothers, Antipholus of Ephesus and his servant, Dromio of Ephesus. When the Syracusans encounter the friends and families of their twins, a series of wild mishaps based on mistaken identities lead to wrongful beatings, a near-seduction, the arrest of Antipholus of Ephesus, and false accusations of infidelity, theft, madness, and demonic possession.

And this:

Twelfth Night, or *What You Will* centers on the twins Viola and Sebastian, who are separated in a shipwreck. Viola (who is disguised as Cesario) falls in love with the Duke Orsino, who in turn is in love with Countess Olivia. Upon meeting Viola, Countess Olivia falls in love with her thinking she is a man.

Twins provided Shakespeare a plot device that allowed for "foils, doubles, misprised identity, and gender confusion."

Of course, the boy and girl twins in *Twelfth Night* are sometimes referred to as "Shakespeare's medical mistake." Today, we know that you can't have identical twins of different genders, but in Shakespeare's day this wasn't fully understood.

The first recorded performances of both plays were at London's Inns of Court – *The Comedy of Errors* in 1594 and *Twelfth Night* in 1602. In both plays, twins are the protagonists. Shakespeare's fictional twins are complex and entertaining, and they make for some great theatre.

As youngsters, Carl and Bob saw a clear career path in theater, specializing in *The Comedy of Errors*. Who better to play twins than twins?

~ ~ ~

"Found the records with Enterprise," reported Police Chief Frank Crenshaw. "One Carl Castor Leicester rented a silver 2022 Toyota Corolla three weeks ago at the Burpyville Regional Airport. He listed a second driver, Robert Pollux Leicester. They used a credit card belonging to Estelle Fiona Grady – a Visa. Car is due to be returned at the end of the week."

"That confirms that," said Chief Purdue. "The twins were driving a Corolla."

"Yeah, but it doesn't put them in that car on your surveillance tape."

CHAPTER FIFTY-FIVE

"Then I, and you, and all of us fell down,
Whilst bloody treason flourish'd over us."
-Julius Caesar

Estelle Grady was surprised when she heard a car pull up in the driveway. She wasn't expecting any company. Had Jeff come home early from work? Or maybe that lady from the Historical Society had come back with more questions about her ancestors?

But it was neither. When she looked out the picture window, she recognized the silver Toyota Corolla as the rental car Bob and Carl were driving. Had they forgotten something on their last visit?

She opened the door before they could knock. "Boys, what are you doing here? I thought you were going to lay low at the hotel."

"Perchance can we stay temporarily with you? The Highliner has kicked us out of our rooms, those varlets."

That had been Carl. She was one of the few people who could tell them apart. His eyes were a tiny bit farther apart than Bob's. He had that freckle near his ear. And his voice was slightly higher pitched, not that anyone else would notice.

"Come in, come in," she ushered the boys inside, shutting the door firmly behind them. "I will phone Jeff to let him know we will be having company. He will be happy to hear it. You boys are his favorite nephews."

"We are his *only* nephews."

"True, true."

"The Highliner has evicted everybody," said Bob. "It caused a riot. We slipped out without paying for our rooms. Just grabbed our bags and ran."

"Maybe we should park our car in the garage where no one will spot it," suggested Carl.

"Why would you be worried about that?"

"We are afraid the police might be onto us," answered Bob. "When we were leaving the hotel, we saw a cop car pull up."

"Pish," said the woman. "That was likely police called by the hotel to evict everybody."

"No, we don't think so. It was a Caruthers Corners cruiser, not a Burpyville unit."

Mrs. Grady shook her head. "Unfortunately, you can't get your car into the garage. The panel truck is still parked in there – remember?"

"That truck belongs to Merry Times," said Bob. "We need to get it back over to the Highliner, leave it parked on the street so the police will find it there where it is supposed to be. Not likely they would associate it with us if they find it there."

"Best you wait till dark, so no one will spot you. I will have Jeff follow you over, give you a ride back. Then you will be able to put your rental car in the garage."

"I'm not sure why we're skulking around," declared Bob. "Other than skipping out on our hotel bill, we haven't done anything wrong."

"Aunt Ceci did. And we know about it. That makes us accessories after the fact."

"Oh."

"And what about that other thing?"

"Oh that. Yes, we had best get rid of the truck."

~ ~ ~

"Can you see anybody?" asked Bootsie, crowding toward the big window.

Maddy and Cookie were peeking over the windowsill, a pose like those World War II *Kilroy Was Here* drawings.

"Not since the twins pulled up in that Toyota Corolla," whispered the historian. "They still inside with Estelle Grady."

Lizzie stood toward the back of the room where she wouldn't be visible from the outside. "You ladies said you wanted a place where we could stake out the Grady house. Well, here you are," she said proudly, spreading her arms like a spokesmodel showing off a prize on *The Price Is Right* – one of her favorite TV programs.

"You certainly delivered," smiled Maddy. "We couldn't have a better vantage point."

The four women were watching from the house directly across the street from the Gradys. Being the largest stockholder in Caruthers Corners Savings & Loan, Elizabeth Kay Ridenour (née Bergamachi) had simply phoned Edward Durkin, the bank's straight-laced manager, and asked him if he had foreclosed on the house for sale at 338 Bluebird Lane, and if so could she pick up a key? Easy as that.

"Hold on," called Maddy from the window. "I see someone. It's Estelle Grady moving around in the living room. She just walked to the picture window and looked out, as if she's expecting somebody."

"Probably her husband," said Bootsie.

Maddy observed, "It's a little early for him to get home."

"Where does he work?" asked Lizzie.

"ZapData," said Cookie. Her perfect memory kicking in. "Jefferson Archer Grady was hired as its manager earlier this year. There was an article about it in the *Burpyville Gazette* on January 12, 2022. That was a Wednesday. The article was on page three. Byline was by a reporter named Ralph Wrightson. He won an Indiana State Press Association award for Investigative Journalism back in 2014. He was recently named Business Editor of the *Gazette*. ZapData has 23 employees. It recently won a big contact with the US Department of Agriculture."

"Thank you, Ms. Rain Man," jibed Lizzie. She was impressed by her friend's talent. Lizzie could barely remember her own children's names. But they were pretty much estranged, so why bother?

"Look, here comes a car. It's pulling into the Grady driveway," reported Maddy, face pressed against the plate-glass like a kid watching a department-store window display. "A white Honda Accord. A man's getting out. Is that Jeff Grady."

Cookie bent closer to look. "Yes, that's Jefferson Grady. His picture ran with that article in the *Gazette*. Thick glasses, big nose, moustache, receding chin."

"What's he doing?" Lizzie was still standing at the back of the room.

"Looking in the mailbox," answered Maddy. "Mostly flyers. I recognize the weekly brochure from Food Lion."

"They're having a sale on turkey breast this week," Lizzie commented. Her mail came earlier in the day, the vicissitudes of Fritz Berber's erratic mail route.

"He's going inside," Maddy continued the commentary. "His wife greeted him with a kiss on the cheek. I can't see anything else."

~ ~ ~

Jefferson Grady had took the afternoon off at ZD and rushed straight home after receiving his wife's phone call. Truth is, he wasn't all that fond of Estelle's nephews. Those boys were bad news. Acting wasn't a respectable profession, in his opinion. Putting on plays was a childish way of avoiding real work.

Aside from that, he'd heard about a blue panel truck running Maddy Madison off the road this week. Could've killed her. As the mother-in-law of the town's mayor, she was a pretty big deal hereabouts. That van parked in his garage was likely the one local police were looking for. The front bumper was twisted into an S. No doubt, Carl and Bob had something to do with the incident.

But he didn't dare ask, for fear they might tell him. Some things were better not to know.

Just what he needed, to be harboring criminals! He'd only been on his new job for less than a year. Moving to a small town to head a struggling data processing operation had been a risky move. He'd given up a cushy position with Google, not to mention stock options and a good 401k plan. He couldn't afford to lose this job over some picadillo caused by those twits. He'd had enough of their puerile antics.

Although he would never admit it, ol' Jeff was homophobic. He didn't approve of the boys' wayward lifestyle. It was his belief that all actors, ballet dancers, and antique shop owners were gay – deviants who needed the tough love of conversion therapy.

His wife disagreed, coddling the boys as if they were pet poodles rather than grown men capable of earning a proper living. She had been secretly subsidizing their acting ambitions for years. If he had all the money she had spent on them, they could be living in a McMansion on the other side of town. That Melon Hill section was considered an up-and-coming neighborhood, lots of fancy new housing that put the shoddy bungalows in Wabash Acres to shame. But money was tight in the Grady household. He'd taken a cut in pay for some attractive stock options with ZD.

Jeff Grady knew his wife had been an actress before he met her. No doubt working with all those weirdos had warped her judgement. She was much more socially tolerant than he was. To her, the twins' fay ways were "cute." To him, it was a sickness. Jeff had been raised in a Pentecostal household, a conservative family that believed in snake-handling, speaking in tongues, and the punishing fires of Hell. He'd thought his wife could be redeemed, but after 20 years of marriage he still feared for her Immortal Soul.

Jeff was stewing by the time he walked in the front door. "Hurry it up," he ordered. "Let's move that blue van. Sooner it's out of here the better."

"I thought we were going to wait until dark," said Carl.

"Yes, that was the plan," nodded Bob.

"Change of plans," snapped Jeff Grady. "You boys drive the van. I'll follow in my car to give you a ride back. We'll leave van down the street from the Highliner. Let the police find it there. Not here."

"Can't we do it later," whined Carl. "I'm having tea."

"Yes, elderberry tea" said his brother.

"I also have elderberry wine if you prefer that," offered Estelle Grady.

Carl said, "Tea's fine."

Bob added, "And Aunt Ceci made some delish watermelon sandwiches."

"*Hmm*, they are yummy," nodded Carl, his mouth stuffed like a chipmunk's.

"Here, dear, have one," offered Estelle Grady, holding out the plate to her husband. "They are quite tasty. A local delicacy."

"I hate watermelon," he said angrily.

"Then you sure picked the wrong town," laughed Carl.

"That's for sure," chuckled Bob. "This hick town all but worships big red melons."

Jeff Grady growled, "Forget your tea and crumpets and watermelon sandwiches. Let's move that van now!"

"But dear –" his wife began.

"No, we're going to do it my way. As they used to say on that TV Western, 'Head 'em up, move 'em out.' I want to get that van out of my garage – right this very minute!"

~ ~ ~

"Move over, let me look," said Bootsie, scooching in, her wide frame pushing Maddy aside. "There he is. I can see Jeff Grady through the picture window. He's speaking to the twins. He doesn't look very happy. One of the twins is trying to say something, but Mr. Grady cut him off. Now he shouting at the two boys, and his wife is tugging at his arm. Darn, I wish I could hear what they're saying. This certainly doesn't look like a happy Ozzie and Harriet household."

"What if I sneak up to the house and listen from under the window," Bootsie suggested.

"Or you crazy?" said Cookie. "You'd get caught."

"Better hold back and see what happens," cautioned Maddy. "We don't want to tip our hand yet."

"That's right, we gotta be careful," Lizzie said. "They've sent us death threats. They've tried to kill Maddy with that blue panel truck. These people are dangerous."

"Uh-oh, they're coming outside," whispered Bootsie, eyes growing as wide as 50¢ pieces. Her brunette pixie cut was standing up like Buckwheat's.

"Heads down," instructed Maddy. "Don't let them see us."

They watched as Jeff Grady and the twins jockeyed cars around in the driveway, then backed the blue panel truck out of the garage, swapping it for the silver rental car. Estelle Grady waved goodbye as the boys drove away in the truck with her husband following in his white Honda.

"Well, we've found that blue truck," said Maddy.

"Should we try to follow them?" asked Lizzie.

"No, we can't do that," explained Cookie. "Mrs. Grady would see us pull my car out of the garage."

"So we're trapped here?" asked Bootsie. Disappointment crossing her moon-pie face.

"Looks like it, at least for the time being," said Maddy. "Maybe they will come back soon. Otherwise, we'll sneak out of here after it gets dark."

"Oh well," said Lizzie. "Anybody want to play Euchre? I brought some cards."

CHAPTER FIFTY-SIX

"Why, 'tis a happy thing to be the father unto many sons."

-Henry VI

Det. Harry Teague's police cruiser was exceeding the speed limit, but Highway 21 thankfully had little traffic at this time of day. Too late for commercial vehicles, too early for rush hour. Harry was on the radio with Elvina Dobbler, trying to reach the Police Chief.

"He's meeting with the mayor," she told him. "Getting read the riot act, I expect. The Town Council wants to shut down this murder investigation for that dead actor."

"Why so?"

"Bad for the town's image. The Council wants to encourage more tourism. Visitors don't want to worry about getting kilt."

"But we can't just walk away from a murder investigation ..."

"That's the whole point. Ain't no proof nobody murdered that Adoofus Anderson. Doc Medford's sticking by his heart attack ruling."

"What about that guy's brother? Toxicology showed *he* was poisoned."

"Ain't our case. He died over in Burpyville. Let them worry 'bout their own tourism – that's the message we're getting."

"Politics!" He hated getting edicts from on high.

"I hear you, sugar."

Harry glanced nervously at his passenger. Vic Davone was hearing all this. He would be backing away from identifying one of those twins as being the customer who dropped that poisoner's cufflink. Fearful of losing customers if he went against the Town Council's decrees. Better get that ID made quick, before orders came down from the top to drop this line of inquiry. Time was ticking out.

"Elvina, I'm trying to find out if those two actors – Carl and Bob Leicester – have any relatives in this area. An aunt maybe."

"You know Chief Purdue don't tell me nothing about cases."

"C'mon, you sit less than three feet from his office door. You hear everything."

"Not me. I don't hear nothing. My ears are closed, my eyes are shut, my lips are zipped. Just like them three monkeys. But if'n I was you, I'd talk to them Quilters Club ladies. They might be able to answer your question."

~ ~ ~

N'yen Madison was still on his computer. "I'm in," he announced. A broad smile crossing his round tangerine face.

"You just broke through the firewall of an encrypted website?" exclaimed Aggie. "That's illegal."

"Me and my online buddies do it all the time. Last week I was inside Caruthers Corners Saving & Loan. Wanna know how much money N.L. Purdue has in his personal checking account? I can tell you."

That was tempting. Newcomb Lamont Purdue was one of the wealthiest men in town, owner of the EZ Seat Chair Factory. But Aggie knew better than cross that line. "No thank you," she demurred. "Aunt Lizzie would kill you if she knew you were poking around inside her bank's records."

"Beelzebub666 got inside First Third Bank last week. They have a much tighter security than the Savings & Loan. A really good firewall."

"Beelzebub – that's Tommy Truehart, isn't it? He shouldn't be doing that. He's a police deputy, for goodness sake."

"I think hackers are cool," said Sissy.

"Black hats are law breakers," countered Aggie. She wasn't taking any pre-law courses yet, but having a father who was an attorney had drilled certain legal principles into her psyche.

"Do you want to see what I've got here, Miss Goody Two Shoes, or had you rather lecture me on the law? You're not an attorney yet."

"Okay, okay," she gave in. "What have you got?"

"Broke into the DNA database of Ancestor.com, one of the most popular family tree sites out there."

"So?"

"Just as I suspected, many of those egotistic actor types have had their mitochondrial DNA sequenced. Deoxyribonucleic acid carries the genetic instructions for all known organisms. As a result, mtDNA is a powerful tool for tracking ancestry through females. It can accurately trace lineage back through hundreds of generations."

"Which actors are you talking 'bout?" asked Sissy.

"I was checking on Estelle Grady's relationship to her nephews. That's when I got the first surprise. She's not their aunt; DNA analysis shows that she's actually their biological mother."

"Do tell," breathed Sissy, staring at the images of double helixes swimming across the computer's backlit screen. She loved scandal.

"No doubt about it," nodded N'yen. "DNA testing is the most accurate technology to determine parentage. The link between Estelle Fiona Bennington Grady and the Leicester twins is indisputable. The probability of parentage comes up as 99.99%."

Aggie wrinkled her brow. "You said first surprise – what's the second?"

"Adolphus Everly Anderson was on the database too. Turns out, he's the twins' father."

CHAPTER FIFTY-SEVEN

"Run when you will, the story shall be changed ..."
-A Midsummer Night's Dream

As Harry Teague raced toward Caruthers Corners, he spotted a blue dot on the horizon. A small truck heading toward him. It was going the speed limit, but at the cruiser's 70 MPH the dot grew into a 2.74-ton Chevrolet Express Cargo Van in the blink of an eye.

"Holy crap," exclaimed Harry as the truck zoomed past. "Wasn't that those Leicester twins behind the wheel?" He'd not met them face-to-face, but he'd poured over their pictures enough with Vic Davone to have their images burned into the circuits of his brain!

Slick Vic paused in his crooning "It Had to Be You." Looking around dreamily, he replied, "Didn't notice."

"That was a blue panel truck, just like the one that hit Maddy Madison's Audi. It had to be the same van. I could see damage on its front end."

Just then, the police cruiser whooshed past a late-model Honda Accord, a white hatchback driven by a single white male. Was it following the panel truck? Sure looked like it.

"I'm turning around," Harry said, hitting the brakes. The Ford Police Interceptor left a dark C of burnt rubber as he spun the wheel.

"Wooooooo," exclaimed his passenger, holding onto the cruiser's interior grab bar for dear life.

Harry felt his shoulders strain against the strap of the seat harness, a force of 5g making it momentarily difficult for him to breathe. Stomping on the gas, he felt the Interceptor jump forward. Flipping the switch, the vehicle's overhead light bar began to flash a staccato red and blue. The siren sounded like the wail of a banshee as he gave chase.

Up ahead, the white hatchback began to pull over, but the blue panel truck seemed to speed up. Foolish if they tried to run. A Ford Interceptor can go from 0 to 60 in 5.5 seconds. It can reach 100 mph in 13.4 seconds – the top speed exceeding 150. A Chevy Express would be lucky to hit 119 going downhill.

The cop car was closing in fast. Siren blaring, it passed the white car, pulling up behind the panel truck like a hound after a hare.

After a short distance, the panel truck gave it up and pulled over. Det. Harry Teague screeched the cruiser to a stop and exited the vehicle. He approached the truck carefully, his hand on his service revolver. Back in the cruiser, Vic Davone was hiding on the floorboard.

One of the Leicester twins – was it Carl? – stuck his head out of the driver's side window of the van and called, "Hello there, officer. Those lights gave me quite a start. I was trying to move out of your way."

Yeah, right, thought Harry.

"Would you gentlemen please step out of the vehicle?" he instructed in his stern cop's voice.

"Certainly, 'tis no problem."

As the two men climbed out of the panel truck, Harry noticed the white Honda Accord pass them at a crawl. A rubbernecker ... or had the car been traveling with them as he'd thought. He made a mental note of the driver: a middle-aged man, graying at the temples, glasses over a bulbous nose, moustache. Reminded him of one of those novelty disguises you used to see advertised in comic books.

"Put your hands against the truck and lean forward," he said. "Stay there while I check your front bumper."

"Is this necessary?"

"Do as I say, please."

Moving to the left, he leaned forward at an angle to glance at the bumper and grill. The damage was apparent, twisted chrome and crumpled metal. No doubt this was the truck that had struck Maddy's car. He was sure paint samples would confirm it.

"I'm afraid I'm going to have to put you boys under arrest," he told them. "Suspicion of hit and run. Let me read you your rights –"

CHAPTER FIFTY-EIGHT

"Like a liar gone to burning Hell."
-Othello

Police Chief Jim Purdue paced back and forth. Det. Harry Teague watched silently. Myrtle Dobbler sat at the front counter, tapping her fingers, her dispatcher's duties forgotten.

"We have to play this carefully," the Chief was saying, mostly to himself. "That truck is definitely the one that hit Maddy's car. You can tell by the paint scrapings. But the trick is placing those Leicester boys at the scene. They claim the truck is owned by Merry Times and was used by all of the actors at will. Said it already had the dent when they picked it up yesterday."

"Maddy said she didn't see the driver, so that leaves the case against the twins purely circumstantial," Myrtle spoke up. Her and Elvina's online University of Phoenix law studies coming to bare.

Jim Purdue shook his shiny head. "They give each other alibis that they were in their room at the Highliner Hotel at the time of the hit-and-run. We've got nada."

"Where is Mrs. Madison?" asked Harry, breaking his silence. He hated to see a "clean bust" get tossed aside for lack of an eyewitness. "Maybe she saw more than she remembers. We could get Ernst Hegler to use his hypnotic techniques to enhance her memory."

"That won't work. Hegler and his sister are out of town, a visit to the Magic Castle in Los Angeles. He's a member, y'know." For most of his life Ernst Hegler had been known by his stage name, The Great Wizardini. Both a hypnotist and stage magician, he and his sister had settled down at the Hoople Senior Living Center.

"Maybe we should interview Mrs. Madison again anyway. She might come up with something she hasn't told us before."

"Good idea, but who knows where Maddy might be. She and my wife and those other two snoops are off looking for clues. Col. Mustard in the Library with a Lead Pipe for all I know."

"Vic Davone identified Carl Leicester as the actor whose hair he cut. Said he never forgets one of his razor styling jobs. And Carl admitted he lost a cufflink. Asked for it back."

"May as well give it to him. Vox couldn't find anything to link it to Adolphus Anderson's death. No trace of poison. Clean as a whistle."

"How about you, Chief. Do you think Carl and Bob Leicester are connected with the murder of those two actors?" pressed Harry.

"A good chance," replied Jim Purdue. "Adolphus and Agamemnon Anderson were their bosses. Maddy and the Quilters Club were investigating those deaths. These boys likely ran her off the road – that's attempted murder in my book. You try to kill one person, you'd likely be willing to kill others."

"But you can't prove anything," repeated Myrtle.

The Chief scowled. "Don't you have any paperwork to do?"

"Just on those two boys locked up back there in the cell – less you plan on cutting them loose for lack of evidence."

Harry Teague was trying to hold onto his collar. "If you let 'em go, they're a flight risk."

"Maybe so, but any good lawyer could spring them in twenty seconds with a writ of *habeas corpus*. Judge Crammer would release them without thinking twice."

"Okay, okay," Harry gave up his argument. "But we need to hang onto the Chevy cargo van we impounded. It's evidence of a crime ... whether they committed the deed or someone else did."

"Where is the van?"

"I had Buddy Flynn tow it in. It's sitting in that fenced-in lot behind his Texaco station."

"What about them twins?" repeated Myrtle Dobbler. You'd think she was their Public Defender.

Chief Purdue sighed. "Go ahead and release Carl and Bob Leicester," he said to Harry Teague. "We'll keep the van. See if there's any place they want you to drop them off."

~ ~ ~

Aggie reached her Grammy on her cell phone. "You won't believe what we turned up on Ancestor.com," she said.

"What *I* turned up," N'yen was shouting in the background.

"What the three of us turned up," she corrected her statement, winking at Sissy Jackson.

"And what's that, dear?"

"Something surprising about Mrs. Grady."

"Oh, really? We're staking out her house right now. Lizzie got us into an empty place directly across the street from 327 Bluebird Lane. I can see right into her front window."

"Well, hold onto your socks. Estelle Grady is not the aunt of those two actors, Carl and Bob. She's actually their mother."

"What?"

Aggie repeated her statement.

"You don't say? Talk a little louder. I'm putting you on speaker phone. I want the others to hear."

She repeated herself again.

"You found this on Ancestor.com?" came Cookie's voice.

"Right. The info was in their DNA database."

"And how did you get into the Ancestor.com database?" asked Maddy. Then added, "No, never mind ... don't answer that!"

"There's more," continued her granddaughter. "Something even bigger."

"Bigger than that?"

"Yes," affirmed Aggie. "Turns out, the father is none other than Adolphus Everly Anderson. Seems Cecelia Connors – that was her stage name – and Adolphus Anderson appeared together in a Broadway production of *Macbeth* some 30-plus years ago. She was Lady Macbeth, he was Banquo's Ghost. Looks like she got a little too much of the spirit in her."

"Aggie!" chastised Maddy. But she had to recognize that her granddaughter was 19 now, almost a grown woman. How time flies.

"Sorry, but you get the drift. Ceci Connors had a pair of love children by her co-star. Raising them pretty much derailed her acting career."

"Addy Anderson didn't step up to the plate?" That was Lizzie's voice in the background. She loved hot gossip.

"Apparently not."

N'yen chimed in. "She passed them off as her sister's children. Married Jefferson Grady a few years later. Switched to teaching. She'd have a lot to be angry about, dontcha think?"

~ ~ ~

At that moment, Harvey Wallace Wallberg was sitting in a jail cell in Burpyville. He was accused of assaulting hotel manager Robert Bob Roberts Jr. during a riot at the Highliner Hotel. Five actors had been arrested in the fracas.

"Zounds! Let me out of here," shouted Harvey Wallberg, hands gripping the bars as if he were about to shake them. "This is all a horrid mistake. I'm a world-renown Shakespearean actor, not a backstreet thug."

"Quiet in there," ordered Deputy Homer Woodall. He had jail duty today. Chief Crenshaw liked to rotate his officers – patrol, desk, guard duty.

"I want a lawyer."

"You got one phone call," responded Deputy Woodall. "Know any lawyers?"

"Unfortunately not. I'm new to this one-horse town."

The Deputy stepped close to the bars and handed Harvey a card. "Call this guy. He'll do you right. Name's Wentworth."

"Gee thanks."

"Just trying to be helpful."

"Why are you doing this for me?"

"I'm a patron of the arts. Admire your acting," said Homer Woodall. But the truth was, he got paid a generous stipend for every client he sent to J. Harold Wentworth, Esq. It was a good sideline. He kept a stack of the lawyer's business cards in his desk.

~ ~ ~

J. Harold Wentworth maintained a hole-in-the-wall law office near the Burpyville Police Department. A convenient location – like Willie Sutton explaining why he robbed banks, because that's where the money is. Well, the jail in back of the PD was where crooks needing a lawyer were found.

The johnny-on-the-spot attorney had Harvey Wallberg and his fellow actors out within a half hour. They paid him with promissory notes, essentially liens against their next performance.

Now there had to be a *next* performance.

Fortunately, Harvey Wallberg had a plan. Claiming to be manager of the Merry Times Players, he hired Wentworth to sue the town of Caruthers Corners for canceling subsequent presentations of *A Midsummer Night's Dream*. Merry Times had a contract, he insisted.

Taking the job on contingency, Harold Wentworth described it as a "Let Them Play or You're Gonna Pay" case. He thought that would make a good headline for the *Gazette*. Now if he could bully the mayor into reinstating the performances, nearly the entire purse would be his. If not, he got 50 percent of any settlement.

What the heck, he told himself. It was worth a shot. He would drive over to Caruthers Corners and discuss the matter *mano-a-mano* with the mayor. Explain that reinstating the Merry Times performance was for the civic good. Either that, or face a major breach of contract lawsuit. The threat usually worked, he'd found. Most folks wanted to avoid going to court.

CHAPTER FIFTY-NINE

"Good counsellors lack no clients:
though you change your place,
you need not change your trade."
-Measure for Measure

Shakespeare wrote his plays in iambic pentameter, a rhythm like a heartbeat, with one soft beat and one strong beat repeated five times. Mrs. Grady liked to impart an appreciation of this rhythm to her students, almost like a music teacher at a piano.

She had coached Carl and Bob since childhood, imparting a love of the Bard that had blossomed into a career. They were still young – mid 30s – but showing promise. Being slender and gay, they were mostly relegated to female roles. They played such characters well, but theatrical success required doing lead roles like Hamlet, Macbeth, or Richard III.

In Estelle Grady's opinion, Carl should have a shot at doing *Hamlet* in a few years. He was the better actor. Bob might be able to do the lead in *Romeo and Juliet* – either one. They were honing their talents with the repetitive performances of a road show.

She was thinking of her boys when the police cruiser pulled up outside. Light bar unlit on top, lettering on the side of the black-and-white Ford Interceptor proclaiming: CARUTHERS CORNERS POLICE – SERVE AND PROTECT. A cop in uniform at the wheel –

– and Carl and Bob in the backseat.

Ohmygoodness!

"Jeff!" she screamed to her husband who was sitting there watching TV. "The police are here with the boys. I thought you said they had been arrested?"

"Don't worry, dear. I've already called a lawyer!"

~ ~ ~

Maddy gestured to her friends, "Come here quick. Something's happening over at the Grady house."

The three women were sprawled there on the polished hardwood floor at 338 Bluebird Lane playing Indiana Euchre. Euchre is a trick-taking card game with two teams of two. The Indiana Euchre Deck includes two full Euchre Decks inside one tuck box. Maddy had been paired with Bootsie, but had gotten up to stretch her legs. She was still sore from the wreck of her Audi.

"What?" said Lizzie, throwing down her cards and racing to the window. Not one to be left out of any excitement. "Look, it's a police car."

"Hey, we were winning," whined Cookie at the interruption. With her unusual memory, she always had the edge in card games. No one would play her for money.

Maddy ignored the complaint. "Harry Teague just pulled up in front of the Grady house with – what did you call them, Cookie? – Rosencrantz and Guildenstern in the backseat of his squad car."

"Move over," said Bootsie, scooching her pudgy form between them. "Let me see too."

"Then I win by default," Cookie announced, tossing aside her cards to join them at the window. "That means I'm the official grand champion – the Euchre Queen!"

"Queen for a Day," said Lizzie. Not one to give up easily. "I look forward to a rematch.

~ ~ ~

J. Harold Wentworth was on his way to see the mayor of Caruthers Corners when he got a call on his iPhone from one Jefferson Archer Grady asking if he was available to represent his two nephews. Turned out, they were colleagues of Harvey Wallace Wallberg, his new client. If he played this right, Wentworth told himself, he could be representing the entire Merry Times troupe of actors – a windfall of new clients.

And best news yet, this Grady guy had money. He'd said he was the manager of ZapData, a big-time data processing firm. He could affirm to pay an upfront retainer, 1,000 big ones. So instead of driving into Caruthers Corners to see the mayor, Harold Wentworth veered his smoking oil-burning 2005 Lincoln LS into the gated entrance of Wabash Acres.

The rows of cookie-cutter houses gave him pause. These pre-fab bungalows were small boxy dwellings with single-car garages. Maybe this Grady guy wasn't as rich as he'd seemed, living in a rundown neighborhood like this. At one time, this may have been a posh area, but those days were long past.

He had trouble finding 327 Bluebird Lane. All the street names sounded like something out of an aviary. He got lost several times. Zigzagging through the blocks, he finally stumbled across the right address.

J. Harold Wentworth was surprised to see a police car parked in front of the house he was seeking. Lucky that he'd been near Wabash Acres when the call came in. He pulled up behind the cruiser and waddled across the freshly-cut grass in a direct line to the front door, shouting, "Don't say a word. Take the Fifth. Your attorney of record is here!"

CHAPTER SIXTY

"Let's kill all the lawyers."
-Henry VI

Det. Harry Teague held up his hands. "No need to get excited," he said to Jefferson and Estelle Grady. "I am just giving your nephews a lift. They asked to be dropped off here at your house."

Jeff Grady had already called a lawyer, the only one he could think of – J. Harold Wentworth, the guy he'd read about in the *Gazette* who was suing the town to change its name. Some descendant wanted to rename it Weasleyville or something like that.

He'd remembered the lawyer's moniker because it reminded him of those TV ads for a loan company – J.G. Wentworth. The ads showed passengers on a municipal bus singing opera, the words being, "I have a structured settlement, but I need cash now."

Well, the Grady family needed a lawyer *now*! Jeff was afraid this cop was going to arrest him as an accomplice to that hit-and-run. After all, he'd been spotted following the boys when they were pulled over in the panel truck.

Once again, Harry Teague tried to explain. "Folks, calm down. Carl and Bob have been released from police custody. No need to get excited."

"Why did you bring them here?" exclaimed Jeff Grady. "This is not their home."

"They asked me to bring them here. So I'm releasing them to you, sir. But I feel obliged to tell you they remain Persons of Interest in a hit-and-run incident."

The bespectacled man took a deep breath, released it slowly. "If you've dropped the charges, where's their panel truck?"

"The truck has been impounded, sir. As I said, it was involved in a hit-and-run accident."

"You can't just take that truck."

"Do you own that truck, sir?"

"Uh, no, of course not."

"Does the truck belong to Carl and Bob?"

"Not exactly. The boys merely borrowed it from their acting company. They were returning it when you pulled them over. I was following along behind to give them a ride home."

"You say you were accompanying them ... I thought I recognized the white Honda Accord in your driveway."

"Hey, I was merely there to give them a ride."

"You're saying you weren't suspicious when your nephews dropped by driving a banged-up blue truck immediately following news reports of the mayor's mother-in-law being run off the road by a vehicle exactly like that?"

"We don't listen to the news. Too depressing."

Harry Teague continued. "You weren't curious how the truck got all that front-end damage?"

"I don't ask any questions. My wife asked me to help her nephews."

"Sounds pretty suspicious to me, sir."

"Wait a minute. You're not going to pin involvement in that hit-and-run on me. I don't know how the front of that panel truck got banged up. I was just storing it in my garage as a favor to Carl and Bob."

"So you were helping them conceal a hit-and-run vehicle?"

"No, that wasn't it at all."

"What was it then?"

"I don't have to answer that," he snapped. "You couldn't make a case against the boys, else you wouldn't be dropping them off here. So how could I be an accomplice, if you can't prove a crime?"

"We're still investigating –"

Just then, as if by magic, Jeff Grady heard a voice calling from outside, "Your attorney of record is here. Take the Fifth!"

Talk about providence!

"In here, in here," Grady shouted, flinging open the front door. "This policeman is harassing me and my family."

Harold Wentworth burst into the room, huffing and puffing, arms waving like a wind-up toy. "Don't say another word," he instructed. "Take the Fifth."

"My nephews were involved in a hit-and-run accident. And now he's asking me questions, threatening to arrest me as an accessory."

"Don't say another word," advised Wentworth. A cash register in the back of his head kept ringing *Ca-ching! Ca-ching!* These people were going to need some serious lawyering. They exhibited all the signs of guilt – exactly the kind of client he preferred. Guilty people paid better than the falsely accused. No moral high ground for them.

"About that hit-and-run –" the detective continued.

"Hey, I didn't have anything to do with that crash," shouted Jeff Grady. "That's on the boys." Throwing them under the bus.

"Take the fifth, take the fifth," urged Wentworth.

Harry Teague ignore the nattering lawyer. "Looks to me like you were trying to help your nephews hide the evidence, Mr. Grady. You admitted the van was locked away in your garage."

"I was just doing what my wife told me."

Estelle Grady turned to her husband with an exasperated scowl. "No, you weren't. I told you to wait till after dark when nobody would see you. You've ruined everything, you motley fool."

~ ~ ~

Across the street, the Quilters Club could tell something was going wrong in the Grady house. They had witnessed the abrupt arrival of a man who seemed to be a lawyer, shouting that they should "Take the Fifth!" And they could hear angry shouts and detect a commotion through the large picture window, people racing about and waving their arms.

"Should we call the police?" said Lizzie. Concerned that violence was imminent.

"The police are already here," Bootsie reminded her. "That my husband's deputy inside with them. Don't you see his cruiser at the curb?"

"I meant backup. The situation looks dangerous."

"Surely the Gradys wouldn't dare harm a policeman," said Cookie.

"Don't forget, they may be murderers," offered Cookie.

"You're right," said Maddy. "We better do something."

~ ~ ~

Harry Teague could sense that something was seriously off in the Grady household. Clearly they were hiding something. It was obvious the Leicester twins were behind Maddy Madison's automotive mishap. And the Gradys were knee-deep in this quagmire. Jeff Grady was overreacting for someone who was innocent. No telling what he would do next. The man seemed on the verge of violence. Harry wondered if he was going to need backup.

"You can't prove I knew anything about how that van got banged up," shouted Jeff Grady. "The boys did that on their own. They've never been good drivers."

"Say no more," repeated his lawyer. He turned to the policeman. "I'm advising my clients to take the Fifth."

"No need for that," laughed Harry. "They're not in a court of law. Nor are they under arrest … yet. Where did you get your degree – Trump University?"

Wentworth went red in the face. He looked like an overinflated birthday balloon. "Officer, unless you're prepared to arrest someone, I will have to ask you to leave the premises," he harrumphed.

"Happy to oblige. But I expect I'll be back with a warrant."

The lawyer followed Harry Teague into the yard. "We're going to sue you for undue harassment," he shouted, waving a fist in the air. "We're going to own the town of Caruthers Corners. You wait and see."

Posturing for his new clients.

Det. Harry Teague recognized J. Harold Wentworth. The sleazy ambulance chaser had been a pain in the butt when Harry worked for Burpyville PD. And he was becoming just as big an irritant at Caruthers Corners. Word was, the man was getting disbarred, but something obviously had gone wrong, sparing his fat neck from the chopping block.

"Get off my property or I'm going to bash your head in," shouted Jeff Grady from inside the house. His voice full of rage.

"Mr. Wentworth," the policeman said, "your clients are threatening a police officer. I should advise you that they are on the verge of getting arrested."

"Threatening a police officer? You have no case. I have five witnesses here that will testify otherwise."

"There's more for you to worry about, sir."

"Like what?"

"Simple facts: Carl Leicester and his brother Bob were in possession of a blue Ford van that was involved in a traffic accident. An attempt to commit murder with a motor vehicle. Mr. Grady here admits he's been hiding said van in his garage; that's interfering with a police investigation. This afternoon, he attempted to help them get rid of the evidence by moving the van to another location. And his wife has just admitted her involvement. Can you tell me, Mr. Wentworth, why I shouldn't place your clients under arrest for conspiracy to commit murder, leaving the scene of an accident, and obstructing a police investigation?"

"They have a right to legal representation!"

"And here you are."

Wentworth looked at a loss for words. He sputtered, looking for a snarky reply, something more effective than "Oh yeah!" or "That's what you say!"

That moment passed quickly. The two men looked around at the commotion taking place behind them.

"You're not going to arrest me," shouted Jefferson Grady, coming out of the front door with a baseball bat.

CHAPTER SIXTY-ONE

**"Sound trumpets! Let our bloody colours wave!
And either victory, or else a grave."**
-Henry VI

The Quilters Club poured out the front door of the empty bungalow, coming face-to-face with the Gradys. The couple had followed their lawyer and the policeman into the yard, the twins trailing behind. It looked like a fight was about the break out. Jefferson Grady was carrying a baseball bat. One of the Leicester boys wielded a closed umbrella like a sword; the other balled his fists. Estelle Grady brandished a rolling pin like a cudgel.

"Harry, are you all right?" called Bootsie. Holding a hand over her brow to shield her eyes from the afternoon sun, providing herself a clearer view. She knew she might be called on to testify about this in court.

"Yes, ma'am. At least for the moment," Det. Harry Teague answered. "I was about to call for backup."

"Don't you worry," said Bootsie. "We're here." Squaring her shoulders, she looked ready for combat herself.

"That's right, we're witnesses," nodded Cookie. "If they try anything, we'll testify against them."

"Who are you people?" demanded J. Harold Wentworth. Face still beet-red, nostrils flaring. He was a rounded man who'd obviously had a few hamburgers too many. The vest on his three-piece suit appeared ready to pop a button.

"That's the Quilters Club," scowled Estelle Grady. "What are you ladies doing here?"

"We heard shouting," said Maddy. "We wanted to make sure everyone was all right."

"We're just fine," asserted Wentworth. "Now move along or I will press trespassing charges."

"I'm standing in the street," said Cookie. "That's a public thoroughfare. We're not trespassing."

"But what are you doing here?" demanded Jeff Grady. "This is a private neighborhood."

"My bank owns this house," Lizzie nodded toward the squatty bungalow behind her, the red **FOR SALE** sign prominently visible. "My friends and I were merely inspecting the property."

"That sounds pretty fishy to me," snorted the lawyer. Eyes narrowed.

"Tell it to my husband," said Bootsie. "He's the police chief."

"Chief Purdue?"

"That's right. I came outside to make sure my husband's deputy was okay. Your voices sounded threatening."

"He was threatening *me*," shouted Jeff Grady. "He can't do that in my own home. I've got right to protect my home and family from fascist police."

"Careful what you say," interjected Wentworth. "Your words may be self-incriminating!"

"Harry, are you safe?" called Bootsie.

"I'm okay, Mrs. Purdue," grinned Harry Teague, amused by this confrontation between his boss's wife and these miscreants. He'd been heading for his cruiser to call Tommy Truehart for backup. This was getting out of control – bats and rolling pins and umbrellas.

320

"Mrs. Grady, you and your husband look pretty intimidating," observed Maddy. "I hope you plan to go back inside your house before something happens that you will regret."

"Intimidating?" the woman said, looking down at the rolling pin in her hand. "Not at all. I was just starting to bake a pie."

"Oh? What kind?"

"Uh, well ... I don't know. Apple maybe. Yes, apple."

"Your sons look like they are ready to do battle."

She frowned. "They're not my sons – they're my nephews."

"Not according to Ancestor.com," blurted Cookie. At times she had no filters, saying whatever came to her mind. A particularly delicate quality for someone who never forgets.

Estelle Grady looked shocked, her eyes focusing on the historian. "What are you talking about? Does this have something to do with the genealogy research you've been doing."

"Ancestor.com's DNA database shows that the twins are the progeny of you and Adolphus Everly Anderson."

"W-what?" stuttered Jefferson Grady, turning to stare at his wife. "You never told me that."

"Sons, nephews, what's the difference?" she snapped, giving Cookie an If-Looks-Could-Kill stare.

"You're our mom?" blubbered Carl. Or maybe it was Bob.

"So what? I raised you, didn't I?"

"But you said our mother was killed in a car accident," whimpered Bob. Or maybe it was Carl.

"My sister *was* killed in a ten-car pile-up. She *could* have been your mother."

"But the DNA –?"

"Who believes that scientific gobbledygook?"

"You believed it enough to sign up to Ancestor.com," Bootsie pointed out. "And DNA evidence is admissible in court."

"That gives you a good motive to murder Adolphus Anderson," said Maddy. "The pregnancy ruined your acting career. And Adolphus walked off and left you behind. Luckily, you met Mr. Grady here."

"You never told me," Jeff Grady repeated. "I had a right to know."

"They weren't your sons," she sneered. "What would it have mattered to you?"

"I helped raise them. I paid for their boarding schools. I financed those degrees from Juilliard. We'd be living in a much classier neighborhood if all our money hadn't gone to support these two fops."

"What's your complaint, my dear husband?" she rejoined. "I settled the score. I killed the man responsible. Yes, I poisoned the blackguard who ruined all our lives. "

"Don't say anything else," ordered Harold Wentworth. But nobody was listening to him.

"So you admit you killed Adolphus Anderson?" pressed Bootsie, trying to get Estelle Grady to repeat her words, She wanted to make sure the confession stuck.

"Verily I did. Slipped *Amanita bisporigera* mushrooms into his Chicken Chasseur at the Cozy Café. Can you believe after all these years, he didn't even recognize me – me, the mother of his sons?"

"Stop! Stop!" shouted the attorney. "Say no more!"

But she continued unabated: "Even more ironic, Addy was working day-to-day with his very own sons and had not a clue who they were. His loss. Their blood coursed with his acting talent – plus my own. They could have risen to greatness with his assistance!"

Maddy interjected, "The Quilters Club was hot on your trail. Is that why you had Carl and Bob run me off the road? As a warning? Or were they trying to kill me?"

Estelle Grady looked confused. "But I didn't ask them to do that. They told me and Jeff that they had hit a fence with the Merry Times van and planned to get it repaired on the sly."

"Yes," the woman's husband backed her up. "The boys said they didn't want their new boss – that Agamemnon guy – to find out about the accident for fear he'd fire them."

"But he's dead. Your wife killed him too," Cookie accused.

"I did not!" the woman hissed. "You can hang me for Addy. That I deserve. But I have never even met his brother."

Maddy turned to the twins. "Then, did you boys kill Agamemnon?"

"Foh! T'was not us. But the name of the true murderer eludes our tongues. That we sayeth not!"

"You know the murderer but refuse to identify him?" said Harry Teague.

"Take the Fifth," shouted Wentworth.

"All I'm saying is that we did not kill either of them," said one of the twins. Carl, as it turned out.

"Then why did you two go after me?" persisted Maddy. "You admit that you were driving that blue van."

"That is true," sneered one of the twins. "Best that you had died."

" *'That the false housewife Fortune break her wheel, provoked by my offence,'* " quoted the other.

"You say you were trying to kill me," responded Maddy Madison. "How very rude!"

Bootsie pointed an accusing finger. "You heard them," she shouted. "They've all just confessed. Arrest them, Harry!"

Det. Harry Teague obliged. "Mr. and Mrs. Grady, Carl and Bob Leicester, you are all under arrest. Mr. Wentworth, stand aside. Another patrol car will be here shortly to help me transport your clients to the Caruthers Corners Police Department. We have some nice jail cells waiting for them."

J. Harold Wentworth bellowed, "I must protest my clients' unwarranted treatment –"

"Protest all you like, sir. But keep talking and it may land you in a cell alongside them. Now I need to read them their right."

CHAPTER SIXTY-TWO

"A man can die but once."
- Henry IV Part 2

Harvey Wallace Wallberg found his luggage stacked in one corner of the lobby. He was no longer considered a guest of the Highliner. Now all the rooms in the hotel were empty, the actors expelled.

Presumably, Mrs. Roberts was putting fresh sheets on each bed, tidying up the rooms for future guests. Not that any were expected. The owners didn't seem to care, the hotel merely a placeholder for a future civic auditorium.

Robby Junior did not come out to greet him, probably hiding in the small office back of the counter. Ringing the little domed silver bell brought no reaction. Nor did pounding on the counter and shouting. The facilities seemed deserted.

No one being around, he walked behind the counter, opened the cash drawer and counted out $212 in various denominations. Not much, but it wasn't like the hostelry had had any paying guests lately. The Merry Times Players had proven to be unreliable clientele.

Pocketing the money, he scooped up his bags (all three of them) and carried them down the street to Adolphus Anderson's car. The rusty green Ford Fiesta was still parked in the same spot where he'd left it. Harvey Wallberg unlocked the car, tossed his bags into the back, and slid behind the wheel. Having filched the keys following Addy's death, he now considered the vehicle his – just like Merry Times Players. No more taxis for him!

Last man standing was always the winner. That was the rule.

Off and on, he'd been sharing a rental car with the Leicester brothers. He had taken them under his wing last season, giving them tips, coaching them – in truth, grooming them.

The twins were probably with their aunt, he told himself. They had told him everything about her, how she used to be a stage actress known as Cecelia Connors (he'd never heard of her), how she now taught drama at a local high school, her talent for foraging and cooking, her knowledge of fungi, her impeccable knowledge of Shakespeare's verse. She had been a surrogate mother, visiting them at boarding school (All Hallows Academy in Vermont), hosting them for major holidays, paying for them to attend that excellent Conservatory Program at Juilliard.

It was through them that he had learned about the Destroying Angel, a common white fungi that could kill you with a single taste. That had sparked his dark fantasies. Blame it all on them! They had facilitated his actions.

Now what to do? The Merry Times Players was disbanded, its members scattered to the winds. He had no idea how to hook up with any of them, even if he'd had a mind to do so. Another problem, the police had confiscated his iPhone and in his haste to leave the jail he'd left it behind. No way to call his young friends or anyone else.

Harvey told himself that he needed to get far away from this part of Indiana. Maybe when he could find a phone he'd call The Bard's Traveling Road Show, apply for the slot abandoned by Agamemnon. That would be quite a jest, him replacing Aggy Anderson, the man who had temporarily been his boss. The sweet irony of it all!

The Bard's Traveling Road Show was still in Phoenix, wasn't it? That was far enough away, the other end of the continent. And the climate was good, warmer weather than the capricious Midwest. A climatic circumstance that provided more outdoor touring dates in the winter. Good for the bottom line of paid-per-performance actors.

However, first things first, he needed to find a safe place to light, catch his breath. Then find a way to phone Phoenix. Everything was going to work out after all.

He recited to himself:

"And whether we shall meet again I know not.
Therefore our everlasting farewell take:
For ever, and for ever, farewell,
If we do meet again, why, we shall smile;
If not, why then, this parting was well made."

One of his favorite passages from *Julius Caesar*.

As Harvey Wallberg pulled the purloined Fiesta into the sporadic traffic of Anthony Wayne Avenue, the perfect place to go occurred to him in a flash: a temporary respite that would offer a good night's sleep, a decent meal, a phone. He would join Carl and Bob at their aunt's house.

What was the name of that development? He'd passed it when he took the taxi to see the mayor. Oh yes, Wabash Acres – that was it.

~ ~ ~

Tommy Truehart A/K/A Belzebub666 sent an email to his gaming pal N'yen Madison, an update that had just come over the wire. Tommy knew he would be interested.

"Holy moly," the Asian boy said, "I was wrong."

The missive read:

BISMARCK, NORTH DAKOTA – In an unexpected turn of events, accused murderer Hugo Merriweather Marston has confessed to a second homicide, that of Northwestern University professor Jonathan Livingston Segal.

Dr. Segal's death in a cave in southern Indiana had been ruled accidental, but Hugo Marston's revelation puts the death of the noted expert on troglofauna in a new light. Authorities are reappraising the situation.

"I brained him with a rock hammer," Marston said. "The cops thought he bumped his head on a stalactite. That's a good one on them."

When asked his motive for the murder of Dr. Segal, he simply said, "Same as the one for Rickie Burke. May they both rot in eternity."

As to why he is now confessing to the second murder, he replied, "They can only hang you once. So what's to lose?"

Aggie read the news release over his shoulder, the light of the computer screen reflecting on her freckled cheeks. "We've gotta tell the Quilters Club," she said.

"Tell them what? That I made a big mistake?"

Sissy slapped him on the shoulder. "You found blood on that rock. You were just wrong about how it got there."

"Likely splattered when Marston whacked him with a rock hammer," nodded Aggie. "Fooled us all, not just you."

"A murderer almost went free," he sniffled.

"Better that than the Quilters Club thinking it almost put an innocent man in prison."

"Innocent – I'd punch him in the nose if he were here."

Aggie laughed. "You weigh maybe 100 pounds soaking wet. That park ranger was way over 250. I'm not sure whose nose would get smashed."

"I know *tae kwon do*."

"How? You've never had any martial arts training."

"I read," he said.

"My hero," declared Sissy. "Neesie may be little, but he's smart and quick. I'd bet on him."

Aggie rolled her eyes. "I'll take that bet," she said, trying hard to keep from laughing. "He doesn't have a Black Belt. He doesn't even have a belt. He usually wears suspenders."

~ ~ ~

The three junior members of the Quilters Club passed along the news about Hugo Marston. For some reason, his murder confession made everyone feel better. Maybe it was the restoration of their confidence in being amateur sleuths.

"We got it right," said Cookie.

"I knew he did it," huffed Bootsie.

"I'm so relieved," said Lizzie.

"Solving whodunits is a great responsibility," sighed Maddy.

"Too bad we don't have the great powers to go with it – like Spider-Man," commented N'yen.

CHAPTER SIXTY-THREE

"Why, I can smile and murder whiles I smile."
-Henry VI

The house on Bluebird Lane looked deserted. In fact, it was. The police had carted away Mr. and Mrs. Grady as well as the Leicester twins. The Quilters Club had returned to Maddy's home on Melon Pickers Row to compare notes. The fat attorney was on his way back to Burpyville to apply for a *habeas corpus* for his new clients.

Turns out, Harvey Wallace Wallberg had arrived thirty minutes too late. "Drat!" he said to himself. Had he driven all way out here to the sticks for nothing?

Wallberg walked up to the front door, studying the 327 number to make sure he had the right house. He had written the address on a scrap of paper. He rapped sharply on the door but there was no answer. He tried again, cursed, knocked a third time. Nobody at home.

Undaunted, he strolled around to the back of the house, used his elbow to break the glass in the kitchen door, and let himself in. He would apologize later.

Checking all the rooms, he confirmed that nobody was there. He went to the refrigerator and helped himself to a bologna sandwich, a slice of coconut cake, and a glass of elderberry tea. The coconut cake was tasty, so he had a second slice.

The Gradys had a landline in addition to cell phones. He used the princess phone on the kitchen wall to place a call to Phoenix, but couldn't get through to the manager of The Bard's Traveling Road Show. He told himself he would try again later. He wanted to claim that open slot in the troupe before someone else snatched it up. He felt very confident he could step into Agamemnon Anderson's velvet shoes with the Road Show. That could have happened here if that two-bit mayor hadn't canceled the Merry Times performances. He doubted that the lawyer he'd hired could reverse the decision. Thus, his interest in Phoenix.

Both Adolphus Anderson and his brother had stood in his path to success as an actor. The death of the first brother had made it clear that the demise of the second would remove all obstacles. As William Shakespeare had said, *"The fewer men, the greater share of honor."*

Harvey Wallberg had that Grady woman to thank. If her nephews hadn't told him about how she'd dispatched Adolphus Everly Anderson with her poison mushrooms, he would have never had the nerve to emulate her with his own pickings. Without their tutoring, he could never have told an *Amanita bisporigera* from a *Leucoagaricus leucothite*.

But everything had fallen apart. Bookings disappeared. Money was not available. The actors had been kicked onto the street as if they were tramps rather than celebrated thespians. Where was the fairness in this distorted world order?

He sat down at the kitchen table to contemplate his next move.

What was this? he asked himself as he took another sip of his libation. This wasn't tea. It was a fermented ale – elderberry wine.

Just what he needed.

He took a biiiiig swig.

Heigh, that tasted good. He took another. And another.

~ ~ ~

"We've just wrapped up another murder," said Cookie, saluting them with her chilled glass of watermelon tea. "Estelle Grady confessed to poisoning Adolphus Everly Anderson. Case closed!"

"Congrats to us," agreed Lizzie. Conveniently forgetting that she was the one who hadn't wanted to get involved in the actor's death.

"Yes, Estelle Grady – the former Cecelia Connors – confessed in front of a zillion witnesses," nodded Bootsie. Proud of solving another case ahead of her policeman hubby. One of those Battle of the Sexes things. *Lysistrata* indeed!

"Not quite a zillion," said Cookie, a stickler for accuracy.

"Half a zillion then."

"You can't count their family, so six witnesses. Us and Harry and Jim."

"Myrtle Dobbler heard her repeat her confession at the station."

"Seven then."

"That should stick in court," Bootsie affirmed.

Lizzie bit her lip, flaking the lipstick. A sign of deep thinking. "Mrs. Grady admitted that she poisoned Adolphus Anderson, but she denied killing his brother Agamemnon. Why's that? Like Hugo Marston pointed out, they can only hang you once."

"Maybe the twins did it," surmised Cookie. "The fruit doesn't fall far from the tree. They certainly tried to kill Maddy. They admitted that."

"Then why wouldn't she have taken the rap for them? She seems truly devoted to those boys."

Maddy had been giving it some thought. "That's because this case isn't solved," she declared. "Someone else is involved. Carl and Bob as much as said so."

"Carl – or was it Bob? – just quoted some Shakespeare. These actors always seem to be doing that. Doesn't mean anything," Lizzie waved the idea away. "Who can understand that gobbledygook anyway?"

"No," countered Maddy. "They said more. How did one of them put it? 'The murderer of Agamemnon Anderson eludes our tongues.'"

"That's just Shakespeare talk for taking the Fifth."

Maddy wasn't about to give up her concern. "Look at it this way: Mrs. Grady wasn't anywhere near Aggy Anderson before he died. She couldn't have done it. Ergo, someone else did. Two murders, two murderers."

"But both men were poisoned by Destroying Angel mushrooms. She admitted that's what she used on Adolphus; and that's what the toxicology analysis said killed Agamemnon," Cookie shared her own logic. "That's statistically unlikely to be a coincidence."

"They're connected, yes," conceded Maddy. "But Mrs. Grady didn't do it alone. She couldn't have."

"Like I said, she probably had help from her nephews –"

"– sons," corrected N'yen. He wanted credit for his find.

"They admitted they were the ones who ran me off the road," said Maddy. "They just wouldn't say why. Or who told them to do it."

"They did have possession of that blue panel truck with the banged-up front end," Bootsie pointed out. "It's circumstantial; we can't put them behind the wheel. But Jimbo will get it out of them. He's good at interrogation."

"Does he use a rubber hose?" teased Lizzie.

"Only to water the front lawn," the pump woman smiled.

~ ~ ~

Carl and Bob Leicester were in fact taking the Fifth, thanks to their lawyer's coaching, but under normal circumstances they were quite talkative. Blabbermouths, in fact. They liked to impress people with their wild tales and insider knowledge. Secrets were not the least bit safe with them.

Even such a risky subject as murder.

While drinking at The Bottomless Pit, a neighborhood bar down the street from Highliner Hotel, they had regaled Harvey Wallberg with a Gothic tale of revenge and murder – how their aunt had fed poison mushrooms to an old lover, none other than Adolphus Everly Anderson, owner of the Merry Times Players. Their former boss.

"Gadzooks! She's the one who kilt him? I thought it was a heart attack," Harvey had exclaimed at the time.

That's when they told him about Destroying Angel (*Amanita bisporigera*), a deadly fungus that grew wild in local forests and swamps. All white, with a ring on the stalk and a large, saclike cup around the stalk's base, the bulbous mushrooms are often confused with puffballs (*Lycoperdon perlatum*), a harmless variety of fungi.

"Of the more than 5,000 species of mushrooms, only about 50 are poisonous for humans," they pointed out. "They contain amatoxins and virotoxins. There is no known antidote."

"You guys know a lot about this."

"Not us. Our aunt's the expert."

"Now explain what they look like again," urged the older actor. A plan starting to formulate inside his head.

Harvey Wallberg had no problem finding some 'rooms himself in a quiet copse of trees just outside of town. For $50, Mrs. Roberts had put them in Agamemnon's sugar cream pie. A joke, he'd told her. And once the fatal results became known, she had kept her silence for fear of being charged as an accessory to the Great Man's murder.

When he'd told that doofus policeman and that chink boy how he would go about committing a perfect murder, he was speaking from experience.

Let them prove it if they could.

This reminded him of another quote by the Bard: *"But 'tis common proof, that lowliness is young ambition's ladder, whereto the climber-upward turns his face; but when he once attains the upmost round, he then turns his back, looks in the clouds, scorning the vase defrees by which he did ascend."*

Verily, that about summed it up.

CHAPTER SIXTY-FOUR

"Farewell, a long farewell to all my greatness!"
-Henry VIII

Deputy Tommy Truehart pulled his cruiser to the curb in front of 327 Bluebird Lane. There was a green Ford Fiesta ST parked in the driveway next to the Gradys' white Honda. That was odd. Where did the Fiesta come from? The house was supposed to be empty.

Tommy had been sent over to pick up a few personal items – change of underwear, denture cream, toiletries, and such – for the new prisoners. They had been hauled in without having a chance to pack for an overnight stay (or much longer).

The police department had two small jail cells in back. The Gradys were incarcerated in one, the twins in the other. Chief Purdue had been forced to evict Jasper Beanie, the town drunk, to make room for them. If Judge Cramer refused them bail – highly likely on a murder charge – the Chief would transfer them to Indy. That was common practice. His cramped cells were only good for overnighters.

Approaching the house carefully, hand on the butt of his service revolver, Tommy called out, "Hello. Who's in there?" He was on high alert. The Chief had told him nobody would be there, to lock the door when he left.

A faint voice came from inside: "Go away. No peddlers, no Fuller Brush salesmen!"

"Who's in there?"

"*'Away, you starveling, you elf-skin, you dried neat's-tongue, bull's-pizzle, you stock-fish!'* "

"Police officer. I'm coming inside. I should warn you I'm armed."

"Absent thee from my presence, *'thou clay-brained guts, thou knotty-pated fool, thou whoreson obscene greasy tallow-catch!'* "

Tommy pushed on the door. It was locked. "Open this door or I'll break it in."

"Leave me be, *'thou leathern-jerkin, crystal-button, knot-pated, agatering, puke-stocking, caddis-garter, smooth-tongue, Spanish pouch!'* "

"Sticks and stones," muttered the deputy, kicking at the door with his boot.

Thunk!

Nothing happened.

He tried again with the same results.

Thunk! Thunk!

"Owwww!" he complained. That was an awfully sturdy door for such a shabby house, he told himself. His toe felt broken, despite his thick service boots. "Open up this door or I will place you under arrest for resisting an officer of the law in the rightful execution of his duties!" he shouted at the top of his lungs. People likely heard him all way over on Woodpecker Way.

"Hold on, *'thou abortive, rooting hog.'* I will give thee access."

The lock clicked and the door swung open to reveal a disheveled man in tight pants, waistcoat, and plumed hat.

"W-who are you?" stammered Tommy Truehart. "You can't be a Trick-or-Treater – it's not Halloween yet."

"I am an invited visitor to these premises – Harvey Wallace Wallberg, at your service."

"Oh, you're one of them actors."

The man's face darkened like a thundercloud. "Not one of, but *the* leading actor of the Merry Times Players." That was essentially true, he told himself. He hadn't yet been offered a job with The Bard's Road Show. Nor had he officially resigned his position with Merry Times. With Adolphus and Agamemnon gone, that made him the lead by default – according to his reasoning.

"What are you doing here, Mr. Wallberg?"

"As I said, visiting my friends."

"But there's no one here."

"Alas, they went for a short stroll. Should be back at any moment."

Now Tommy knew the man was lying. Neither the Gradys nor their two boys had gone for a walk. All four were locked behind bars at the Caruthers Corners Police Department.

As Tommy stepped closer, he could smell alcohol on the man's breath. "Sir, have you been drinking?"

"Just a nip of the ol' vino. A man can drink in his own home, can he not?"

"But this isn't your home."

"It's not? Oh, right, this is my friends' home. No, that's not right, it's their auntie's home. As the Bard said, '*Is it thy spirit that thou send'st from thee So far from home into my deeds to pry, To find out shames and idle hours in me, The scope and tenor of thy jealousy?*' "

"I'm going to have to ask you to come to the station with me," said the deputy. "Y'know, to clear this up."

"Clear what up?"

"We have two murders of your fellow actors –"

"I can clear *that* up," he railed. "I only did in the one of them. Carl and Bob's auntie did the other. Simple, see?"

That's when Deputy Tommy Truehart drew his pistol and said, "Sir, I'm placing you under arrest. Let me read you your rights –"

"Yea, do that, thou lily-liver'd boy. But first, I need to have another sip of that delicious elderberry wine."

"Sorry, but –"

That's when Harvey Wallberg caught the deputy with an uppercut, knocking him sprawling into the grass. The sprinkler – *tick*! *tick*! *tick*! – drenched his tan uniform. "What the –?" he groaned, rubbing his chin.

But by then the drunken actor had jumped into the rusty green Fiesta and backed into the street, barely missing the police car, then wheeled up Bluebird Lane at an increasing rate of speed.

He was making an escape.

CHAPTER SIXTY-FIVE

**"The dove pursues the griffin; the mild hind
Makes speed to catch the tiger; bootless speed,
When cowardice pursues and valor flies."**
-A Midsummer Night's Dream

"You wanna drive my bug, d'you?" grinned N'yen Madison. He was very proud of his first car. The 2003 Volkswagen Beetle was in good shape, the 2.0L FI 4cyl engine almost as pristine as the shiny yellow paint job. His Grammy had chosen well.

"I've never been behind the wheel of a Beetle." His cousin Aggie walked around the VW as if inspecting a vehicle on a used car lot. You might have expected her to kick the tires.

"It drives real good," said Sissy.

"He's let you drive it?"

"No, of course not. I don't have a driver's license," she replied. "But it's a mighty smooth ride, I can tell you that."

"What say you let me drive it up Main Street and back?" Aggie suggested.

"No way you're driving it without me along."

"Me too," echoed Sissy.

Aggie sighed, exasperation showing in her knitted brow. "I've been driving nearly three years now. I have my own car, but it's back in New Haven. I know what I'm doing, you idiot."

N'yen held firm. "You wanna try out my bug, me and Sissy come along."

"Okay, gimme the keys," Aggie held out her hand, palm up.

Aggie eased the VW up Main Street, stopping carefully at each red light. With the whirring and grinding of the little 4cyl engine in the rear, she thought it was like driving a washing machine.

Upon reaching the end of South Main, the town limits, where you merged into Highway 21, she gunned the vehicle. 0 to 60 took about 14 seconds, as if moving in slow motion. "Yahoo!" Aggie shouted, but she was being more sarcastic than not.

"Watch it," said N'yen, but he didn't sound overly concerned.

The yellow bug sped along the double-lane asphalt highway, ignoring the posted 55 MPH speed limit. With a long enough run, the VW was approaching 65. "Not exactly a Lamborghini," Aggie said. "But fun nonetheless."

"A Mini Porsche," corrected N'yen, referring to Volkswagen's history of being designed by Ferdinand Porsche to satisfy Hitler's demand for a "people's car," an inexpensive vehicle capable of transporting two adults and three children at 100 km/h (62 MPH), one that every German family could afford.

Traffic was light, only one car heading their way. A green Fiesta, it was weaving all over the road. "Hey, what the heck?" said Aggie. "That guy's gonna cause a wreck."

"Watch out," squealed Sissy. "He's heading straight for us."

As it drew near, N'yen's sharp eyes recognized the driver. "Holy moly, that's that crazy actor we followed – Harvey Wallberg. I think he's recognized our car. He got a good look at it when we followed him the other day."

"He's gonna ram us head-on," shouted Sissy, curling into a ball in the backseat, her uncontrollable reaction to impending danger. "*Eeeeik!*" she screamed.

"Hang on," said Aggie between clenched teeth. Her fantasy of being racecar driver Tony Stewart returning with the blink of an eye. Swinging the steering wheel hard to the right, she slid the VW into a side road that suddenly appeared – the entrance to the old Star-Lite Drive-In Theater, now used as a weekend flea market and site of a Sunday morning ministry.

"Whooa," wheezed her cousin, clinging desperately to the overhead hand grip. Sissy rolled around like a loose ball in the backseat. Aggie wasn't sure, but she thought she may have screamed too. They were lucky the VW didn't turn over with the sharp turn.

"Is that green car still back there?" Aggie shouted.

"Yep, it turned in behind us. Coming on like a bat out of hell." Not that the little agnostic Buddhist believed in an afterlife.

"Well, he's not gonna catch us!"

"I'm not so sure about that. This car's only got a lawnmower engine."

"It's not the car, it's the driver," she replied.

As the VW bounced down the graveled road, Aggie could see a wide field ahead, like a cemetery of abandoned speaker poles. To the right was a tumbledown ticket booth; just to the left, a cement projection booth with adjacent concession stand. A tattered poster on the concession stand's wall advertised the last movie to play here, 2014's *Transformers: Age of Extinction* starring Mark Wahlberg.

A quick glance in the rearview mirror told Aggie that the green Ford had turned into the drive-in theater's entrance, still in pursuit of the Beetle. "What would Tony Steward do?" she asked herself.

When N'yen stuttered, "W-who?" she realized she had been speaking her thoughts out loud.

"Never mind," she snapped. "Just hold on tight."

"Please don't wreck my car!"

"Harvey Wallberg is out to get us, dummy. If that green Fiesta catches up to us, he'll ram it into your precious little car like a torpedo."

"Drive faster," he gulped.

Aggie aimed the VW down a narrow row flanked by silvery speaker poles, an off-kilter grid that allowed parked cars an unblocked view of the screen – not that there was a screen left, just a skeletal frame that used to hold one. Closing in, the green car followed them down the row.

"Okay, here's where it gets interesting," she shouted over the mechanical whine of the engine.

"W-what?"

"Just watch."

Swinging the wheel, she wove the VW between the poles, turning this way, skidding that way, making sharp right turns, impossible left turns, zigzagging in a random pattern. Like driving an obstacle course.

The green car tried to follow. However, Harvey Wallberg was not an experienced driver. And he was still inebriated from those extra helpings of elderberry wine. In short order, he clipped a pole, taking off his side mirror. Then he hit a pole straight-on, busting his radiator – steam billowing from under the rusty hood, blinding the windshield with its roiling cloud.

Just after that, the Fiesta mowed down a half-dozen speaker poles in a row, one finally lodging in the wheel housing, grinding the vehicle to a stop. The 1.6 *EcoBoost* engine clunked to a stop, then burst into flames. In 2017, Ford had recalled all 2014–2015 Ford Fiesta ST vehicles because of a risk of engine fires. The owner of this vehicle must have ignored the warning.

"Keep going," yelled N'yen. "Put some distance between us. That car's gonna explode."

Harvey Wallberg stumbled out of the flaming car and got about ten feet before the Fiesta gave off an ear-splitting roar and was enveloped in a huge orange fireball. Wallberg was knocked off his feet, thrown forward another five feet before being stopped by a metal speaker post.

Sissy uncurled from her ball-like position and said, "Quick, use your iPhone to call the po-lice."

"No need," said Aggie, breathing raggedly. "Here comes Tommy Truehart. The deputy must have been chasing Harvey Wallberg."

"Beelzebub666 to the rescue," grinned N'yen at the sight of his online buddy.

CHAPTER SIXTY-SIX

**"So we grew together,
like to a double cherry, seeming parted,
but yet an union in partition,
two lovely berries moulded on one stem."**
-A Midsummer Night's Dream

Carl and Bob didn't like sharing their cramped cell with Harvey Wallberg. He was as drunk as the worm at the bottom of a tequila bottle. He smelled of alcohol, elderberries, and – strangely, coconut. *"The rankest compound of villainous smell that ever offended nostril,"* as the Bard would have described it. And he displayed a large purple-red knot on his forehead, the result of that speaker pole. The overcrowded conditions were temporary, for tomorrow a transport would take them to state police holding cells in Indianapolis. An accommodation between state and local authorities.

"You bloody sod, you confessed," snarled Bob Leicester. "Now we're all going to the gallows."

"They don't hang people in Indiana," Harvey waved away the younger man's words. "Besides, I'm not worried. My lawyer will get me off."

"You have a lawyer?" Carl looked up from the bottom bunk. "Who might that be?"

"A fearsome warrior by the name of J. Harold Wentworth. I hired him this very morning. He sprung me from jail then, he will spring me from jail now. No matter what I say, he will turn the words back on them like arrows.

Fortified by wine, I speak freely and I laugh at them. I blow my nose in their general direction!"

"Wait the briefest moment, my good fellow. Wentworth is our attorney also. Uncle Jeff hired him this afternoon. But the lawyer told *us* to keep our mouths shut, to take the Fifth Amendment in order to avoid self-incrimination."

"Are you certain we are speaking of the same counselor?" Harvey Wallberg looked woozily down at Carl, seeing two of him. But, of course, there *were* two of him – Harvey was looking at twins.

"A man of fat guts and red countenance? Waves his arms like a penguin?"

"Verily, that is he," nodded Harold Wallberg. He found this coincidence perplexing, that they should share the same lawyer. Could Wentworth represent two opposing sets of murderers at the same time? Who would the litigator favor if one party ever need be thrown like carrion to the wolves?

Bob cut into these thoughts. "J. Harold Wentworth's sage advice to us was silence. I would recommend that you follow suit. Else you will pull us down the hillside with you."

"'Tis true," nodded brother Carl. "Aunt Ceci – our mother, that is to say – it's difficult to get used to those words – poisoned Addy Anderson on her own. But we are knee-deep in quagmire with you, my treacherous friend. Not only did we tell you how she did it, but we helped you pick the mushrooms."

Wallberg offered his sweetest smile. He recalled his favorite Shakespeare passage: "*Look like the innocent flower, but be the serpent under it.*" He said, "My dear lads, that was because we three are fast friends, willing to rise and fall together."

"Rise, for sure," replied Carl. "But fall may be another matter."

"Come now, my boys. You thought you would profit from Agamemnon's imminent demise. That I would take over Merry Times, and thus move you to better roles – Hamlet, Titus Andronicus, even Lear."

"Little chance of that now." Bob looked sad, like a boy who had lost his puppy. "Adolphus's death threw Merry Times asunder. And Agamemnon's dying rendered the company unsalvageable. Your attempt to take the reins has failed so very miserably."

Carl looked equally despondent. "The murder you committed was for naught. Now we are all headed to prison. And us being so much younger, our life sentences will last longer than yours, you stinking old man."

"Hark! Who can prove my guilt?" responded Harvey Wallberg. "Perhaps you boys will bear the entire weight. It could as well been you two who created the crime on your own."

"Not so, you drunken sot. You confessed to the murder of Agamemnon to the police. Do you not remember?"

"Perhaps I had too much elderberry wine ..."

"You have ruined the lives of us all," moaned Bob. "My days on the stage but begun, have ended."

"Wait now –"

"'*Thou art unfit for any place but hell,*'" quoted Carl. Leaving the last word to William Shakespeare himself.

EPILOGUE

"The evil that men do lives after them."
-Julius Caesar

Autumn in Caruthers Corners was as spectacular as a blazing bonfire at night. Estelle Bennington Grady and Harvey Wallace Wallberg (A/K/A Harvey Wallbanger) each were charged with Homicide in the First Degree, both poisonings being premeditated.

Carl and Bob Leicester faced Accessory After the Fact charges for their knowledge of Mrs. Grady's murder of Adolphus Everly Anderson, as well as Accessory Before the Fact charges for helping Harvey Wallberg choose and collect the poisonous mushrooms that were used to murder Agamemnon Anderson.

Jefferson Archer Grady escaped prosecution, but was quietly dismissed from his position with ZapData by its owner.

Estelle Grady and Harvey Wallberg were probably looking at life terms. In Indiana, the death sentence is given only in murder cases that involve extreme circumstances such as rape, robbery, arson or if the victim was a child or law enforcement officer.

The twins would likely get life, also. According to Indiana Code 35-41-2-4, you can be charged with complicity if you intentionally or knowingly aid, induce, or cause another person to commit a crime. If you are an accessory to murder, your penalty could be the same as the person who committed the deed, even though you yourself did not kill anyone.

Complicit in two murders, their goose was cooked.

At their hearing, the Leicester brothers got into a shouting match with their former mentor.

"*'Thou clay-brained guts, thou knotty-pated fool, thou whoreson obscene greasy tallow-catch!'*" bellowed Carl. Shaking his manacled fist at Harvey Wallberg.

"*'Thou subtle, perjur'd, false, disloyal man!'*" shouted Bob. Equally focusing his ire on their one-time colleague.

The twins blamed Wallberg's drunken confession for their fate.

"*'I'll beat thee, but I would infect my hands!'*" retorted Harvey Wallberg.

Carl spat, "*'I scorn you, scurvy companion.'*"

"*'Thou art a boil, a plague sore!'*" added Bob.

Wallberg wasn't through with his return invective. "*'You scullion! You rampallian! You fustilarian! I'll tickle your catastrophe!'*"

Shakespeare talk.

"Save it for the stage," bellowed Judge Horace Cramer, banging his gavel. "I'm sure there will be a theater group at Michigan City." Lifers and Death Row inmates are incarcerated at Indiana State Prison at Michigan City.

~ ~ ~

Maddy Madison flew by a private charter from Burpyville Regional to Bismarck Municipal Airport in North Dakota. Chief Jim Purdue had arranged for her to have a private interview with convicted murderer Hugo Merriweather

Marston. Pleading guilty, he had been fast-tracked to incarceration in the North Dakota State Penitentiary.

NDSP is a maximum custody facility that houses men sentenced to the Department of Corrections and Rehabilitation. Located in Bismarck, it holds 1,550 inmates. Although hanging is a possibility in a murder trial in North Dakota, Hugo Marston had received a life sentence. If ever released, he would be extradited to Indiana to face murder charges there also.

Maddy was ushered into a room with a heavy glass separating her from the prisoner. Marston looked haggard, none of the he-man swagger she remembered from their previous encounters.

"Well, well, a visitor from afar," he said over the phone that connected them. "I expect you want to know how I escaped detection by the famous Quilters Club, right?"

"Just wanted to satisfy my curiosity – how did you do it?"

"There's no reason not to tell all. I'm already in this cement box for life or longer. Killing Jonathan Segal was really quite simple. That scumbag had been messing around with my wife. Nobody does that and gets away with it. I showed that to Ricky Burke ... which is why I'm here. When me and the prof were coming out of that cave, he paused at the top of the crawl to pull off his hard hat and wipe the damp hair out of his eyes. I'd picked up the rock pick he'd dropped. Saw my opportunity and I took it, whacking him on top of his head. He stumbled forward, banging against the low-hanging ledge, leaving a trace of blood there. That's what that stupid cadaver dog smelled. You ladies took it from there. Despite all the evidence against me, I walked."

"Why confess now?"

"Why not? But mainly, I want Trudy to know I stood up for her *both* times. That little gal's the love of my life. I pledge my heart to her – always."

Note: Trudy Mae Marston remarried two months after receiving a quickie divorce in Reno. Her new husband was (ironically) Hugo Marston's public defender.

While in North Dakota, Maddy took time to visit Fort Abraham Lincoln State Park, where Marston had worked. She knew that her friend Cookie, a historian par excellence, would want a full report. After all, Lieutenant Colonel George Armstrong Custer and his wife had lived at the fort from 1873 until Custer died at the Battle of the Little Big Horn in the summer of 1876.

At the state park, Maddy met one of Marston's former co-workers. "He was a hothead," recalled the ranger. "Smacked me in the jaw one time for mentioning his wife had nice hair. She was a bleached blonde, but she wore it in a cut like that Jennifer Aniston on *Friends*. I meant it as a compliment, but he was touchy about that woman. He would have gone berserk if he'd known she once asked me out for drinks."

~ ~ ~

Aggie and N'yen returned to school. Sissy got the lead in *The Sound of Music* (the high school had hired a new drama teacher). Beau continued to fish with Edgar Rideneur and have his weekly lunches with Chief Jim Purdue. Ben Bentley took his wife Cookie on a vacation to visit Fort Abraham Lincoln State Park and the site of Little Big Horn.

Mayor Mark Tidemore was pleased with what was now called the Herb Shiner Summer Concert in the Park. Shriner was a Hoosier celebrity who'd been known for a folksy television quiz show ("Two for the Money"). People had enjoyed the concert's homegrown music sprinkled with Old Standards and Golden Oldies. It sometimes seemed that Caruthers Corners existed in a time warp.

With the success of the summer events, the Town Council was looking for something in the Fall. Beau Madison suggested a carnival. The town already had a Ferris wheel at the back of the Town Square, beyond the gazebo and the koi pond, almost at the edge of the Pleasant Meadows church property. Rides were 25¢.

This was a perfect venue for a carnival, a fundraiser that would feature an amalgam of local folks and traveling carnies and professional circus acts.

Thus launched the Caruthers Corners Crazy Carnival. Everybody had a good time – until Barffy the Clown died under mysterious circumstances. Nobody could ascertain the cause of death. Was this going to be a case for Maddy and her Quilters Club pals?

Thank you for reading.
Please review this book. Reviews
help others find Absolutely Amazing eBooks and
inspire us to keep providing these marvelous tales.
If you would like to be put on our email list
to receive updates on new releases,
contests, and promotions, please go to
AbsolutelyAmazingEbooks.com and sign up.

AUTHOR'S NOTE

The first production in America of a play by William Shakespeare took place in 1730 in New York City – an amateur performance of *Romeo and Juliet*.

Puritan and Quaker religious beliefs prohibited acting because they disapproved of the "rude jokes and raucous atmosphere." Nevertheless, Shakespeare's plays began to crop up in Philadelphia and Charleston.

In 1751, after the ban had been lifted on the immigration of actors, the London Company of Comedians came to Virginia. Their first production was *The Merchant of Venice*, but over time they added *Richard III*, *King Lear*, *Romeo and Juliet*, *Othello*, and *Hamlet* to their repertory. They toured Fredericksburg, Williamsburg, and Annapolis, then spent four years playing Jamaica. They returned to Philadelphia and New York in 1758 with new productions of *Cymbeline*, *The Taming of the Shrew*, and *Macbeth*.

George Washington was an avid theatre-goer and attended one of the London Company's performances in Williamsburg. Despite continuing animosity towards the British, citizens of the new nation loved the plays of Shakespeare. During his presidency, Washington encouraged theatre-going. Virginia and Maryland seem to have been the

Romeo and Juliet

two colonies that never banned theaters as immoral and a public nuisance.

During the 19th Century, traveling companies spread the plays into every corner of the United States. By 1810, theater companies had been established from Montreal to the Gulf of

Mexico. They produced their own plays, but often welcomed such touring stars as Charles Kean and Ellen Tree.

William Macready arrived in Philadelphia in 1843. Charles Calvert and Charles Rignold came in the 1870s, followed by Sarah Bernhardt in the 1880s, offering her own renditions of Hamlet and Cordelia to eager audiences.

Touring continued into the 20th Century, featuring such well-known performers as Johnston Forbes-Robertson – the definitive Hamlet of his day. Edwin Booth arrived in California for the 1848 Gold Rush, performing *The Taming of the Shrew*, *Othello*, and *Hamlet* while standing on a tree stump. Ben Mouton took his production of *The Taming of the Shrew* from mining town to mining town, traveling in "a wagon decorated with scenes from the play."

Junius Brutus Booth took his *Hamlet* to San Francisco in 1851. His three sons – John Wilkes, Junius, Jr., and Edwin – toured in the South and mid-Atlantic. But the careers of the entire family were ruined when John Wilkes Booth shot President Lincoln in 1865. Edwin Booth built a theater in New York City, but it failed.

In the first decade of the 20th Century, Shakespearean productions declined because of the large casts and high production costs. However, the 1909 opening of *Antony and Cleopatra* at the New Theatre in New York City revived the plays of Shakespeare, bringing him back into the mainstream.

During the '20s, acclaimed productions with John Gielgud, Maurice Evans, Lunt-Fontanne, Margaret Webster, and Paul Robeson reestablished the Bard's popularity in America. Orson Welles' 1939 production of *Julius Caesar* in Nazi uniforms proved Shakespeare's modern relevance.

In 1953, the festival at Stratford, Ontario, opened, with a similar company springing up in Stratford, Connecticut, two years later. The Connecticut company's 1960 tour of *A*

Midsummer Night's Dream set the style for modern tours. The play stopped in 13 cities between Boston and San Francisco, including an evening with the Kennedys in Washington, D.C.

The Shakespeare Theatre Association of America (STAA) was established in 1991 to "provide a forum for the artistic and managerial leadership of theatres whose central activity is the production of Shakespeare's plays; to discuss issues and share methods of work, resources, and information; and to act as an advocate for Shakespearean productions in North America."

There are nearly 100 members.

ABOUT THE AUTHOR

Marjory Sorrell Rockwell says needlecraft arts –
quilting, crocheting, knitting – are pastimes every woman can
appreciate. And she particularly loves quiltmaking. "It's like
painting with cloth," she says. But when not quilting she
writes mysteries about a Midwestern sleuth not unlike herself,
a middle-aged lady with an unpredictable family and loyal
friends. And she's a big fan of watermelon pie.

Quilter Club Mysteries

Visit Maddy's new website...

quiltersclubmysteries.com/

Take a tour of Caruthers Corners and the surrounding countryside. Meet Maddy's family and friends. Get a complete list of all the characters who have appeared in the entire Quilters Club Mysteries book series. Well, practically all.

What's more, you'll learn lots about quilting. There's a free quilt pattern. A dictionary of quilting terms. Even a Quilt Gallery showing some of Maddy's favorite quilt patterns.

No fees, no charges. Just fun.

For sales, editorial information, subsidiary rights information
or a catalog, please write or phone or e-mail
AbsolutelyAmazingEbooks
Manhanset House
Shelter Island Hts., New York 11965-0342, US
Tel: 212-427-7139
www.AbsolutelyAmazingEbooks.com
bricktower@aol.com
www.IngramContent.com

For sales in the UK and Europe please contact our distributor,
Gazelle Book Services
White Cross Mills
Lancaster, LA1 4XS, UK
Tel: (01524) 68765 Fax: (01524) 63232
email: jacky@gazellebooks.co.uk